Turning Inside Out

Lisa Marie Feringa

This is a work of fiction. Names, characters, places, and incidents are the product of the author's imagination or are used fictitiously. Any resemblance to actual persons, living or dead, events, or locales is entirely coincidental.

NIV: Scriptures taken from the Holy Bible, New International Version®, NIV®. Copyright © 1973, 1978, 1984, 2011 by Biblica, Inc.™ Used by permission of Zondervan. All rights reserved worldwide. www.zondervan.com The "NIV" and "New International Version" are trademarks registered in the United States Patent and Trademark Office by Biblica, Inc.™

NKJV: Scripture taken from the New King James Version®. Copyright © 1982 by Thomas Nelson, Inc. Used by permission. All rights reserved.

Jesus Paid It All (1865) by: Elvina Hall (1822-1899) copyright - public domain

Text Copyright © 2014 Lisa Marie Feringa

Cover Design and Copyright © 2014 Lisa Marie Feringa

All rights reserved.

ISBN:1495277240
ISBN-13:9781495277245

to Isabel (izzi)

You are fearfully and wonderfully made, knit together in my womb.

contents

Acknowledgments	i
chapter 1 ali	pg 1
chapter 2 reece	pg 12
chapter 3 leah (lee-lee)	pg 17
chapter 4 ali	pg 23
chapter 5 mideah	pg 27
chapter 6 ali	pg 35
chapter 7 reece	pg 44
chapter 8 ali	pg 52
chapter 9 mideah	pg 58
chapter 10 leah (lee-lee)	pg 76
chapter 11 ali	pg 82
chapter 12 leah (lee-lee)	pg 95
chapter 13 reece	pg 101
chapter 14 mideah	pg 110
chapter 15 april fool's day	pg 116
chapter 16 leah (lee-lee)	pg 132
chapter 17 april 2nd	pg 140
chapter 18 sylvia	pg 149
chapter 19 ali	pg 155

chapter 20 mideah   pg 160

chapter 21 leah (lee-lee)   pg 168

chapter 22 ali   pg 174

chapter 23 mideah   pg 180

chapter 24 ali   pg 190

chapter 25 ali   pg 211

chapter 26 mideah   pg 221

chapter 27 reece   pg 225

chapter 28 jason   pg 232

chapter 29 reece   pg 236

chapter 30 reece john wheaton   pg 244

chapter 31 ali   pg 247

chapter 32 ali   pg 251

chapter 33 ali   pg 254

chapter 34 mideah   pg 265

chapter 35 ali   pg 271

chapter 36 ali   pg 279

chapter 37 ted mideah vanessa trista   pg 288

chapter 38 jeff   pg 294

chapter 39 ali   pg 300

chapter 40 leah (lee-lee)   pg 306

acknowledgments

Jesus. Lover of my soul. My Shepherd. My Savior.
Steve Feringa. Keeper of my heart. My supporter. My encourager.
Denice Goldschmidt. Thank-you for your kindred friendship. It was you that encouraged me to write. Your keen eyes, listening ears and prayerful heart inspired and impacted this book and also my life. You are a treasure. "Many women do noble things, but you surpass them all."
Proverbs 31:29 (NIV)
Leanna Bolden. Thank-you so very much! You gave me the gift of your time and valued opinion during a very busy season of your life: raising a toddler, church planting and other creative endeavors. Your input was invaluable.

Genesis 3:6-7 (NIV)
⁶When the woman saw that the fruit of the tree was good for food and pleasing to the eye, and also desirable for gaining wisdom, she took some and ate it. She also gave some to her husband, who was with her, and he ate it.
⁷Then the eyes of both of them were opened, and they realized they were naked; so they sewed fig leaves together and made coverings for themselves.

chapter 1 ali

Ali eats the lie and her eyes are open wide. The food looks delicious and harmless —so promising. Lies flood her head and torment her new day. She wants a new beginning, a fresh start. Yesterday was a failure. Today her hope rests on another promising lie, that she can *will* away her starving soul. Today she *will* stick to the rigid rules of her latest diet.

She undresses and stands naked in the secret corner of her bedroom, where she hides the scale. She already went to the bathroom twice and doesn't dare read the digit on the scale without being relieved of all bodily waste. The lower the digit, the higher her worth. The bathroom scale disappoints and decides her mood for the rest of the day. Ali was hopeful and empowered, before she suddenly became fat.

In front of a full length mirror she criticizes the flabby lumps that magically appear when stepping on the scale. She can't find enough clothes to cover her shameful body. The jeans she wore yesterday seem tighter today. This realization makes things worse; they are stretched out and still tight! No way will she select clothes from the fat side of the closet! She wants to disappear into size zero, not blimp out of size eight.

Her stomach growls when she smells the rich aroma of toast and bacon that lingers in the kitchen. Standing with the refrigerator door open, Ali calculates the cost of her choices for breakfast—calorie overload. Nothing is worth it. She opens the pantry door —all forbidden food.

Her mother is reading a magazine. Not looking up, she mumbles, "Good morning Ali. There's some bacon left and you can make more toast."

"No thanks, Mom, I'm kinda in a hurry."

Ali grabs her travel mug and fills it with black coffee, no cream and sugar today. She rushes out the door, leaving her home feeling empty.

Ali is lucky to find a parking spot. Nine o'clock, and the college campus is already swarming with students. Monday is always busiest, which adds to Ali's aggravation. Hugging her backpack like a teddy bear, she shuffles into the classroom and hopes to blend in. She's too late for a back row seat and is forced to sit near the front.

She believes everyone is watching her.

Nobody is.

She is afraid everyone will reject her ugliness.

Nobody does.

Ali is embarrassed for no reason. Negative thoughts consume her. Words cross her arms and slouch her low in the chair. She hates the clothes she chose to wear. Her jeans are uncomfortable sitting and need to be unbuttoned. They are biting into her waist. She can't keep her mind off her belly that bulges over the rigid denim waistband. She wore her mother's shirt today, because it is opaque and loose. It drapes and ruffles over her like a tent. *What was I thinking? I cannot believe I am wearing this! People will think I have no style. Who wants to be friends with a loser?* Ali wishes she was home, safe and unnoticed in her warm bed. She wants to cozy soft blankets around her neck and not wake up until she is skinny.

After class, Ali hurries to the lounge to find a remote place to study what she missed while daydreaming hatred towards herself. It doesn't take long for the lounge to fill with students. Two unfamiliar girls join her table. This scares Ali. Her heart races and she blushes. These girls are invading her space, her cave. She wants to be alone. They are sitting too close. One of the girls has a Bible with her. Who invited them anyway? They remind her of the 'witnesses' that show up at her house. Her mother always crawls across the floor beneath the front windows and doesn't answer the door. *I hope these girls don't start preaching to me. Why do they have to sit here? There are plenty of tables with extra seats.* Ali crawls behind her book and keeps music plugged into her ears, pretending not to be home. The girls respect her need for privacy and talk amongst themselves while working on an assignment. Ali peeks over her book long enough to determine: They are pretty. They are skinny. They are happy. That is why friendship is easy for them.

Envy creeps into Ali's green-eyed heart. A good friend is missing in her life. She is usually the third wheel, the tag-a-long. Most of the time she is too cowardly to join other girls. *When I lose 15 more pounds and can wear cuter clothes, things will be different. People will like me better. I will be happier, popular even.* Her thoughts are obsessions. She slouches behind the biggest book in her backpack. She really isn't reading. She is holding up her Government book to fence in her yard. The grass looks super green across the table where the two BFF's are chatting and giggling non-stop. *I wish I had a best friend. I bet they tell each other everything. They seem really nice. But they wouldn't like me. Right now, I have nothing to offer. I feel like a dork. Besides, I am not about to start carrying a Bible around.* When Ali gets up to leave, the young ladies smile at her sincerely and say, "Bye." She smiles back, soaking in their warmth. For a moment she feels special —noticed.

Ali decides to cut through the University Center building instead of staying outside and walking around it. In the crowded lobby she spots him right away —Mr. Perfect, her biggest crush. He is walking towards her, flirting with two gals that flank his sides. Her heart races as he approaches. She smiles and tries to look attractive, but nerves tighten her face. She looks like she is in pain. *Quick Ali, think of something to say. I want him so bad. Oh, he looks gorgeous! If I say something, maybe he will stop and talk to me. I can do this.* She is standing in their path.

As they are passing Ali says, "Hi," in a weak voice. She stares dreamily at his face and doesn't move out of their way. Mr. Perfect looks at her without expression or response. He and his gals continue walking past. The gal on his right bumps into Ali and almost knocks her down. Ali is horrified. She thinks the whole campus saw her acting like a geek. Caught up in the moment, she rushes through the crowd and forgets where she is going. She stays in motion to survive self-disgrace. Her reprimands are relentless. *Just great! How can I be so stupid? Why did I say anything? I should have waited until I looked good before I opened my big fat mouth! He was with other girls, so why would he notice me? Was one his girlfriend? I hope not. If I lose some weight....he might ask me out. I wish I didn't wear these jeans today, or this ugly shirt. He wouldn't ask someone like me, anyway. Why did I let myself get so fat? I am not going to eat for the rest of the day. Sheesh! I must have looked like an idiot... stupid, stupid Ali. Why did I have to see him today? I shoulda stayed home. Where am I going? Oh crap, I better hurry. I'm gonna be late. I'm not sitting in the front again.*

Ali tries to calm her thoughts, slouching in the rearmost table of History class. Her stomach keeps making loud noises. She presses her fingers into her belly, hoping to stop the gurgling. She is bent forward and studying neatly organized notes, preparing for a pop-quiz. Everyone in the room is feeling pressure, with notebooks open, eyes down, quietly speed-reading and memorizing. She blends in. This relaxes her. She ignores her hunger and the sharp pains that fight her willpower. *I am not going to eat! Especially not today.*

Ali finishes first and walks to the front of the class to turn in her paper. She is confident she aced the quiz. She needs this positive reprieve to give this day some value. The professor corrects the papers during class while everyone reads the next lesson. Soon he returns the quizzes and dismisses the group. Ali smiles at her 100%, before neatly tucking the paper in her folder.

Before her last class of the day, Ali loiters by a vending machine. She window shops candy and snacks, bantering decisions in her head and coming very close to giving in. She is so hungry. But fat people aren't supposed to eat. The vending food is more forbidden than what was in her pantry this morning. A candy bar will surely plunge her day into the sewer. Chocolate has the power to kill an already lifeless existence. She ends up bringing a Diet soda into Math class, hoping this will curb cravings. Another battle won. Value —up another notch.

She doodles in her notebook, waiting for class to begin and doesn't look up until she hears the professor talking. *Oh! No! I can't believe it! What's he doing here? Oh my! How long has he been sitting there?* Ali's face flushes deep red. Her armpits are instantly wet. In clear view from where Ali is sitting, a ray of hope brightens her day. Her biggest crush, Mr. Perfect, is sitting two seats ahead. Ali doesn't know what to make of it. They are one month into this semester. Hope and dread mix, as she fantasizes the love opportunities in future Math classes.

Ali is attentive to his every move. She wants to know his name. She discerns his style and admires the back of his dark hair. She notices the tan on his thick neck and the silver chain around it. His burgundy shirt and dark jeans look new and expensive. Head to toe, he wears the latest brands and pricey labels. Even his backpack appears luxurious. His energy is like gravity. It pulls at Ali. She feels tangled in it.

When class is over, she lingers until he is clearly gone. She hides because she is afraid of what she might say to embarrass herself and also because she is ugly today. Besides, she can't breathe right now. Math just became very interesting! Ali carries a full can of Diet Pepsi out of class. Her cravings are fulfilled by dark brown hair and strong shoulders. Ali forgets she is hungry. Lust is a powerful distraction.

Later, at a popular coffee shop downtown, Ali turns the pages of a fashion magazine while sipping coffee and nibbling on a bran muffin. She feels guilty for eating after being so determined not to. Maybe high fiber and tiny bites will eliminate the calories. She will do extra sit-ups to make up for weakness of will. She devours Hansel and Gretel's crumbs, nibbling down their path and fearing she will find the house made of sweets. It is so easy to lose control. Ali will eat the whole house if she is not careful.

Whispers hiss from the booth behind her and claw at her back. Two beauty queens are poisoning the room with ridicule, gossip, fashion trends and men. They purposely talk loudly so that others will overhear. They are making fun of everyone. The littleness of others proves that they are Big, Powerful and Important. A chunky girl is in line for a doughnut. The queens mock and say, "Haven't you had your share of doughnuts? You are what you eat, muffin-top." Humph. "If I had teeth like his, I'd keep my mouth shut." Snicker. "That guy keeps looking this way. I winked at him. He's cute, puppyish."

Ali feels sorry for the chubby girl, even though the girl doesn't hear the insults. Ali is half the size of the muffin-top girl and still believes she is chunky. Life is for the beautiful. The queens behind her confirm it. Fat invites ridicule. *Are they talking about me now?* She holds still and listens to the queen holding up a cosmetic mirror. *Did she just say my hair is flakey? Too dark? I have a mole on my neck?* Ali turns her head to look back and the cosmetic mirror snaps shut. She catches the queens spying on her. Embarrassed to eat another bite, she puts a dollar next to the half-eaten treat and slides out of the booth.

When Ali stands up, one queen shouts and points at her, "Hey you with the granny shirt, your pants are unbuttoned!" Several people hear and look over at Ali. "Seriously. Look, they are wide open!" The queens giggle and hope others are laughing with them.

Ali's feet are not moving fast enough. She rushes to the nearest exit. Her tears prevent her from noticing the sign, "Please use other door." Bam! Too late. Her forehead slams against the glass. Everyone in the coffee shop looks to see what happened. The room is silent, except for two girls giggling and snorting without mercy.

Before turning and walking out the proper door, Ali glances at the queens that mock. One is stunning, expressing a condescending beauty that makes people afraid to approach. The other wears a paid-for beauty—store-bought lips, bleached hair and large breasts. Ali notices how attractive they are. Everyone notices. Men turn their heads and women monitor their man's reaction. One glance makes Ali feel insignificant, worthless, but mostly.... FAT.

Outside the coffee shop, a soft breeze washes her face. She senses something warm and wet on her upper lip and chin. It feels silky —warm and sticky. She licks her lips. A familiar taste jolts her into a panic. Automatically, she strokes her fingertips across her mouth. Blood. She looks down and sees red splotches across her frumpy blouse.

"Your nose is bleeding. Let me help you. Your nose is bleeding...." a gentle male voice is repeating.

The young man is beside her. He is touching her arm and offering her his linen shirt, holding it near her face. This startles Ali. She turns her head to face him.

"Just lean your head forward," he coaches. He presses the fabric onto her nose and pinches her nostrils together. With his arm across her shoulder, he helps Ali to a nearby bench, holding his shirt on her face.

"Sit here. Relax. It should stop in a few minutes." Above the cloth, he sees big brown eyes blinking at him. His arm is around this pretty girl's shoulder. This awareness makes him instantly nervous and his movements awkward. He steps back when she sits down and allows her to take over holding the shirt herself, pinching her own nose.

"Thank-you." Ali's voice has a strange nasal sound. She laughs nervously.

"Oops, you better stop laughing. It's making things worse."

"Okay, sorry," says a nasal voice. Ali suppresses her giggle and snorts instead. Now they both laugh.

"Come on, really. Laughing is making it worse."

"I can be serious," Ali sits up taller and tilts her chin in.

He can tell she is smiling beneath his shirt as she holds it against her face. Her eyes are warm and sincere with gratitude. "By the way, my name is Reece."

"I'm Ali," she muffles, still pinching her nose.

After a minute, she is aware the bleeding has stopped. She doesn't take his shirt off her nose right away. She is breathing better and can smell a mixture of cologne and sweat in the threads, a pleasant sexy scent. *Why am I pretending my nose is still bleeding?*

She wants to check out her hero without him noticing her gawking. She gets her chance when Reece looks the other way and watches an old man pick treasures from a trash can. She feels guilty for looking at his body when his head is turned. He is thin and has attractive muscle tone, athletic, but not macho. His brownish hair curls at his neck. He has an impressive tan, with a couple of pimples on his shoulder blade. When he looks back at her, she sees a boyish face with piercing green eyes. Friendly, gentle and comforting eyes convey his honesty and settle her nerves. She instantly trusts him.

"Let me check your nose. It should be better now."

Ali lifts her head from the cloth, conscious of him looking so closely at her face.

"Cured!" declares Reece. He smiles at her, then catches himself staring. "Okay, um... well, I'll let you get back to what you were doing." He stands awkwardly, with his hands in the pockets of his worn jeans. He shuffles backwards a couple steps, says, "Bye Ali!" and jogs across the street.

She waves at his back and watches the wind blow through his curly hair, lifting it off his ears. She's in a daze, anxious and confused.

Reece is gone when she realizes she still has his shirt. It is streaked and blotted with her blood, permanent stains for sure. She walks over to the trash can, where the old man is still rummaging, and tosses it in. The old man bends into the can and pulls it out. Ali changes her mind and grabs the shirt from the man's hands in a tug of war.

She feels childish and guilty for taking the shirt away from a homeless man. Not looking back, she wads it up and squishes it into her backpack.

The old man mumbles to nobody as he pushes a squeaky cart down the sidewalk, away from the mean girl that took his things.

Alone in her car, Ali adjusts the mirror to access damages to her nose and forehead.

She shouts, hoping no one hears, "I am such a klutz! How embarrassing! Why am I so stupid?" She touches her tender nose and red forehead.

"Well, it probably isn't broke. Geez, right in front of everyone."

She fights negative thoughts the entire way home and believes every lie.

Her mother is making dinner when she gets home.

"Hi Mom."

"Hi Ali, how was Spanish class?"

"Mom, I don't have Spanish this semester, remember? I tell you all the time. Government-History-Math. Maybe you should say it five times."

She knows her mother isn't listening. "I did all my homework. Aced my History test! Tonight... I am just gonna relax." Ali stands at the stove and waits for her mother to see the conspicuous wounds glaring from her face.

"I am making fettuccine for dinner. You better be eating tonight," her mother warns, watching the spoon as she stirs the sauce.

"Oh." Ali responds without enthusiasm and heads to her room.

Ali's mother finally looks at her when she walks away. "Make sure you do your homework," she commands in a lazy voice.

Ali leans toward her bedroom mirror. Her face is red and sore. She picks at some acne on her chin and speaks to the girl she hates the most.

"Ow!"

"Zits, a swollen nose, a bruised head, aren't I lovely!" She picks harder at her chin, making it worse.

"Ow! I should just leave these alone." Pinch. Rub. "Okay, okay."

She steps back to scrutinize her figure, grabbing chunks of her belly, "Fatty."

She prods her rump, lets out a sigh and squeezes the flesh beneath her upper arm. She remembers how her teacher's arm would jiggle when she wrote on the board. The class would snicker and poke, thinking their instructor was unaware. Ali waves her arm in the air and watches to see if her triceps are flabby, then gasps, thinking she saw some fat wobble. She tries to imagine what she looks like to others. There are words she cannot say out loud —words that murder the girl she hates. *Everyone must think my body is grotesque and ugly. I hate it. Look how awful I look. I let myself go! I should not be seen in public. I'm getting a double chin. Yuck, no wonder I have no friends.*

She sucks in her tummy and turns sideways. *Better, if I keep my stomach held in like this.*

She slouches and walks over to a chair, trying to keep her abs held in as she sits down. Her belly barely lumps over her belt. An unavoidable amount of fat settles over her tight pants. Most women would be pleased with this waistline. But not Ali, not only is she displeased, she is ashamed. Ali grabs and squeezes at fat again. Frowning, she sinks deeper into the overstuffed chair. She feels a lump jabbing her back and remembers. *Chocolates.* She reaches behind, ready to throw the bag across the room. Just one? She digs in for another and another, eating her sorrows.

She eats without feeling. She eats without thought. She begins to forget. Every bite seduces her, leading her to a place where nothing matters, the place where she hates herself the most.

The bag is almost empty when her mother calls her. "Ali, dinner's ready!"

She is eager to keep indulging. These calories will not matter, anyway. She has no choice. She already ate too much chocolate. She wants to eat dinner. She doesn't want to get to her last bite.

Her mom and little brother are already eating when she sits down at the table. Ali heaps a sizable portion on her plate and smothers it with alfredo sauce.

"Hey, save some for me!" her brother whines.

"You have more than I do." Ali defends. She is angry at him for discovering her shameful appetite.

"Do not. It's all on your plate. I might want seconds, ya-know."

Ali ignores him and takes an extra piece of garlic bread. She leaves the table to eat in privacy and watch TV. Her mother nibbles while reading the paper, making humming sounds as a response to non-stop stories told by her son. This is their typical family meal.

Ali is last to finish eating. She returns to an abandoned kitchen and puts her empty plate on the counter. The leftover food isn't put away yet. Ali gets another fork and begins helping herself to more, eating directly from the serving dishes. She eats with numbing sadness. She feels defeated. Again, she loses the battle. Fork-full after fork-full, she punishes herself. Watching and hiding, she eats with a madness, trying not to make any noise or leave clues behind. Indulgence is her secret.

Full beyond discomfort, Ali manages to drink a glass of water. It is customary.

Music is part of her disguise. It will mask the sound of what she needs to do next. She turns the volume up just enough, but not so much to draw attention. In the bathroom, she also turns on the faucet and leaves it running. She lifts up the toilet seat, then kneels before the throne.

Ali is afraid of so many things right now. Fears come easy when you shield yourself from God. She is afraid of being fat, afraid someone will hear what she is doing right now, afraid of the smell and taste of the food she is purging, afraid of the damage she is doing to her body, afraid of love, afraid of hate, afraid of herself. Now she is afraid of God. Like Eve hiding her shame with fig leaves, Ali feels naked before God, the only one who knows her secret.

"I am a fake." she whispers as she closes her eyes and bites her bottom lip, determined not to cry.

Tears slip through the cracks anyway. Her heart pours into trembling hands that shield her face. She weeps. Her painful release squeezes her chest so tight it suffocates. Hot regrets soak her face and crawl down her cheeks. Sorrow is pushing from her inner most part as she leans her bruised forehead on the toilet seat —in desolation and defeat.

The End.

Now she is numb.

She wasn't really hungry.

It is rarely about hunger, food hunger that is.

James 1:5-8 (NIV)
⁵ If any of you lacks wisdom, he should ask God, who gives generously to all without finding fault, and it will be given to him.
⁶ But when he asks, he must believe and not doubt, because he who doubts is like a wave of the sea, blown and tossed by the wind.
⁷ That man should not think he will receive anything from the Lord;
⁸ he is a double-minded man, unstable in all he does.

chapter 2 reece

Interesting. Smart. Shy? A shy smile. Attractive. Attracting me! Messy straight hair. Dark hair. Yeah. I want to mess it up more. Huge brown eyes. Sad eyes? Why is she always alone? I want to see her again.

Reece noticed Ali a couple of weeks ago at a coffee shop where college students and young professionals gather. Now, he looks for her whenever he goes there. Finally, his timing is right. She is sitting alone in a booth with a drink and a muffin. She seems uncomfortable, tilting her head to hear the conversation in the booth behind her and trying to be discreet. He can tell the two girls behind her are taunting her. They are jealous. Reece saw the gals stare at Ali when she walked by. Competition. The gal with her back turned is holding up a cosmetic mirror, spying with it. *Women like you annoy me! I'm not blind. Don't blink your hollow eyes at me. I won't be your victim.* The women are attracting attention and know it. He doesn't know what was said, but the women are laughing and people are staring in Ali's direction. *What happened? She's crying? Wait! I want to talk to you...*

Ali. Reece is tapping his chin with a pencil, sitting at a desk in his campus apartment, trying to concentrate on homework. *Hey brown-eyes! You have my favorite shirt!* His mind replays the scene at the coffee shop a few hours ago. *Do you need a friend? Why are you always alone? I will sit with you anytime.* Reece is staring at a blank sheet of paper next to an open book. *Forget those stupid girls. I will be the best friend you will ever know.* He is sure of this. He knows they will run into each other again. The town is not that big. Besides, he has to get his shirt back. *Or she can keep it. That would be okay, too.*

Forget the homework. Reece changes into bicycling shorts, then grabs his helmet, music and water bottle. He loads his bike on the car-top rack and drives out of town. He needs to release some energy into the wind.

He peddles to the rhythm of songs. God songs. Some friends tease him about his taste in music. *You like that stuff? Grandma music!* He doesn't care what they say. It calms him. He doesn't know how to explain worship. It is his way to experience Love, another way he prays. How can he explain an intense emotion that doesn't exactly make sense?

Reece catches himself singing loudly and remembers no one can hear the music, only his pitchy shouting, that is, if anyone is around. These country roads seem to belong to him. He laughs at himself and apologizes to God for the awful singing. *Okay God, does it sound better when it gets to You? Did you just say it's awesome? Hey, thanks!*

The aroma of fall rides on the wind. Sometimes it smells so pleasant that Reece stops his bike and closes his eyes to experience it fully. It sings to him like the music in his ears. He worships God for it. Love showers down on Reece as he coasts down a winding stretch of shady road. This is all he needs right now.

He breezes by people doing yard work and enjoying the outdoors. Reece always waves and shares his genuine smile. Not everyone waves back, but most do. Some turn away or look down. He wonders about this, how a person he doesn't know can boost him with a wave and a smile. They make him believe this world is a good place, a safe place. But what about the others? Those who turn away? The space around certain people is uncomfortable. He feels uninvited as he petals past an older woman with a small dog. He nervously holds his breath and waves. The lady turns away and scowls. *What makes her so mean? Why panic, all I did is smile and wave. Are you afraid?* He realizes his response was fear. After all, he did hold his breath and peddle faster to get past the awkward moment.

He turns around in a big circle and rides back towards the lady. He looks directly at her. She purposefully turns her back. He says it anyway.

"Have a great day!" he yells, and means every word. She never turns around; but he notices that she stiffens. In his rear view mirror, he sees her pick up her dog and wave at him with the dog's paw.

Reece parks his bike outside the convenience store where his best friend is working. Jeff is busy filling up the cup dispensers at the frozen drink machine.

"Hey Reece!" he says holding out his hand. They give each other a manly-man hug while shaking hands.

"Here's one on me." Jeff says and hands Reece a large cup.

"Alright! Thanks." Reece takes the cup, fills it to overflowing with frozen coke and helps his friend restock cups and lids.

"I talked to her today," Reece says with a big grin.

"No. Really?" Jeff is surprised. "When? What did you say? What's her name?"

The questions come faster than the answers. Jeff always supports Reece, knows him like a brother. So he understands the gravity in Reece's declaration.

"Her name is Ali."

"Ali. Nice. So that's the name of the girl you are stalking," Jeff jokes. "Ali who?"

"Ali. I-don't-know-her-last-name-Ali." Reece states shyly, knowing exactly what Jeff is thinking. "And I am not stalking her! I like coffee, too."

"What? What do you mean? You don't know her last name? Do you have her phone number?"

"No, I bailed before I had the guts to ask. No phone number either."

Jeff looks at his friend and laughs. Given a similar situation, he'd do the same thing. Reece bites his bottom lip, smiles and shakes his head.

The store isn't very busy, so Reece stays for another hour and helps Jeff put together a new display. Slowly the whole story comes out about seeing Ali, the bloody nose and how he gallantly rescued her.

Jeff keeps the conversation light by teasing Reece about being a hero. "And don't rush off next time. Just wait 'till she gets to know you."

"I'll need to get my fish shirt back sometime."

"What? I don't get it. Why does she have your fish shirt?" Jeff is confused.

"Oh. I left out a detail. I took my shirt off to stop her nose from bleeding everywhere."

"You took your shirt off in front of her? And let her use it as a Kleenex?" Jeff is surprised. "And here I thought you were some shy dude!"

"Come on. It was embarrassing. But she's so cute, I got over it fast."

"That's your favorite shirt!"

"Yeah. I know." Reece schemes, "I can get it back later."

Jeff hopes there will be a 'next-time' for the sake of his friend. He hopes that Ali will give Reece a chance. She needs to get to know him. Hopefully she is deserving.

Riding his bike back to the car, Reece can't stop thinking about Ali. He loves the way she bites her bottom lip while she is reading and the way her dark hair falls across her chin. He feels compassion for the loneliness she emanates. He rehearses conversations and pretends Ali is falling in love with him. Reece knows he is behaving masculine, protective and over-romantic. He doesn't care. He enjoys the fantasy. And he lets it expend him. *God, is she the one for me? I hope so. I don't want to be alone. Will you help me run into her again? I want to be smart about it, that's all.*

Four years earlier, Reece and his father visited Grandpa in Key Largo. They chartered a boat and entered an all day fishing tournament. His Grandpa purchased three white linen shirts for them to wear. He had the words *'gone fishin'* embroidered on the bottom hem of one sleeve, on the other sleeve, a sailfish. These were their team shirts. His grandpa was energetic and vibrant, enjoying his seventh year of retirement.

Reece vividly remembers that day. It was the first time he felt like a grown man. He was seventeen. It was as though he entered his rite of passage and accredited it to the way his father and grandfather treated him —as their fishing partner, confidant and friend. They listened to his ideas and comments as an equal. He felt strong and valued. They took turns navigating the boat. They joked with each other. Some of the jokes would make his mother blush. They had serious conversations where Reece was included, instead of waiting until he was out of earshot. Reece witnessed his grandpa asking advice from his dad. Grandpa trusted and respected his son. Reece wondered if the relationship with his father evolved to this place, where a father humbly asks his son for advice. Reece was confident in the man he was becoming and pondered about his future, which seemed so vast, like the waters surrounding their boat. The years ahead of them felt endless, as if they were invincible.

Who would have guessed that the photo of this day would be the very last one of himself, his father and grandpa? This memory is framed and displayed above their fireplace mantel —three men woven together by the threads of white sailfish shirts that say *'gone fishin'*. Four months after this tournament (where they took third place) his grandpa died from a massive heart attack while deep sea fishing. They couldn't get him to shore in time to save him.

Reece clings to the memory of his grandfather and wears the shirt often. His mother is convinced it's his only shirt. She teases him about it. For a joke, she made photo-copies of the shirt, cut and pasted them over every shirt in a clothing catalog, then mailed it to Reece. Reece took the same catalog, pasted his head on every model and mailed it back.

This is the shirt that Reece gave to Ali to stop her bleeding nose. It is the shirt he willingly left behind, not knowing when or if he would ever get it back. This shirt is still important to him and still making history.

Jesus Paid It All (1865) by: Elvina Hall (1822-1899)
I hear the Savior say, "Thy strength indeed is small;
Child of weakness, watch and pray, Find in Me thine all in all."

Jesus paid it all, All to Him I owe;
Sin had left a crimson stain; He washed it white as snow.

Lord, now indeed I find Thy power, and Thine alone,
Can change the leper's spots, And melt the heart of stone.

Since nothing good have I Whereby Thy grace to claim,
I'll wash my garment white In the blood of Calvary's Lamb.

And when before the throne I stand in Him complete,
I'll lay my trophies down, All down at Jesus' feet.

chapter 3 leah (lee-lee)

Now I am alone with Mr. D. It scares me. I don't know why. He is Meggy's daddy. I like Mr. D. I think. I'm ap-sposed to, right? He takes me to fun places with Meggy. Meggy is at the doctor with her mama today. I hope she gets back pretty-soon. We're going to wear princess dresses and make cookies for our dollies. Mr. D. said that someday he will take us on an airplane ride in our pretty dresses and we can bring our dollies too. I am going to wave at mama from the sky. Mr. D. said that people look like ants when the airplane flies up really high. I don't look like an ant. So what if I have brown hair. I won't even be scared, cuz mama said Mr. D. will keep me safe. Mr. D has to go away lots, just like my mama. Mama says she will bring me a surprise when she gets home. I hope it's gum or a purple sucker.

Leah is sitting on the living room window seat, holding a stuffed lamb and looking out. She is missing her mama more than usual today.

Mr. D seats himself in the corner chair. Enough out of view, yet he can still see the driveway. Wearing only a pair of thin shorts, he watches Leah while pretending to read a comic book with pictures of animals. Finally, he invites Lee-Lee to join him. Leah hesitates and resigns, finding no alternative. He points to animal characters and talks with funny voices. Lee-Lee is having fun, laughing at the funny things Mr. D says. Her heart pounds a bit faster when Mr. D. takes hold of her hand. First he just holds it. Sensing something isn't right, she begins to pull away. She wants to get out of the chair, but he holds her tighter. Pulls her closer...

From the plush chair they are sitting in, Leah notices her lamb flopped over on the window sill. She stares at it for a while, then closes her eyes. She sees a valley of green grasses waving under a yellow sky. There are sheep on the hillside, grazing. The wind sings and forms patterns in the grassland. One of the sheep is missing, the new lamb. Looking down from the sky, Leah watches the lost lamb running from a fox. A lamb of purest white is seen dodging through waves of green —vivid white, like cotton balls. Except now, the whitest wool is absorbing blood in bright red steaks across the lambs back, scratches in lines of four. This fox is beautiful and looks like fire ignited by the warm sunshine. It chases the baby lamb until suddenly, as if planned, the lamb lays down and offers itself to the pursuing fire. Alive then dead. Blood is pouring from its side. Now Leah is running in the grass. The sun is down and it is cold. She rushes to the lamb, *"It needs me, it needs me!"* she whispers. Leah is following an obscure path, the only path, trampled like a tunnel, in the grass. The path ends where the lamb offered his life. Confused, Leah waits alone in matted grasses, the shape of the lamb. *Did it die? Where did the lamb go? Why did it go away?* In a panic, Leah looks down and notices. She is standing in the lamb's blood, thick and sticky, gluing her bare feet to the grass. *I won't be afraid anymore.* Here I Am.

The sky is yellow all around the green grassy hilltop. The rigid profile of a child stands at the highest peak. Her white cotton dress is blowing in the wind. *I need to stay here, by the yellow light.*

Unexpectedly, a car door slams. Mr. D. abandons Leah in the chair and rushes to the bathroom. Meggy rushes into the room calling, "Leah, Leah, I brought you a Barbie sticker! Look at mine. It's a princess one!" Mrs. D is in the kitchen putting away the bag of groceries she carried in. Leah silently accepts the gift from her trusted friend and goes back to the window seat. She picks up her lamb and strokes its back, smoothing down the fur and inspecting it for wounds. Curling up close to the corner of the window seat, holding the lamb tightly in one hand, the sticker in the other —Leah waits. Meggy sits at the other end of the window and watches her friend.

Eventually, Meggy slips away to play by herself. Outside, a basketball is heard bouncing on pavement, banging off the backboard and vibrating the metal rim. It is Mr. D, erasing his sins. Meggy's mom is annoyed with Leah for ignoring her daughter. She goes to the window sill several times to persuade her to go and play. She finally gives up when the phone rings. It is Leah's mother Jodie, with more excuses to leave her daughter there longer. Jodie assumes it is okay, doesn't ask, just directs the time Leah will be picked up. *Tomorrow!* Leah will be staying another night. When Mrs. D hangs up the phone, she calls the elderly neighbor to let her know Meggy won't be coming over tomorrow. *This really messes up my schedule!* Next, she calls the hair salon and cancels her appointment. Even though she allows it, she is angry at Jodie for taking advantage of her and wrecking her plans.

Eventually, Leah rests her head against the window and falls asleep. Mrs. D slides Leah's small body over, puts a pillow under her head and covers her up. When Lee-Lee awakes, the house echoes in ghostlike abandon. Empty chairs surround the table. Dinner plates are crusted with casserole. The main dish, which is centered on the table, is scraped down to crispy black edges of unrecognizable elbow noodles. Leah walks around the desolate house, hugging her lamb, thinking she is left alone.

Where did everyone go? I want my mama. They left me here all by myself. Mrs. D is mad at me. I want my surprise. Mama's bringing me a purple sucker. She hears a noise in the basement, then shoes tapping on wood treads ascending the stairs. It's Mr. D. I don't want to see Mr. D. right now. Leah runs and hides behind a door, peeking through the crack between hinges. She sees Mr. D. walking with a magazine folded in his hand. She holds her breath when he walks past, then darts into the dining room and crawls under the table. Leah shivers in a forest of chair legs. Soiled dishes still litter the roof of her shelter. Leah pretends her lamb is lost in these woods, bouncing four stuffed feet on the floor between square tree trunks. The lamb climbs a small tree and sits in the branches. The lamb is waiting for mommy. What did you say? Someone is coming? The lamb is whispering into Leah's ear. She sits cross-legged, watching pretty bare feet with red toenails walk around the table. Dishes clunk and slide above her head. When the table is cleared, Leah crawls out on all fours, the lamb's leg squeezed in her hand and bouncing along beside her.

Mrs. D is in the kitchen filling the sink with sudsy water. Leah watches her from behind, then taps her fanny. "When's my mama gonna be here?"

Startled, Mrs. D turns around, her hands dripping with bracelets of bubbles. "Oh honey, your mom called to say she won't be here until tomorrow."

Leah bursts into tears and runs away. She crawls back under the table and buries her face into her lamb. Mrs. D exhales loudly, dropping her shoulders. She doesn't follow Leah or even think to console her. Instead, she plays the victim, overscheduled and exhausted, surrounded by ornery children and a distant husband.

"Why am I always the one still working while everyone is playing? Maybe I'd like to just sit for a while, or do something fun for a change!"

Dishes bang louder, water splashes higher and cupboard doors slam. Mrs. D's tantrum lasts as long as her pitiful thoughts. When it is over, she is sour. Her family is disregarded while she frequents the refrigerator to fill her empty wine goblet, exiting the kitchen and reality.

Leah stops crying and freezes when she hears the first cupboard door slam. *I did something really bad. I made Mrs. D. angry.*

Leah will avoid Mrs. D and be small when she is near. Leah is hungry, but doesn't dare say so, doesn't dare come out of hiding. The kitchen grows quiet. Ugly red toenails approach the table. The sound of the wine goblet hitting the tabletop echoes above. Wooden chair legs screech, as they pull away from the table, putting a temporary hole in Leah's cave. Chair legs push back under the table. A knee almost bumps Leah's head. She scootches away from the bare legs and the ugly red toenails that keep wiggling and tapping. Leah waits and waits, planning an escape, but doesn't dare move, doesn't dare breathe, just sits squeezing the lamb against her neck and ear. After several more taps of the wine glass bumping the tabletop, the wooden legs push back and the red toenails disappear. Leah scrambles out and crawls towards familiar voices of cartoon characters muttering from the other room. She joins Meggy on the floor, sharing her pillow. This is how the little girls remain, engrossed and unaware of their surroundings until they are forced to get up. It's Bedtime.

Getting ready for bed makes Leah want to cry. She holds her tears. The routine of brushing teeth and putting on her princess nightgown reminds her of another night spent without her mama. This isn't her sink. Her toothbrush goes in the holder on the wall, first slot, not in a plastic baggy on the counter. She misses her penguin sheets and the way her mattress sinks beneath her. She needs her mama's kisses. *Mrs. D's breath smells like hairspray!* She misses the familiar sounds her own house makes. This house squeaks and scratches, and lots of cars go by. They aren't allowed to talk or get out of bed or Mrs. D will yell. Mrs. D. doesn't read three books like mama does. She doesn't read any. She doesn't let them have a nightlight on. The room is dark and filled with shadows.

Leah curls up and pulls the covers over her head. She feels alone, as if Meggy disappeared. She hears snorts and deep breathing coming from across the room. *Is Meggy dreaming of feeding ducks with grandma?* Eventually, Leah falls asleep. She doesn't dream of ducks or grandparents. In her sleep, an incubus leads her down a path, darker than a child's room absent a nightlight.

Nighttime drama on TV turns into infomercials as Mrs. D. lays on her back, departing the day in oblivion. Her mouth is wide open. One arm is stretching off the bed, floating above the floor. Her husband has spent much of the evening at the computer, behind locked doors —his self-made prison cell. His secrets are easily kept when his wife's bottles are empty. He tip-toes to his marriage bed to the side his wife sleeps. He flicks her hand that is suspended off the bed and watches it bounce, then folds it across her chest. He makes sure she is fully asleep before he quietly leaves the room.

Slow deep breaths, from two little girls, sing to the moon glowing through a tall window that is stationed between twin beds. A warm breeze is dancing with the sheer curtain. The monster is not under the bed or in the closet this time, nor in the shadows that scratch the walls. It is across the room, peering its head from behind a slightly open door, his evil hand clutching the knob. This monster is primed and ready to devour. Beady eyes skim the room identifying the prey —a disinclined child asleep in the guest bed. Sly and crouching, the monster moves with practiced grace and ease, so as not to awaken his victim. In premeditated fashion, it slithers up against Leah, inflicting wounds that will fester for years.

    The fiend is full and content. It sleeps peacefully through the night, his spine resting against Mrs. D's belly, her arms protecting and accepting. Both their secrets depart with the moon. By morning, Mr. and Mrs. D are ready for their masquerade.

Psalms 63:1 (NIV)
¹ O God, you are my God, earnestly I seek you; my soul thirsts for you, my body longs for you, in a dry and weary land where there is no water.

chapter 4 ali

Ali pushes a pillow into her neck and squishes it close to the sides of her head. She tries bending one leg off the edge of the bed. Nope, that didn't work. She turns to the side and hangs an arm off the edge. Nope. She pushes the pillow aside and rolls onto her belly, face down with one leg bent and stretched out as far as possible. Three hours later, Ali still hasn't fallen asleep. She is hungry. In her mind she is touring the kitchen cabinets, remembering hidden snacks, and willing herself not to give in and eat. Her stomach moans. Her throat is raw and sour tasting. Anger is sleeping with her tonight. She curses herself, calling out degrading names. Remembering is unpleasant. She hates who she is —the girl that does disgusting things.

In the darkness of her bedroom, she lies there, eyes closed, breathing in and out and harboring a madness. This is her eternity. Most of the night is behind her. She is really thirsty, but doesn't want to move from her cage. Endless streams of wicked thoughts flow into her lake of dreams.

Ali's eyes twit rapidly behind their lids. She is in a huge rocky canyon. She tries to climb out, but as she nears the top her footing gives out and she slides back to the bottom. After a while the canyon turns white and slippery, like a glass bowl. Over and Over she climbs toward the top only to slip every time. She looks up from the bottom of the canyon at people wandering around the edge of the cliff. They stare down at her. Nobody helps her.

She doesn't know how long this dream plays. Was it her only dream? Did she spend the past four hours in sinking frustration? It feels like it.

Ali wakes up the next morning feeling like she is crawling up a steep hill. Her body is heavy, not wanting to roll out of bed. When she finally sits up, her head pounds with every heartbeat. She walks over to her bedroom mirror and notices that her eyes are puffy and her face is mildly swollen. *I can't go to school looking like this!* Feeling desperate, she searches for an excuse to skip school, while holding a cold wet cloth across her face.

Her momentum is slow, going through the motions of morning —the beauty ritual of brushing teeth, showering, make-up, and hair. The mirror doesn't convince her of any improvement. *Mirror, mirror on the wall, who's the ugliest one of all?*

"Why do I bother?" Ali snips aloud, as she digs through a basket of folded laundry, searching for something to wear. She pulls out a clean bra and panties from the bottom of the basket and picks up a folded shirt that fell out of the pile onto the floor. On the chair by her bed is a pair of jeans she wore a few days ago. She puts them on because they are already stretched out. They won't remind her how fat she is —hopefully.

Her backpack is still where she left it the day before. She can hear her mother upstairs, yelling at Brandon. "Hurry up kiddo! I don't have time for this nonsense! And wear something clean today!"

He is whining defensively and slamming dresser drawers. It is a typical morning. Ali skips breakfast, fills up a mug with black coffee and heads out the door, swinging her backpack at her side.

Her mother is in the kitchen, shortly after Ali leaves, making Brandon toast and scrambled eggs. She doesn't really notice that Ali has already left. She sets two plates on the table. One is for herself.

At the bottom of the stairs she yells at Brandon again. "You better not make me late again, buster!"

Ali floats through her morning classes, hiding in the crowd, never making eye contact, mostly staying deep within herself. Later in life, she will not have much memory of this time of her life. Because she didn't allow herself to take part in this day and many others like it. She floats like a cloud far above everything going on around her, never letting anyone see what is behind her veil.

Ali has time to kill before Math class. She wanders around campus, in a zombie-like pout. She forgets that Mr. Perfect will be in class today. Otherwise, she would be rushing to get the best seat. Just before class starts, Ali wanders in behind a tall boy with thick glasses. She is hesitant to enter the room, nearly walks back out, because the only open desk is next to "Mr. Perfect". Normally she would be excited for the chance to sit by her secret love. Not today. She feels exposed. Ali's secret is too near the surface.

She unzips her backpack and pulls out her Math book, unaware that the shirt used for her bloody nose yesterday falls out and lands at the feet of "Mr. Perfect".

Ali feels someone nudging her arm. "You dropped something."

She turns towards "Mr. Perfect" and notices what he is holding out to her. It is a soft, white shirt, crusty with stains of blood. It looks spotted and scary. It seemed strange to expose it, something you normally wouldn't want to touch, yet he is handing it to her.

"You dropped...."

Quickly, Ai grabs it from his hand, with a look of horror on her face. She instantly stuffs it deep into her backpack and dares not to notice who is watching her. What seems like hours is only seconds. She feels like she is on stage with beams from a spotlight heating her face. Ali can tell when people are deliberately looking at her. And she senses every eye as if they are stones thrown at her. She imagines what people are thinking. *What is that? Is that blood? Why does she have a shirt with blood all over it?*

Ali lowers her head and tries to shield her face with her hands. *That was so stupid. I bet he wants to wash his hands now. Why did I forget it was in there? I should have stayed in bed.* The memory of what happened yesterday distracts her. She sits in heated embarrassment next to her secret crush and runs an ink pen over the wood-grain pattern on the desktop. When class is over, she licks her finger and smudges the ink.

Later, sitting in her car, Ali takes the shirt out of her backpack. She holds it up by the shoulders. Now that she is alone, this bloody shirt looks innocent. She brings it to her face and smells it. She remembers his face. *Reece?* She smells it again, then smoothes it across her lap. *Does he want this back? I'm sure it's ruined.* Ali holds his shirt all the way home, lifting it to her nose, liking that it smells masculine.

A week later, Ali finally attempts to wash the blood stained shirt. First she soaks it in cold water mixed with a stain removing solution. The stains she always has trouble with are coffee, ketchup and especially blood. By mistake, she leaves it soaking for three days in the washing machine. She forgets about it until she has a load of cloths to wash. Ali lets the machine spin out the old water, before starting over with a fresh load of whites. When she takes it out of the washing machine, she is amazed to see no trace of blood. His shirt is brighter than ever, fresh and new. Then it dawns on her, *How will I give him back his shirt? Chances are I will never see him again. Who knows if he even lives around her?* She irons it anyway. *Why am I doing this?* While ironing the sleeves, she notices that there is writing on one sleeve and a fish on the other. This makes her wonder if Reece is a fishing kind of guy, or if the shirt is just branded that way. She smells it again before hanging it in her closet. Strangely, that strong masculine smell is absorbed into the threads of his shirt. The stains are washed away, but Reece remains, weaving into Ali's future.

Proverbs 9:13-18 (NIV)
[13] The woman Folly is loud; she is undisciplined and without knowledge.
[14] She sits at the door of her house, on a seat at the highest point of the city,
[15] calling out to those who pass by, who go straight on their way.
[16] "Let all who are simple come in here!" she says to those who lack judgment.
[17] "Stolen water is sweet; food eaten in secret is delicious!"
[18] But little do they know that the dead are there, that her guests are in the depths of the grave.

chapter 5 mideah

If there is a mirror, she will find it. Mideah likes to be reminded of how attractive she is. And attracting attention is what she does best. She is very skilled at walking in a sultry way, sitting statuesque or fluttering her long, perfectly manicured fingernails. She loves to flip her long hair or slide her hands down her hips, especially when wearing a sexy dress or short skirt and always-always when dancing. Most of the time, she cakes on too much makeup. She really doesn't need any. Her natural features are stunning beneath the mask she paints on each morning, adding more brush strokes to her face throughout the day.

Everything beautiful stops at surface level. Like the outer layer of an onion, the wise can easily see through it's transparency. Fools cannot. Mideah cannot see through this layer. An onion will rot from the inside out.

"Gina! Urgh! Get a life! Keep out of my things!" Mideah is angry. She found her expensive skin treatment in her roommates vanity drawer - AGAIN!

"If you're going to sneak into it, it seems like you would be smart enough to put it back," she says under her breath, then adds loudly, "You'll probably just deny it, as usual!"

Mideah is certain Gina can't hear her and wants to vent. This morning is not going well. She slept too long and has to rush. She would rather miss her class than go looking frumpy.

There is nothing special about this particular day, yet she tends to herself as if preparing for her wedding day. *All eyes on me!* is her hidden agenda. Mideah has her language class at the University and will go to work afterward. She is learning to speak Italian, hoping it will advance her at the travel agency. The underlying reason for taking this class and also geography, besides career reasons, is that she hopes to impress others by being multi-lingual and worldly —well traveled. *Dumb-blonde* is not a label she wants to wear, but will act the part if it is to her advantage. Sometimes she even stoops to baby-talk, especially to older men, who seem to like it — she thinks.

The bathroom door opens unexpectedly. "What... are you... talking about?" Gina asks, popping her head in the bathroom.

"THIS!" sneers Mideah, holding up her acne cleanser. "You were using it again! It only took half the morning to find it... in YOUR drawer."

"I am glad you found it," Gina says quietly, before shutting the door. She is not willing to argue this morning. Mideah will get over it anyway, until she finds it missing again.

Gina and Mideah are both very selfish. It is amazing that they manage to stay close friends and even roommates. Gina is always borrowing her roommate's things, mostly without any intention of returning them. Mideah does the same. In fact, today Mideah is wearing a pair of jeans that Gina had recently bought. Gina apparently didn't notice. Mideah took them from Gina's closet last night when she was home alone, ripped the tags off and hid the evidence deep in the garbage. She hid the jeans under a pile of clothes thrown on the chair, and dug them out this morning.

Bitterness is rooted in Mideah as she paws through the top drawer of her dresser, searching for matching jewelry to wear. She just doesn't have all the things she wants. She decides that she hates the shirt she is wearing and changes it for the third time this morning. *Now my jewelry doesn't match!* On the chair, the pile of discarded clothes is growing as she narrows down what to wear. She stands at her closet and pulls out a yellow, sheer blouse and baby-blue camisole, freckled with teeny white flowers. She slides the lightweight fabric over her arms and boney shoulders. She likes what she sees in her three-way mirror. Mideah practices posing and making facial expressions —a sexy pout, a smile, puckered lips, then a blank look, staring deep in thought. Uninvited fear creeps into her gut. She denies it, doesn't want it. It is easily dismissed with the shake of the hips, her 'model' pose.

"Okay, you're ready girl." Mideah tells her best friend in the mirror. She transfers all contents from one purse to another, one that better matches her outfit. She tugs a pair of tall boots over the tight legs of Gina's jeans and hurries out the door before her roommate notices what she is wearing.

In the car, Mideah adjusts the rearview mirror, turning it on her face. She drives to school, fixating on her guise and imagining that every woman wishes they could look like her. While driving through the parking lot, she inspects her face with admiration, adds a bit more lipstick and blows the mirror a good-bye kiss. She exits the car as if jumping out of a cake. Surprise! Showtime!

She will be tardy, but doesn't feel the need to rush. The way she is walking invites stares from 'the boys', a name she likes to call her male colleagues. Acting like a snob is her way to maintain power and control. It matches the mood she is in. She loves to widen the space around her, bulldozing everything in the way, making more room for herself. She attracts attention by being sassy, proud and charming —whatever works at the moment. Mideah is smart! She is a master manipulator. She gets her way every time. People get tangled in the strings attached to her. They become her marionettes. Mideah doesn't realize that she is the puppet and Vanity is her puppeteer.

The young Italian professor has already begun his lecture when the classroom door slams shut. He is annoyed —until he sees which student is late. Mideah owns the class from the time she walks through the door, all the way to her seat. The professor backs up and repeats his last few sentences, partly because the class stopped listening, and mostly because she eclipses his next thought. He struggles to keep his mind in focus when she is present. He wants to impress her, and adds more energy to this specific class.

After language class, Mideah has an hour to kill before geography. Ignoring her tight, uncomfortable boots, she walks to a clothing store near campus. Shortly after she enters the store, the young man working that day timidly asks her if she needs help finding anything.

"No, I'll be fine on my own," Mideah answers, not looking at him.

She purposely brushes against him as she squeezes around a display rack. She notices that he is watching her look around the store, staying at a distance, pretending to refold sweaters on a nearby table. His eyes turn to stare, but not his head. She touches some watches that dangle from a spinning clear plastic display. She tries on one, holds out her arm for a better look, then puts it back and walks away. After looking through some nearby racks of clothing, she strolls back to the watches for another look. She purposefully lets her favorite watch slip into her open handbag. Mideah glances toward the boy working and sees him turn away nervously. This time he doesn't look at her as her boot heels drum across the wooden floor to the door.

Mideah utters, "Thank you," without looking back. She pulls the screen door open, stretching its springs.

"Come again," he invites. Twang. Slam. The springs pull the old wood door shut, dividing the space between his lusting eyes and the seductress. He hides at the front window, with curtains as his shroud. His pupils secretly wander over her body as Mideah waits to cross the street. When Mideah is out of site, he wonders if he should have mentioned the watch, then reasons the idea away. *Maybe she didn't know it fell into her purse?* He knows it was intentional, but denies it until he believes his own lie and hopes she will shop this store again —soon.

The city clock towers against the sky and bongs loudly eleven times and reminds Mideah of something.

"Oh!" she shrieks and reaches into her handbag for the new watch.

She peels off the price tag, sets the time to 11:03, a few minutes fast, before clamping it to her wrist. She races the clock, entering Geography ten minutes late. The woman professor ignores her, used to this interruption from Mideah, who is notoriously late for her class. She has eighteen other students who arrive at a respectable time, eager to learn.

The guy sitting next to Mideah notices that she forgot her text book. Truth is, she didn't bother to take it out of her backpack. He slides his chair until it touches Mideah's and pushes his book in front of her. He sits closer than he needs to. Mideah doesn't mind, because he is good looking and smells sexy. The hairs on his arm tickle hers as they turn pages together, half listening to their professor. During class, he almost writes his name and phone number on her notebook without her permission, but doesn't have the courage. Later his thoughts will convince him that she is interested in him. After this class ends, Mideah will have no thoughts of him. He is disposable. Same situations can have entirely different meanings.

Employees are hard at work at the agency, except for Mideah. She is bored. Her mind keeps drifting and losing focus. She wishes that she wore a different pair of pants. Gina's jeans are too tight, cutting into her abdomen. This bothers her, so she unbuttons and unzips them, just a little. *No way is Gina this size. She is fatter than me! I bet she is trying to lose weight to fit into these jeans.* Her feet are sore and getting hot, so she takes off her boots. Now she is ready to work. She needs to get busy putting together a vacation package for a family of five, frequent clients of hers. He and his wife have three girls, an eleven-year-old and eight-year-old twins. Mideah doesn't remember if he has a grown daughter. She is afraid to ask at this point. Maybe it was a niece that traveled with them that one time? His wife has only mentioned the three girls. That's his family as she knows it.

She enjoys planning trips for him. *Why am I procrastinating? Why can't I focus?* She is confused about her lack of motivation. Hunger is causing the apathy, but she doesn't make the connection, just ignores her body's signals to eat each time her stomach asks for food. Earlier, she passed on lunch and decided to go straight to work. On her desk, a diet soda is ignored. Next to it is an apple with a few bites missing.

She daydreams about the father of this family. She knows he is forty-one from his passport. He looks much younger, is athletic and very attractive. He is a commercial pilot and flies his family all over the world. His wife is much younger than he is and pretty. Mideah contemplates this woman's appearance for a moment, making comparisons. *I am hotter than she is.* Mideah boosts herself by uncovering greater defects on the woman, judging his wife's legs as chunky and her butt as wide and flat!

She fantasizes what it would be like to be his wife, where they would go, how he would surprise her with exotic retreats and lots of gifts and pampering. She pictures herself sipping cocktails on sugar sand beaches while reading romance novels, or shopping exclusive stores and eating in expensive restaurants —or in bed! Her lips lust for him. Her stomach growls again.

Mideah jolts in her seat when the phone rings.

"Good afternoon, Schaffer Travel. How may I assist you?" She speaks professionally.

"Hello Mideah, it's Ted. I'm calling about the winter break trip."

"Oh Ted, hello! I was just thinking about you. You really need to come in. Is it possible to schedule a meeting this afternoon? The sooner the better." Then she adds, "I am all yours."

"Great. I can be there at three." Ted decides as he writes himself a reminder.

Mideah confirms, "Three o'clock it is. Looking forward to seeing you."

With renewed energy and focus, Mideah thinks about Ted's twin girls, what eight-year-old girls do for fun, then compiles a list of amusement parks, festivals and special events aimed for kids. She adds a few teen activities to entice his eleven-year-old daughter. Mideah pretends to include herself in their vacation to plan his romantic evenings. She is jealous that her spicy ideas will be wasted on his wife. *This should be my vacation.* She compiles all this information together, makes extra copies, then packages it neatly into a bright translucent pouch with her business card displayed.

This business card has a large, close-up, professional photo of Mideah's face, head tilted provocatively, overshadowing the agencies contact information that is written in tiny print. She hands out this card just to show off the photo. Later, she will get some social cards made with this same photo, but printed on lip-shaped card stock. *I'm sexy!*

Mideah glances at the new watch that wraps her guilt-less wrist. It is approaching three o'clock. She pushes each foot back into leather boots, folds the hem of her jeans neatly around each ankle, traces the zipper up her calves. *Time to get beautiful. Oops. More beautiful.*

The restroom is her transformation booth. She gazes into her eyes, falling more in love as she re-applies makeup and primps. She dabs perfume on her neck and between her breasts, adds lip gloss as a final touch. Transformed.

Coworkers who enter this restroom will find evidence of Mideah's recent visit, smelling makeup and lingering perfume. Brown powder is dusted over the counter and white vanity bowl. She entitled herself to a drawer in this public vanity and made it her cosmetic toy box. The other two drawers are used to store extra soap, toilet paper and cleaning supplies. Everyone else keeps personal items at their desk. Mideah left her toy box open, exposing a pink hairbrush, its bristles tangled in long blond strands. Whoever uses this bathroom next will shut her drawer after snooping through her things, then wipe Mideah's spills off the counter.

Poised, ready and waiting, Mideah adorns her office chair. Although Ted is a few minutes early, Mideah is prepared for their meeting, always prompt and on time when it is to her advantage.

"Good afternoon, Ted," she greets, her professional voice edging on sexy. "I am ready for you. Will you please follow me to the conference room?" She walks in front of him, crossing her legs in front of each foot, like a model on a runway. She is hoping that Ted is walking his eyes all over her. He is.

Mideah pulls out a chair for him, "Please have a seat. May I get you something to drink?"

"Coffee, if it is already made." He smiles nervously at her. "And only if you're having some."

"I made a fresh pot just before you got here.... cream, no sugar, right?"

"You remember!" Ted feigns surprise.

"I pay attention." Mideah flirts as she leaves the room.

Ted doesn't restrict his lustful thoughts. He fantasizes about what is beneath the fabric of her tight jeans.

In the kitchenette, Mideah pours two mugs of coffee and puts fresh cream in both. She carries them to the conference room, pushing the door closed with her knee. She selects the chair right next to Ted, instead of across, as she would for most other clients.

"Here is the preliminary packet. I'd like to go through the itinerary, get your approval, then we can finalize." Mideah talks while opening the packet, her hands shaking nervously as she pulls out the brochures and assorted paperwork.

Ted notices her anxiety, rapid speech and blatant professionalism. He pats the top of her hand and holds it for a moment, comforting her. "Relax, we've been through this before." He squeezes softly before letting go of her hand.

Mideah looks at Ted's face, allures him with the pout she often practices in mirrors, then smiles. She continues her presentation at ease, explaining options for travel and entertainment. She dares to go further in her flirtations, saying, "I am excited for your family. You will all have a great time..." Mideah hesitates and gives Ted a sideways glance at her prettiest angle, "Now if I could just get you to adopt me..."

Ted eats up her words, raises his eyebrows and smiles with his eyes partly shut. They continue the meeting with small talk of unrelated business. Often her knee *accidently* bumps his and vice versa. While progressing their flirtatious comments, Mideah or Ted will lean over to bump shoulders, suggesting a nudge, but really implying the unspoken. Both parties are aware of the ulterior motives they are expressing, in covert fashion, yet in denial of the harm being done. Both are guzzling the thrill and rush of serotonin, love's natural drug, and not thinking beyond the closed door. Neither are thinking beyond themselves.

On the conference table, two mugs of coffee are left behind, never touched until the evening cleaning crew pours them out.

Psalms 77:16-20 (NIV)
[16] The waters saw you, O God, the waters saw you and writhed; the very depths were convulsed.
[17] The clouds poured down water, the skies resounded with thunder; your arrows flashed back and forth.
[18] Your thunder was heard in the whirlwind, your lightning lit up the world; the earth trembled and quaked.
[19] Your path led through the sea, your way through the mighty waters, though your footprints were not seen.
[20] You led your people like a flock by the hand of Moses and Aaron.

chapter 6   ali

Ali has her entire outfit picked out the night before Math class. Mr. Perfect is in the audience now. She tries on clothes for almost two hours. A pile of clean clothes is forming in front of her closet. She knows what jeans she wants to wear, but they are too tight. To stretch them out, she pulls them on over another pair and does squats and lounges. She believes that baggy jeans depict the illusion of skinny. Skinny means value. Skinny means confidence. Skinny means self-control and perfection. Skinny will get Mr. Perfect to notice her.

She fantasizes his name. Several girls do. They whisper it. *Jason.* They secretly write it in notebooks, next to hearts and flowers. To have him love you means you are special, better than other girls. Ali no longer calls him Mr. Perfect. Saying *Jason* is so much sexier. She obsesses to know everything about him. He wears Polo cologne. He has a mole just above his collar, right side. He is a Math genius and refined comedian. Ali practices the perfect giggle, to be ready for his witty remarks. She has pretend conversations with him, whispers between lovers. She speaks up in class, hoping to sound smart. Her makeup and hair are always perfect for Math. He never notices. All the girls drooling over him, including Ali, fail to realize that he doesn't actually see them or hear them. He receives. He absorbs. He cannot fathom giving. His ego is so hungry, it instinctively devours. He stockpiles hearts and stores them, easy to discard when they pass their expiration date.

Ali gathers with the other chicks, waiting for the scraps he throws. She arrives to class early, trying to guess which his seat he will take. Sometimes she pretends to look at a bulletin board, stalking discreetly in the back of the room, ready to melt into the seat behind him.

Today, a white cotton shirt spans endlessly across Jason's back, tight-fitting. It follows contours of muscle and pinches into the grooves of his biceps. Ali studies the topstitching of Jason's yoke and stares at the thin, red stripe edging his sleeve. *Ahh, his arms! Tanned. Bulging. Sculpted.* She desperately wants to pluck the strand of black hair gracing the back of his shirt —not to groom him, but for a keepsake.

Slouching into the desk directly behind Jason, Ali keeps her mind busy with self-doubt. She hates the scene in front of her. She draws an equilateral triangle on notebook paper and labels it *The Bermuda Triangle*. She puts the letter "J" in the center of the triangle. At the tip of the triangle she writes G1, then adds G2 and G3 to the other corners—naming the female dogs flirting with her J. This is the seating arrangement in front of her, the shape of the Bermuda Triangle, with Mr. Perfect centered and looking like a Greek statue —the eye of the storm. He is enthralling goddess G2 and G3. They keep touching his arms. Without permission, Jason rakes his fingers through the waterfall of blond hair in front of him. G1 swishes her hair, hoping the chiseled marble likes her best —Touch-me! Touch-me!

Ali gives her brown hair a swish but it seems to stick to her scalp, too short to be fluid. She wishes that her thighs didn't rub together when she walks and that crossing them was easier, like it is for the bare legs of Goddess G2. Ali pinches her own ear without realizing it. She rubs the soft tissue where an earring should be. She stares at the twisted silver hoop tangled in red curls of the bare-leg girl. A week later, Ali will notice a similar pair of hoop earrings on her mother's nightstand and wear them to Math class.

Goddess3 giggles and leans over, bouncing her temple off Jason's broad shoulder. She blinks mascara lashes at him. This happens right after Jason writes something on her notebook.

The teacher asks a question. There is a hesitation before a show of hands lift, eager to answer. G3, the black haired goddess with fat red lips, waves her manicured fingernails like a flag, while bouncing in her seat. The teacher points to her. All hands go down. She picks up her notebook with pretty fingers to read Jason's handwriting. Before she recites the stolen answer, Ali butts in and says it loud enough for everyone to hear. G3's fat red lips form a childish pout. She huffs and slaps her notebook down. The spiral wires hit the desktop with a deliberate bang. Blue eyes, with a thick umbrella of mascara, shift over her shoulder and squint at Ali like a poison arrow. Ali slumps low in her seat, until Jason turns around to deliver a look that means 'I am impressed.' The power of his grin pulls Ali up. She sits taller and leans forward, allowing pride to swell her balloon of hope.

After Math class, Ali sharpens her pencil at the door, timing her exit just right, preparing her opening statement. *Here he comes!* Her witty comment is memorized and polished. *...And there he goes.* Ali is cut off after, *"Hey, I...."* He lunges ahead of her words to tickle the sides of G1, the blond water fall. Suddenly, the leggy-girl speeds up and slips her arm around Jason's bicep. As if in a race, the girl with pouty red lips bumps Ali out of the way and gropes into Jason's right side. The Bermuda triangle has returned. It storms down the corridor, swallowing up Ali's confidence, leaving her crushed against the door jamb, held by waves of students vacating Math class. Ali's opening statement is left behind with the pencil shavings. Now she is doing a dead-man's-float, swept by a current through her next two classes. She does not want to notice anyone or be noticed. She is drowning.

At three o'clock, Ali pays for two bags of chocolates, ice-cream, chips and a liter of spring-water. She avoids eye contact with the cashier by keeping her head down and shoulders curled forward. Her soul mourns inside her chest and calls her away from the choices she is making. Ali doesn't believe in a better way. Her mouth craves the taste of sugar and fatty-greasy food. She trusts that gorging will help her disappear. It will sedate her. It will eliminate her cravings. She craves Love. Craves Jesus. She just doesn't realize.

She convinces herself that this is her final time of giving in. It will be the last time of weakness, her final good-bye. She is super embarrassed when two people get in line behind her, aware that they are analyzing the items she lined up on the black belt. The cashier jerks the belt forward a few times, jiggling her junk food as if calling Ali names. *Junkie! Addict! Pig!* The chip bag crunches and echoes when it hits the liter of water. Ali thinks the cashier knows her dark secret, as she presses judgments into her palm, *Twenty-six cents makes sixteen, seventeen, eighteen, nineteen and twenty.* Instead, Ali hears, *No wonder you are so fat! Are you really going to eat all that? Get a life!* Anxious and uncomfortable, Ali wishes she had her cart full of items to mix in with her sins. Healthy decoys would make it look like she is just there for groceries and a couple of treats. Ali watches the cashier's hands to avoid eye contact. She takes the receipt and mumbles gratitude. She picks up her two bags of indulgence faster than she realizes and hurries out the automatic door.

In the car, Ali finally relaxes and breathes again. Alone and hidden she bites her thumbnail, trying to remember what she did last time. *Should I get some or not? I hate that stuff. I hate buying it. It is obvious and embarrassing. What if I can't throw up? I will be so fat! I hate this! I hate this! I hate me. I have to... can't risk it.* Shame crushes her when she chooses to do it this way. It is humiliating to buy this last item. Using this product to purge is a testimony of her desperation. Walking into a store and buying this is worse than going to Math class naked. It exposes her to the bone and allows a window into her secrets. She passes a few Pharmacies before stopping. She cannot keep going to the same one or they will suspect. Quite a few miles down the road, she pulls into the parking lot, glad there are only a few cars. Once inside, she browses the isles for other items to be her decoys. Nail polish, polish remover, nail files and shampoo samples will surround her real purchase. Hopefully, these items are distracting enough to keep the cashier and other customers from noticing she is buying a special syrup that comes in a tiny brown bottle. She positions the bottle just right, thankful the price tag is on the back, so she can block its label with her shampoo samples.

Ali doesn't realize she is holding her breath when the cashier picks up the syrup. He is an older gentleman wearing a long white jacket. He peers over half moon glasses that rest low on his nose, looks directly at her, then punches in the price. She silently gives him cash for the exact amount. And he silently finishes the transaction. The man puts each item in a brown paper bag and tears the receipt.

He looks into her eyes compassionately and finally speaks, "Do you understand the danger in using that?"

Ali is dumbfounded. She did not expect confrontation.

"What?" she says weakly.

"What is meant for poison, can become the poison —if misused." He tells her, realizing the irony.

"Huh?" Ali says, pretending to be confused. She does not know how to respond.

"The stuff can kill-ya," he says bluntly, but with a tender voice, as if talking to his granddaughter.

"Thank you." she says and walks away before he confronts her again.

The pharmacist just happened to be the cashier for Ali. Usually he is at the back of the store in the pharmacy. He watches Ali leave, hoping she understands what he is trying to say to her. He is concerned that so many young ladies are coming in to purchase ipecac. The store manager is ignoring his request to have it removed from the shelves. *You worry about your area, I'll take care of mine!* The manager keeps telling him.

When the cashier returns from her break, the pharmacist tells her, "Another one today."

"Really!" she shakes her head, "I think I will just start hiding those bottles behind other products."

"Go ahead, my lips are sealed," says the pharmacist, then returns to his area in the back of the store to fill prescriptions.

Just before leaving the parking lot Ali transforms the passenger seat of the car into a buffet. Her smorgasbord of salvation generously serves chips, chocolates and the doughnuts she picked up after buying the little brown bottle. She drives along with her food in easy reach.

I'll never go in that store again! Anxiety rushes through Ali's nerves each time she re-lives the words the old man said. *It is poison. It will kill you. Dangerous.* Swear words repeatedly slip past her lips. Anxiety is controlling her as if she has tourette syndrome. She feels like a pressure cooker where words and groans need to escape. Otherwise, she would explode from all the negative thoughts pressing against her skull. *He knows. It is so disgusting. And he caught me. Stupid. Stupid. Stupid. I am weak. I am awful. Horrible. Another day —ruined! My life is a waste. I can't keep living like this. So out of control. I have no will power. None! I am just a fat jerk-loser-pig! Cow!*

Ali's car is moving along in a steady line of traffic as she slowly fades from living. Calories aren't exactly enjoyed. There is false pleasure in food that has no consequence. What is the point then? Punishment! That is the point. Faults, too many to name, become bites of chocolate, glazed apple fritters and mouthfuls of chips. Comfort! *I feel worthless. Make me feel better or help me forget* Greed! Another point. Ali is not satisfied with normal portion sizes. *I want more, so I will eat more.* Eat the whole bag. Hog it all. *I want to gorge on food and still be skinny. I don't want to exercise.* Selfishness! Her key point. *I want to be noticed. I want to be great! It want it to be about me! I want to be the pretty one. The smartest. The nicest. The sexiest.* Fear! Always fear. And then comes the emptiness. The relief. She is a perfectionist, a perfect failure. this is what she believes in. Ali desires something to worship, so she makes food her idol. And it becomes a controlling relationship.

full stomach-empty soul-empty stomach —Bulimic Poetry.

She pulls her car into the driveway, gathers up the evidence of cartons and wrappers, and hides it in her backpack. The ice cream she bought is melting. Her mother is not home yet, as expected. She knows her little brother is in the basement, based on the sound of his video game echoing in the stairwell. Each weekday after school, Ali is required, by Mom, to be home watching Brandon "a couple hours," so she says. Most of the time a couple hours is three or four hours, depending on her mother's social duties for work. Ali's step-father, Brandon's dad, keeps the same work hours as her mother, except when they travel. Right now Dad is on a business trip. He set out a small package for Brandon on the kitchen counter earlier today (a video game). Ali quit hoping for non-existent surprises from her step dad a long time ago. Dad always leaves one present and it never has her name on it.

Ali feels safe, yet still tip-toes around the kitchen. She grabs a bowl and spoon and takes them, along with her backpack, to her bedroom. She turns on her TV to a program about nothing. She thinks about nothing, sees nothing, hears nothing, while she finishes most of the ice cream. She is a zombie, slow moving and robotic, controlled by dark thoughts about her nothingness.

The last thing she does before she sinks to the bottom, is drink from the little brown bottle. Now she waits. Ten minutes later, her punishments, faults, greed, selfishness, perfectionism and fears are flushed down the toilet.

Her demon, Shame, is hiding while all this is going on. He didn't get flushed! Shame is making himself known, lurking inside Ali's soul.

He is whispering in her ear, *Worthless.*

He is calling back his companions, *Fear, Doubt, Greed, Vanity, Envy, Despair and Discontentment!* He gathers his army and says, *Skulk with us!*

The demons cling to Ali, talons gripping her shoulders. He neck is stiff. Sore. It hurts to turn and look another way.

Desperate and in need of intervention, Ali will fight her battle in private. Across the nation, food will be purchased, never intended to be digested, but tasted twice. Ali is unaware that right now someone several miles from her home is drinking syrup from the tiny brown bottle for the last time, departing life with the words 'accidental death' written on the form filed at the coroner's office.

She cannot imagine this reality: dying in her own vomit.

Little brother, Brandon, does not stay in the basement for long. He heard Ali come home. After a while, he decides to show his sister the game his dad bought him. Brandon sees that Ali's door is cracked open. He pushes it open the rest of the way. She is not in there.

He squints, curls his lip and says, "Huh?"

Brandon is confused to see a carton of ice cream melting on her dresser. Wanting some too, he picks it up and carries it down the hallway, past the bathroom. He stops, motionless at the door when he hears Ali coughing and toilet water splashing. Brandon moves slowly, soft-footed down the stairs, swallowing several times. He notices that he is carrying the carton of melting ice cream. Appetite lost, Brandon hides the ice cream deep into their freezer and pulls the curtain over his eyes.

Ali returns to her room believing her secret is kept. For the most part it is, since her family turns a blind eye. Denial is so much easier than confrontation. She does not detect that her door is open, different than she left it, or that something is missing off her dresser. She feels oddly renewed, trusting a lie. *This will be my last time!* Thankful that what she ate won't make her fat.

She doesn't feel Shame right now. It is resting and gaining power, chanting *worthless, worthless, worthless...* Ali is not hearing it yet. This voice will become piercing later on, when her will weakens and she submits to instinctive hunger, real and legitimate hunger. Her body needs nourishment. That is when Shame will scream, *Just eat! Food is all you have!*

Ali binges again, hours later, after skipping dinner with her family. She waits until everyone is sleeping and ends her day with her self-destructive ritual, unaccountable for the food she eats and using the remaining syrup for an encore purge. She is afraid of her last bite. She hates getting to the end of her comfort.

In bed, Ali stares at the ceiling with tears edging her eyes and getting ready to spill over. Her body is still and lifeless, heavy with grief. Her heart is pounding dangerous patterns against her chest, likely from an overdose of ipecac. Ali knows she is out of control, knows that she needs help, yet convinces herself that she can do it on her own.

Her thoughts teeter-totter between burying secrets and telling someone.

"Who? Who can I tell?" She keeps asking herself. "I have no one to tell."

She has no relationship able to carry this burden with her. Her 'loved-ones' will be crushed under the weight of her load. They are emotional weaklings, not capable of this news. That is why they run from Ali, why they don't see. They live under the same roof, with eyes squeezed shut, lips sealed, backs turned and fingers in their ears.

So Ali gets her shovel and starts digging! Her secrets need a grave.

Job 39:27 (NIV)
[27] Does the eagle soar at your command and build his nest on high?

chapter 7 reece

Brandon hands the school bus driver a crumpled note with his Dad's handwriting, his permission to ride the bus with Luke. Brandon staggers down the aisle, his duffel bag bouncing behind him, hitting seats and students along the way. At the back of the bus, he pushes into the seat with his buddies, Luke and Carl. The boys fumble through their hand shake ritual, that ends with bumping fists together.

They do a victory dance sassing, "we're going kayaking!" Luke is the instigator, Brandon and Carl are the imitators. The boys all talk at once, shouting over each others' voices.

"Dude, I see you flippin' out of yours!"

"No way! It's you who's swimmin'. After I tip you with my paddle!"

"You won't catch me!"

"My Gramma is faster en you!"

"If I tip over, it will be on purpose!"

"Where's Jordan?" Brandon asks Luke, who is having the party.

"Doo-ude, he's meetin' us there."

The contest continues, jabbing each other with boyish insults, all three afraid to admit they never kayaked before.

Luke fogs up the window behind him, cupping his hands over his mouth, puffing moist air onto the window. He draws a kayak in the haze. It looks like a banana. The other two boys copy, drawing stick figures posing with half circles for biceps. The fog on the window dissipates, leaving faint finger smudges, while Brandon passes out candy that was stashed in his duffle bag. After several bubble gum blowing contests, the bus stops in a residential area near the water sports store. Several young kids herd down the narrow aisle and exit the bus.

The bus driver is looking over his dark rimmed glasses and into his oversized rear view mirror. Chomping nicotine gum, he shouts to them. "Hey boys! Time to get off the bus!"

The boys snap to attention and say, "Huh?" then stumble down the aisle in one big wad.

Jordan is sitting on a bench outside the store, wearing muddy shoes and using his gym bag as a foot stool. The three boys run over to greet him, heaving false punches to his shoulder. They trail behind Luke into the store, over to a young man that is working that day.

"We're here for kayaking." Luke tells the man.

"Hello men! I have you all set up. We need to go over a few things before we hit the water." The man motions with a head nod that means follow me.

The boys are led like a timid train through a locker area toward the back door.

Before the man goes out, he turns and says, "Over there are changing rooms and lockers if you need them. I'll be holding onto your locker keys. So have them ready when I get back." He points and says, "Bathroom's over there. Come on out when you are ready."

The dimly lit locker room smells moist with a faint odor of Pine-Sol cleanser. The bare concrete floor is cold on the boys' feet as they change into shorts, long sleeved t-shirts and flip flops. They each select a locker and pile their belongings at the bottom, cloths hanging out and jamming in the door. Brandon doesn't realize when he wads his clothes, that his locker key is mixed in with it. He accidently shuts the key inside.

Luke is ready first and waiting near the door. After the last metal door slams shut, he reminds his friends, "Remember to give your key to that guy."

Brandon pats all the pockets of his khaki cargo shorts, not feeling his key. Both of his hands are face up in front of him when he says, "Dudes, I can't find my key!"

"Braaaannn-don!" They all sing at once and start searching the floor, bench, bathroom and changing rooms.

Luckily, Brandon's locker door is still slightly ajar, lodged with clothes. He yanks on his locker door until it breaks free and opens. Brandon pulls his belongings out of his locker and feels around the bottom of his bag.

The kayak guide pops his head around the back door and says, "Hey, did you guys get lost?"

"No, but Brandon's key did!" Luke tattles, handing the man his own key. Carl and Jordan do the same.

"Don't worry about it. We can look for it later. I want to get you men on the river!"

The missing key is barely visible, standing upright off the bottom of the locker and wedged against the metal sidewall. "Hey! Here it is!" Brandon slides his hand down the inner metal wall and peels the key off with his thumbnail.

Their instructor fakes an angry voice, but is grinning at Brandon when he grabs the key from the kid and says, "Gimme that key!" He adds, "Hey men! Grab your jackets."

The kayak guide opens their lockers. Four boys dig through their bags once again and pull out wrinkled jackets.

Just outside the door, lined up on the weedy grass, red kayaks are balancing inches off the ground, resting snuggly in carpeted wooden holders. Six kayaks have a paddle teeter-tottering across the cockpit and life vests folded in the seats. Two women in their late thirties are chatting near the end of the row.

Everything is a race with these boys, including picking out a kayak. Carl trips over the back of one and falls onto the grass. The women smirk and lift eyebrows at each other, sharing the same thoughts.

"Now that everyone is here, I'd like to introduce myself. My name is Reece. I started kayaking when I was six years old, with my Grandpa and Dad. I have been instructing and giving tours for three years now." He is standing with his legs wide apart, holding a paddle across his thighs. Intent faces are staring at him. He points his paddle toward one woman and says,

"We'll start with you. Tell us your name and briefly describe how experienced you are at kayaking."

Both women state their names, Brenda and Cathy, and say they have been canoeing, but never kayaking. Reece points to Brandon next. Brandon shifts on his feet a couple of times, biting his lower lip. He doesn't want to be the first to admit he has never been kayaking, or even in a boat before.

"Well, I already know your name is Brandon and that you are good at finding keys," Reece encourages, "And I will give you boys a refresher course, just in case. What are your friends' names?"

Brandon exhales, smiles at Reece, points and introduces, "This is Luke. It's his birthday party today. That's Carl and Jordan."

Reece looks at Luke, "Birthday-boy? How old?"

"Eleven," Luke answers proudly.

"How about you, Carl?"

"Eleven."

"Jordan?"

"I'm twelve." He stands up straighter, but is still shorter than the other boys.

"Are you twelve, Brandon?"

Brandon is pleased to be mistaken as a big-kid, but is honest. "I'm only ten," He says while kicking his left flip-flop into the dirt. "Oh!" He remembers. Jerking his head up, Brandon quickly corrects, "Actually. I'm almost eleven."

The women are amused by the four young boys, but are melting over Brandon's boyish charms. His appearance has traces of a baby-face, with straight blonde hair curving outward over his ears and thick bangs, almost covering his green eyes. Light brown freckles speckle the bridge of his nose. His cheeks expose dimples with the slightest movement of his lips. They notice that Brandon often flashes shy half-smiles, timidly curling up only the right side of his mouth, tilting his chin into his chest. Brenda and Cathy both have nine year old daughters at home. One whispers to the other, "My future son-in-law." Both women giggle. The boys are unaware, but Reece overhears and smiles.

Reece demonstrates how to properly strap on the life vest and how to loosen it first, allowing it to slip over their heads. Everyone puts theirs on, off and then back on, except Brandon, who rushes to pull his off without loosening the straps. The boys giggle and tease as they watch a headless Brandon struggle inside the life vest. He is trapped with it covering his face, wedging his arms against his ears. Wiggling out from the neck of Brandon's vest are two hands bending at the wrist, grabbing air. Reece laughs to himself, walks over and lifts the vest off Brandon's head, exposing a blushing, embarrassed face. Reece resists teasing as he loosens the straps, slides it over Brandon's head and pulls the straps snug, across his chest.

"Okay, Brandon slide your thumbs into these loops and pull forward." The vest opens and hangs loosely off Brandon's shoulders. "Put your thumbs under the shoulder straps and lift." Brandon is successful as he flips the vest instantly over his head.

"That's it. Slip it back on and pull it snug again," Reece instructs.

Cars slow down, their drivers gawking at the row of kayaks lined up, each carrying a passenger pretending to paddle in the grass. A young man is standing in front of them twirling a figure eight with a paddle. Reece ignores the honking and waving from the street as he continues the lesson. He gives each boy a chance to demonstrate for the others, to keep their attention. He shows them techniques for entering and exiting the kayak, gives options of paddle gripping, and explains how to steer. He goes over rules of safety and explains the importance of staying in a group and what to do if someone tips over. This most likely will happen with these boys and probably on purpose.

Everyone pitches in to load the Kayaks on a trailer that is ready and waiting, hitched behind a navy blue van. The logo *'Bluewater Adventures'* is painted in big letters across the entire side. A red-head girl, wearing a t-shirt with the Bluewater logo, helps them load, then rides up front with Reece.

Their destination is a wide, slow moving river six miles out of town. The van pulls out of the parking lot and heads down the street adjacent to the grassy area where the kayak instruction recently took place. Laying in the grass is a forgotten life vest. One of the women spot it.

She yells out, "We might need to stop! I think someone forgot their vest."

Reece is patient as he drives the van near the curb and puts it in park. Distractions are a common occurrence with his groups of young paddlers. The lost and found box is always overflowing, keys are lost and he is constantly inventing new ways to keep their attention and energy focused beneficially.

Brenda hops out of the van to retrieve the vest. The boys watch out the window as she jogs across the grass. At first they blame Brandon for leaving it behind. He insists that it was not him. When they realize it was Luke who left it, nothing more is said, no teasing, no blaming. Brenda hands the life vest behind the seat to Jordan, who squishes it down on the floor and rests his feet on it. The ladies have their vests stacked neatly between, while absorbing the kicking and punching felt through the back of their van seat.

It is relatively warm for early fall, hot when the sun peeks out of the thick cotton clouds, but cool in the shadows. The group is thankful they all brought jackets to wear when the sun hides its heat. Two of the boys, Luke and Carl, struggle at balancing their kayaks. They climb in feet first and immediately fall bottom first into the water, like slipping on ice. They will be kayaking wet from the waist down, consequences from ignoring instructions. Jordan manages okay, but is sitting stiff and timid as if frozen to his paddle. Brandon surprises Reece with his grace and natural ability from the start and is now paddling confidently ahead, looking back to zap his friends with pride beaming off his face. The women are talking while snapping photos of a turtle sunning on a rotten log.

Reece hangs back at the rear of the group, available for necessary help. Familiar as this river is to him, it never ceases to tranquilize him with calming beauty —in sight, sound and fragrance. The more intentional he listens, the more he hears. If he searches, the landscape offers him something new to see. If he closes his eyes, the sounds grow louder and the aroma more intense. An eagle soars above them. Reece yells three times to get the groups attention, pointing to the sky. The eagle is gone and his kayakers paddle on in oblivion. Ever since he can remember, his grandpa would give him a dollar for every eagle he spotted on his own, a quarter for hawks and two dollars for porcupines and owls. What he really received from grandpa was awareness —priceless awareness!

Everyone is more confident, moving downstream at a faster pace. Even Jordan is slouching and relaxed, trusting his kayak when it tilts from side to side. Reece paddles by the women to tell them to pull out of the river at the sandy clearing, after the next bend ahead. He steers across to the other side and repeats this information to the boys, asking them to follow him.

Autumn, the co-worker that rode with Reece to spot the van, is waiting by the shore, ready to hold the watercrafts steady as the novice kayakers climb out. She pulls each boy's kayak completely out of the water and onto the sand where they get out on dry ground. She has a portable table set up with beverages and snacks, including a birthday cake, scripted with Happy Birthday Luke. Blue icing forms a river holding a plastic miniature kayak. Luke's parents are waiting for him, lounging in camp chairs. Mom is ready with her camera, Dad with matches.

Birthday rituals of singing, making a wish and candle blowing are complete. The boys jump up at once, eager to get back into the water.

Wait!" Dad says, "Go over to the truck, Luke." He points to the parking area. "There's a surprise for you in back."

The boys rush to the truck, pushing and bumping into each other, before breaking into a sprint.

"Dude!" They shout in unison, all standing on the rear bumper, peering over the tailgate.

Dad is smiling and Mom is snapping photos of Luke and his friends crouching in the truck bed, petting a brand new yellow kayak as if it were a dog. Luke will finish the last leg of the river in his own kayak, with a new paddle and life vest.

While Autumn and Luke's parents clean up and drive back, the group returns to the river. Luke is cautious with his new toy and bosses his friends if they get too close. A new kayak cannot get scratched. And it is better admired from behind by three jealous boys.

Reece remembers the day he received his first kayak. He was nine years old. He checked his savings account weekly, until he had enough money. Grandpa took Reece to the store the day he reached his savings goal. The kayak just happened to go on sale that morning, giving Reece extra dollars for a better paddle and some gear. Scratches were not allowed on his kayak either.

Brandon and Luke race to shore. Satisfied and exhausted, the group doubles up to carry each kayak to the Bluewater van. Autumn jumps out to help when she sees heads bobbing through the trees. The drive back is quiet. In the far back seat, four boys have their eyes closed and mouths wide open.

Standing next to the van, Brenda and Cathy gather belongings and say goodbye, leaning in to hug their young friends. The boys pull away with reluctant grins. Brandon gets an extra squeeze from Brenda.

Carl's dad leans his head out the window and yells to Brandon, "Are you sure you don't need a ride?"

"No. My mom is always late. I can wait." Brandon responds.

Reece sits outside on the bench with Brandon as he waits for his ride home. After forty-five minutes, they both go back into the store and call his mom. No answer. Brandon leaves a message, looks at Reece and shrugs his shoulders.

"Wanna help me get some packages ready for shipping?" Reece asks.

Brandon likes this idea. He follows Reece around the store, holding a box as Reece reads from a clipboard.

Deuteronomy 5:7-10 (NIV)
[7] "You shall have no other gods before me.
[8] "You shall not make for yourself an idol in the form of anything in heaven above or on the earth beneath or in the waters below.
[9] You shall not bow down to them or worship them; for I, the Lord your God, am a jealous God, punishing the children for the sin of the fathers to the third and fourth generation of those who hate me,
[10] but showing love to a thousand [generations] of those who love me and keep my commandments

chapter 8 ali

The phone keeps ringing and ringing. Hang up. Ringing again.

Finally, Ali answers the phone, "hello?"

"Ali, it's Mom."

"Yeah?"

"Look, I need you to pick up Brandon from that kayaking party, ASAP!"

"Mom, I am right in the middle..."

"You need to go now! He called a while ago and has been waiting."

"Alright. Where is he?"

"It is called adventure, ah, blue-something. Just look it up to get directions. Gotta go!" Click. Her mother hangs up on her.

Ali turns off the stove and leaves the pasta soaking, as the boiling water dispels. She just put the noodles in. Feeling sorry for Brandon's abandonment, she rushes out the door wearing a yellow sweatshirt with a glob of ketchup dried up on her chest and duck print flannel pajama pants. She has been rubbing her right eye. Now mascara is smeared from the under her eye to her temple. She doesn't look in the mirror and doesn't care that her hair is uncombed and greasy. *No one will see me. I'll just stay in the car.* She expects Brandon to be waiting outside as usual and will hop in the car before she even parks.

She starts her car, turns on her headlights and pushes the gas pedal with a clumsy foot. She is wearing her stepfather's brown corduroy slippers. They were closest to the door, easiest to slip on. Her neighborhood is turning shades of gray from the sun dropping towards the horizon. Ali drives out of the cul-de-sac reading directions off the back of the invitation she found tacked to the bulletin board. In bold, it says, *'Please pick up at 6:00 in the parking lot of Blue Water Adventures.'*

The clock in her car glows 7:09 p.m. when she pulls into the parking lot. Brandon is not outside waiting. Yellow light from inside the store warms up the windows and spills onto the pavement. At the entry doors, Ali reluctantly motions to Brandon, who doesn't seem to notice her. He is standing holding a box, laughing and talking to someone bending down at a display rack. Her first thought is to go back to the car and honk, but dismisses the idea. She combs her fingers through clumpy hair, tucks it behind her ears and forces herself to go inside.

"Hey! I know you!" a familiar voice remarks.

Ali turns towards the voice and immediately her face heats up and turns deep red. She is regretting a series of choices. Getting out of the car is her biggest regret. She bites her lower lip and squeezes her eyes tight, her common instant reaction to surprise and embarrassment. Without speaking, her brain spells out a four letter word, emphasizing each letter.

"Remember me from the coffee shop? Ali, right?" He holds out his hand, "I'm Reece."

"Reece?" Ali asks, faking a question.

She knew who he was the moment he stood up and turned around. She shakes his hand shyly and purposely grabs a handful of her yellow shirt, the part with the ketchup stain. She wishes she could hide her entire self in her fist. She wishes the store lights weren't so bright and hopes his eyes don't look down at her feet. *Oh yeah, and the pants! What was I thinking? How hard is it to comb my hair and put on some decent clothes?*

"Hi Al." Brandon chirps, "We're almost finished with this order. Wanna help?"

Reece is grinning at Ali, sensing her embarrassment. Her body language shouts, *I am uncomfortable! Don't look at me! Get me out of here!* He has a hunch she doesn't know her makeup is smeared across her eye. If he knew her better, he would say, 'first a bloody nose, now a black eye!' and maybe even sing the rubber-ducky song. Looking at her under-done appearance compels him to like her even more. It makes her authentic. He appreciates seeing who she is when she thinks no one is looking.

Reece gives Ali a quick escape by saying, "Thanks for your help, Brandon. I can finish it up," but really wishes she would stay.

"Aww-right," Brandon resigns.

"Sorry we're so late. Thanks for being patient with him." Ali says, rescuing her mother by apologizing.

"No problem. He's been a great help," Reece squeezes Brandon's shoulder and adds, "We'll kayak again sometime. Bring your sister if you want."

"Really? Aw-right!" Brandon's dimples deepen from the huge grin on his face. He looks over at Ali and says, "Maybe she can come, but she can't kayak as good as I can."

"Well, she has us to help her out," Reece tells him, then turns to Ali, "How 'bout pick a day next week and give me a call?"

Reece walks just a few steps over to the counter and picks up his business card. Brandon looks at Ali and lifts his eyebrows up and down, making an overt statement.

Ali elbows him. "Stop it!" she whispers with teeth clenched.

Reece holds out the card to Ali, "Call me here. I can set both of you up with equipment —on the house."

"Why on the house?" asks Brandon, confused about stuff on a house.

Before Brandon gets an answer, he changes the subject, "Al, why are you wearing Dad's slippers?"

Her embarrassment intensifies. Ali gives Brandon a tug. "Were leaving."

She glances back on the way to the door, waves and says, "Thanks again. Bye."

Reece has his arms folded on his chest and lifts his hand in a quick good-bye. He is still smiling as they drive away.

In the car Brandon is sitting in the backseat, a habit formed by his mother. Ali usually lets him ride in the front with her, but doesn't mention it this time. As soon as they are out of site of Bluewater Adventures, Ali pulls down her mirrored visor and dares to see what she looks like.

"Oh great!" she sighs, noticing her black eye and matted hair. "Just great!"

"Ali's in laaa-of." Brandon sing-songs, leaning forward, grabbing the back of her car seat. "With Reece-eee." He makes kissing sounds near her ear.

"I am not in love. I don't even know him," she defends. *Why do I care if he sees me so... sloppy.*

Ali's toes curl and release inside the fleece lined corduroy slippers floating on her feet. It feels like she is wearing shoe boxes. *Thanks a lot Brandon for pointing them out in front of everyone!* She ignores the teasing by turning the radio up louder, drowning the words escaping from the back seat. As Brandon mocks, Ali sings falsetto and off key as possible.

A fast food restaurant is in the distance, "Hey! Stop there! Stop there!" shouts Brandon in the backseat, "Please. Please. Please. Please." nonstop, like a steady pounding of a drum.

Ali puts her right-turn blinker on.

"Thank you. Thank you. Thank you. Thank you...."

"Okay, Brandon! Stop!"

"Okay. Okay. Okay. Okay..." in perfect rhythm to the blinker.

Ali turns off her blinker, pretending to change her mind.

"Sorry! I'll stop," pleads Brandon.

At the drive-through, Brandon yells his order past her left ear, towards the microphone. She reads the backlit menu, suddenly getting cravings for everything advertised by photographs. The burgers look bigger than life, with meat, cheese, fresh lettuce and tomatoes pushing past the edges of the bun. The french fries are a perfect golden hue and stacked neatly in a cardboard pouch, similar to a fresh box of yellow crayons. They can smell the entire menu, thanks to the kitchen that is venting temptations into their rolled down window. Ali's stomach begins to ache for food. She badly wants to resist eating. She was almost going to binge when she started boiling pasta. Her mother's phone call saved her from it.

Victory! She pulls out of the drive through without ordering for herself. Brandon's fries are calling her name. She asks for one. He hands her three long crispy, salty, picture perfect, yellow crayons. They melt in her mouth and melt her resolve.

Back in the same fast food drive through, Ali orders anxiously.

"Man! You must be hungry!" Brandon comments.

"Shut-up!"

French fries and cola romance Ali, while the cheese burger whispers sweet nothings in her ear. The hot apple pie and sundae are getting jealous, waiting for attention, believing they are getting the last word. Dessert. Ali thinks they will get the last word, then changes her mind. One more stop at a convenience store should just about do it. *Brandon, stay in the car!* She is this far gone, might as well go all the way. She comes out with a grocery bag, that hides her lovers. These beaus will be invited behind closed doors, into Ali's bedroom. Thinking they will be spending the night. Ali knows otherwise. Her lovers will be flushed down the toilet. Relationships do not last for those who fear intimacy.

Late that night, Ali is still awake. She is simmering in self-condemnation while she mentally plots out a new game plan. Each goal is designed to deliver her from this horror. Each goal is vain. Each goal ends in ruin.

1. Tomorrow, I will only eat celery and carrots and exercise for two hours.
2. I will look at skinny girls in magazines for motivation, maybe make a collage.
3. I will dress nicer and look like I am put together and confident.
4. Maybe I will take laxatives. (scribble that idea out) (no, pretend to scribble out that one) (no, I won't do it.) (probably, I will) (I am fat. I need it, just this time.)
5. Avoid people until I can get some of this weight off. I can't let people see me this fat.
6. Skip classes tomorrow. Should I? I will be puffy and ugly. Ugh, Math class!
7. Wear dark clothes tomorrow. What am I going to wear tomorrow?

I hate being so fat. Nothing fits me. Sweatshirts are good at hiding fat tummies. Stretchy yoga pants and baggy sweatshirt. Settled.
8. Lose two or three pounds each week. I should be at my goal weight before Christmas. Won't it be nice to start off the new year thin? Just think, I won't have the typical lose weight resolution!
9. Get rid of temptations. As soon as I get up, I will throw away all junk food.
10. Starting tomorrow. I will do this! Maybe I should eat my last bit of chocolate right now, seeing how I won't be able to have any for a while.

Ali gets out of bed at 2:00 a.m. and feels her way around her dark room. She pats the chair until she locates the familiar plastic bag of Snickers Bars and carries it to bed. She worships and adores her chocolate lover. He takes her away from this place and time. His sweetness deceives her — soothes her and tells her lies and says he will always be there. She keeps wanting more. There is never enough. Only two left. *It just isn't enough. I don't want to be done already. Can't I back up time? How far back should I go? To the beginning of the bag, so I get to eat again? Or to the beginning of this madness, before I was hungry?* The bag is not as empty as Ali. There is a void in her soul. Food has become her god. She reaches for it when she needs love. It punishes her. No matter how much she eats, it is never enough. The food-god she worships crowds out all joy. Ali begins her mental list again. With false hope and a false god, she searches for a way out of this cave.

1. Starting tomorrow, I will...

Proverbs 5:3-11 (NIV)
[3] For the lips of an adulteress drip honey, and her speech is smoother than oil;
[4] but in the end she is bitter as gall, sharp as a double-edged sword.
[5] Her feet go down to death; her steps lead straight to the grave.
[6] She gives no thought to the way of life; her paths are crooked, but she knows it not.
[7] Now then, my sons, listen to me; do not turn aside from what I say.
[8] Keep to a path far from her, do not go near the door of her house,
[9] lest you give your best strength to others and your years to one who is cruel,
[10] lest strangers feast on your wealth and your toil enrich another man's house.
[11] At the end of your life you will groan, when your flesh and body are spent.

chapter 9 mideah

Bzzz. Bzzz. *Not again!* Mideah glances at her phone and lets out a huff. Annoyed at the seven messages from the same man, she completely turns off her phone and picks up her pace on the stair-stepping machine. Beads of sweat gather over her face and soak through her skimpy spandex top. She wipes her face with the soft pink towel draped around her neck without losing a beat. Music pounds her eardrums, intending to motivate this workout. But Mideah's thoughts screech over the lyrics, muting every word. She isn't hearing, but the man next to her can list the songs squirting out the tiny ear buds corked in Mideah's ears. It is not music motivating him. It is her figure, plus intrusive liberties of his imagination. She encourages violation when she dresses provocatively, whether fair or not. Of course she has the freedom to choose what she wears. And he has the freedom to look, to lust and undress her!

Mideah is struggling to come up with a good excuse to back out of her date tonight. Jason bought tickets to a sold-out rock concert. He surprised her weeks ago, excited that she agreed to go with him. Lately, Mideah is distracted, not wanting to be with him much. This is driving Jason crazy. Other girls fawn at his feet. He is sure this concert will change their relationship back to better days. Jason even has new clothes and new cologne to wear on this date. He could care less about the band they are seeing. He only likes it because they are Mideah's favorite. Jason has been compulsively fantasizing about this date from the moment the tickets were purchased, at a hefty price too. *She is worth it*, he reasoned. *She will be excited.* Mideah's reaction to his surprise was a letdown.

Before Mideah headed to the gym, she called Jason. She planned her call when he wasn't available and left a cowardly message. All she said was, "I can't go to the concert tonight," Forgetting her excuse, she quickly added, "I'll talk to you later," and hung up.

The voice message caught up with her and she needs a good excuse. Dreaming up lies has benefits; it gives energy to her workout. The more she spawns excuses, the faster she is stepping. The truth will not be told; because truth is: Mideah is dropping her commitment for a better offer. Ted called late last night and suggested dinner, whispering hushed tones into her ear, quick and to the point. "Can we talk a bit more about this vacation? I can meet you at Queen Anne's Lace. Dinner. Seven o'clock?" Ted rapidly hung up when Mideah consented. This business meeting is a hoax and they both know it.

Queen Anne's Lace is an exclusive club and restaurant, part of a posh resort. It is an hour away from the conference room at Schaffer Travel Agency. The inconvenience is convenient, discreet and premeditated.

Mideah reduces the volume and her pace. Moving slower gives her time to conjure a lie. She calls on her inner nymph. *My aunt died? No. He'll wonder why I am just telling him now. I could tell him that I am sick. Nah, then he will want to come over to take care of me. I'll tell him I have a work emergency! That excuse has promise. I won't even be lying!* She misleads herself first, Jason second.

In the locker room, Mideah showers, moisturizes and dries her hair. She pulls it back into a tight ponytail and paints her face before leaving the gym. Outside the building, she brushes the snow off a bench and sits down. The man stair-stepping next to her walks out of the gym a minute behind her. He approaches Mideah, ready to say something. Mideah quickly fumbles through her purse for the phone, turns her side to the man and speed-dials. He shifts his feet and taps his thighs until his courage diminishes. Mideah is glad he walks away. Peering behind the bench, with her chin resting in her palm, she stares at frost and ice patterns glazing over a decomposing apple core. After the sixth ring, someone picks up.

"Mideah!" Jason says quickly, almost breathless.

He was talking to another woman when Mideah's call beeped in. He tried to end the conversation, but the gal kept jabbering. Finally, he had to say, 'I'll call you later. Bye.' He is eager to talk to Mideah, hoping he can change her mind about their date tonight, hoping everything is okay. She is the only woman that challenges him, that he has to make an effort with; the woman he is most brilliant for and nicest to.

"Hey Jay-cee, it's Itty-bitty-middy." Honey is dripping through the phone line, sweetening Jason's ear, as Mideah uses their pet names to control her man. "I am so disappointed I could cry." (fake sniffle-sniffle).

"Bitty, what is it? Is everything ok? Don't cry." Jason is sincerely worried as he strokes Mideah with his voice.

"It's just that, well, we have an emergency at work," She whines. "In fact, I'll be going into the office shortly. Work has been crazy. It is an emergency meeting. The only time my client is available." Mideah spits her excuses on Jason, relieving herself of the miniscule guilt she is feeling. *What? I told him the truth.* Indeed.

There is a silence between them, pricking at their skin and growing awkward.

"Jay? Are you still there?"

"Yeah," Jason interjects with an abrupt pout.

More silence.

"Hey. I said I was sorry. What am I supposed to do, quit my JOB?" defends Mideah.

She never apologizes. She is above apologies. Later that night, Jason will pour this conversation into his mind one-hundred times. Drink it up. Forget to taste it. Pour again. *What am I missing? She wants me. I know it. She is just shy sometimes and works too hard.*

"It's okay, Middy. I understand. Don't get upset. I'll make it up to you. We can plan something special later."

"You're so sweet. We'll do that." The phone is getting sticky again.

"How about tomorrow? Will that work out? Maybe we can..."

Mideah interrupts, "Oh! I gotta go. We can talk later." Click.

"Mideah?" Pause. "Mideah? Hello?" Puzzled, Jason is staring at his phone, rearranging thoughts in his head to be in his favor. *Did she just hang up on me? I bet we got disconnected. She is probably trying to call me back right now.* He holds his phone for twenty minutes waiting for that call while thinking, *What could we do tomorrow? I wonder why she isn't calling me back?* He phones her several times, but hangs up when her recorded voice asks him to leave a message.

There was a time no more than a decade ago, that Jason was a wall flower, picked last, *You're really nice... Let's just be friends...* too-skinny, too-short, a thick-glasses, shy-guy. The summer before his senior year of high school, with the aid of a super cool older cousin, Jason redefined himself and swallowed his painful past. His parents had recently split, unable to handle the fact that his little sister is among the missing. Her pretty face is featured on post office bulletin boards and milk cartons. The only thing found was her rag doll, stained with chocolate —bait. A local hunter found the doll in a wooded area, an hour away from the park where she was last seen. This nightmare numbed his family and dissolved it. Six years later, his dad moved to California to live near his only sister, Auntie-Sheryl. The arrangement was for Jason to go with his Dad, which translated to living most of the summer with Auntie-Sheryl and her son, Brett. Brett was a player, your typical ladies man. For Jason, Brett was a godsend. Jason became his disciple, following the teachings of narcissism —arrogance, vanity and pride. Thick glasses were replaced with contact lenses and Ray Ban Aviators. His braces came off gleaming white teeth, perfectly straightened. He left the salon with a new hairstyle and the mall with a new wardrobe. Jason went through a natural growing spurt, increasing his height by seven inches, and gained unnatural muscle mass with the help of anabolic steroids. Brett and Jason hit the gym by day, downing huge glasses of protein-power drinks; then the clubs by night, downing huge mugs of beer on tap. They worked out with several body-building club bouncers who guarded the doors at popular nightclubs. The bouncers would wave them in without checking the date on Brett's young cousin's I.D. card. The bars are where Jason's night classes took place —Lessons with the Ladies 101. Jason had the best teacher, Brett, who was smooo-thhhh as butter and fake as the Easter bunny. And they found their share of bunnies to reproduce with. By the time Jason enrolled for his senior year of high school, he forgot who he used to be. Even years later, he denies the homely, awkward boy he was. Dirty-Old-Man-Jason will tell stories, through brown stained teeth, to willing ears, proud to say he was *Born a ladies-man and will die a ladies-man!* And his ex-wives will certainly agree.

Realizing that Mideah isn't going to call back, Jason shrugs off his feeling of rejection and rings the same gal he was talking to earlier. She picks up immediately and agrees, without hesitation, to go to the concert. She is honored to be Jason's last minute date, canceling plans with her best friend to oblige him. The date will end terribly for the poor girl when she wakes up the next morning, abandoned in a strange bed. Feeling like a castaway, she reads the note taped to the door as she leaves the unfamiliar apartment:

'Make sure you lock the door ~J.' Is all it said.

This gal sinks her feelings and holds them down by piling heavy hopes and expectations on top of self-lies. She lives and breathes Jason. His name is scratched into the bark on her heart, a tree lost in a forest of lies. She will forever anticipate his next call, even after marriage and three kids.

Mideah hangs up on Jason for no reason, except to jettison his plans for tomorrow. She has Ted to dream about. Maybe he will give her a better offer. If not, Jason can be her back-up plan. She tosses the phone into her gym bag and scans the parking lot for clues to where she parked her Spyder convertible —paid for by Daddy.

Halfway home she realizes that she forgot to stop by the office to pick up Ted's vacation packet. She really believes it's unnecessary, but doesn't want to blow her cover, or his.

Her co-workers look perplexed when she walks into the office. "I thought this was your day off?"

"I just need to pick up something I left behind," Mideah explains and rushes past.

The ladies spy on Mideah, who is standing on tiptoes and looking over the tall partition in front of the boss's office. His door is shut, lights off. Mideah sneaks to her desk to prepare for her affair, printing copies of Ted's itinerary. She inserts them into a large brown envelope. Using her best cursive, she writes his name with a sharpie marker across the front.

When Mideah is at her desk, the ladies scoff and exchange questioning expressions. They act busy when Mideah walks past swinging the envelope in her hand.

One woman peeks at the name on the envelope. "Humph," she snorts. The other ladies look up on cue, roll their eyes and shake their heads.

Mideah is unaware of how much gossip is shared on her behalf. Her office is private and remote, with taller partitions forming her cubicle. Mideah assumes she has a higher position in the hierarchy. She doesn't know that an employee with more seniority gave up this cubicle for Mideah to maintain peace in the workplace.

Mideah charges out the door. No good-byes. No one even looks up. When she is gone, the chatter begins —juicy gossip to defame their narcissistic co-worker.

The tub steams with water that wafts sweet floral smells to the ceiling and condenses on the mirror. Mideah rests a tray near the tub containing a mug of herbal tea, a magazine and small a bowl of cucumber slices. She sinks in and lets the water bite her skin with intense heat. The pages of Cosmopolitan wilt and curl as she turns them with wet hands. When she is done sipping tea and comparing her body to images of airbrushed models, Mideah rolls a small towel behind her neck and leans back wearing cucumber goggles. She sinks her chin deep into the water and falls asleep dreaming of Ted.

Before getting out of the tub, she exfoliates, rubbing gritty cream over her body, giving her elbows and knees extra attention. Her hands and feet are crinkled white and waterlogged.

Her body is weighed down and knees shaky as she towels off. She steals through Gina's drawer for some lotion. Hiding way in the back, beneath a washcloth, is the goldmine. Mideah's eyes widen when she sees the price tag. She carefully slips the small tube out of the narrow box and generously applies it to every inch of skin. Back in the drawer, it is meticulously placed exactly how it was found. Now however, the metal tube is crinkled and almost empty.

Before putting on her robe, she admires her body from every angle, adding a hand mirror to inspect herself from behind. She empathizes with Ted's eyes, certain he will find the sharp angles of her body alluring. Robe on, hair in a towel turban, she wipes a small round pad over her pores, feeling her cheeks and forehead tighten and cool. She sprits on toner to give her face a glowing appearance, according to the advertisement, and pats it dry with a soft towel. Mideah applies her own, very expensive, face moisturizer. She lets it soak in for a few minutes before massaging it deep into her skin. Mideah pays top dollar for products to improve her appearance. She is ignorant that a cold wet washcloth, eating plenty of vegetables and drinking enough water will give her better results. Beauty starts on the inside and radiates out. Mideah thinks it soaks in or is applied. She thrives on the opinion of others, gets angry when people don't notice her. She needs to turn heads, requires it to survive.

Mideah's top drawer is full of makeup in loose disarray, piled up like cookies in a jar, three layers deep. The upper layer is used most. The bottom layer is forgotten. Mideah needs to stir the contents of this drawer so she doesn't keep replacing makeup she already has. She rakes through tiny compact containers to find concealer. She turns the bottom dial on the tube and a beige finger rolls out to point at dark circles and blemishes. She puts beige smears under each eye and highlights her cheek bones. She draws a straight line down the bridge of her nose to make it appear narrow and dots the tip of her chin. A very dark concealer stick is used to contrast the lightened areas. She chisels her face by darkening the edges of her nose and the hallows of her cheeks. She darkens her temples to make her eyes look wider. A foundation cream is layered over these extreme lights and darks and blended to look *natural*.

Mideah focuses on her eyes next. She adds several applications of brown eye shadow in varying shades, from her eyelids to her brow. With eyeliner, Mideah draws a pretend eyelash, curling out from the outer corner of her eyes. Meow. She uses this same liner pencil to outline her vaporous green eyes, then applies thick layers of mascara, *Black/Black*. Her lashes are like awnings shading her soul, fluttering and blinking deceit. She plucks a few stray brown hairs to arch her brows, hoping tears won't run her makeup. With a tiny comb, wet with hairspray, she positions her eyebrows perfectly.

Mideah peels off the whitening strips capping her teeth. These strips have been fading already white teeth for forty-five minutes. Brush. Floss. Mouthwash. She swishes the intense mint-medicinal flavor back and forth, cheek to cheek. Her head tilts into several angles for inspection and approbation. Spit. Ah, fresh breath. Smile. Bing! Teeth so white, they let off a spark.

The turban comes off and wet hair is massaged with styling gel. *Specially formulated gel, made with naturally-derived moisturizer for a healthy scalp, promoting hair growth.* A wide tooth brush is combed repeatedly down long lengths of highlighted blond hair, while a warm wind oscillates from the *ionic* blow-drier. *(Ionic*—of course! Because *ionic blow dryers utilize one-half the heat in half the time, drying hair quickly, thus reducing frizzy hair and heat damage, while leaving your hair fuller and shinier!* Mideah rubs finishing cream between her fingers before combing them through her reduced frizz, fuller, shinier hair, *to give her tresses a smoother look*. She pulls her hair into a loose ponytail at the base of her neck, then twists and pins her hair, creating a modern-day bun, puffy and loose, with some hair spiking out.

Before leaving the bathroom, she mists pricey perfume directly in front of her. Opening her bathrobe wide, she walks into the floating particles, feeling the cool sting.

She is happy to have an occasion to wear the little black dress. Mideah smiles at the silky fabric draping on the hanger that is hooked over the top of the open door. Last night, she pulled it out of her closet and placed it on display to fantasize possibilities with Ted. There is nothing business-like about this dress, especially the back of it, where the dress divides and exposes a risqué strip of skin. The back is cut so low that another sort of cleavage is divulged. Mideah's long platinum gold chain, stranding a single pearl, will be worn backwards on her neck. The chain is severely long and hangs between boney shoulder blades, playing peek-a-boo between black silk curtains. The tiny iridescent ball will roll across the small of her back throughout the night, advancing her fantasy. Mideah's apparel is hazardous.

Queen Anne's Lace is calmly busy when Mideah approaches the maître d' podium. A tall, thin, distinguished looking gentleman rolls out his questions with a heavy Italian accent.

"Madame." He pauses. "Do you have a reservation?"

"I will be joining the Schaffer party this evening," Mideah articulates in a fake elite tone. She clenches the leather tote in tightening fear, turning her knuckles white inside her small, black-lace gloves. The tote is her alibi, containing Ted's brown travel envelope, just in case his intentions are strictly business. She worries she is misreading his signals.

The maître d' scans the table diagram for her reservation. Ted left her a message earlier, "Our reservation is under *Schaffer*." Short for Schaffer Travel Agency —to remain anonymous.

The maître d' motions to Mideah. "Right this way." Pause. Slight bow. "Madame."

He holds her bare arm, tenderly, just above the elbow with a thumb and pointer finger, guiding her to a table in a darkened corner. Mideah discretely glances around the dining room at the formally dressed guests. Eyes are turning while heads remain stiff and proper. Most of the men in the room are older, silver haired or dyed a younger color. Some are balding. The demographic of women vary in age. Many appear to be twenty-something. She notices Ted, looking smart and handsome in a black dinner jacket worn over a crisp white shirt. It is unbuttoned and gapping apart to bare the silver St. Christopher pendant hanging between sculpted pecs. He nervously scratches the sexy, midnight shadow of hair that sharpens his jaw. Light flicks from his sleeve. *Cufflinks? Really Ted?* Mideah giggles silently.

Ted stands, adjusting his lapels and shrugging his shoulders as Mideah approaches.

"You look incredible," he compliments, pulling out a chair for her.

The fabric of the back of her dress pulls apart slightly as she seats herself, gifting Ted with a seductive view of milky soft skin. He restrains himself from tracing his finger along the edges of the silk V on her back. Instead he places this image in memory on the surface of his brain, easy to recall and embellish later.

Ted idles behind her, leaning on the back of her chair and breathes a compliment into her ear. "Your dress is ravishing," he extols in hushed tones, her hair tickling his cheek.

Dating a forty-year-old, seems mature, distinguished. She doesn't thank him for the compliment, just smiles, slightly turning her head toward him with seductive eyes. She allows him to adjust her chair before he seats himself.

The table decor is white-on-white, with accents of silver and crystal. Lace fabric is layered over a thick, bleached white, cotton cloth. Mideah unfolds the lace napkin that is folded into a flower blossom next to the silverware. She delicately smoothes it across her lap. An open bottle of wine is already on the table with two glasses poured and waiting.

Ted sipped some of his wine while waiting for her arrival. He lifts and tilts his goblet towards Mideah.

"Cheers," he says. Their glasses clink.

"Thank you for ordering the wine." This is all she can come up with to say. She is surprisingly nervous.

"My pleasure," responds Ted. To fill in the awkward silence, he begins, "I appreciate your taking time to meet me here."

Mideah is not sure how to respond and hesitates. *Is this a business meeting?*

"Of course! I always take the time for..." She pauses to scheme. "For..." Almost says *my clients*, but stops herself and says, "For my friends."

She decides to allow Ted to take the lead in directing the evening towards work or play.

Ted is still not sure they are on the same page when he says, "Shall we enjoy the atmosphere and dinner before getting down to business?"

Ted, are you flirting with me? Did your eyebrows raise up? Mideah wonders. Hopes.

"I agree. Why rush," Mideah says. Her hands tremble when she touches her wineglass to her lips. She notices Ted watching and pointing his glass at her. So she stops and pulls her glass away, leaving a red lipstick smudge on the rim.

Leaning closer to her, he says, "Life is an adventure. Dare it." Clink. He smirks at his genius. He memorized a quote last night to intrigue her, plagiarizing Mother Teresa. Mideah is captivated, willing to be led into dark cracks.

The waiter approaches their table with menus. He introduces himself and recites the specialty items featured by the chef. They are not ready to order, so he bows and leaves. A tall, slender, young woman wearing a lace apron around her waist, approaches their table to fill water glasses.

Mideah and Ted study their menus. Ted lays his menu on the table first and folds his hands on his lap. He watches Mideah flip through the leather bound pages, fanning them back and forth in indecision.

"Hmm..." She says. Flip. "Ah..." Flip. "Well..." Flip back.

"I can order for you, if you prefer," offers Ted.

"I'll handle it," determines Mideah but changes her mind. "On second thought, why don't you surprise me?"

When the waiter returns, Ted orders confidently, bordering on condescension, requesting certain items to be prepared *just so*. Their waiter listens patiently, memorizing their selections and special requests. Mideah sits tall and superior. This waiter is her servant. She nods at him with pursed lips, backing up Ted's demands. The waiter leaves Ted and Mideah sipping expensive fermented grapes that alleviate fear and doubt.

Appetizers are brought to the table. Ted is excited to introduce Mideah to the exotic delicacies he proudly ordered, to amaze her with his diverse tastes.

"You have got to try this," He expresses, holding a small bite at the tip of a miniature fork, his other hand cupped beneath.

Instead of taking the fork from him, Mideah opens her mouth to be fed intimately. Ted indulges, then temps her with another dish, this time feeding her with his fingers. The seduction is blatant, yet both deny it happening. Innocent is the plea. Business. Strictly business.

Eyes closed, "Mmm...delicious."

Beneath the table, Mideah's shoes lay toppled. Her bare toes wiggle freely. She even dares to rest her naked toes —briefly, on the wing-tip of Ted's polished black shoe. The sensation, electrically charged, does not go unnoticed by either party. Somewhere, inside the bubble they are lost in, an invisible deceitful finger motions to both of them. *Follow Me.* Its hand is palm up, with the pointer finger flicking towards the bad idea. They are led without a fight into the gravitational force of pleasure. The leather tote is ignored, leaning on a chair leg near Mideah's shoes. Forgotten.

Mideah takes her turn to feed, by allowing Ted to sample from her plate. She holds her fork near his lips to nibble on a bite just her size, but too small for a man. She wipes a crumb off the corner of his mouth with the side of her thumb. Each touch is sinking them deeper. Main course meals are placed on the table, each plate displaying an artistic arrangement of food, small in portion and unrecognizable.

Mideah slices and rearranges food on her plate, delicately, taking very few bites while Ted impresses her with his travel log.

"South Africa!" Ted exhales, "What beauty —and the animals. Seeing them in their natural habitat. Up close, without fences. No zoo there!"

"Africa is high on my list. I hope to go someday. Have you ever been to Denmark?"

"No. Have you?"

"Not yet. My mother is Danish. I am planning a trip for us."

Ted beams, watching her facial expressions as she talks, "When will you be going?"

"Probably not for a year or so. Mom has a busy schedule. She cancels every time I try to set something up."

Ted nods.

Mideah continues, "Danish people were voted the happiest people in the world."

"Really?" responds Ted.

"Also, one of the most peaceful."

"Well, I wonder what's their secret?"

"We'll have to find out," hints Mideah.

"Yes *we* will!" Ted bursts, trying to picture her mother and wondering if she is as hot as her daughter.

They stare at each other, nerves calmer now, with both elbows on the table and hands cupping empty wine glasses. Led by the power of suggestion, they look to the bottom of their goblet, tip the last drip into their mouths, set the glasses down, lean back in their chairs, and fold hands in their laps —perfectly synchronized.

Ted slides his plate aside, placing the lace napkin on top. Mideah imitates, pushing her plate of rearranged food, barely touched, near the edge of the table. They are done with the meal. Now what? Ted is studying Mideah, plotting ways to accelerate their covert foreplay. Mideah does the same. She considers asking Ted to share a dessert. The space between them is growing awkward. A bus boy, who smells like a mixture of coffee and dish soap, is clearing dirty dishes from their table. He fills his black tub with wasted expensive food.

Ted sees the waiter approaching. *Quick, Ted, come up with something!* He panics. Now Mideah notices the waiter and opens her mouth to speak. Ted beats her to it.

"Shall we order another bottle of wine?" He asks impatiently, wishing he didn't sound so desperate.

Mideah is relieved, "Excellent idea!" She says with too much enthusiasm. "I was thinking the same thing."

"May I interest you in coffee or dessert? Or shall I bring you the check?" The waiter asks, standing with hands folded behind his back and leaning forward.

"We'd like to try a dessert wine. Any suggestions?" Ted requests,

"Something that compliments the Chocolate Molten Cake?"

The waiter is quick with a solution. "I will bring you a couple samples to help with your selection."

"We would appreciate that." answers Ted.

"May I assume you will be ordering the Molten Cake?"

"Yes. And we'll be sharing," explains Ted, who is still making meal choices for Mideah.

They sample tiny tumblers of wine while the sommelier stands proudly and patiently. Ted encourages Mideah to choose.

"We'd like a bottle of this one," she says, pointing, not pronouncing the name.

The sommelier nods and says, "Excellent. I'll be right back with your wine." He turns and stiffly walks away.

When the waiter arrives with their dessert, he recognizes the wine label and asks, "How is the wine?"

"Perfect." - "Excellent." They both answer differently.

"You'll find it goes well with this dessert." He places the plate between the couple and lays out a fork on each side. "May I get you anything else?"

"We're good," retorts Mideah.

When the waiter turns to leave, Ted stands up slightly, lifting his chair by the seat, and scoots closer to Mideah. He picks up the nearest fork, eases it's edge into the moist dark chocolate and pulls off a small bite. He offers it to Mideah, holding the fork close to her lips. She touches his hand, drawing it to her mouth.

"Mmm..." she groans, "scrumptious."

Chocolate blankets her tongue, stimulating taste buds. The first bite is always the most intense. Ted feeds her more, before taking a bite. They push the plate aside, leaving the last few crumbs nested in syrup.

Several goblets of spirits soothe and relax them, body and soul, escorting risks. They secretly study one another to strategize ways to direct the evening to forbidden places. Although they have already eaten, they both hunger for fruit from a forbidden tree.

Awaiting him at home, the Garden of Eden is within Ted's reach, if only he would work the soil and plant good seeds in his immediate family. His wife and children are ready. They wait for Ted to shower *them* with love and dedication, so they may bloom. His girls are craving a man's love and will search desperately for it. If their father cannot give them true, honest and appropriate love, they will soon be mislead by lust and be in grave danger. His wife needs to know that he loves her deeply. She cannot identify the sadness, this internal awareness that he is not fully hers. It gnaws on her soul. She will fake her way, in denial, believing they have a picture perfect life.

Mideah is performing for Ted now. She pretends to be ignorant that he is watching her slip on black lace gloves. In true geisha fashion, she slowly slides delicate silk on each finger, then smoothes the long gloves up to her elbows. Ted absorbs the show while leaning back, resting his wine glass on his chest. When her hands are finished dressing, fingers walk spider fashion, across the tablecloth towards Ted. The black-widow finger stops at the bottle and taps the label, motioning for a refill of blood-red wine. Ted pours red fluid into her cup and offers it to her. Lace spider legs slide from his wrist and over the back of his hand, to gently remove the offering —a near bite. Ted desires to be wrapped in the spider's silk, unaware that it will become a trap. A black window will puncture her prey with gnashing fangs, turning its victim into liquid. This is part of Mideah's ruse, wearing a black silk dress, its sinuous movement eager to wrap up Ted, killing his family with red manicured nails, masked by lace bristles. He is enticed, yet blind to the web spun across his chosen path. Mideah is watching and waiting, blinking eight eyes across the tablecloth.

A platter crashes to the floor, smashing Ted's focus on Mideah. He looks over Mideah's shoulder to see what happened. Now aware of who is across the room, he instantly squirms, suddenly anxious and uncomfortable. He wonders how long those two have been sitting there. *Did they see him?* He watches the back of the woman's head for clues. He is suddenly distracted, no longer watching Mideah as she continues her geisha-like poses. He slides his chair over, away from his travel agent. Mideah notices.

Her posture stiffens, squeezing her eyebrows together in confusion. Ted is making nervous jesters —looking away, taking quick drinks of ice water, bouncing his knee. He is clumsy sitting the glass down —ice jingling.

"What's wrong?" Mideah asks with concern.

"Nothing," Teds says too quickly.

Mideah turns to see where Ted is looking, then stares back at him, analyzing his discomfort.

"You seem nervous all of a sudden," she accuses.

"Huh? I'm okay. The dinner might not be settling well."

"Humph," Mideah mews quietly. Her mind is racing to uncover reasons for his change of mood.

"Well," says Ted in bogus nonchalance, "It is time to call it a night. Got a busy day tomorrow."

He arches his back, stiffening his arms, acting like he needs to stretch. "Ah, what an excellent meal. Thank you for joining me."

What. The. Hell? Mideah is trying to figure out what just happened. She turns her head and squints in the direction Ted seems to be watching. *What is going on over there? What does he keep looking at?* She doesn't ask.

Alone in thought, Ted quizzes himself on how well this couple knows his wife. Sitting across the dim lit dining room, they are invading his lie. The woman is seated with her back toward him. He has never met her husband, and her, only a couple of times. His wife doesn't really mention her very much. Her husband wouldn't have a clue who he is. *Would he? How would he know me? Guys don't pay attention to their wife's friends. Do they?*

Mideah leans back in her chair, slouching. Her legs are crossed and on display. She is holding her wine glass close to her lips, taking furious sips and watching Ted. Something across the room has stolen him from her. He is glancing in that direction while rearranging the table, making it look more like they are finished with the meal. He pours the last bit of wine into his own glass and sits the empty bottle at the table's edge to be a subliminal signal, *We are finished. Check please!*

He doesn't notice the unrestrained pout of Mideah's countenance. Nor does he notice the long, bare leg waving at him. Mideah nervously swings her crossed leg, with her stiletto pumps back on. Her shoes are glossy black, except the soles and spike heels, which are bright red —distinct markings of the black widow. As her foot bounces, red is flashing Ted an ironic warning signal. Planning an escape is taking all his attention. The only way out is right past that table. *She will see us for sure.* When he thinks Mideah isn't looking, he buttons his shirt so that only the top two are undone.

If the crowd could hear both Ted and Mideah's thoughts right now it would be quite a scene. Ted is sweating in his tailored Armani suit and rapidly tapping the heel of a Gucci wingtip oxford. Suddenly, he gets up.

"Would you please excuse me?" he says to Mideah, sounding more like the waiter than her dinner partner.

"Are you okay?" she asks to Ted's back as he hurries off.

Mideah watches Ted rush away. She picks at the lace on her fingers and curses into her lap. She doesn't see the woman across the room look at Ted as he walks by. She doesn't see the man turn to look, after the woman says something to him. Mideah doesn't feel the woman staring at her back, wondering where Ted's wife is. The only thing on Mideah's mind is the empty chair next to her. This forsaken chair is laughing at her, mocking and teasing. It is spotlighting her abandonment to all the guests dining at Queen Anne's Lace.

The maître d' speaks softly and formally to Mideah. "Mr. Schaeffer has asked me to escort you out when you are finished."

"What?" She is confused. "Where is he?"

"He was feeling ill and had to leave. He asked that I send you his apologies. The bill is paid, so you need not worry."

"He what?" says Mideah, trying to process what just happened. "He's gone? He left me here?"

"I am very sorry, Madame." Feeling uncomfortable, the waiter attempts to pacify her. "May I get you coffee? Tea?"

Eight ferocious eyes pierce him, "Are you kidding?"

The maître d' is forcing composure, his folded hands fisting. Mideah turns and looks in the direction Ted was last seen, then back at the man standing stiffly, waiting for a response. She takes a deep breath and lets out a quick exhale, the kind that makes a statement. Down by her feet is the decoy, her black leather tote, containing promises. Her job guarantees that she will be seeing Ted again. She yanks the lace gloves off, picks up her tote, shoves the gloves inside and lets the magnetic clasp embrace its partner. Click!

When the maître d' tries to lead her by the elbow, she jerks her arm away and hurries a few steps ahead, all the way outside.

The night air is moist and crisp. The pearl on her necklace is biting her lower back as wind whips between the folds of black satin. The plan was for Ted to offer her his warm jacket and hold her close as they walk to her car. Unless they stay the night, which was 'Plan A'. She isn't prepared for 'Plan C'.

The walk to her car is barren and cold. Her skin is goose pimpled. Her soul shivers. She bats her eyelashes at the darkness around her, but it doesn't respond. No amount of beauty can remedy this loneliness.

Isaiah 1:18 (NIV)
[18] "Come now, let us reason together," says the Lord. "Though your sins are like scarlet, they shall be as white as snow; though they are red as crimson, they shall be like wool.

chapter 10 leah (lee-lee)

Jodie calls Mrs. D to let her know the plane's expected arrival. She promises Mrs. D that she will pick up Leah at twelve-thirty. Latest! The airport is thirty minutes away from where her daughter has been staying. Mrs. D is getting impatient with Jodie for all the imposing.

On the plane, Jodie is seated next to their new sales rep, Matt, handsome and three years her junior. During this business trip, Jodie is thrilled to know Matt progressively better. On the plane, business casual turns into a flirtatious banter between eager Jodie and lusting Matt. They wait at the baggage claim and stand closer than necessary. Matt remarks how hungry he is and asks Jodie if she wants to go somewhere for lunch? She agrees without hesitation.

During lunch, Jodie never mentions Leah, nor is she anxious to pick up her only child. Lee-Lee has been waiting three days to see her mama. Jodie is too mesmerized by Matt's dark brown eyes, flashy smile and designer shoes. She has his attention and intends on keeping it. Does he know she has a daughter? Probably not, since she hasn't mentioned her once during this trip. Matt is so busy impressing Jodie with his adventurous bachelor life, that he fails to ask the most obvious questions. *Are you married? Do you have children?* If he asks, Jodie will answer 'no' to the first question and 'yes' to the second. Maybe she will even elaborate and tell him she is divorced and has a five year old daughter. Instead, Jodie plays the role of single bachelorette, young and carefree. That is who she wants Matt to believe she is, while baiting him and hoping to hook him.

She orders a light lunch and eats daintily for Matt. She ignores the time. Her love life is reviving. Her daughter can wait. It is past one o'clock. Jodie is only concerned with Jodie... and Matt of course.

Not far from where Matt and Jodie share dessert, Leah is perched on the window seat holding her lamb's front leg, ready to wave at Mama. Five minutes equals one hour to Leah.

As each hour goes by in Leah-time, she asks, "When's my mama gonna be here?"

Mrs. D repeats, "Anytime now." After a while, she changes her answer to, "Who knows!" and then to, "Probably never!" This makes Leah start to cry. So her new answer is, "Go play. Your mama will be here before you know it."

Leah tries to play. But every time she hears a car door slam or door click open, she runs back to the window, scans the driveway, then walks away disappointed. After seeing an empty driveway several times, Leah goes to where Meggy is playing with snap-together blocks and kicks over her tower. Meggy starts screaming and throwing blocks at Leah. Mrs. D rushes in, angry and frustrated with the girls, who have been fighting all morning.

"What now?" she snaps.

"Lee-Lee kicked over my tower," tattles Meggy.

Mrs. D growls and grabs Leah's arm tighter than necessary. She pulls her across the room to the corner, points and shouts, "Sit!" giving her a helpful shove.

While Leah is crying with her forehead resting against the wall, she notices the wallpaper edge is curling up. She picks at it and tears off a chunk, leaving white backing exposed. She scratches at more edges and pulls off a few more pieces, rolling the paper between her fingers and flicking them behind the baseboard heater. She names each piece as she snaps it off her finger.... *Mrs. D! Monster! Daddy! Meggy!* The piece called *Mommy* she grips in her hand. Too many emotions want to scream from her chest. Her body wants to pound on things and kick real hard. Leah holds her breath and tightens every muscle in her body, letting herself shake. When she relaxes, she feels better. Her thoughts are empty as she sits like a zombie —still and staring.

Leah's punishment doesn't last long. Mrs. D doesn't want her to be crying in the corner when her mother arrives. *If she ever gets here!*

Mrs. D approaches a calmer and quieter Leah and recites, "If you think you can play nice now, you can come out," then walks away.

Leah is slow at getting out of her corner. She finds Meggy and sits near her. She won't touch any of Meggy's toys. Whatever Leah wants to play with, Meggy suddenly wants, claiming she had it first in a tone meant for her mother to hear.

A car door slams shortly after two o'clock. Heels click on the wooden porch.

Jodie stands just inside the door and sing-songs, "Lee-Lee? Where are you?"

"Mama!" Leah shouts. She grabs her lamb and rushes to the door, wrapping her arms around Jodie's hips. "I miss you bigger than the world, Mama!"

Mrs. D and Meggy walk over to the door and watch.

Jodie bends down and briefly gives Leah hugs before she stands up to list all her reasons for being tardy. "You know how it is..... waiting for bags, traffic. I really needed to break for lunch. The waiter was so slow. Maybe Meggy can come over sometime and give you a break? Unfortunately, today doesn't work. I have to get caught up after being gone so long. You know how the laundry piles up. Oh and I just remembered driving over here, we need groceries! Never ending. Isn't it?"

Mrs. D is insulted by Jodie's selfishness. She doesn't respond to the excuses. She is just ready for them both to leave. "Leah's things are all right here."

"Oh good. Thank you so much for watching Lee-Lee." Jodie picks up a suitcase, pillow and a bag of books. She leaves with arms overloaded, pushing the door open with her hip. "Bye. Thanks again. I really owe you this time!"

Leah tags along behind her, hugging her lamb and repeating, "Mama, did you get me a surprise? Mama. Mama? Did you..."

Jodie doesn't hear her. She's too busy to listen, too busy daydreaming. She pops open the trunk to load Leah's bags.

"Come on. Get in your car seat."

"But Mama, did ya remember..."

"Come on! Leah, get in."

"Mama, did ya remember..."

"Leah! Get in!" Jodie firmly cuts off Leah.

Reluctantly, Leah submits and climbs into her seat. "I can buckle," she assures, fumbling to click the pieces together. After a few tries, her mother takes over and quickly clicks the safety belt.

Inside the car is silent as Jodie maneuvers through traffic. Several minutes pass before Jodie remembers to ask Leah about her fun time with Meggy and Mrs. D.

"Sweetie, did you have fun at Meggy's?"

No answer.

"Lee-Lee?"

No answer.

Jodie turns her mirror to the back seat to see why Leah isn't talking. Leah's head is tipped sideways, mouth softly open, eyes shut. Jodie stares at her longer than she should while driving. Her daughter looks so small and babyish, resting in the car seat. Jodie implants this image into her memory, forever seeing the face of baby Lee-Lee as she sleeps, even when Leah is grown. She feels the most love for her daughter when she watches her dream, and wonders why that is.

Lee-Lee is afraid in her own house now. Doors that close off dark places are scary. The basement door is frightening when no one is down there. Lee-Lee will push it shut, especially when it is open only a few inches. Her house has more sounds, different from before. They bump and echo in new places. Her bare feet are uncomfortable when near a dark open crack, such as under the bed or couch. Something might sneak out to bite her toes or grab her ankles. She wonders if the night monster in Meggy's room followed her home? She feels it clinging to her spine. *What is that stink behind my neck? Is it the creature? What is that moving shadow. It grunts. Go away! You make me shiver.*

Where is Mama? Leah hears footsteps down the hall, so she gathers her dolls and follows the sound. The shiny red suitcase lays open on the bed. Jodie is unpacking it. Lee-Lee plays at Mama's feet, tucking her babies in blankets, kissing doll faces that smell like powder. Next, Jodie is at the washing machine loading clothes. Lee-Lee is sitting in a laundry basket bouncing the lamb along the rim. She follows mama outside to the clothesline, handing Mama wet items to be hung. Puzzles are put together at Jodie's feet, as she sits opening a stack of mail. Leah asks for the stickers Mama found in an envelope and decorates her shirt with dots of address labels. Mama is making dinner. Lee-Lee pulls up a stool, standing beside her to watch. When Jodie is in the bathroom, Leah waits in the hall, staring at the strip of light that shines across the bottom edge of the closed door. Mama turns on the TV. Leah tries to crawl on her lap, but Mama tells her to go put pajamas on. She scurries and grabs a nightie off the floor, then back to mama to dress herself. Lee-Lee wants Jodie to watch her while she brushes her teeth. *Mama, stay by the door while I go potty. Please read me more books. Mama, will you leave my light on? Mama, I'm thirsty. I just came out to hug you. Mama, will you help me put socks on? Mama, can I sleep with you? Mama, I'm scared!*

Jodie speculates about her daughter, who is usually independent, ascribing Lee-Lee's clinginess to Mama being away too long, possibly working too much. Jodie feels like it is all her fault, then dismisses her guilt by reasoning, *What else can I do? I have to work!* Her daughter has gotten out of bed several times, with poor excuses. Finally, Jodie resigns by carrying Lee-Lee to bed with her. Both toss and turn all night. Both wear dark circles under their eyes and frowns on their faces the next day —a day not worth repeating.

The next two days are re-runs, with Jodie wearing Leah as her shadow. Extra effort to accommodate Leah has subsided, due to waning guilt and shifting the blame back on her child. Jodie is ready to have her routine back, meaning Monday through Friday. Grown-up world. She is behind schedule this morning and rushing. *Leah, go potty. Hurry up and eat your breakfast. Go brush your teeth. Stay still, it is hard to brush when you are so wiggly! Find your shoes. What do you mean you have to go potty? Didn't you go already? We don't have time to look for lamb. Leah, get moving! If you don't hurry up, I'm leaving without you! I'm leaving...*

In the car, "Mama, I don't want to go."

"Well, you have to."

"Can't we stay at home?"

"You know we can't."

"Mama, turn around. Go back! I don't wanna go there." Leah is crying.

Jodie turns up the radio to drown out the voice behind her. Her hands are gripping the steering wheel, knuckles white, face red. *Deep breath, slow exhale. Deep breath, slow exhale.* Jodie reminds herself how to calm down, her thoughts rapidly flip through channels: Leah. Work. Matt. The time! Self. Traffic. The time! Quit crying. Drive faster. The time!

Leah did not stop crying. In Mr. D's driveway, Jodie is peeling her little girl's fingers off the seat belt, one at a time and dragging her to the door. No kisses. No hugs. No goodbyes. The time!

Matthew 23:25-28 (NIV) (Jesus words)
[25] "Woe to you, teachers of the law and Pharisees, you hypocrites! You clean the outside of the cup and dish, but inside they are full of greed and self-indulgence.
[26] Blind Pharisee! First clean the inside of the cup and dish, and then the outside also will be clean."
[27] "Woe to you, teachers of the law and Pharisees, you hypocrites! You are like whitewashed tombs, which look beautiful on the outside but on the inside are full of dead men's bones and everything unclean.
[28] In the same way, on the outside you appear to people as righteous but on the inside you are full of hypocrisy and wickedness.

chapter 11 ali

Beep. Beep. Beep. Beep. Beep...

You might as well get up instead of hitting the alarm so many times. Get out of bed and do something. You're just wasting away the morning. Are you going to sleep all day? You need to quit being so lazy.

"Okay! Okay! I'll get up." Ali groans away her Mother's imaginary voice.

Ali turns off her alarm, annoyed by the sound that pushed away the steady dream she was having, a strange dream where she was floating down a river and tame animals were drifting with her.

Ali is leaning into the bathroom mirror. *I knew it! I look like crap!* Last night she predicted she'd wake up with a puffy face and droopy eyes. She pokes at the swollen skin, expecting it to magically shrink back to normal. She sucks in her cheeks and leans close to the mirror. *Scary-face, you still look fat.* Ali puffs out her cheeks like a blowfish and makes fun of the fat girl in the mirror —the girl she insults.

She turns on the water, holds her hand under the flow, feeling the coldness. Hot is on the way, after it wastes all the cold water settled in the length of pipe. She keeps putting her finger in the stream to check the temperature. When it is super hot, she wets the washcloth, squeezes excess water out and spreads it across her face. Her head is tilted back and steam is lifting off the white terrycloth mask, warming her entire face, waking her up. She rubs her face with the cloth and pats it dry.

The bathroom smells like cherry-almonds and fabric softener. The washcloth she is using is soft and thick, still new, from the linen closet in the master bedroom suite. Ali found it the other day while delving through her Mother's things. She also helped herself to a new bath towel and pearl earrings. Eventually her Mother will notice. *Ali, you are a selfish, thoughtless daughter! You have no right to be snooping around and taking my things!*

The part of the day Ali dreads, especially today, is finding something to wear. Her clothes reiterate that she is plump and unfashionable. The pants she wants to wear are in the dirty clothes. Ali digs them out. She shakes out the wrinkles, smells them, and irons them clean again. They are still warm when she wiggles them over her hips. She zips and buttons them, her belly fat pushes over the front edge. Oh no, she has outgrown her biggest pair of jeans. *Disgusting*. This day just got harder.

Usually morning is a fresh start, a renewal, with the entire day ready to unfold. Ali's willpower is strongest at the beginning of every *tomorrow*. Last night she made a mental list of the new person she would be today. She is afraid of the day ahead (afraid of herself, if she is truthful). She doesn't trust herself to make good choices. She is struggling to not loath herself for the torture she inflicted last night. Her negative thoughts bang against the power of this new morning. The battle started with despising her reflection in the mirror and continues when she denies physical hunger. Now her pants are too tight. She hates the way her hair dries. Her arms feel clumsy and knees a bit shaky. There is fuzziness in her thinking along with a tugging sadness hovering over every thought. Time will tell if this day will sink her deeper or be a motivational *yesterday* to fuel her towards a better life. She has no joy to bind the days of the week together so that she can say, *I have a good life*. She needs to find meaning and purpose in serving others, doing her part to make this world a better place. Instead, each day is an effort to survive, despite her bad choices. Ali's life is mostly about Ali. She desperately needs validation and tries to get it from everyone around her. Even strangers! She obsesses about what others think of her. Only

God can show her true value, what a treasure she is. She needs to quit performing. Actress! Hypocrite! Inside, Ali is full of greed and self indulgence —to suppress her fear of people.

This will be her abyss, until she lays down her life. God will raise her up into something beautiful. She won't go there. It's too weird. Too hard to believe. Improbable. *What will people think?*

Ali is going through the motions of living. She is biding time until she finally gets to the bright day ahead when she has a picture perfect body, a beautiful face, where she loves herself and people love her. That is the day she will join the party. The future is when she will participate in her own life. This day doesn't matter. She doesn't really want it.

Her closet is full of sweatshirts, most are gray and have her college emblem printed across the chest. She plans her attire like a hunter, dressing to be unnoticed. The heavy sweatshirt she selects will cover her bloated tummy. It will cover the fact that her pants are unbuttoned for comfort. Drab gray will blend her into the concrete corridor walls that connect her classrooms. She stares into her closet as she pulls the sweatshirt over her head. Out of the corner of her eye, she sees the crisp ironed shirt, Reece's shirt. It makes her blush to look at it. Suddenly she realizes Reece never asked about it. *When I picked up Brandon from the kayaking party last night, why didn't he mention it?* She never thought about it either. She still suffers from embarrassment. He saw her so gaudy, in a dirty shirt and Dad's slippers. *I should have thrown the shirt away. I don't want to see him again! Maybe not. Maybe? I think tomorrow I'll call him and pick a day to go kayaking. What will I wear, though? I can't let him see me in shorts! Not until my legs are skinnier.*

Rummaging in her sock drawer, she remembers the laxatives she hid in a pair of black socks. Holding that pair of socks, she considers several scenarios. Today she has classes all day. *It might be inconvenient.* Part of her feels strong and part feels desperation. Just in case, she puts several pills, triple the recommended dose, into her jeans pocket and puts the socks on. She only makes it as far as the kitchen. Ali fills a glass of water and swallows three laxatives, hoping to time it right and thankful she doesn't have to work tonight.

The whole campus is unusually somber today. Or maybe it is Ali's interpretation. She isn't paying much attention to her surroundings, only to the ground she walks on. She plans her steps so that her feet miss all the cracks in the sidewalk . *Why am I doing this?* She wonders. After that, she makes sure she steps on every crack.

Ali avoids eye contact and ignores people. She walks alone. Sometimes, she lets herself really *see* the life outside her closed heart. This is when she notices that other people around her have friends. It seems like everyone is happy and living the good life —except her. Everyone else goes to parties, clubs, football games and movies. Girls call each other, sometimes several times a day, to talk about relationships, a new dress or a haircut. Stuff. Girls need to bond. She doesn't make the connection that loneliness is part of the reason she keeps filling herself with food. *I forgot how to make friends. When did this happen?*

Ali tries to remember the last time she had friends. *Was it really Jr. High? Was Kari really my last friend?* After her friend Kari moved away, the summer before her freshman year, Ali had a hard time connecting with other girls. It seemed like everyone established cliques. Ali was on the outside of all her circles of friends. Her main friends were paired off with boyfriends. Ali felt like a tagalong. After she graduated, this group of friends drifted apart quickly and moved away, pursuing dreams. Ali is the only one still living with her parents in her hometown. Sometimes she runs into her old girlfriends. They shriek and hug her with exaggerated enthusiasm. They reminisce about the good times they had together in high school, as if it were so long ago. Ali's memory is different from theirs. They embellish and retell stories that sound more fun than what actually happened.

Mr. Perfect is absent from Math today. Ali is glad. She can relax in her ugliness and not threaten their relationship. Their teacher sails through the lesson. Everyone is quiet and paying attention. The class dismisses ten minutes early.

Lucky to get curbside parking, Ali parallel parks a block from the coffee shop. Rain is splattering on her windshield. The wipers squeak forward and rumble back in steady rhythm. Her umbrella is not in its usual place, in the passenger seat pocket. She feels beneath the seat. Not there either, nor is it in the backseat. *Dang!* Ali puts on the hood of her sweatshirt. *This is going to ruin my hair.* She counts change out of the ashtray, slings her backpack over her shoulder and steps out in the rain. She hurries to feed the parking meter, before she jogs a few yards and rushes into the coffee shop for shelter.

The brick floor has a wet a trail up to the counter. Ali is second in line, behind a business man holding a folded newspaper with his armpit. She asks the barista for a tall cafe-latte and grabs some napkins while she waits. After paying, she puts her change in a clear glass mug that has 'tips' written in marker across the side. She sees that her favorite booth is available and claims the whole space by sprawling out her backpack and jacket across the bench seat.

She has her Math book and calculator ready. Folded open is her notebook, to crispy white pages with faint blue lines. Ali writes equations neatly, in pencil. She numbers each new Math problem, lined up in exact rows and columns. The upper right-hand page has her name and date, written precisely how the teacher requests. Sometimes, instead of erasing, Ali will start over fresh and re-write everything to keep it neat and tidy. She doesn't fold or crinkle the paper. She carefully rips along the perforations right before handing in assignments. In the same fashion, she files her returned papers into the same notebook, categorized in color coded pockets.

The lead of her pencil scratches into the paper, number fifteen with a dot beside it. Ali always puts a period after number lists. She likes the way her five looks and practices making it the same way on scratch paper. A line of 5's march across the paper. She does a row of 2's for practice, but stops halfway across after deciding to get back to the homework assignment.

She hunches over her open book and rests her head in her palm. Problem number twenty-three has her confused. Someone pushes her jacket and backpack over and sits down on the seat across from her. She doesn't notice and keeps writing, never looking up.

"Hi Ali."

Ali jerks her head up, drops her pencil. Her elbow bumps into her coffee, tipping it. Reece catches it just in time. A little bit of coffee drips onto the paper she was writing on, soaking to a few pages beneath.

"Reece! You scared me!"

"Sorry. I didn't expect that reaction," he says and sets her coffee down. "Do you care if I sit here with you?"

"No, that would be great." Ali blushes. "I am almost done anyway."

"Go ahead and finish."

"No, that's okay." Ali shuts her Math book. She is bothered by the wet stain on her notebook paper and blots it with a napkin.

"Sorry about that. It should be okay after it dries."

Ali contemplates redoing the whole page. *Maybe later.* She shuts the notebook and stacks it at the end of the table next to her Math book, pushing the cream and sugar packets over to make room.

"It will be okay," she assures him, nervously sipping coffee.

"Nice day, huh," Reece comments sarcastically, glancing towards the windows.

Rain is crashing down in sheets across the glass.

"Wow, this is turning into a real storm!" Ali is amazed at how fast the weather changed, surprised she didn't notice until Reece pointed it out. The sky is dark and looks like night.

"Good day to be at a coffee shop," he decides. "I had a group going out today, but we cancelled. There is a severe storm watch right now."

"A group for what?"

"Oh. For work. I had kayakers scheduled this afternoon. We were super slow in the store today, so they let me leave early."

"That's nice for you. I mean, to get the afternoon off, but too bad for the group."

"Yah, they can reschedule. I don't mind, really. Working. I love my job. Love the water. Being outdoors. I get to be around people when they are out to have fun."

Ali just looks at him and smiles. She isn't good at talking to people she doesn't know. While she is thinking of something to say, Reece drinks coffee and carries their conversation.

"Have you ever been kayaking before?"

"No." There is a brief silence.

"Canoeing?"

"Nope," answers Ali. She waits for Reece to talk again.

"Well, we need to change that. Remember, I offered. Brandon and I said we would help you out."

Ali rolls her eyes and says sarcastically, "Yeah, Brandon is su-uch an expert."

"He did great the other day. Caught right on. Was fearless. His friends had a hard time keeping up with him."

"Really?" Ali is surprised. Usually Brandon is timid when trying something new. "I'm sure he was scared, probably just pretending not to be in front of you and his friends."

"How 'bout you?" Reece teases, "Are you going to pretend not to be scared in front of me?"

"Did I say I would go?" Ali gives it right back.

"No, but I think you will."

"When?" Ali asks. "When is this day you decided I would go?"

Ali is getting more daring with her words. It surprises her how relaxed she feels and how easy it is to talk to him. Reece drums his fingertips across his lips, pretending to be thinking. He looks at his watch, then towards the door.

"How 'bout right now?"

"It's raining!"

"So."

"We'll get all wet."

"You are going to get wet anyway, when you tip over."

"Who says I am going to tip over?"

"Ya-might."

"Well, I guess if I do, that would mean that I didn't have a very good teacher."

Reece laughs. "Okay. You got me. I may tip you over to teach you how to get back in. And you might have to tip over again, with my assistance, for practice. Your paddle might *accidently* get pulled from your hands and thrown down-river."

"I'm having second thoughts."

Unexpectedly, a huge flash of lightning streaks across the sky, brightening the coffee shop with a flash. A split-second after, thunder roars with force and violence. They both jump.

Ali laughs and says, "You screamed like a girl!"

"Did not! That was you!"

"You screamed too. I heard you." Ali is still laughing hysterically.

He leans in and says in a hushed tone under his breath, "We're both going to pretend that didn't happen."

Ali laughs even more, "Oh, I will definitely be reminding you how that sounded." She looks him in the eye. Her expression changes. She looks so serious. Slowly, in her most solemn voice, "Reece..."

"What?" He asks with compassion, eager to know. He wonders and fears what she is going to say next.

"Never. I mean. Never. Ever. Scream. In front of anybody!" She is in hysterics again, proud of her joke.

Reece is embarrassed about the way he yelled, scared by the loud thunder-crash, but knows it sounded funny. He never heard himself make that kind of noise before. He makes a mental note to pretend-scream a few times for Ali, if they ever do go kayaking. *Scream! ....a turtle!* he will exclaim. *Scream! ...sharks! Scream! ...a butterfly! He* will find every opportunity to do his girl-scream in front of her.

"What are you smirking about?" Ali asks.

"I was thinking of ways to practice my new way to scream."

"If I were you, I'd make sure nothing ever scared you again. Except screaming like a girl. That should scare you the most!"

The lighting flashes again. Reece covers his mouth with both hands and fakes screaming. Muffled squeaks are coming out from behind his hands as the thunder crashes. Ali also has her hands on her mouth, to suppress laughter. Her face is getting red and tears are forming in her eyes.

Reece changes the subject back to setting up a kayak-date with Ali. "It looks like today won't work. How about Friday? After Brandon gets out of school? You bring the snacks —and Brandon, of course. I'll set us up with equipment." He winks when he says, "Rain or shine or thunder-screams."

"Shine only!" Ali says too quickly, then pauses to consider. "That might work. I'll have to check with my mom about Brandon going. She'll most likely have other plans and be glad to have someone to watch him."

"Let's plan on it then. I'll call you Friday morning to work out the details."

Suddenly the lights flicker and go out. All patrons are motionless, in momentary silence, followed by surprised murmuring. It is not completely dark. The emergency lights are on, illuminating the exit doors, but not the tables. Gray light filters through the windows. It is a romantic type of darkness. Another flicker, and the lights are back on. An employee switches on the TV near the bar area and turns up the volume. Everyone's attention is on the weather forecast. *Severe storm warning in effect until ten o'clock tonight, high winds, thunder showers, stay tuned. News 8. Keeping you informed...*

Ali and Reece are holding their coffee with both hands, watching the news with the crowd. A barista comes by the table with a basket of candles and matches. She hands them each a tea-light candle and a book of matches.

"This is just in case we lose electricity. We'll stay open as long as we can. Hopefully, the coffee stays warm. We don't have a backup generator."

They hear her repeat this same statement as she delivers a candle to every customer. Reece lights both candles with a single match and shakes out the flame. The room smells like coffee mixed with sulfur and cinnamon, from everyone lighting candles.

Shortly after the candle delivery, lights flicker once again. This time they stay out permanently. Flames from several small candles glow, their light speckling across the room. People are giddy, talkative and friendly in this circumstance. Strangers turn and acknowledge those sitting at other tables and make comments about the weather, the dim lights. They hint about free coffee.

The barista overhears the murmurs and yells out, "Free coffee! While it lasts!"

People crowd the counter to warm their paper cups with coffee and cream, hoping the supply doesn't run out before their turn. Ali and Reece are last in line and get their share. The employees fill their own cups with the remaining coffee and sit with the regulars.

"I'll have to say, this is the most romantic cup of coffee I ever had here," Reece tells Ali.

Ali blushes in the dim light. His comment scares her. *Is he hitting on me? I'm not ready for this.* She doesn't respond, instead looks at her cup and picks at the plastic cover.

"Don't worry. I'm not trying to seduce you!" he defends, as if reading her mind. "I just think it's funny. I sat down to talk to you and suddenly we are having candlelight-coffee."

Ali can look at him now. She feels better about the situation. "Yeah. I can't say I've done this before, either." She hesitates and agrees, "It's kinda fun, ya-know."

Reece takes the cardboard ring off his hot paper cup and rolls it across the table. Ali flicks it back with her finger. Reece flicks harder and it flies across the table onto Ali's seat.

She picks it up and rolls it back to Reece asking, "Do you go to the University here?" finally initiating a conversation.

"Yup. Third year. I'm in Business Admin. How 'bout you?"

"Sophomore."

"What are you studying?"

"Hmm." Ali ponders, "I can't decide. Probably graphic design. Right now I am only taking three classes, ones I know will transfer."

"Graphic design. So you're artistic. Are you living on campus?"

"No, with my Mom and Stepdad." It embarrasses her to admit this. "They're never home, so it's almost like my own apartment. Plus, it helps save money. Gotta pay for school, ya-know? Where do you live?"

"Campus apartments."

"What's that like?" asks Ali, exploring her future options. She lies, saying living with her parents is okay for now. But really, she is ready to move out the first chance she gets.

"It's alright. I have a great roommate. Close to everything. I can walk or ride a bike pretty much everywhere. My mom would love it if I still lived at home."

"Are you and your mom close?" Ali asks, comparing her relationship with her mother, which is typically strained and distant.

"Very." Reece says and nods his head. "We talk almost every day. She's an amazing woman." Then as if feeling guilty for only promoting his mom, Reece includes, "My Dad's a great guy too."

Already, Ali can sense that Reece lives in her fantasy family, the family she pretended to have as a child. She remembers how she used to imagine herself living in the country with barns and lots of animals, and that her father would read to her every night, while she curled in his lap, her head on his shoulder. She used to wish her mother wanted her around to help bake and clean; and would dance, twirl and sing into hairbrushes. *Silly! Make believe. What will I want next? Seven dwarfs!* Ali reprimands her childish dreams.

"What's your family like?"

"They're okay. I guess." Ali is abrupt and doesn't elaborate.

"Brandon seems like a nice kid."

"Yeah, he is. Gets on my nerves sometimes, though."

"He'll grow out of it. I did. I used to purposely drive my sister nuts. I knew every button to push."

"How old is your sister?"

"Twenty-seven. She's married. My nephew's two."

"Aww. So you are an uncle. How old are you?"

"Twenty-one," answers Reece. "You?"

"Nineteen. Your sister has the same scenario I do. A pesky little brother."

"Yep. I tried to tag a long wherever she went. I'd hide in her room when she had friends over. After a while, the first thing she would do is search her room, push me out the door and lock it. I liked to play jokes on her. One time, I switched all her clothes in her dresser with my Dad's. Another time I hid her clothes is a trash bag. They accidently were thrown out with the trash."

"Oh no!" Ali sighs. "You were a brat."

"I was. I really got punished for that one. My Dad made me take all my savings to buy her new clothes. And he took my bike away for two weeks. He is super big on respecting each other."

"Sounds like your sister put up with a lot."

"Yeah she did. She's an inspiration. For Christmas that same year, she gave me a gift certificate for the full amount I gave her for clothes. It was for a sporting goods store. I was saving for my first kayak. She knew how bad I wanted one." Reece reflects while looking at the table. "It made my mom cry when she did that."

"Wow," says Ali, somberly. She has a pang in her chest, a longing. Normally she is jealous of families that seem so picture-perfect. But not this time. She is happy that Reece has what she always dreamed of.

Outside the rain is still coming down in sheets, blowing against the glass. Much of the coffee crowd has already left. Not one new customer has walked in the door since the power went out. Ali and Reece turn and watch the flashes of light outside. Both are sitting sideways in the booth, legs stretching out on individual benches. Their backs rest against the low privacy wall that separates them from the empty booth on the other side. Two candles flicker on the table between them. Thunder rumbles in the distance, out of sync with the lightning. It has been over two hours now. Reece looks at his watch.

"What time is it?" Ali asks.

"Five-twenty."

"Already?" She is surprised at how fast the time went. "I should get going soon. Hopefully the rain will let up long enough to make it to my car."

"I should get going too."

Reece thinks about his bike, leaning against the wall a couple stores away, beneath a canvas canopy. When he left his apartment earlier it was a light, misty rain, nothing like now. He detoured downtown after school to get some exercise. He stopped in the coffee shop when it started raining hard, to wait for it to pass. He wasn't expecting this much rain. He wasn't expecting Ali.

They wait another fifteen minutes before mutually deciding it isn't going to clear up.

The rain sounds louder when they open the door to leave the coffee shop. It is coming down fast and furious. There is a river gushing along the curbside and pooling at the drains. They huddle together, beneath the small overhang that shelters the door.

"I'll count to three and we make a run for it," Reece strategizes.

"Ready anytime!"

"One. Two. Two and a half..." Ali jumps out in the rain. Reece pulls her back.

"Hey! Not fair." Ali gives Reece a polite shove.

"Three!"

Ali runs this time. Reece watches her. "Let me know about Friday!" he reminds.

"Okay!" she yells, running with her hood covering her head and leaning forward to keep the raindrops off her face.

Reece watches her unlock her car and dive inside. Ali doesn't see him sink against the wall near his bike, waiting to be out of sight before hopping on his bike. Ali might offer to drive him. He wants this bike ride. Unlike Ali, he allows the rain to wash his face and drench his hair. His tires spray a river up his spine as he deliberately steers through puddles.

I can't get any wetter than I already am!

Luke 15:3-7 (NIV)
³ Then Jesus told them this parable:
⁴ "Suppose one of you has a hundred sheep and loses one of them. Does he not leave the ninety-nine in the open country and go after the lost sheep until he finds it?
⁵ And when he finds it, he joyfully puts it on his shoulders
⁶ and goes home. Then he calls his friends and neighbors together and says, 'Rejoice with me; I have found my lost sheep.'
⁷ I tell you that in the same way there will be more rejoicing in heaven over one sinner who repents than over ninety-nine righteous persons who do not need to repent.

chapter 12 leah (lee-lee)

Jodie is looking forward to her break from work. It's been a while. She has planned all the things to do for the next five days. It is Friday, late morning. The weather is agreeable for the first day of summer. She outfits Lee-Lee in a new yellow sundress and covers it with a dainty, white sweater. Jodie has all the right things for her only child, two-year-old Leah; the trendy stroller, which is meticulously clean perhaps from underuse, popular children's books, appropriate high-fiber/low-sugar snacks, educational toys, name-brand baby shoes, all neat and tidy, bright and shiny. This means she is a good mother. This shows the world that her daughter is beautiful, cared for and financially blessed. Hopefully passers-by will notice them and think, "aww, what a perfect family." Secretly, Jodie hopes to burden friends and strangers with envy.

Am I a good Mom? She buries self-doubt under her busy schedule. *At least I don't drink like my mother did. Look at the nice things Leah has. I sure made a cute baby.* Jodie requires that others notice she is a fabulous mother. Of course, it is true on some levels. Like every good mother, she will fail her child in some way. Jodie falls short as a mother by not being available emotionally, but mostly unavailable physically. Her job often takes her away for days at a time. When not traveling, she works long hours. Deep down she knows this is affecting her relationship with her husband and daughter, but denial and selfishness tell her that the family is well provided for and that they can have it all. Her job makes her feel important, powerful and elite.

Jodie wears her *elite-ness* today. It stretches across her body in spandex with an expensive logo. It hugs her feet with mesh-ultra-light running shoes. She tore the tags off this outfit early morning. She jogs along the lakeshore park, pushing Lee-Lee along. Stopping to catch her breath, Jodie locks the breaks of the stroller after parking it next to a picnic table. She rests the heel of her running shoe on top of the table and uses it for support as she leans forward to stretch. Lee-Lee is quiet in the stroller, entertaining herself. By now, she would normally be climbing out. Jodie is glad she has a moment to herself to view the water and people watch. Before long, she is off running again. Destination playground. *Fall asleep Lee-Lee, so I don't have to go to the playground.*

Approaching the swings, Jodie locks the stroller again and bends over to lift Leah out. Something unusual catches her eye.

"Lee-Lee, where did you get tha-aat?" she says, contorting her face in disgust.

"My lamb Mommy," announces Leah proudly.

"Well, we need to put it back. Where did you get this?" The stuffed animal looks worn and filthy, with something dry and crusty on its belly. Jodie takes it away from Lee-Lee by pinching the ear with one finger and thumb, not wanting to touch it too much.

The child pulls it to her chest and hugs it tightly, screaming, "No Mommy! I keep it!"

Not wanting to make a scene, Jodie speaks politely, with exaggerated articulation. "Please give the lamb to Mother. It is not ours. We need to return it," then tries to take it away again.

"Mommy, Mommy... you hurting it!"

People begin to stare. Jodie is aware of this and is confused how to respond to Leah. She needs strangers to believe she is handling the situation with motherly excellence, taking advantage of this teaching opportunity.

She exaggerates more, "Please sweetheart. We cannot keep it, because it would be stealing. Please give me your lamb." Oops, she said *'your'* lamb.

Leah continues the tantrum with loud dramatics. Jodie's smile turns fake as she glances around the park to see if anyone is looking for their lost lamb. No one appears to be searching, as far as she can tell. The children playing are too old to be carrying stuffed animals. Plus, they would have noticed it by now. Isn't everyone looking at her hysterical daughter and the lamb she is clinging to?

Embarrassed, Jodie reaches into the stroller and lifts her child while Leah clings to the lamb. She hugs her daughter close, whispers into her ear, "It is okay, sweetie, you can keep it. Shhh. It's alright. Shhh."

Tears and whimpering stop abruptly, like an on/off switch. Leah is satisfied with the outcome. Crying means *I get what I want*.

The remainder of their outing, Leah includes the lamb in all her activities. She is gentle and motherly, often kissing her baby lamb, protecting it and helping it to be brave on the slide and swings. On the way back, they pass the park from earlier. Lee-Lee holds the lamb's leg and pretends it is waving *bye-bye* to the picnic table, where it used to live.

"My lamb," she whispers into a furry ear. She kisses the back of its head.

The next day Jodie puts the lamb into the washing machine. Sanitary cycle, with bleach! This occasion to de-grime the lamb does not come easy. Lee-Lee has not put this stuffed animal down since she found it. Jodie has to slip it out of Lee-Lee's arms while she naps. It is not quite dry when her daughter wakes up.

Leah frantically searches her bedcovers, patting and screaming, "Mommy! It gone! Mommy! Gone!"

Jodie quickly removes it from the dryer and rushes it into Leah's room. "Here it is."

"Oh... look! She white. Like snow!" smiles Leah, impressed with the transformation. "Why it wet?" she asks, then runs off to play before Jodie answers.

The phone rings. It is her husband, Dan. "I forgot to tell you this morning... I'll be home late tonight. The guys from work want me to sub for the basketball game again. Two of their players can't make it."

Jodie is disappointed. "Tell them to get someone else!"

"I can't. I already committed."

"Well, un-commit! What about your responsibilities here? I sure could use some help! This is my vacation, you know! Sure, I'll just keep working around the house while you're out playing all night!"

Dan has the phone turned away from his ear to tune out his wife's whiny voice. Before she is finished, he cuts her off and asserts in loud monotone, "I am playing ball. I will be home late tonight!" He hangs up on her shouting.

Jodie is fuming. Her angry eyes glare at the phone as if it were her husband. She mutters a few choice words, that hopefully Leah does not hear, before she slams the phone onto the table. *Why does he always do this to me? He knows I have the day off! He probably knew about this all week. Sure, wait until last minute to tell me! Why is it ME left to raise our daughter, to do housework, yard-work and everything-else-work?*

This is the mood she sports for the rest of the day, dwelling on Dan's defects to the finest detail. Dan left his socks and designer-underwear on the bathroom floor. She calls him a nasty name and throws them in the trash. Punishment outweighs the crime. He has a tendency to leave a trail throughout the house; dirty dishes by the couch, empty soda cans, unboxed DVD's scattered on end tables, clothes in piles at his side of the bed and shoes toppled wherever they happen to be removed. Leah watches her mother carry a laundry basket through the house throwing Daddy's things into it. She stays at a safe distance, fearful to get in the way. *Mama is mad.*

Jodie continues to castigate Dan as she fills the basket with only his belongings. She takes the basket to the garage, planning to hide it on the shelves. His mess is even worse in the garage! More colorful words are expressed. Jodie huffs, places the basket on the floor and begins to rearrange a shelf, making room to hide the basket containing Dan's treasures. She pulls an XL sweatshirt off a heap of Dan's junk on the shelf. *I'll use this sweatshirt to cover the basket. Even though he wouldn't notice it if I dropped it on his head!*

Jodie freezes, puzzled at what she sees under the shirt. Dan's red duffel.

Sitting right here. On the shelf. She nervously unzips the flap. Jodie fears she is going to find the expensive basketball shoes Dan just *had* to buy, the only pair he has right now. She donated his previous like-new shoes to charity, shortly after he splurged on the pair in the duffel. These are the amazing shoes he will *supposedly* wear to *supposedly* play basketball tonight. Jodie dismisses thoughts that Dan is lying and defends him by believing, *He probably plans on coming home to pick up his things later.* She takes the duffel off the shelf, making room to hide the basket, stuffs the XL sweatshirt on top and neatly slides everything discretely into place. Dan's duffel, containing the pricey basketball shoes, is propped on the kitchen table, ready for pickup.

Emotions stir in Jodie's chest at every glimpse of the red bag waiting on the table. Time is ticking slow, with no calls from Dan to apologize or at least to say, *Oops, I forgot. I will stop by later.* Or, *Will you drop off my duffel bag?* More time crawls by. Jodie and Leah eat dinner alone, with a red bag for their centerpiece. It is not until after Jodie finishes reading Lee-Lee three books and tucking her in bed that suspicions surface. Her mind is ready to connect the dots that have been there for a while. Jodie pours herself a glass of wine and waits in the dark. She only drinks one glass, wanting her mind to be sharp and ready to chop her unfaithful husband into pieces. As she waits, her fury intensifies.

Lights sweep across the house at three A.M. Her husband opens the side door discretely, like an intruder. Still sitting in a dark room around the corner, Jodie listens to the heavy sound of dress shoes tumbling off feet. She hears Dan flick on the dim light above the stove. She waits quietly in the dark, ready to pounce, listening to drawers open gracefully, cupboards gently closing, shuffling pitter-pat like a rat stealing crumbs. All movement suddenly stops and a four letter word is whispered by Dan.

Tick-tock..... tick tock... The world is still.

Outside a car slowly whooshes by, tires splashing through the wet street, while the rain drips from the edges of the roof. A dog is barking in the distance.

Tick-tock... tick-tock... Jodie hears Dan pick the duffel off the table and take it back out to the garage. He closes the door with a soft click, pulls out a chair at the table and sits down to bite at his thumbnail. *Think Dan. Think.* Both knees are bouncing wildly. *Who gives a...*

Leah jerks and sits up in bed. She hears a loud crash in the kitchen, glass breaking and yelling. Mama and Daddy are fighting again. She needs a safe place and someone to hold her tight. She needs Mama and Daddy. They are not reachable. So close. So distant. Her lamb is all she has. It keeps her safe. It tells her everything will be okay. Leah pushes the lamb hard into her belly and curls her knees up tight.

The tiny toddler whimpers under pink butterfly blankets, while her parents stoop to new levels. In the morning Daddy is gone.

Jeremiah 33:2-3 (NIV)
[2] "This is what the Lord says, He who made the earth, the Lord who formed it and established it--the Lord is his name:
[3] 'Call to me and I will answer you and tell you great and unsearchable things you do not know.'

chapter 13   reece

Reece has beef jerky and trail mix held in the crook of his arm, waiting in line at the convenience store where his friend Jeff works. He scans the display, meant for impulsive shoppers, to purchase chewing gum. How many flavors of mint do we need? Icee. Wintermint. Wintergreen. Doublemint and Spearmint, now those are classic, Grandpa's fishin' gum. Reece selects Spearmint, the vintage gum that was Grandpa's favorite. This gum is mostly for Brandon, to move the legacy through time. Reece will put it into his shirt pocket just like Grandpa did, to take out only when they get to the water. He remembers the cigarette package bulge in Grandpa's pocket, that was really his large packet of gum. Grandpa never smoked with the rest of his generation, never chewed tobacco or used profanity. He would however, clink his beer bottle with his buddies, but never to excess. He was a beloved mentor since the day his only grandson, Reece, was born.

Jeff is standing behind the cash register, attending a customer buying a 12-pack. Fridays are busy at the store, with a steady stream of people all day. He wants to talk to Reece and ask him about Ali, but can't with so many customers. The person in line before Reece is asking Jeff for directions to the high school. Reece is waiting patiently, hearing Jeff retell the route three times.

"Too bad you can't go with us," Reece says to Jeff as he pays.

"Yeah. Wish I could," Jeff agrees. "Kayaking, right? Who's going?"

"Ali and Brandon."

"Brandon?"

"Ali's little brother. I took Brandon and his buddies out a couple weeks ago."

"Ali too?"

"No. Just kids. It was his friend's birthday party." Remembering, Reece explains, "Ali came to pick him up after. I didn't know Brandon was her brother 'till then."

"Wow, Reece. Meeting the family, already?"

"Only by coincidence." The image of duck flannel PJ's and corduroy slippers pops into his head. "She was embarrassed because..."

The person behind Reece starts tapping on the counter and shifting his weight to imply, 'hurry up'. Reece takes the brown paper bag off the counter and nods at Jeff.

"Have a good time, Reece. Wish I could go."

Autumn and a co-worker load three kayaks and gear onto the trailer, to help Reece out. He has been anxious about this outing all day. Ali will arrive soon. Reece left to pick up some snacks. He is relieved to find everything ready upon returning.

"Thanks for helping, you two! I owe ya."

"We'll move the van down-river for you. Later on, when Joe gets back," Autumn offers. "How far do you want to paddle?"

"You're so sweet to me, Autee," Reece flatters. "Ali and Brandon are following me to spot the van. But thanks anyway. We're ending at the portage, just before Dead-Man's-Curve."

"Okay, thought I'd offer. Because you're the one that's always helping me."

"Naah."

"Naah, yourself."

"Ali should be here any minute." Reece keeps watching the parking lot. "Look at the perfect weather we're given. Sunny. No wind."

"Beautiful!" Autumn agrees.

"Well, I better finish packing my dry-bag."

Ali told Reece she would pick up Brandon from school and come right over. They walk in while Reece is putting neoprene gloves to his backpack, just in case it cools off.

Ali and Brandon follow the 'Bluewater Adventures' van to the river, where they unload kayaks off the trailer, leaving them at the edge of the parking area.

"Will they be alright here?" Ali worries about leaving them unattended.

"We'll see." Reece shrugs. "We haven't had a problem yet."

Next, they follow the van to their destination downstream. After parking, Reece gets into the backseat of Ali's car.

"Brandon, switch seats with Reece," Ali demands.

"Why? I was here first."

"Braaan-don!"

Reece pipes in, "I'm alright back here. We'll be there in a sec, anyway."

Ali glares at her brother and drives on, music muffled by the wind pouring through cracked windows. Their only conversation is Reece giving directions back to their kayaks; since Ali didn't pay attention when following Reece.

"Take a left at the dirt road, just beyond that state park sign. Oops! Stop!" he says, when she almost drives by.

"Whoops!" Ali slams on the breaks, throwing her passengers forward.

"Where'd ya learn to drive?" Brandon criticizes, leaning against the dashboard, bracing himself.

Reece is amused. "There's a two-track about a mile up, on the right," giving Ali plenty of warning this time.

"I'll make sure you see it," Brandon says, sounding like a hero. "Slow down. It's right there!"

Ali pushes the breaks a little too hard again, looking to the right. No road is in sight. Brandon is pointing towards her window at an overgrown trail —on the left.

"The road is up a little further. On the right," Reece reminds, for Brandon's benefit.

"Oh." Brandon plops back into his seat, quieter now.

Instead of helping Reece and Ali with the kayaks, Brandon races ahead, off trail, down a rocky decline to the river. Reece has the traditional mint-bulge in his shirt pocket. The beef jerky and trail-mix are packed in a dry-bag, along with extra gloves, binoculars and two long sleeve shirts. Earlier he noticed that Ali had on leather slip-on loafers, jeans and a thin, silky blouse. Reece forgot to mention clothing. *Oops! What not to wear. I knew she never kayaked before. Shoulda told her. She's probably out of her comfort zone. Just wait. I'll get her hooked on nature.*

Reece takes a paddle over to Ali's kayak. Autumn's dry-bag is tucked inside. He never saw her put it in there. *Good ol' organized Autumn.* Thinking of Ali, Autumn packed it with water shoes, a spandex shirt and capri cargo pants —all her own gear, Ali's size.

Understanding Autumn's intention, Reece hands the bag to Ali, "You might want to change into something else," he mutters, not knowing the best words. "Autumn packed you some stuff to wear."

Ali looks at him puzzled and glances down at herself, turning her ankle as if her shoe is agreeing with Reece.

"Oh," she says and reluctantly takes the bag.

Ali feels nervous and afraid. *What if Autumn's clothes are too small?* This would be the end of the world, for Reece to see Autumn's clothes squeezing her fat rear end, possibly ripping the crotch. She doesn't want her size compared to another woman's, unless of course, the other woman is bigger. *Please fit. Please fit. What am I going to say if they don't? I hate this. I wanna go home.*

Reece balances her kayak above his head and walks it to the river. He wants Brandon to help him carry the other two.

"Hey buddy. Come back up. We could use your muscles." Brandon flexes his biceps for Reece. "That's what I'm talkin' about."

Ali is in her car pulling Autumn's clothing out for inspection. The first things she checks are the size tags. *Wow, she's a size larger than me?* When she first saw Autumn, Ali admired her figure, athletic, yet feminine and slender.

How could she possibly be bigger than me? Ali is still reluctant to put on Autumn's pants. She doesn't want to be reminded how obese she is. When Reece and Brandon are out of sight, she slouches deep into the back seat and changes shirts. It is a little tighter than she hoped, but comfortable. *I guess spandex is supposed to hug the body. I feel like I am on Star Trek!* "*Ambassador Ali, you are on a collision course... Your specie is even weaker than expected...*" Ali is used to wearing loose fitting, shapeless tops. Next, she wrestles on the pants. They slide up easy over her hips and are simple to button even while sitting down. She looks at the shoes for a moment, wondering if she is supposed to wear socks with them. She leaves her socks on.

Ali feels strange in someone else's clothes, like dress-up when she was a little girl. She opens the car door and steps out. The kayaks are no longer on the grass. *Must be Reece and Brandon are waiting for me at the river.* She role plays her Star-Trek top, "*There seems to be no sign of intelligent life anywhere..*"

The capris are loose on the hips and waist. Ali pulls them up and they fall back down her hips a tiny bit. This sends her spirits soaring. She feels so skinny right now. She walks down the bank in her new sexy, athletic body —that is smaller than Autumn's. Smile.

Brandon's laughing his head off at something Reece said. Reece pats his shirt pocket and pulls out a packet of gum, offering a piece to Brandon. Ali watches Reece start to put it back in his pocket, until Brandon says something. He nods, takes out two more pieces and hands them to her little brother.

Reece hears sticks and gravel crunching. He looks over at Ali coming down the hill. *Whoa. She looks good.* When he notices she still has her socks on, he turns around, trying not to laugh. Oh, he wishes that he knew her better, with all the opportunities she gives him to tease. *Kermit. It's not easy being green.* He never intends to hurt her feelings. He really loves to see her smile and laugh. He doesn't fault her for not having experience. But she does look funny with bright green socks and water shoes. *Definitely a Kodak moment from the knees down.*

"You look great! ...Autumn!" Reece smirks.

"Thanks. At least I 'appear' to know what I am doing."

"Are you ready for this?"

"Guess so."

Reece scoots the kayak into the water until it floats freely. Holding the back end, he instructs Ali to straddle it just above the cockpit.

"Where's that?" she asks, "the cockpit." She wants to giggle.

"Oh. It's the opening at the seat."

"Right. Of course." Ali stands over the seat, feet in the water, green socks soaking up the river.

"Sit into the opening and stay low. Bring each leg inside," he says, still holding it steady for her.

After she is sitting, Reece lets go. It wobbles freely side to side. Ali grips the edges tightly. "Help, I'm going to tip over," she panics.

Reece steadies it again, allowing her to get used to it. "I'm going let go and have you lean side to side, here, on the shore. So you can get the feel of it. You'll notice the boat moves side to side easily, but only to a certain point, then it stops tipping."

He lets go of her kayak and instructs, "Okay, now lean. I'll catch you before you tip over."

Ali trusts what he tells her and tries it. She relaxes more when she realizes it is not going to tip over as easily as she imagined. When she is confident, Reece hands her the paddle and pushes her off. She grips the paddle way too tight and pokes short choppy strokes into the water, moving downstream.

All this time, Brandon is acting like a pro, chiming in with expert advice for Ali to ignore. Reece pulls Brandon's boat to the water and lets him show off, in little brother fashion, all his natural abilities, outshining his older sister as he rapidly paddles past her. Reece goes in last and floats over to Ali's side. From his kayak, he continues to help her. Ali listens and applies his instruction, gaining confidence. Soon she progresses ahead and catches up to Brandon. Not to be outdone by a girl, Brandon splashes his paddle, fast as he can, in short ineffective movements. Ali allows him the glory. She holds back and relaxes as the river carries her downstream with her paddle balanced across the cockpit. She dips her hands in the water and feels the current flow against them. It calms her.

Reece glides next to her to encourage, "You're doing great! How do you like it so far?"

"This is amazing!" Ali shines. "I see why you love this. I'm getting hooked. It feels like I'm part of the water."

They watch Brandon, who is way ahead. He is holding his paddle at one end, trying to knock something off a log, probably a turtle. Reece offers Ali some beef jerky. She takes a small piece from the bag and chews on the edge.

"Ali. Look," Reece whispers, motioning to the river-edge.

"What?" she says too loud, glancing in the direction he is facing.

A beaver is startled and dives into the water, flapping his tail against the surface.

"There's the lodge he was building for winter shelter," Reece explains, pointing to a pile of random sticks and mud.

"That's what it is? I was just wondering how that pile got there."

Brandon is getting farther and farther ahead.

He looks back and says, "Hurry up slow-pokes!" His voice echoes off the water.

Ali and Reece ignore Brandon's pace and let him play at a safe distance upstream.

"How often do you come out here?" Ali asks, attempting to fill the silence.

"Quite a bit in the summer, almost every weekend. Not so much this time of year." Reece leans back in his seat and touches the top of Ali's kayak with his paddle. "There's a lot of trails around the river that I hike or mountain bike."

"You are so... Mr. Outdoors!"

"Absolutely! This is where I find peace... in all this beauty."

Find peace? Beauty? How cheesy. Or maybe it's mature? She isn't used to hearing guys talk like this. Guys she know only use slang for adjectives.

Reece knows he's odd. Knows Ali is figuring it out, so he says, "Hang with me for a while. You'll know what I am talking about."

"Well. You're right. It's beautiful. Thanks for doing this for us, Reece."

Reece grins at her, biting his lower lip with a beautiful row of straight white teeth. It is the first time she noticed how perfect his smile is. She stares briefly, until it is uncomfortable, then jerks her paddle into the water. She paddles faster to catch up with Brandon. Reece watches her timid movements, the way she stiffens her body when the boat tips slightly, just like a beginner. He enjoys her shyness, her way of holding back. This intrigues him. It challenges him to draw out the real Ali. So far, he only gets glimpses of her.

Reece is the only one in Ali's life right now who detects the way she hides. Sadly, nobody close to Ali cares enough to notice, except Millie, her co-worker. At work Ali has a different personality. Millie often speculates what is causing Ali's moods, but keeps it to herself. Millie is worried about her and wants to tell her why. She keeps her lips closed, knowing her opinion would be uninvited and most likely denied.

Time escapes them. Reece frowns at his watch, almost six o'clock. *How can we be here already? Let's start over.* The air has cooled and shadows are long. Ali and Brandon are wearing the extra shirts and gloves that Reece brought for himself —always prepared. He hopes they don't notice the goosebumps dimpling his bare arms and legs; and how he is pretending that he isn't cold.

He yells to Ali and Brandon, "Follow me. We're at the end."

"Really? Already?"

"Oh man!" says Brandon, disappointed.

"Sorry. It goes fast," Reece sympathizes, paddling towards shore.

He wades back into the river to pull out his companions, Brandon first, who says he doesn't need help, then proceeds to tip over. Reece catches him just before the cockpit dips into the current. Brandon changes his mind and allows Reece to drag him to shore. Reece does the same for Ali, who patiently waits for help.

"Ya don't want to get those green socks wet again." Reece cannot resist.

"I know. I know. I get it now. Don't rub it in."

Reece and Brandon are at each end of a kayak, climbing the bank. Ali tries to lift hers over her head, similar to the way she saw Reece carry it. Bang. It comes crashing down, too heavy for her to handle. Brandon and Reece look back.

"Gee Ali, don't wreck it!" Brandon scolds.

"Sorry," she apologizes, sheepishly.

"It's okay. Just wait a sec and I'll be back down to help."

Instead of waiting, Ali grabs the paddles and vests. She follows Reece back down for another kayak, while Brandon starts the van for heat.

"So, did you like it? Do you think you will go again?" Reece asks her.

"Sure," Ali tries to think of more to say. Nothing.

They stand in awkward silence until Reece says, "That was some storm we had the other day." He points to trees that were uprooted. "Look what it did to those trees over there."

"Wow." Ali spots several trees lying about. *How did I not see those before? Am I that ignorant?* "I sure got soaked running to my car that day."

"Me too." Reece doesn't tell her how wet he actually got from riding his bike home in the storm. "Candlelight coffee. Nice."

"Best coffee I ever had," she says, then hopes she doesn't sound flirty.

"Not me. I've had better." Reece watches Ali's smile droop. "Just kidding," he assures. "Did you finish your Math?"

"Yes I did. And on coffee stained paper."

The van is toasty warm by the time Reece finishes tying down and loading everything on the trailer. Brandon takes the passenger seat again, leaving Ali in the backseat. She doesn't want to argue her way next to Reece, so she resigns next to a pile of life vests.

The ride is bouncy on the two-track leading to the main road. Ali slips off Autumn's water shoes and her own soggy socks to let shriveled white feet dry off. Brandon is full of questions for Reece. He hands a stick of gum back to her. Minty freshness cools her sinuses and makes her sneeze.

"Bless you," says Reece automatically.

Romans 13:11-14 (NIV)
¹¹ And do this, understanding the present time. The hour has come for you to wake up from your slumber, because our salvation is nearer now than when we first believed.
¹² The night is nearly over; the day is almost here. So let us put aside the deeds of darkness and put on the armor of light.
¹³ Let us behave decently, as in the daytime, not in orgies and drunkenness, not in sexual immorality and debauchery, not in dissension and jealousy.
¹⁴ Rather, clothe yourselves with the Lord Jesus Christ, and do not think about how to gratify the desires of the sinful nature.

chapter 14 mideah

Ted's vacation file is at the bottom of Mideah's inbox, untouched, but not unnoticed. At first Mideah put it there because she knew Ted would be crawling back on hands and knees, begging, pleading.

In the meantime, her current work piles on top of it as a reminder of the time and distance between her and Ted since their supposed dinner meeting. Mideah frets for three long weeks of no communication, not one phone call. Several times a day, she stops herself from calling him. She could use the excuse that she needs to either confirm or cancel the vacation plans she was working on for his family. *Ya know what, idiot, I'm going to call you and find out what your deal is! Are you going on this trip? Or what Ted!*

Mideah uses the office phone to speed-dial his familiar number. One ring. Hang up. She waits until coworkers are distracted, in meetings or out to lunch. She strategizes to ensure a private conversation. She dialed his number four different times today. Each time, halfway through poking his number into the handset, Mideah hangs up and stares at the phone in nervous relief. *He can just leave me alone, for all I care! Jerk! See if I ever plan a vacation for you again! I have better things to do than wait around for an unfaithful old man! I can have my pick, and I don't pick you!*

Mideah growls around the office in anger, as she pillages from coworkers, pens, post-its, notepads, the extra tape and stapler from the copy room. She switches chairs with an absent intern. Mideah's chair squeaks and the hydraulics no longer work. She returns the same chair a few days later, when four new chairs are delivered.

Days pass. No word from Ted. Finally, the office phone surprises her. Mideah is not expecting it this time. She is over her fervent hopes of hearing Ted's voice.

After Ted deserted her that cold night at Queen Anne's, Mideah came to work anxious and furious with hope. *Ted will be sorry. I'll pout and act mad. Make him grovel. He misses me, I just know it.* For the first few weeks, Mideah answered the phone with her sweetest voice, "Good afternoon, Schaffer Travel, Mideah speaking," She was determined to be ready for Ted's call.

Now she is tired of being disappointed. When she picks up the phone, her voice is sour.

It's lunchtime. She is about to leave when her phone lights up. Ring...Ring...Ring...Ri... She almost doesn't answer it. She is right in the middle of adjusting her leggings and pulling her boots up to her knees. The phone stops abruptly and begins again. Ring...Ring...Ring...

"Oh come on! Just leave a message," she huffs, annoyed. "Schaffer. Mideah." Her voice sounds bored and gruff.

"Mideah?" utters the person on the line.

Mideah is shocked to silence. She is unsure. *Ted?*

"Mideah? Is that you?"

Adrenaline pounds into her torso. Her head squeezes. Her voice is shaky when she answers, "Yes. Yes, this is Mideah. Who's calling, please?"

"It's Ted!" he says enthusiastically. "Don't you recognize my voice?" He jokes and acts naive, "Has it been that long?"

Mideah, still caught off guard, yet encouraged, doesn't know how to respond. Miniscule silence is a canyon between each breath, and between herself and Ted.

"Mideah? Are you there?" Ted is desperate for her. He wants his way. He rehearsed his manipulation before calling. Stage fright, he forgot his lines.

Finally Mideah says, "Yes. Uh. Ted. Yes, it's been a while. What's going on?" Before he answers she asks, "Are you still on for that vacation we were planning?"

The ice between them melts as Ted pours on the heat. "Oh. Yeah. The vacation. There's been a change of plans. I'm thinking Mexico. Warm. Sunsets. Beaches. I'd like your opinion." He makes it sound like she's the one going and trying to get her excited about it.

"Sure-Sure," Mideah says all buttery. "I'll dig up a few destinations. When would you like to meet?"

Ted hesitates. "Well. Humph. How about right now?"

"Now? As in right this minute?"

"Yes, if that works for you. I'm a couple of blocks away."

"That's fine. But I don't have anything to show you."

"No problem. I'll help you. See-ya in a bit." Click.

Mideah stands dumbfounded holding the receiver, shakes her head and hangs up. She rushes into the bathroom to primp. She repaints her face, untucks her blouse, adjusts her bra to enhance cleavage, then undoes another button. She re-tucks her blouse, pushing fabric towards her back, to make it tight across the front.

Ted opens the door and enters the empty office. Everyone must be out to lunch. Without hesitation, he wanders back to Mideah's cubicle. She is not at her desk so he sits down in her chair and waits for her while nosing around the photos tacked to her wall. Most of them are of Mideah and friends. One is with handsome men on each side of her. They toast the camera with party faces. Mideah is in every photo. Ted does a quick scan over the tall partition, then quickly steals a photo off the wall and puts it in the inner pocket of his jacket. It is a picture of Mideah standing in the sand on the ocean shoreline. The sun is setting in an orange glow, through the shear white dress she is wearing. The wind blows her hair and lifts her white dress up in swirls behind.

Mideah is seconds after his theft of her photo. She rushes to her cubby and is startled to see him sitting at her desk.

"Oh!" She squeaks.

Ted laughs. "Sorry I scared you." He stands, takes her palm in a makeshift hand shake and holds it in his gentle grip. "I let myself in. I hope it's alright."

They release hands. "That's fine. I am the only one here anyway," she cunningly hints.

Mideah does not mention his abandonment the last time they were together at Queen Anne's Lace. That is a dangerous zone. It might ruin the mood, or worse, send him fleeing again.

Ted takes her chair and twists it around to face her. "Have a seat."

Mideah sits down and he positions her at the computer. She clicks around the internet, chatting on and on about exotic destinations and package deals. She sometimes leans to the side so he can look at a picturesque landscape on her computer screen. Ted is hearing only enough to mask his fantasies. From behind, he leans close to the side of her head, supporting his upper body on the back of her chair. His face purposefully brushes against her hair. His eyes walk down her sternum as far as her shirt allows. Her perfume intoxicates him and triggers him to lose inhibition.

The sun is setting above sugar sand and turquoise water, the image on her computer screen. "What do you think of this one?" Ted asks. It reminds him of the photo in his pocket.

"Yes! I've been there!" Mideah says with excitement, "You will love it."

"Well then, let it be our starting point," he says, tipping his head to clunk hers, playfully.

Mideah enjoys every second of their blatant flirtations. It reassures her of his intentions. She likes where all this is going and does her best to push it along to illicit territory. She has an itinerary for their relationship plotted and hidden in her inner world. In this inner world, she is queen. If you start with her, you will end with her. There is no running away, because every road you flee to will confuse you and lead you right back to her kingdom. She knew Ted would be back. It just took longer than it does for most of her subjects.

She decides to bate him. "So. When are we going?"

"Well, I have the first week in May off."

Her next comment catches him by surprise, in a good way.

"Let me check my schedule. I think that works for me too." Mideah clicks the computer screen over to her planner.

Does she think I meant her? Ted cannot believe her mistake. *Can it be this easy?* He goes with the idea, forgetting a major detail —his wife. It will take some careful planning and solid lies to pull this one off. *Wow! An entire week with this gorgeous young woman! What a lucky guy. I'm game!*

Mideah highlights the entire week and types 'VACATION DAYS' across the dates. She pats her shoulder where Ted's hand is resting, caresses it and says, "I'll put my vacation request in today."

The office door opens and invades their privacy. The receptionist plops her purse on the floor and rolls her chair up to her desk, unaware of the visitor in the rear cubicle. Two more coworkers stroll in. Ted and Mideah's risqué moment pauses. They are anxious to resume playtime somewhere secrets can be kept.

Mideah follows Ted to the front door. She hands Ted printouts in a brown envelope. Her demeanor now business professional, she shakes his hand firmly and says, "I will verify those dates in a couple of days."

"Sure thing," Ted supports. He nods and walks out the door.

Back at her desk, Mideah immediately prepares and submits her vacation request. She busies herself by crafting her vacation for the rest of the day.

Parked across the street for Mideah's lunch hour, Jason gapes nervously out his car window toward the entry door of Schaffer Travel Agency. A few women walk out together with purses strung over their shoulders. Jason is relieved that Mideah is not with them. He plans to *accidently* pass her on the street. He will offer to buy her lunch. It seems as if everyone has left. The building appears sleepy and empty. Disappointed, Jason starts his car to leave. He hesitates. An unexpected, sharply dressed gentleman is walking swiftly towards the agency's door. The handsome stranger adjusts his collar, takes a deep breath and enters the agency. Surely this man will turn and walk out after realizing everyone out to lunch. When this doesn't happen, Jason leaves his car, walks to the door and slowly opens it like an intruder. He tip-toes next to the receptionist's empty desk, holds his breath and listens. He cannot make out their words, but recognizes her voice, confirming his suspicion. Jason wants to march boldly to Mideah and catch her in action, or at least ask her to lunch. Instead, he cowardly sneaks out the entry doors and rewinds his steps.

Jason doesn't leave his parking spot. He is furious and wants to punch something or someone. He spies towards the office door. His head feels the pressure of every heartbeat. Employees begin to return to work. Soon, he sees Mideah behind the large storefront glazing. She is shaking the good-looking man's hand. Jason studies their body language for clues. All appears professional. Good thing.

That night, Mideah finally returns Jason's calls. He never mentions seeing her at the office, nor does he mention watching her at the mall after she left work. He pours his unfailing charm on her. But his clever and flattering words seem to bounce off Mideah. She sounds distracted during their conversation. He is doing all the talking while Mideah hums responses. "Mm. Ah-huh. Oh"

He semi-jokes to her, "Hello? Where are you? Yoo-hoo... Do I need to come and get you?"

"What are you talking about?" Mideah snaps, finally using words.

"You sound preoccupied."

"Well. You know. I've had a busy day. A lot going on at work."

"Like what?" Jason furthers his investigation.

"Spring break is coming up. You know how busy I get." She is barely tolerating their conversation and says abruptly, "Hey look, it's getting late. I need to go."

"Already?" Jason whines, "We hardly talk anymore, baby..."

"Some other time. Bye." Click.

Jason's intuition bellows through the night. It keeps him awake and drives him toward desperate measures. He is losing his grip on Mideah and will take it out on other women.

Luke 7:37-38 (NIV)
[37] When a woman who had lived a sinful life in that town learned that Jesus was eating at the Pharisee's house, she brought an alabaster jar of perfume,
[38] and as she stood behind him at his feet weeping, she began to wet his feet with her tears. Then she wiped them with her hair, kissed them and poured perfume on them.

chapter 15 april fool's day

Ali steps off the scale encouraged. Lately it's been good to her, displaying a smaller number each week. *Seventeen pounds so far.* She visualizes a chart with a downward jagged line of weight loss. Every morning after emptying her bladder, she strips down and is nearly naked before a three-digit number determines her worth. And for the past couple of months, she has been worthy of a social life, trendy clothing, a new hairstyle and men. Ali is turning the heads of young men on campus. She walks taller, chin lifted, endorsed by loose fitting jeans.

She had value. She was worthy of love, long before she lost weight. She just didn't believe it. Resting her significance on losing weight will gain her temporary fulfillment, but is a shaky foundation to balance on. She still doesn't know or understand the truth. She has no one that tells her how much she is worth.

Ali skipped dinner. Now her stomach rumbles while waiting for Jayne near the entrance of a popular pub. She shivers in the cold, regretting that she left her coat in the car. She considers going back to get it, but doesn't want Jayne to think she is late. Instead, she endures the chill with arms folded across her chest and legs tight together.

Ali met Jayne at the fitness center she joined last November. Jayne, who was also new to the club, was frantically pressing buttons on the electronic panel of the treadmill next to Ali's. She couldn't get it to start. Jayne gently squeezed Ali's elbow to get her attention. This startled Ali. She twisted, tripped, fell on the belt and rode off the end of the treadmill. Instead of sympathy, Jayne burst out laughing and accidently peed her spandex pants.

"You made me pee my pants!"

"Yeah? Well, you made me fall off the treadmill!"

Instant friends. Jayne was talkative and easy to get to know, just what Ali needed. They began to set up times to meet at the gym and eventually started hanging out with each other on weekends, chasing after men, per Jayne's influence.

It befuddles Ali that men are attracted to Jayne. Jayne's body is soft and curvy, what Ali would consider plump. If Ali had Jayne's percentage of body fat, it would ridicule her back into the shameful cave she finally brought herself out of. Jayne's hair, face and lips are beautiful and lush, although she has thunder thighs and a large butt. Jayne doesn't seem to mind. She doesn't try to hide her imperfections. She still wears short skirts and tight dresses. Whenever they are together, men typically buy Jayne drinks, luring her into conversation and dancing. They try to guilt her into going back to 'their place' when the bar closes. In all the time Ali has known her, Jayne has only gone as far as heavy flirting, getting drinks for free and leaving her men at the bar.

Ali is startled from a daydream when she hears Jayne approaching, her loud spike heels hacking quickly onto the cold pavement.

"Hey Ali!" Jayne calls out, breathless. "I had to park so-oo far away. Sorry to keep you waiting."

Ali looks at her watch for the tenth time, annoyed to be waiting for forty-five minutes. She is sure that Jayne isn't parked forty-five minutes away, so her excuse isn't valid. Not wanting to dampen the evening, Ali pretends she isn't bothered.

"You look amazing!" compliments Ali, admiring her friend's metallic silver dress. "Where did you get the pink pumps? Adorable!"

Jayne lifts one leg and points her toes to display her shoe. "Oh, I cleaned out my closet recently. Forgot all about them. Wow Ali! You're wearing a dress? I am like, so-oo shocked!"

Ali smoothes her hands across her thighs, as if spreading a napkin. She lifts the draping silk of her navy dress and waves it across her legs. "Yeah. I got this a couple days ago. Does it look okay?"

"Love-it!" Jayne sing-songs. "Of course, it could be a bit shorter to show off your sexy legs! Woo-wee"

Ali indulges the idea before deciding that if her dress were any shorter it would look like she forgot to wear pants. Four inches above her knee is enough leg.

They approach the antique oak doors of the pub. Ali grasps and pulls the fat wooden handle that has worn smooth over the years. It feels grimy and sticky. She envisions creepy-crawly germs waxing over her palms, transferring to everything she touches. She steps toward the doorway, but Jayne cuts her off and walks in as if the door were held open for her. Heated air melts the goose-pimples off their skin as they parade past the long wooden bar where several stools are occupied. There are no vacant seats. Ali watches heads turn towards her friend. All eyes teeter-totter up and down, checking out Jayne's metallic hourglass. Ali doesn't realize that their eyes are on her also when her back is turned.

There are two seats available at a tall, round table between the wooden bar and the booths. A cute waitress wearing a lime-green t-shirt and skimpy shorts bounces over to ask what they'd like to drink. Jayne talks, while Ali stares at the waitress's thick brown ponytails with green ribbons near her ears. She wants to copy her hairstyle. *Would it be too childish? She looks cute. Would I?*

"Corona Light with lime," decides Jayne, after asking the waitress to describe their various craft beers.

"Same here," copies Ali, not realizing she divided her hair and is holding it in chunks by her ears. She flings it back into place when the waitress leaves.

The waitress is back immediately with their orders. She places their beers on two round cardboard coasters. Both girls squeeze the lime into the bottleneck and poke it down with pink fingernails. Ali's nails are short and natural. Jayne has fake nail extensions that are lumpy and conspicuous. Ali wonders why Jayne doesn't notice that her nails look awful. She actually seems proud of them.

They sip beer and study the crowd for prospective partners. Most of the patrons of this pub are doing the same. When the bells on the entrance door jingle, Jayne glances to see who is walking in.

"Whoa. Who's that guy?" Jayne provokes.

Ali turns to look and knows immediately who Jayne is talking about. Her face heats up just by seeing him near the door, looking around the room.

"I know him," brags Ali.

"Well, intro--duce me!" demands her friend.

"He's taken."

"By who?"

"Me," Ali claims sheepishly.

"You wish!"

"You're right. I do wish. I've had a crush on him for a long time." Ali points her finger at Jayne. "So hands off!"

"We'll see," challenges Jayne. "What's his name, anyway?"

"Jason."

He walks right by their table. Jayne cannot resist saying, "Hey Jason," in a soft sexy voice.

He turns and plays his sly smile on Jayne. "Do I know you?" he asks, putting his hand on her shoulder.

"No, but you should," Jayne flirts with a common cliché.

"Yeah, I probably should," he flirts back and gives Jayne's shoulder a gentle pet.

Ali clears her throat. Jason looks over and notices Ali.

"I know you from somewhere." He squints and looks sideways at her.

"Math class. Last Semester," She says to jog his memory.

"Yeah. Yeah," Jason says in his cool-dude voice. He thinks it elevates his status above everyone. "Maybe I'll see you ladies around? I am here with some buddies," he continues with the same pretentious voice, looking at Ali and raising both eyebrows at the end of sentences.

Jason rubs his palms together as if his hands are cold. He presses his fingers together, prayer-like and draws his hands to his lips. He kisses the fingertips and directs the kiss towards both women before he walks away. When he is out of earshot, both girls giggle. They lean towards each other to say, "Whoa!" and turn to see where he went and who he is sitting with.

Jason smashes into a booth with three other guys about his age, all good looking. But Jason is definitely a stand out. From across the room, they hear the manly-man grunt-and-groan greeting. They snicker again, childishly, still watching with hopes rising.

Shortly after Jason's grand entrance, the waitress shows up with two unexpected beers. "These are from the booth back there," she explains and points at the manly-man booth. Jason and the guys wave to them to take credit for the favor. Ali smiles and Jayne blows back a feminine kiss.

"So, how do you know Jason?" Jayne asks, digging for some gossip.

"I see him around campus. Plus, he was in one of my classes." Ali picks at her fingernails and doesn't look up at Jayne.

"Does he have a girlfriend?" Jayne asks and leans secretively towards Ali.

"I'm not sure. Probably not. I never see him with the same girl." Ali wonders the same thing.

"Do you know the other guys he's sitting with?" Jayne's head is turned and looking over her shoulder. "Like the one with curly blond hair?"

"No. And I don't really know Jason that much."

"Well, I wonder why they bought us these drinks? They aren't coming over to talk to us!" Jayne taps her manicure on the table and stares at the curly blond.

"We all just got here. Maybe in a while?" Ali sounds optimistic, but doesn't really believe they are interested.

Ali and Jayne look around the room and make comments about the crowd. They nurse their beers and wait. Every few minutes, Jayne glances over to Jason's troupe, waiting for a signal. Nothing in the room looks as inviting as that table.

"I think we should make the next move," she tells Ali.

"What should we do?" Ali is now onboard with any scheme of Jayne's. She is desperate for Jason's attention.

"Let's buy them a drink."

"Good idea," Ali agrees with hope renewed. "What are they drinking?"

Both look over at the table and say, "...a pitcher of beer."

Jayne waves the waitress over. "What are the guys at that table drinking?"

"Bud. On tap," she says and flicks one ponytail with the back of her hand.

"We'd like to buy them a pitcher," Jayne tells her. "But could you deliver it to our table? We want to bring it to them ourselves."

"Sure. I'll be right back..."

She hurries off and returns right away to deliver a worn, plastic pitcher of beer. Suddenly Ali is very nervous. *This is real. Are we really going to invite ourselves to their table? What if they don't want us there? How embarrassing. Let's forget the idea, Jayne.*

"Ready?" Jayne asks.

"Let's wait a minute," Ali stalls. "What are we going to do, exactly?"

"We are going to walk over there and tell them we have a present for them."

"Then what?" How can Jayne be so confident?

"Then we are going to sit down."

"What if they don't want us to?" *This is a stupid idea. We will look like desperate idiots!*

"Girl! Why wouldn't they? Look at us!"

Ali isn't convinced. She fears rejection and is getting uncomfortable. As they walk, Ali ducks behind Jayne, who is leads the way. The guys see them coming, Jayne first, holding the pitcher, Ali next, holding their two bottles of Corona.

"What's this?" the guys ask.

"It's a thank you gift," Jayne flirts, "for letting us join you."

"Hey thanks!" They scoot closer in the large booth and make room for Ali and Jayne to sit opposite each other. Ali slides the Corona smeared with thick lipstick across to Jayne, who happens to be sitting next to Jason.

"So, are you going to tell us your names?" blond curly-hair guy asks.

Jayne pipes in right away, "Jayne." She holds out her hand like a dog paw, ready to shake.

He clasps her fingers and says, "Kevin." He rubs his thumb across the top of her hand.

Kevin points and names his friends. "Gary. Seth. Jason." He sits back and asks, "And who is your beautiful friend?" looking right at Ali.

Jayne and Ali speak at the same time. "Ali."

"I'm Ali," she repeats, then feels embarrassed for assuming she is the 'beautiful friend'.

Ali is hyper-aware that Jason keeps looking at her. They talk about school majors, classes, past and present teachers. Small talk. Big talk is on the way, after a couple more pitchers of beer. Jayne is flirting across the table with Kevin and getting a favorable response. Jason focuses on Ali. He wants to satisfy his hunger. Every so often his shoe taps the top of her foot, gently and purposely, which makes Ali's uterus whimper.

Until finally he says, "Switch spots."

Jayne is glad to trade places. She stands immediately, crosses over to Ali's spot and nuzzles next to Kevin. Ali is shy going to Jason. Unsure, she scoots onto the worn vinyl and folds her hands between her knees, sitting stiffly, not daring eye contact. Jason immediately wraps his arm across her back and squeezes at her waist. Ali secretly hopes he doesn't feel any fat when he touches her belly. They toast away nerves and inhibition. Each person aims the conversation on themselves. *All about me. I want to be special. I am special. Did you notice? Should I say it again, in case you didn't hear?*

Soon, Ali and Jayne leave the table to use the restroom.

Girls crowd the mirror with purses open. They layer on makeup and primp hair.

"Jason's here," one girl says to a friend.

Ali's eyes dart towards their conversation, keeping her head steady. She lingers, filtering out the invasive noise of toilets flushing and water running, while pretending to touch up lipstick.

"Is he with Mideah?" the friend asks.

"No. Some other guys."

"Fair game for us then," the girl says as they leave.

Who is Mideah? Ali wonders almost aloud. Jealousy chews through her chest as she waits and waits for Jayne to finish admiring, dabbing, wiping and applying. Ali's toes are wiggling in the tips of her shoes, releasing anxiety. She is worried Jason will move on if she is gone too long, worried that Jason is being lured and trapped by the huntress that preceded her at the mirror. *Is Mideah Jason's girlfriend?* Ali speculates. *Who is Mideah?* She is jealous of a girl she doesn't know. *Do I know her?*

"Are you coming or not?" Jayne asks loudly, "Ali! Hell-low?"

"Oh!" Ali jerks her head towards Jayne. "Yeah, I'm ready." she dashes past Jayne, out the door and into the orchestra of loud conversations.

Gary and Seth are buried in the booth, ignored, pushed-in and unnoticed behind Jason and Kevin. While Jayne and Ali are gone, they both attempt to talk the other guys into leaving.

"Let's get-outta here! And go to Boomtown." Gary suggests, referring to a dance club two blocks away.

"Yeah," Seth supports the motion.

But Jason and Kevin are tuned out, distracted by two scantily clad women approaching them. Jason scoots over, allowing one gal to sit down. Kevin copies. Gary and Seth's shoulders scrunch together more and press against the wall.

Seth rolls his eyes at Gary and says, "Lets book!"

"We're leaving," Gary says to Jason.

"In a few," Jason says from the side of his mouth.

"Ten minutes. Tops. And it's Boomtown!" Gary demands. But Seth is the only one paying attention.

Ali rushes from the bathroom to reclaim Jason, when she hears a familiar voice shout, "Hey Ali!"

She turns and sees Reece sitting at a table with Autumn.

"Oh! Hi Reece. Hi Autumn." Ali points to where Jayne was standing, ready to introduce, "This is..."

Where is she? Ali glances around and sees that Jayne is already back at the table. She watches Jayne point a thumb in hitchhiker fashion at the gal who invaded her space. The girl looks at Kevin, back at Jayne, then stands up. Alpha Jayne claims her spot and sits in uninvited warmth on the vinyl seat.

"How's that cute little brother of yours doing?" Autumn asks.

Ali is distracted and doesn't hear the question, is too busy guarding Jason. Fear swells as she watches the flirty girls from the bathroom mirror standing by Jason. The girls definitely have his attention. *Did he just touch her leg?* Ali's jealousy thickens.

"What's up?" Autumn changes her question, attempting to engage Ali.

"Oh. Um." Ali reverts her eyes to Autumn and back to Jason. "Not much. Just school," she says in a mechanical voice.

"Keepin' ya busy?" Autumn asks, politely.

"I've been buried in homework." Still preoccupied, Ali asks, "You?"

"Classes are easier this semester so I have more time on the trails. I started...," Autumn doesn't finish. She knows Ali isn't paying attention.

"Okay," Ali says automatically, tapping nervously on her thighs with fingertips and not daring to ask Autumn to repeat herself. There is an awkward silence, before Reece rescues the conversation.

"Are you here with anyone?" he asks. "Do you want to sit with us?"

Ali looks back at Jason. She hopes he doesn't see her talking to Reece and think she's not interested. Jason never notices, still sidetracked by the same girls.

"Well. Um." Ali shifts her weight. "I'm here with another group."

Reece tries to figure out what she keeps looking at. He kindly says, "Okay, another time. We'll see you around."

"Yeah. Bye." She turns swiftly and rushes to Jason.

The two girls are blocking the place next to Jason where Ali wants to sit. They are chattering nonstop and touching his shoulder and arm. Ali slouches behind them, feeling small, and waits for Jason's cue. She was there first. *Tell 'em Jason. You're here with me now.*

Reece and Autumn watch Ali across the room. They notice her standing stiff and gawping at Jason. It is obvious she is waiting in line for her turn.

"Oh no," Autumn says, "Not him!"

"Yup, you're right," agrees Reece. "The writing's on the wall."

"Do you know him?"

"Why? Are you interested in him too?" Reece taunts.

"Oh...Nooo." Her voice is low and exaggerated.

She explains, "He dated my cousin for a while, until she found out he was leaving their dates early to be with another girl."

Autumn thinks about how he hurt her cousin. "He's a creep."

Reece looks over at Ali again. She is still waiting for the creepy guy and still ignored. He wants to grab her arm and pull her away from danger. *Can't you see? You're nothing to him.* He wants to shout. *You can do better than that! He doesn't deserve you!*

Ali must have finally said something. The two girls glance at her, as if taken aback. They look at Jason for confirmation, then step aside. Jason pulls Ali onto his lap and whispers in her ear. The two kittens pad away in disappointment.

Reece is frustrated to see Jason wrap his arms around Ali and how she responds by leaning her head close to his. Both he and Autumn are reading between the lines. They watch the group at Ali's table get up to leave, throwing dollar bills on the table. In a chortling herd, they head to the door. Reece shrugs his shoulders and downplays his emotions. *Whatever. She'll figure it out.*

The music is loud and the dance floor crowded. Sweaty bodies are in creative motion, celebrating lyrics and drumbeats. Hips sway suggestively to siphon the attention of peers. At the chorus of a familiar song, hands fly in the air and fists pound, replacing the song's words with swearing. This is how to party! They shout obscene words into the air. —To get attention? This young group is generating short-term memories of stumbling feet and slurred words, memories that disappear in their sober minds. Most people at the bar tonight are just a drink away from remembering loneliness. Happiness gained from grinding hips, conjuring spirits and swearing, rarely lasts the length of the car ride home.

Young bodies dance away repressed fears that are hiding under carefully selected clothes. The crowd that surrounds Ali is heated and eager for pleasure. Gathering here is more than a mating ritual for Ali (and others). She needs this validation. The drop-dead-gorgeous man seated at her side means she actually might be pretty and kinda fun to be around. The glow of happiness rises in her, burning off her fear of rejection. The group from the pub is sharing a round table near the dance floor. Jayne and Kevin are dancing. Seth and Gary have their backs to the table, finally getting some attention from two girls they know. Jason keeps groping Ali, inappropriately, as if he owns her body. To Ali, it isn't demeaning. It is reassurance. *Yes Ali —you're sexy. Yes Ali —you're worthy of a guy like Jason. Yes Ali —he wants you... Yes Ali —someone can love you.* Ali misinterprets his actions.

The music changes to a slow and seductive ballad. On cue, singles abandon the dance floor and stand at the sidelines, waiting to be noticed. Couples wander onto the worn wooden floor. Jason tangles his fingers with Ali's and slyly leads her out to dance. As they move in fluid rhythm to the song, his hands are moving down her back and nearing the curve of her buttocks. Her heart panics. Intuition speaks to her, scraping memories off the edges of her brain. Her flesh sends an invitation to Jason, yet her soul is hesitant to his advances. Somehow, her inner wisdom knows something is off. She ignores it. Jason embraces her with his hands and gropes nearby women with his eyes. He gives her bottom a squeeze and winks at the guy he caught gawking at her cute butt. This gesture is a victory dance. *Look what I'm taking home!*

Throughout this evening, Jason weeds the crowd for clues of Mideah's whereabouts. He hopes she'll show up or maybe her friends will. He can interrogate them. Earlier, he noticed that Mideah's car was parked at the agency. Yet when he called Schaffer Travel, he was told, "Mideah's unavailable, I'll let her know you called." He tried to phone her several times and is still waiting for her to return his call. Before going to the pub, he drove by her office again. Her car was still there. Schaffer Travel was closed, lights out. Vulnerability and rejection set him on the prowl! Mideah clawed his ego and it is bleeding. Tonight, Ali is there to lick his wounds and keep him occupied, until he upgrades to Mideah.

They dance three songs in slow embrace and leave the dance floor when the music livens up. Back at their table, everyone is drinking a fresh pitcher of beer. Jason pours a glass for Ali and encourages her. "Drink up!" This time he winks at Seth. Her peers are watching. So Ali takes deliberate gulps, catching her breath between.

"Bottoms up!" Jason cheers.

Ali clanks her glass on the table.

"Slow down Ali," Jayne persuades.

Ali leans in, whispering at length into Jayne's ear. Jason seizes the moment to beg Seth for the keys to his van.

"Come on, Seth!" he whines, "Switch up with me."

"Aw-right." Seth reluctantly surrenders, knowing what he is consenting to. He stands, digs keys out of his jeans pocket and slides them over to Jason. "It's parked in traders alley."

Jason pockets them and flips his own car keys to Seth. "South end, easy to spot."

Jason purposely parked his car in a noticeable area, just in case Mideah comes looking for him. He explores the crowd again. His eyes flick to every blond head, hoping to see silky hair, spread across the back of his desired lover. She is not here. He thinks about sneaking out to see if Mideah's car is still parked at the agency. Instead, Jason crouches down to check his cell phone for messages. None are from Mideah. This angers him and softens him, all at once.

Still fixated on Mideah, he leans towards Ali. "Hey Middy," he says into her hair. Ali's back is turned. So he tickles her ear and neck to get her attention.

"What's *hammidy*?" Ali asks, shrugging the tickle off her neck.

"I said follow me," Jason lies after realizing his mistake.

"Oh."

"Did you drive, Jayne?" Jason asks. "Ali's coming with me."

"Huh?" Ali says, with a quizzical expression, "Where we goin'?"

"We drove separate, baby," Jayne answers in her natural raspy voice.

Without hesitation, Jason tugs Ali like a child who walks too slow. He grips her by the forearm and leads her to the door. Ali is confused, looking back and forth at Jayne and Jason.

When they exit the building, she asks, "What're we doin'?"

"I thought it would be nice to get some fresh air," Jason grins. "Plus I want you all to myself." He kisses her cheek.

"Awright. Ya-got me. " Ali slurs, stumbling beside Jason. "Oopsie."

They walk through rows of parked cars at the side of the building, near an alley.

Jason scans the parking lot, stops suddenly and says, "Oh! Wait!" He flattens his palm on her chest and directs, "Stay here!"

He quickly runs through a couple rows of cars, believing he sees Mideah's black convertible. Ali watches and wonders what is going on? She doesn't see Jason kick the tire of an arbitrary black car in disappointment. He returns quieter and diminished.

Bugs swarm and battle for light beneath a single streetlamp that illuminates only a few rows of cars. Jason draws Ali close to his side. He leads her to a burgundy van, parked discretely in Trader's Alley. It's beady headlights stare out of the dark alley. 'Traders Alley'—notorious for exchanges of illegal substances.

"Are we goin' somewhere?" questions Ali. She leans against the side of the van as Jason fumbles with the keys.

The door of an unfamiliar van magically opens for Ali. It slides along the track and echoes a *click* into the silent night. Mildew mixed with stale fries wafts into the cold, damp air, slapping Ali's face. The van's interior squeals adolescent neglect, with fabric seats worn and covered with papers. Empty soda bottles litter the seats and floor, along with books, shoes and a sweat filled duffle bag.

"Is this your car?" she wonders aloud.

"Seth's."

"Where's your car?"

"Shhh," he says, warming her ear with his breath, "just relax." Behind her, he saddles his hands across her lower back, pressing thumbs into her spine, prodding her into the van. She stumbles over a travel mug on the floor, attempts to sit, but the seat is covered with garbage. Instead, she steadies herself with one hand on top of the seat and crouches with her back nearly touching the ceiling. Jason climbs in, squeezing past her and into the back seat of the van. He scoops everything cluttering the velour bench, onto the floor. He pulls familiar levers and folds the rearmost seat into a flat bed. Ali is still crowded and standing like Alice in Wonderland, overgrown and hunched over, in too tiny a space. Jason presses a button and the van's door clicks shut, imprisoning Ali.

"Climb on back," he incites.

Ali denies where this evening is heading. She is trusting her safety to a man with character of her own invention. He is the prince of her charming fantasy. He is paying attention to her! It is erasing her logic —erasing the warnings every mother tells her children. *Do not take candy from strangers! What do you do when a stranger asks you to get in his car? ...you RUN!*

Instead of fleeing, she falls into his snare by crawling on her hands and knees to Jason. The velour upholstery feels dirty and smells dank. A dark sensation ripples through Ali, an endless shiver, a whisper saying —*follow me, you coward!* She abides. Jason's thick hands grip her upper arms and impetuously pull her to him, goading her into position. There is no getting to know each other. No conversation to bridge the river of fear inside Ali. No securing her trust. No gentle kiss. No intimacy spawned from love. He is crafty and quick. He pulls her dress up. She instinctively clasps the hem and attempts to hold it down.

"Hey-hey, now." His breath fogs her ear. He squeezes her hands so she will release her grip off the dress. It hurts. He movs the silky fabric up her back.

Ali tries to pull her dress back down but can't reach it anymore. His hands feel rough and dry against the tender flesh of her spine. The bristles on his chin scrape against her neck as she referees his roaming hands. She fights his leathery palms, tries to block their path.

"Come on. Loosen up!" he says, using more force to invade her body.

The words she wants to speak are not reaching her lips. Screams push against the walls of her chest with a massive force. Her teeth are clenched. And just like that, her dress is off and tossed over the seat, blanketing a wadded bag of stale french fries. By the shoulders, he holds his frightened rag doll, whose embroidered eyes are sewn tightly shut. Jason flops his doll beneath him. The elastic of her panties stretch in a tug-a-war, then snap free, in Jason's favor.

Their lips have never met. Her stitched on heart has not been melted by the sound of her lover's voice. He isn't tender. He doesn't cherish her. He doesn't protect her. He harms! He is a thick storm cloud that hovers above her and blocks all light.

Jason fumbles with something, —clink, snap, zip.

"no," she whispers. *Is this what I wanted?*

"Hey, girl," he exhales and forces his knee between her tightly clamped legs.

"no jason." She manages to murmur again.

"It's what you want," he says.

Her mind swirls with confusion and indecision, as she flushes her self-worth like vomit. *But I don't want this. Stop! Please. Why?*

His movements are raw and harsh. Absolutely robotic. He robs a virgin's alabaster jar of her sacred perfume.

She burns. Like fire. Consumed.

In fetal position, Ali cowers against the hard vinyl shell of the van's rear door —where Jason left her whimpering. He drives her to a street corner near the pub where she and Jayne met earlier. He ignores her while she turns herself into a zombie —a corpse that forgets. *Who is that man in the driver's seat? When did he start the car? Where am I? Where is he taking me?*

Ali tips and rolls with the abrupt turns of the van, bumping her head against the hollow plastic sidewall. The edges of her mind are blunt and deadened —yet they scream with fury.

"This good?" Jason asks in monotone. He presses the button to slide open the automatic door. Anxiously strumming his fingers on the steering wheel, he waits for Ali to leave Seth's van.

Ali staggers out the door and stands exposed beneath the streetlight. Her crumpled blue dress hangs inside out off boney shoulders —covering her frailty.

She walks several blocks before sitting down on a park bench at the playground. Ali is forsaken and trembling. The moon throws shadows across the grass. She stares at ghostly swings, swaying barren, on long chains. They invite her. She positions herself onto the U-shaped rubber seat. The chains feel cold under the grip of her hands. The black rubber phantom hugs Ali's hips as she readies herself to fly away. She presses her feet harder than necessary into the sand to gain momentum. She needs to forget. The sand absorbs the force of her anguish and sucks it down with every stomp.

Ali propels the swing high into the air, disappearing each time her navy dress fades into the sinister sky.

2 Samuel 12:1-4 (NIV)
[1] The Lord sent Nathan to David. When he came to him, he said, "There were two men in a certain town, one rich and the other poor.
[2] The rich man had a very large number of sheep and cattle,
[3] but the poor man had nothing except one little ewe lamb he had bought. He raised it, and it grew up with him and his children. It shared his food, drank from his cup and even slept in his arms. It was like a daughter to him.
[4] "Now a traveler came to the rich man, but the rich man refrained from taking one of his own sheep or cattle to prepare a meal for the traveler who had come to him. Instead, he took the ewe lamb that belonged to the poor man and prepared it for the one who had come to him."

chapter 16 leah (lee-lee)

The children, in Miss Nancy's first grade class are crying. Their beloved teacher has lost her temper and shouts fuel on their fears.

"Enough!" She slams a heavy hard cover book onto the table. "I said enough!" Stomp. "I will NOT tolerate anymore crying!"

The children cry harder with faces buried into open palms. They are scared and do not want to see their teacher's face so angry. Miss Nancy storms out of the room in tears, slamming the thick wooden door. Bam! The glass rattles.

Silence.

Minutes later, the principal calmly steps into the classroom, allowing the door to click shut, softly. The children are frozen to their chairs. He walks to the edge of a carpeted area, sits down with legs crossed and begins to read from the large book he carried in.

"Alone in a faraway land, lived a child of noble birth..."

As he reads, the room begins to thaw. One by one, the children quietly form a circle around him and listen intently. No one asks about their teacher. No explanations are offered. Leah is the only student not in the circle. Instead of joining the comforting story, she is in the locker hall, scribbling purple tornados on everyone's backpack. She grips the permanent marker her teacher uses to make smiley faces. No one noticed

Leah at the teacher's desk, or saw her leave the room.

It was Leah who started the commotion that lead to Miss Nancy's breakdown. Leah provoked and prodded each child, turning the air sour, until everyone was fermented.

The night before this first grade disturbance, Jodie is shocked to hear that a six year old girl (Leah's age) is missing. She watches the parents, somber and lifeless as wax, all over the news. Photos and videos of the child bleep into regularly scheduled programming, over and over. The special alert warns parents to supervise their children. All children under the age of 16 shall be accompanied by an adult after the newly set 7:00 curfew, until further notice. Jodie is frightened by unknown dangers. *The missing girl looks just like Leah!* ...Last seen on the swings. *That is the park we play at all the time! How does a child just vanish? With so many people around and watching?*

"Lee-Lee," she explains, "There are bad people that want to hurt little girls."

"Where Mommy?"

"Everywhere."

"Who wants-ta hurt me, Mommy?"

"I didn't say someone wants to hurt you," Jodie huffs. "Look. Never take candy from strangers. If someone you don't know wants you to go with them... Run! Away!"

"Didda bad guy hurt that liddle gurl?"

"I hope not," Jodie says under her breath. "I'm sure she'll be okay."

"Why didn't *she* run?"

"I don't know, Leah."

"Is Mr. Bags a bad guy?" Leah wonders, thinking of the scruffy old man that puts garbage bags in his shopping cart and pushes it around town.

"No, and you shouldn't call him that. It's not nice."

"Should I call him Carter, instead."

"That would be better." Jodie tries not to laugh at the names her daughter comes up with.

During that same night, Leah wakes up several times, crying. Bad guys are poking lambs with sticks and making them bleed. The worst dream, the one that never wakes her up, is about Mr. D. He is covering her face with a pillow, making it hard to breath. He pokes at her with sticks until she is small and shriveled. After that, he picks her up like a raisin, pinching her between his thumb and finger. His big face says, *"Shhh... don't tell anyone about our games, not even Meggy. Your mama will say you are a bad girl and punish you."* Mr. D. holds out his shoe to her. A red gumball is rolling around in it. He won't touch it. He tells her to eat it. Leah takes it out and puts it in her mouth. Mr. D. whispers into her ear, *"Watch out for bad guys, they want to hurt little girls,"* and crawls under her bed.

Leah is sitting next to Tommy at the big table. They each have a sheet of paper in front of them. Leah pulls Tommy's paper away every time he tries to write. Tommy presses harder, until he breaks the lead.

Tommy says, "Gimme your pencil."

"No!" Leah sasses.

He pokes her in the side with his broken pencil. Immediately, Leah picks up his paper and rips it in half. He pokes her some more, harder, and doesn't quit when she struggles to get out of the way. She tips Rachel over in her chair. Rachel cries. She pinches Tommy so hard that he cries too. Leah is on the rampage, grabbing papers from other children and wadding them up. More kids are crying.

"You're being naughty!" Sarah riddles.

"I am not a bad guy!" Leah screams. She runs away and seats herself in a far away corner, pressing her palms against her ears. Kids are yelling and crying.

Miss Nancy storms out of the supply room. She is astonished. Her migraine sends bolts from her temples and down her spine. Events starting at home and leading to this moment, have pecked away her serenity. She is a pressure cooker. Next to her is a large dictionary. She lifts it above her head, as if holding a boulder... Slam!

* * * * * * *

Jodie's car finally rushes into the driveway. Mrs. D glances at the wall clock that's across from the chair her body is melted into. She huffs her annoyance at the little hand resting slightly left of the six. Before hauling herself out of the chair, she puts her wineglass on the floor and screens it with a pillow.

Meggy and Leah are in the backyard trying to catch a toad. Warty skin is pressed into the crotch of tree roots at the base of a large tree. Meggy grabs a stick to poke it out of hiding.

"Don't hurt it!" Leah yells. She is crouching with her face close to the hole, watching the toad march his front legs into the dirt, unable to back up.

"Shut up. Yer scarin' it!" hisses Meggy, then accidently pokes it too hard in the belly.

"Ewe!" They scream.

Meggy drops the stick. She puts the pads of her fingertips across her lips. Wide eyes raise her hairline. The little girls look at each other, stand up, and run towards the house. Leah's buckle shoes pound into the dry lawn. She marches froglike, away from their cruelty. Her inner thighs sting hot, then feel cold and wet. Meggy scuttles into the house. At the back door, Leah looks down at her feet and watches a wet drop roll down her leg and soak into the ruffle of her white sock. She hears her mother and Mrs. D both yelling her name. Meggy leads them around the house to the backyard. They find Leah standing at the back door staring at her feet.

"Leah!" her mother yells. She waves a piece of notebook paper at the air, in sync with her words, "When I call you! I. Expect. You. To come! Immediately!"

Mrs. D shakes her head 'no' and clicks her tongue several times. She is holding Meggy's hand and gives it a pious squeeze into her chest, as if holding her little girl's arm up in victory. Leah's arm gets yanked to the car with the note from her teacher crumpled into her sleeve, beneath her mother's grip.

Jodie's cordial *"goodbye"*, her sweet *"thank-you"* and poetic *"see you tomorrow,"* is sucked out of the car by the wind and floats over Mrs. D's driveway. Her mother's public voice is replaced with broken glass, cutting and fragmented.

"What am I going to do with you?" Jodie quips, after she whacks the top of the steering wheel.

Leah sucks her bottom lip in and bites it.

"This is the third note from your teacher. And school just started!" Her mother adjusts the rearview mirror.

Leah notices that two angry beady eyes are squinting back at her, telling her not to speak. Jodie's anger spills into the backseat in the form of several questions —pauses between, never expecting answers.

"What is wrong with you! Why are you so naughty now? Well? What happened to my sweet little girl? Is this how it's going to be? Is my daughter the playground bully?" She continues with more questions and never notices how mean she sounds. This is her usual selfish outpouring of leftover anger at Leah's father. Since age two, Leah became the scapegoat for all her father's sins.

Leah holds her breath to keep Mama's words off. She squeezes her tummy in to push them back out of her ears. This way, she won't get the urge to cry, won't feel the cuts from her mama. She stares at the rings on Mama's hands, wants to kiss them and say, *"I am sorry, sparkly fingers. I love you pretty rings."*

Finally, tension inside the car is soothed and washed away by wind pouring through open windows, refreshing this mother-daughter relationship. Leah smiles at the eyes in the mirror. Her mother reaches back and pats Leah on the knee. Leah grabs Jodie's hand to squeeze out warmth, prolonging her mama's touch.

When they arrive home, a familiar car blocks their driveway. Matt is in the kitchen pulling a box pizza out of the oven. Jodie dances in ahead of Leah. As the grownups hug, kiss and giggle, Leah piles her shoes, coat and backpack in the middle of the floor and runs out of the room.

In the living room, Leah feels the empty chair that is still warm from Matt. Leah curls into his heat and pretends the chair is her daddy with his protective arms wrapping her up. She reaches to the armrest for the remote control that is resting on it and switches the channel to a cartoon. The volume is kept down low. She is spying. With careful measurements, Leah records the pitch of her mama's voice, how often she giggles, the length of each quiet interlude that changes her breathing. She is jealous *for* her mama... Leah wants to be the one that brightens her mama's face, who captures her eyes and makes her laugh. She wants to be the one Mama closes her eyes to hug. She takes the data she is gathering and measures it against herself. Leah is the germ, Matt is the antidote. She is jealous *of* her mama... Leah wants Matt to scoop her up and twirl her pink shoes off. She wants him to lean toward her and listen to all her words. She wants to live between their hands, holding a Mama and Daddy.

A commercial comes on the TV that peels Leah's attention off kitchen romance. In the commercial, a little girl dressed in a pink ruffle nightie feathers down a decorative staircase in dim light. It is the middle of the night and she is looking for her daddy. A stuffed dog held by the ear, bounces beside the curly blond child. Light from the television flashes shadows on the daddy's face as he eats from a yellow bowl. When his face softens to a smile, his teeth glow in the dark. He is gazing at his little daughter standing next to his chair, hugging her stuffed dog. He holds his strong palms out to her. She climbs onto his lap and takes his spoon. The daddy holds her with one arm and the bowl with the other. He lets his little girl finish the ice cream. The product brand is flashed on the screen and a deep voice says, "Share the Love."

"Lee-Lee. Come and eat," her mama sings, sweetly. "Leah?...Leah! We're eating!"

Leah doesn't hear her mama until the commercial ends and the cartoon resumes. She bounces off Matt's chair and sits in her usual spot. Matt reaches for his second piece of pizza, moving the box towards himself, just as Jodie tries to get a piece for Leah. Before she puts a slice on Leah's plate, Jodie picks off all the toppings except for pepperoni.

As she chews, Leah does not take her eyes off Matt sitting across from her. She stares at his thick eyelashes and counts how many times they blink at her mama. She wants to pet the thick black hairs on his arm. When he comments on how good the olives are, Leah puts olives back on her slice.

She takes a bite and says, "I like olives too," inviting herself into their bubble.

Matt looks over at Leah, by accident of thought, before he continues his story to Jodie. Leah smiles at him, not realizing he looked right through her. She pulls the pizza over and puts all the olives from the remaining three slices onto one piece. *This can be Matt's piece of pizza.*

Jodie notices and says, "Leah! Stop! It is rude to touch other people's food."

Leah sinks into her chair, but watches to see if Matt will eat his special piece of pizza.

He will like what I did.

Like most nights, Matt stays past her bedtime. Leah is told to put on her jammies and brush her teeth. She picks out a ruffled nightie and runs to the mirror to see if her hair is curly, like that little girl's. It isn't. Leah finds her lamb sticking out of a tousled blanket on her bedroom floor. She picks it up and carries her lamb by the ear to the TV where Matt is sitting. Cradled at his chest is a huge bowl of cereal, which he rapidly dips into with a soup spoon. He sets the bowl on the table where Leah is standing and picks up the remote to flip through channels. Leah moves towards him, still holding her lamb by the ear. Gingerly, she takes his huge spoon, scoops up some cereal and starts to eat —waiting for his teeth to glow.

"Hey! What-are-ya doin'? That's my spoon! Get your own." Matt's lips are pressed tight against his teeth, holding in the light.

His reaction startles Leah. She drops her lamb and runs to the kitchen where her mama is wiping off the stove. Matt enters the kitchen behind Leah and puts his bowl on the counter next to the sink. It still has cereal in it. He rinses off his spoon and puts it into the dishwasher. Leah will never share a spoon with anyone again.

Alone in her bed, Leah's eyes roll into a dream. Lambs are lined up single file at two buckets. They each take one bite of grain from the silver bucket, and one sip of water from the red bucket. Leah is last in line. When it is her turn, the grain is gone and the water has bits of cereal floating in it. She reaches into the red bucket to scoop out the debris. The water turns hot and burns her hand. She runs for help, holding her burnt fingers. There is an explosion behind her that causes her to look back. She sees a baby lamb running from a roaring fire that is pouring out of the tipped bucket of grain. Leah reaches out her palms to the lamb. It runs to her. She picks up the living ball of wool and folds it into her chest.

Isaiah 1:29-31 (NIV)
[29] "You will be ashamed because of the sacred oaks in which you have delighted; you will be disgraced because of the gardens that you have chosen. [30] You will be like an oak with fading leaves, like a garden without water. [31] The mighty man will become tinder and his work a spark; both will burn together, with no one to quench the fire."

chapter 17 april 2nd

A full moon illuminates the poison dark air. A misty fog settles over the town and compresses light into distinct round shapes. Street lamps lining the sidewalks look like dandelions turned to seed. A burgundy van is prowling the town, searching for someone. It deliberately avoids the park. The driver does not like to be near places where there are swings. A mistaken turn takes him by the wooded backside of the city park where Ali buries recent memories in the playground sand. As if driving by a graveyard, he holds his breath and looks away. The swings are not visible, but he knows they are there.

The six-pack on the floor clanks and rattles with every turn. Jason is holding one bottle between his thighs. Mideah is nowhere to be found. His bottle of courage helps him brave ringing her apartment buzzer with impatient jabs. No one is home. He is sure of it, can sense it. Anxiety thickens as Jason rushes back to Schaffer Travel Agency —a scheme brewing.

Safely disappearing in a haze of fog, Jason positions Seth's van where he has a clear view of Mideah's black convertible. He is close enough to hear conversation, yet discreet enough to go unnoticed. He doesn't expect Mideah to return to her car alone. It frightens him when he doesn't know where she is at all times. His imagination is feral, motivating his exploitations.

He waits, aware of every pound of his heart, reclining in the rearmost seat so the van appears abandoned. And waits. And waits. The windows facing the black convertible are cracked open. He can hear sounds of the night... random barking, trees rustling, sporadic traffic, a drunken shout. All these sounds dwindle to silence as morning approaches.

Dissatisfaction chips Jason into a defeated statue that slumps with throbbing head resting against the back window. Finally, there is an abrupt splash of light. Redeeming headlights travel across the side of the van. Jason perks up so quick that he fears discovery. A car pulls into the parking lot. It moves slowly past the van and parks directly behind the black convertible. The engine continues to run and lights stay on, enhancing the fog and making it hard to see if it is Mideah. Frozen and breathless, Jason gapes out the side window, head low and eyes squinting. Seconds are like hours as he searches for answers. *What are they doing in there? Why is it taking so long? Come on! Its gotta be her. I know it is!* He wants to confront her, but restrains.

Finally the car door opens. The dome light silhouettes two adults behind steamed windows. The unknown driver is leaning toward the passenger, arm extended and touching near the woman's face. The woman's hand reaches up and pats the driver's arm before turning to climb out of the car. Jason recognizes her the moment she stands up. The moon outlines her tall slender profile and glows off her long hair. She bends one knee and leans level to the window, her hip jutting out in a curve familiar to Jason. He wants to own her. He does not share.

Her voice is faint, yet her words vibrate Jason's ears. "I had an amazing time." Pause. "Really?" She shifts her weight to the other leg.

It frustrates Jason to hear only one side of their conversation.

Mideah speaks again. "It's so hard to leave."

She is still leaning her head down, behind the open door. "Aww. That is so sweet."

Mideah reaches into the car to take something. "What is this? Can I open it?"

She stands up holding a small gold box. After fumbling with the tight ribbon, she lifts the top off and peers inside.

Mideah hesitates before her fake response, "My! They look irresistible!"

She hides her disappointment. The stranger is saying something so Mideah tilts down again.

"Oh! I kno-oow!" She sighs, lengthening her words.

She stands up, opens the box again and says, "Mmm. Yes, they do smell delicious!"

She blows a sexy kiss into the car. "Bye Love."

In runway, spiked heel fashion, she saunters across the car's headlights to her convertible. The mist smokes and dances around her, akin to a graveyard scene in a scary movie. Her legs are bare and extend like a spider's under the short knit dress she is wearing. Both Jason and the stranger in the car watch her, caught in her beauty, unable to move. The slam of her door permeates the van. The still night suspends time, before her engine rips to a start. Mideah drives away, angling through empty parking spaces. The stranger in the other car waits for Mideah to turn out of the lot, before departing in the opposite direction.

Jason is perched and ready with keys in the ignition. He strategically starts the van after the stranger pulls his car out to the street. Jason watches covertly to see which way he turns, and follows surreptitiously behind.

The stranger drives several blocks across town to the suburbs. The distance between the houses widen the further they travel. Front lawns get deeper and are edged with ornate fences. Steep roofs of multi-story homes point at the sky, with chimneys reaching higher. All the homes in this suburb have unique, yet similar features; dormers, balconies, wide porches with pillars, turrets, manicured landscaping flanking several steps that zigzag up to prominent entry doors.

Jason stalks the stranger Mideah was with by staying two blocks behind. He drives cautiously with the headlights off. The man's silver Lexus turns left into a driveway. Jason catches up to it before the garage door closes. He briefly studies the lit garage. It is tidy and empty, without a second vehicle. Before the overhead door closes, Jason reads the car's license plate. He pulls over and parks across the street, repeating the plate number to keep it fresh, then types AV84KNG into his cell phone, along with the house number and street name. He relaxes and studies the large home with a shroud of envy veiling his eyes. Inside lights turn on and disappear, mapping out the stranger's route through his home. The last light to click off is in an upper dormer, near a balcony.

Jason's imagination runs wild. *Has Mideah been in that bedroom?* He visualizes her naked in satin sheets, motioning her lover into an ornate oak bed. He wants to plow over the picket fence with the van and throw rocks at the lead-glass windows. *How often does she come here? Does he pay her?* Instead, he drives away in early morning light.

Mideah yawns at her desk and moves at a snail's pace. She arrives at work an hour late, but doesn't care. Her boss is out of town this weekend. Plus, she hates working on Saturday, even for a half day. A mug of coffee is pressed against her chin. She closes her eyes and inhales the aroma of morning. Concentrating on work is difficult today. Her mind circulates to last night's chain of events. Her remembering is so vivid that a tender *sigh* escapes her breath. It startles her, hearing her voice like that. She hopes nobody was listening.

Reluctantly, she scoots up to her computer screen to check today's schedule. There are two pink notes taped to her keyboard.

One reads:

French Club stopped by for package pickup - 2:30 pm.

The next note is written with a heavier marker:

Call French Club! A.S.A.P.

It is in the receptionist's handwriting.

They called four times!!!!

(Written across the bottom and underlined with several scribbles.)

Mideah crumples both notes into one ball and pitches it over her shoulder onto the floor.

The cell phone in her purse interrupts her bitter attempt to start working. The ring is loud. She hurries to shut off the tone before looking to see who is calling. Jason. His white teeth gleam from the lit display on her phone.

His pearly-white smile once melted her into submission. Mideah's stomach fluttered when she snapped this picture. It was the day she first met Jason at the pier. He was by himself, holding a book while walking across large boulders at the edge of the lengthy concrete pier. She caught him staring at her. This prompted her to walk over and stare back, with one hand on her jutted hip and leg bent in her sexiest pose. She stood and watched him stumble and trip, overcome with insecurity and extreme shyness —feelings he had not experienced since eleventh grade. Mideah couldn't resist teasing him, saying, "Really? A nice day like this, us hot women over here. And you're going to read a book?" According to Mideah, she was all it took to convince Jason to join her and the three girls she was with. She spent the rest of that day with Jason. She teased, charmed and lured his complete devotion.

"Urgh! You have got to be kidding!" Mideah scrolls through her messages from last night.

"Why do you keep calling me?" She grumbles and deletes the twelve messages Jason left her last night.

The phone vibrates in her hand. Once again, white teeth gleam and burn her eyes. Mideah huffs and throws her phone back into her purse.

Yesterday... Ted contrives the day to his favor. Right after his wife leaves for her annual girl-weekend, he is out the door wearing a tight shirt, jeans, and a dabbed on masculine scent. He arrives early and parks down the street —hoping. In the pocket of his leather coat, he has a gold leaf box with four expensive chocolates. He smoothes his hair and walks boldly to the door of Schaffer Travel, geared up to surprise Mideah.

In the copy room, Mideah organizes two rows of paper the length of the counter. As the machine cranks out sixteen copies, she sorts them face down onto each pile. It angers her that the copy machine is still broke. It will not collate or staple. All morning She prepares a trip for the Senior Ladies French Club. She promised to have their package complete by 2:00. This deadline is approaching way too fast. She contemplates calling them, to postpone pickup time to the end of the day.

Mideah lays papers out, counting in her head as she stacks them. *eek!* She is startled by large hands tickling the sides of her tiny waste. Her instant reaction is to throw her arms up. Papers go flying. They scatter over her neat assembly line and drop to the floor. As she turns around, a masculine cologne wafts across her face —familiar aroma of passion.

"Hey, I'm sorry," he apologizes. "Didn't mean to scare you."

"What a surprise!" Mideah smoothes down her dark green sweater dress. "I wasn't expecting to see you today."

"I came to steal you away for a while."

"Ooooh. How criminal of you," flirts Mideah.

"Come on. Can you take a break now? I have a surprise for you."

Mideah looks at her watch. It's not quite lunchtime.

She wavers and says, "Well Ted, I um..." She glances to her piles of paper on the counter and at the papers cluttering the floor.

"Let me help you," he offers before she finishes her sentence.

Ted stays with Mideah to finish collating, stapling and stacking. "Looks like we're done. Let's go."

"I'm not quite finished," She worries.

"Oh, come on." Ted leads her out the door to his car.

"Hungry?" He asks.

"A little. Why, what are you thinking?"

"I could use a bite to eat. Drive-thru or sit down?" He is hoping she says *drive-thru*.

"Either. Whatever you want."

Ted drives for a few blocks and decisively parks at a Chinese restaurant.

"Wait here," he tells her. "I'll be right back.

Alone in the car, Mideah snoops inside the glove compartment. Sunglasses, car manuals, mints, a hair brush with strands of feminine hair curling off, red lipstick, a city map. She notices the vinyl car manual is wedged slightly apart. She pulls it out and opens it. Two condoms fall into her lap. She looks up and sees Ted walking out of the restaurant carrying a large white bag. Mideah quickly stuffs the condoms back into the manual and returns it to the glove box.

"I know where we can go," Ted tells her, shutting his car door.

"Where?"

"How 'bout I surprise you?"

They cruise out of town, flirting and enjoying the scenery. After thirty minutes of endless road, Mideah asks, "Where are we going?"

"You'll see. We're almost there."

Mideah waits twenty more minutes. Ted turns down a long, gravel driveway that curves through the trunks of lofty cedar and oak trees.

"We're here!" he says, as they approach a dark log cabin.

Not far from the cabin, a bright-blue lake glitters between the trunks of barren trees, waiting for the rebirth of spring.

Mideah walks up the woodchip path towards a screen porch. When she notices the red door, she compliments, "What a cute cottage!"

Ted passes in front of her. He hands her the warm, white bag, before rolling over a large rock to retrieve a brass key attached to a yellow rubber coin pouch. He unlocks the door and steps aside to let her enter.

Stale damp air breezes into Mideah's face as she walks into the kitchen and puts the bag of Chinese food on the countertop. Ted gathers dishes and utensils, then neatly displays the food across the counter.

"Help yourself."

"It looks really good." Mideah compliments and dots her plate with small samples.

After Ted loads his plate, he leads her into the family room. They sit shoulder to shoulder on the couch, using the coffee table to rest their feet.

While Ted eats, he thinks about the real reason he brought Mideah to the secluded cabin. He barely tastes his food. His next move is critical — doesn't want to scare her away. Plus, his cravings are out of control. He is in dire need to vent his obsession, before the pressure turns to craze.

Empty plates rest on their thighs as their nerves digest. Ted dares a fraught move by lifting his arm and wedging it behind Mideah. Poor timing makes this gesture gauche and clumsy. He brushes his lips to her hair and suggests, "Do you need to get back right away?"

Mideah needs to work. She has a two o'clock deadline. It is almost that time now. But she really wants this moment with Ted. Her mood is ambivalent.

Ted misinterprets hesitation, so he tries another lure. "How 'bout I show you around the place first?" He takes her plate and places it on the coffee table. "I'll take you out to see the lake. Then we can come back and warm up with fresh coffee."

Mideah doesn't answer.

"And I'll build us a fire?" Ted squeezes her thigh just above her knee. "Well? What do you say?" Pats her leg. "...Let's relax for a while."

No worries. I can go back to work tonight. Big deal. So they have to wait a day!

"A fire would be nice," she commits. "The office can do without me for an afternoon."

Mideah carries both their dishes to the kitchen sink. Ted follows behind. Together they shove leftover food into the refrigerator.

He leads her down the path, toward the lake, to a break in the tall trees. A bench is facing the water, soaking in sunlight. Mideah plops down and feels immediate warmth on her face. Ted sits next to her, leaving more space between them than he wishes. He's not sure if she is willing. Desire overwhelms him and turns into fear. He grows desperate and does not want to lose control. Manic is closing on him.

"Are you cold?" He asks, pretending concern.

"Just a little. The sun helps."

Ted takes this as an invitation and scootches against her. He wraps his arm across her shoulders, holds her tight and promises, "I'll warm you up." His hand gropes the shivers off her upper arm.

Mideah leans into his advances and solicits more by resting her forearm along his thigh. Both their bodies are reeling to burn a hotter fire. Groping evolves, masked by conversation while they remain facing the lake. The wind picks up and rustles decomposing leaves off the sparse branches hovering over them. An oak leaf swirls free, just when Ted courageously tilts Mideah's face towards his. He reaches his hand beneath her chin and the leaf floats past her lips and settles into his palm.

"Whoa!" He jerks back. "I can't believe this leaf landed right in my hand." He looks up and sees very few leaves on the branches.

"It is just a leaf!" Mideah is frustrated. "Big deal!" She is sure he was about to kiss her. *Are we going to sit out here freezing? I should go back to work!*

"Here, you can have it." Ted hands her a crisp brown leaf.

"Why do I need this?" She tosses it to the dirt. "Let's go. I'm really cold," she whines.

They walk back to the house holding hands. Ted leaves Mideah at the door.

"Go on in. I'll be right back."

Waiting inside, Mideah lounges on the couch with her head against a pillow. Ted is sitting in the passenger seat of his car taking something out of the glove box. He puts it into his jeans pocket.

From across the room, he sees Mideah reclining in a provocative position. "You look comfortable."

Mideah winks, puckers her lips and kisses the air. Ted fights going to her. Patience is key. He gathers wood and builds a fire. He kneels in front of the hearth until the flames are hot and consistent. He does not want to be interrupted, doesn't want the fire to burn out. He opens a wooden trunk, removes a red and black, checkered, blanket and spreads it onto the floor in front of the fire. Mideah watches in anticipation. She is happiest when she gets her way. Right now, she is elated.

He kneels and stretches his arm to Mideah, lounging on the couch. He teasingly pulls the pillow from under her head and tosses it onto the blanket by the fire. He grabs two more floor pillows from the trunk and positions them just right. Ted turns his face and delightful eyes invite her, just before he lays down on his back, one knee bent, hands behind his neck. He closes his eyes and waits. Ted is crafty. He sets Mideah up to make the first move. He temps her, blames her, reduces her.

Mideah straightens up on the couch, cranes her neck to look beyond the coffee table. Ted looks like he is faking sleep with a sarcastic grin on his face. She crawls to the floor and shimmies next to sleeping Ted. He waits longer, grinning, facing the ceiling. It is Mideah that kisses him first, and warms herself by the fire inside Ted.

Ecclesiastes 7:15 (NKJV)
[15] I have seen everything in my days of vanity: There is a just *man* who perishes in his righteousness, And there is a wicked *man* who prolongs *life* in his wickedness.

chapter 18 sylvia

Her dress is stuck in the chains and she is crying. I run to the swing to help her, but the dress is so stuck that I rip the fancy ruffle. She tells me it's okay, her mommy will fix it. She wipes her hands where I wrecked her the lace and gets back on the swing.

"What's your name?" she asks.

"ReeceJohnWheaton." I say it like it is one piece of a word. It sounds like I have a really long name when I say it that way. I forget to ask what her name is, but she gives it to me anyway.

"I'm Sylvia. Wanna be my friend?"

I'm a lot older than her, because I am eight. I don't want to hurt her feelings, so I say, "Okay. Want me to push you?"

"Yes please, JohnReeceWheaton,"

She says my name all wrong. But that's okay, because she's just little. So I get her swing started by holding the chains and run forward and backward. She drops her doll in the sand and I run right over the top of it by accident.

"Watch out! Dolly! Dolly!" she says.

I stop and pick up her doll. Before I give it back, I brush the sand off the yellow hair and pink dress and hand it to Sylvia.

"Ain't she purdy? She looks just like me. I'm her mama."

I look at the doll and back at Sylvia, "Yup," is all I say. Cuz my mom comes and tells me we're leaving.

"Bye ReeceJohnWheaton!" She yells.

I walk behind my mom down the park trail. She got my name right that time. I look back at her and smile. She is pumping with her legs and swinging higher and higher. Sylvia didn't need me to push her.

"Why do I always have to watch her?" Jason whines to his mother.

"Just stay here while I run some errands. Is that too much to ask?"

Jason and Sylvia get out of the car and run off to the playground. Sylvia heads straight to the swings. Jason runs a short distance until his mother's car disappears from view. The park is full today, kids running and parents sitting on benches and picnic tables. Three boys are kicking around a soccer ball.

They spot Jason and yell, "Hey-yea," in a high pitched girl voice.

One teases and walks like a prissy girl. The rest of the boys laugh, then copy the girlie walk and point at Jason.

"Nah-nah-na-naaah-na," they say.

Jason slumps forward, drops his eyes to the dirt and tries not to hear their mocking. His glasses slip down and rest at the end of his nose. He leaves them there, unaware that his nose is pinched into a funny shape. He searches for a place to belong, but cruelty coils the playground. *There is nothing to do here but baby stuff! Soccer is stupid! Swings are for sissys.*

Envy alienates Jason further when he sees that his sister has already made a friend. A boy, a couple of years younger than Jason. He is wiping Sylvia's doll and handing it back to her.

"He can just watch her. I don't care!" Jason mumbles and shoves his fists deep into his pockets. "I don't even want to be here!"

From the city park, a sidewalk threads past historic houses for several blocks. Jason remembers the five dollar bill crumpled in the pocket of his nerd pants. He purposely steps on cracks in the shaded sidewalk, never looking back. He doesn't think of Sylvia, left alone in the park. Instead he obsesses about the boys that tease him all the time. *I have five dollars and you don't!* A curt gust of wind blows, shaking tops of trees. An oak leaf floats down and lands in Jason's left hand. This coincidence bewilders Jason — stops him on a crack. After some scrutinizing, he wads it into his palm, shoves it into his pocket next to his five dollars and walks toward his selfishness.

Familiar faces crowd the park on this day when it became unreliable. The usual parents are unwinding their kids on monkey bars, swings and slides. A young man, wearing a baseball hat with aviator wings on the brim, walks past the swings. The little girl is flying higher and higher, back and forth. The ripped ruffle of her white dress flows behind her like a banner.

"If you go any higher you'll get caught in the clouds," he tells her, ducking away from her feet as she lifts above his head.

"Aw, this ain't nothin'," she says and digs deeper.

She watches him walk away and sees something drop from his military jacket. Sylvia leans back, holding her legs out to slow down. She tries to make out the object lying in the grass near the wooded trail.

"Hey!" she yells only once, but his navy jacket blends and disappears into the dark trees.

The little girl drags the tip of her shoe in the sand to stop, drawing a snake shape, with the full tread of her sneaker shaping the serpent head.

At the edge of the forest, the label 'king-size' is face down in the dirt. The chocolate bar is big in Sylvia's child hands. She runs down the trail, holding it up in the air.

"You dropped this," she says, merging the high notes of her voice with rustling leaves.

"Thank you," says the dark. "I'll share it with you. Take a bite."

"Aw-right," she sings, "It's already opened some."

Sylvia pins her dolly between her forearm and chest and peels the wrapper off. The chocolate is soft and melts between her chubby fingers. She takes a few bites before she holds it out.

"Mmmm... want some?" she offers.

"No, you can have it. Do you want one for your brother?"

Sylvia looks carefully at the man's face with a puzzled expression. She decides, "Okay."

No one contemplates this stranger walking out the other side of the trees with a tiny child sleeping on his shoulder. It is a beautiful sight to see a father kiss his child's cheek, holding her in a protective embrace. Blind assumptions. Everyone is distracted the day the wolf prowls across the grass, where little lambs dance and play. Today, parents and chaperones exist in the moment, yet live outside of it. They are sightless and busy with mental to-do lists. They rush and daydream. They trust the park to keep a little lamb safe, while pausing for a cup of coffee or spending a crumpled, five dollar bill.

That night, two men visit his parents. ReeceJohnWheaton is asked confusing questions about who he talked to at the park that morning. They make him sit on the couch. They kneel in front of him. When he says things, one man makes simple comments and the other man writes notes on spiral bound paper.

Her name is Sylvia. I pushed her on the swings. I don't know who else was by the swings. I don't know what time it was. She had a doll. A stuffed doll with yellow yarn hair. I accidently ripped her dress and she didn't cry. I didn't see anyone with her. Her dress was stuck on the swing. I don't know her brother. I never saw her before. I just pushed her on the swings. My mom said it's time to go. No, I didn't see her go anywhere. She was alone. Her doll was on her lap. I didn't see anyone talk to her. I just pushed her on the swings.

Grownups shelter him from the news. His world stays safe and naive. He forgets Sylvia. He gets to visit Grandpa! With a batman suitcase packed for two weeks, Mr. and Mrs. Wheaton drive five hours out of town. Reece is in the backseat sleeping on a pillow propped against the window. Sirens and helicopters wake up the night in their hometown. Beams of light, that normally shine for deer, flicker through the surrounding woods. Volunteers link arms and walk anxiously with noses pointing at the ground. Dogs sniff the dirty laundry in Jason's house and bark memories that echo the towns ears. Nocturnal creatures of the woods watch in fear as their world is invaded by these sleepwalkers, the blind individuals from the park, slapped awake by tragedy.

Exact timing: Sylvia runs into the woods with a king size chocolate bar, while Jason is wooed by light that glows from tall colored windows. He stares at the mosaic composition of jagged glass, a shepherd carrying a little lamb. He walks to the front of the structure and stands at the bottom of several steps leading skyward, ending at a pair of heavy doors. Holding the railing, he climbs toward the top, challenging himself to skip steps. He reaches his leg up high as possible, pulling up the railing in a tug-a-war, hand over fist. At the top he holds the big handle and presses the thumb down to release the latch. It takes both hands to pull the large door open. It clicks and echoes at his back. The foyer turns black except for a strip of vertical light pouring from an inner door that's jammed open. He hides in the shadow listening to a tapping noise —like the edge of a pencil hitting against wood. The music starts. This startles Jason, but piques his curiosity. He allows one eye to look into the strip of light. A group of adults stand in an arc beneath a huge wooden cross. A lady stands at a podium facing the adults, swooshing a thin stick in steady motion. Their song tugs his soul through the lightened crack. The pressure of his tears are ready to reveal him. This angers Jason. Only sissies' cry. *I don't need my dad and I don't need you. Who cares if he hates me. Stupid drunk.* He feels the light burning him and quickly closes the door. Here is where he grows his shell. He tucks in his head and legs to hide in the empty skeleton. Nothing will ever penetrate.

Exact timing: Sylvia is out cold, sprawled across the vinyl backseat of a green Oldsmobile, bumping over a discreet country road, while an elderly cashier rings Jason up for the third time. Five dollars is still not enough to cover his greed. This time, Jason decides to put one magazine back and replace it with another candy bar. The cashier shakes his head and counts thirteen cents into the boy's unsatisfied hand. Without regard for time, Jason idles back to the park.

Exact timing: Sylvia is held in the arms of a Mighty God —*Vengeance is Mine, I will repay*. Jason perches himself on the top of a picnic table and uses the bench for a footstool. His face is buried in the new magazine. Two candy bar wrappers blow off the picnic table and get tangled in a nearby wrought iron fence.

"Jason!" his mother beeps from her car at the curb, "Get Sylvia! We're going!"

Jason walks to the car and starts to get inside.

"Where's Sylvia? I said go get her!" she repeats.

"Oh," Jason groans. He slides into the backseat and shuts the door.

"You are really pushing it, buddy!" His mother exhales and sneers at him. She gets out of the car, stands in the V of the open door and yells, "Sylvia! Come on!"

"Sylvia!"

She walks around the park, looking in all directions, and tries to remember what she dressed her daughter in that morning.

"Sylvia!" She shouts again and again.

Frustrated, she stomps to the back seat of her car and pounds on the window with a clenched fist.

Jason rolls it down a few inches and shouts, "What!"

"Where is Sylvia?"

Jason scowls, shrugs and turns his attention back to his magazine. His mother growls and storms off, calling his sister's name. She finally remembers the white dress and searches the park for her curly-haired, little girl. Utter panic stirs the contents in her stomach. She bangs on the car window with an infuriated fist. Jason rolls his eyes as the window descends.

"Where is your sister?" She screams, accidently spitting on Jason eyelid.

"Wherever you put her!" he spews.

Suddenly, his cheek is burning. Blistering light, from the crack in the church door, cannot match this sensation. A red imprint the shape of his mother's hand tattoos Jason's face, permanently severing their relationship. Jason seals the deal by naming his mother with a word, scraped off filth, that should never be spoken. Every sidewalk has a crack.

Jeremiah 29:11-14 (NIV)

[11] For I know the plans I have for you," declares the Lord, "plans to prosper you and not to harm you, plans to give you hope and a future.
[12] Then you will call upon me and come and pray to me, and I will listen to you.
[13] You will seek me and find me when you seek me with all your heart.
[14] I will be found by you," declares the Lord, "and will bring you back from captivity. I will gather you from all the nations and places where I have banished you," declares the Lord, "and will bring you back to the place from which I carried you into exile."

chapter 19 ali

Ali locks herself behind her bedroom door, more than ever. Her family doesn't acknowledge her absence. They also don't notice the extraordinary amount of food she is consuming. She is in the upstairs bathroom every night, sometimes twice. And the shower is always running while the toilet is flushing.

Ali's house is a catacomb. Every family member has their tomb. Mom's is in her office. Dad's is in the basement, where he fiddles. Brandon's tomb is electronic, a digital grave. Nobody hears one another other cry, "help!" from six feet under, among worms, hands folded, beneath the living. They exist —angry and glib, selfish and proud, afraid and sad. Impenetrable.

Brandon is the one most aware that something is *missing* in his family. He is too inexperienced to know what it is, or what to do about it. He is their cheerleader, hoping to raise his parents and sister from the dead. It is getting harder to pretend happiness. He tells jokes, bathroom humor, mostly funny to eleven year olds. He offers Ali his music and tells her, *Keep it*. When she walks by his open door, *You can use anything in my room you want*. He asks her about Reece and begs her to call and ask if they can do something again. He helps his dad in the yard and follows his mom around the house, until she tells him to find something to do. They don't understand what is happening to Ali, and blame it on selfishness. *It's just a phase.*

Her parents think she is rejecting them, because she hides in her bedroom, or is never home. They accuse her of not participating in the family and then exclude her. Instead of helping their daughter, they hate her instead —and love Brandon more. They need to notice her. Her mother needs to leave her comfort zone and talk to Ali! Their daughter is deeply wounded. When Ali was young, her mother overreacted for lesser things than this! She would rush over to Ali, scoop her up, clean and tape cartoon characters over scraped knees. She would kiss her owies better. Now her mother rolls her eyes and judges things Ali says. She wounds Ali with sarcasm. She blames her daughter for ruining their mother-daughter relationship, and waits in the shadows for Ali to repair the damage.

Ali is getting fatter despite her efforts to lose weight. Coping is becoming impossible. She needs to sedate the screams inside her chest. Her self esteem is trembling. It scares her to death to be unattractive, yet it scares her more to be pretty. *People pay attention to me when I am beautiful.* Ali has strong needs to be noticed, loved, and pleased with what she sees in the mirror. Yet, she cannot handle being stared at, touched inappropriately, rejected by jealous girls and used. *People damage me when I am beautiful.* She is confused. Ambivalent. She loves the food going down, but hates it after. Ambivalence again, there is a connection. Always, she hates this out of control activity. She rips into food with gnashing teeth, killing her memories, killing her embarrassments and killing her existence. She needs to be raised from the dead, —born again. Cringe. What a freaky word. She needs a new life, one that prospers and has hope and a future. She needs to be brought back from captivity. *You will seek me and find me when you seek me with all your heart.*

Ali skips classes when her vices drag her into a shameful closet. She will get in her car and drive around until she is sure that her parents are at work and Brandon is at school. She carefully plans ways to sabotage her life.

She spends the day, today, driving to stores for intoxicating food, then returns to her empty house, to binge and purge in secret. After this ritual, she is forced to participate in life, when she goes to work later.

Ali's coworker, Millie, is already at the service counter. She spreads her arms wide and embraces Ali with a friendly hug and asks, "Ali dear, could you help me out by sorting all these hangers? They are in such a tangle."

Ali hates it when Millie hugs her, but never expresses it. Millie's old-lady perfume, applied in heavy doses, rubs off on Ali's clothes and gives her a headache. Brandon once told her she smells like a granny when she comes home from work.

The hangers are untangled. The money orders are sold. Unwanted products are returned to shelves. Ali gets another granny hug before she punches out, freshly scented with "Posies of Millie"

There is an envelope stuck under the wiper of Ali's car. She open's it and laughs at the magazine cutouts pasted on the paper. Her mood is lifting.

"Reese! What are you up to?" she says to the note.

She deciphers the ransom note of letters and pictures.

A big letter "H" + (fish eyeball picture).

Individual cut letters, spell her name. *aLi,*

A thick mascara eye, followed by cutout letters, *wAnT.*

The number '2'.

Next word: M+(beet) - B.

She decodes his clever message and reads it out loud: "Hi Ali. I want to meet you tonight. Look for me at the car wash."

He signs the letter with a newspaper heart and a wrapper of Reece's Piece's taped to the bottom.

She glances toward the carwash at the far end of the parking lot. His car is parked facing her direction. A shadow inside the car moves and a hand waves out the window. Ali leaves her car and walks over to the car wash. Reece pops out and gives her a tender hug. She doesn't cringe the way she does when Millie hugs her. She allows him to hold her before she steps away.

She feels self-conscience of her granny smell, *Posies-of-Mille.* "Do I stink?"

"Oh yeah! That's why we are at the carwash. You're gonna need a full service wash to get rid of that stench. P. U." he teases.

Ali lifts her smock to her nose, inhales Millie, and curls her nose in disgust.

"You don't stink! Why would you think that?"

"Because the lady I work with wears so much perfume it soaks into my clothes."

It dawns on her, she still has her red smock on, name tag and all. "Oh! I forgot I was wearing this!" Ali says, lifting the lapel of her smock.

"You look good in red. Plus, I might forget your name. I think you should keep it on."

She takes it off anyway. "What are you up to?"

"Are you busy tonight? Do you want to go to a movie or something?"

She feels shy and wavers before saying, "A movie sounds good." She looks at her hands and picks at a fingernail. "When?" *Is this a date?*

"Right now?"

"Oh! Um." Ali watches a car, with three young ladies in it, drive by. She doesn't want to go home and be alone while everyone else is out having a good time. She asks again, "now?"

"Yes! Let's go, Ali."

"Alright."

"Do you need to park your car somewhere?"

"No. It should be okay here."

Reece approaches her to open the passenger door.

"Am I driving your car?" Confused, she walks toward the driver's side of Reece's car.

Reece laughs, "Ali, I'm opening the door for you."

"Whoa. That's a first."

"Really?" Reece is surprised. His mother taught him to open the door for her and also his friends. *It is just good manners, Reece, a nice thing to do.*

Ali returns to the passenger side. Reece presents the open door with a chauffeur's sweep of his hand. He grabs the tips of her fingers, pats the top of her head as she sits down and recites, "My-lady" with a British accent.

"Funny guy!"

He drives around the carwash and joins the lineup.

"Now what are you doing?" Ali asks.

"Carwash first."

"Your car isn't that dirty."

"I thought you would want to go through the suds and wet carpet strips with me. Romantic, huh?" He laughs at the end of his sentence, becoming embarrassed for saying romantic. *Is this a date?*

Ali dwells on the word, romantic. It scares her. "I love the carwash. It's like a stormy day with soapy-rain and spinning-thunder."

"What is it about us? We attract storms..."

After her evening with Reece, Ali stays awake on purpose. Everyone in her house is asleep. She has new energy. *How long has it been since I felt like this?* —this elated feeling. She relives her day, starting with the ransom note, the carwash and watching a double feature. They laughed through the first movie and sat on edge for the second. Strange thing, they held hands during the second movie. It was full of surprises and kept Ali jumping in her seat. Reece reached over and squeezed her hand. He didn't let go. Her hand got a little sweaty, but it was nice. She isn't sure if the hand gesture was intended for intimacy or innocent friendliness. Reece is harder to figure out than anyone she knows. He is simple, direct and honest —free, relaxed and confusing.

Isaiah 2:12-14 (NIV)
[12] The Lord Almighty has a day in store for all the proud and lofty, for all that is exalted (and they will be humbled),
[13] for all the cedars of Lebanon, tall and lofty, and all the oaks of Bashan,
Isaiah 2:17-18 (NIV)
[17] The arrogance of man will be brought low and the pride of men humbled; the Lord alone will be exalted in that day,
[18] and the idols will totally disappear

chapter 20 mideah

"Someone keeps calling you. But he won't give me his name," Gina tells Mideah. "He said, 'Don't have her call me back. I'll catch her another time.' I think it's a phone solicitor."

Mideah and Gina usually tell each other about the men they date, in detail. Not this time. Mideah keeps this new romance to herself.

"Yes, probably a solicitor," Mideah lies. "What time was the call?"

"Which call? He's calling non-stop!" Gina rolls her eyes and exaggerates a sigh. "He just called. Again. Right before you walked in."

Mideah rushes to her bedroom to charge her phone battery. When she gets a display on the screen she checks for messages, with the phone corded to the wall. Five missed calls. She doesn't recognize the number and tries calling it. A digital voice tells her: *Subscriber is unavailable.*

"Huh?" I wonder what that's all about?"

She is curious and obsesses to find out who keeps calling her. Gut instinct hints that Ted is trying to reach her. He hasn't returned any of her calls in over two weeks. *Maybe his flight schedule changed?* Mideah can't figure out why he has been avoiding her. They have routine-visitations for their affair. On Tuesdays and Thursdays, Ted leaves his car at the library or the church nearby and walks to the park in his jogging suit. Mideah picks him up at a grove of trees, the backside of the park. They ride out of town to consume a couple of hours in front of a fire that burns in the little brown cabin, lost in the woods.

Lately, Ted isn't at the park. He's not at the library or the church. Every day, Mideah stalks park benches, steeples and books. She waits in the gap between his wife and children. *When is it my turn?*

Ted gave her strict instructions not to call him using her personal phone. *Only call from the agency. Period!* Mideah is ready to break his orders and call him. (At home even. And from her cell phone.)

Mideah is sure the phone solicitor is Ted. *Okay, I will call him.* Before she conjures courage, the phone rings in her hand.

Without checking who is calling, she answers with optimism, "Hello?"

A panicky voice jabbers, "Mid. It's Ted. Hey. I can only talk a sec. My wife suspects. I can't go into details right now. But she found the Mexico trip stuff. Don't ask me how! I told her it was a surprise. She's watching every move..."

Mideah interrupts, "I don't get it. What are you saying?" Before Ted has a chance, she asks, "And what is wrong with your cell phone? I can't leave messages."

"I got another phone. She keeps close watch on my old one, now."

"What's going on? You know we leave for Mexico in four days!"

"That's what I'm trying to tell you. We can't go. I need to come into your office. Switch things. She found out. I have to take her."

Mideah exhales with force. Her face tightens and she squishes her furious lips together. She doesn't know how to respond reasonably.

Ted waits for Mideah to say something. Anything.

Behind their silence, a muffled voice interrupts, "Ted, honey? Were you talking to me? I thought I heard you say something..."

Click. The phone is dies in Mideah's palm and kills her plans. *This is so not fair!* She throws her phone on the bed first, herself second. She cries into a crisp satin pillow. Her face makes a smeared imprint across the satin canvas, black splotches for eyes, brownish cheeks and bright red lips turned down.

Hurt feelings morph to anger. She rises off the bed and stomps across the floor. Mideah picks up a cotton blouse and snaps it at objects in her bedroom. She yells at Ted in an agitated voice, that presses against the back of her throat. She hopes he hears, somehow. *I hate her!* Snap! Cotton hits the bedpost. *I am going to tell your stupid wife to leave us alone!* Snap! The shirt whacks the chair. *What right does she have, ruining my vacation? I worked so many hours on that trip... and for what?* Snap! The chair cushion. *To watch you take another woman?* She hits her favorite lamp and knocks it over. It shatters. Swear words dart off her designer lips.

Gina hears the crash. She taps her fingernails on Mideah's door. "Hey? Is everything all right in there?"

No answer.

"Mideah?" Gina waits, then calls louder, "Mideah?"

Gina opens the door a sliver and peeks through the crack. Her best friend's eyes are red and puffy, smeared over with black mascara. Gina raids the room without invitation. She sees the lamp tipped sideways on the floor, unplugs it and starts to clean up broken glass. Mideah crushes her pillow against her chest. She plops down on the bed and watches Gina pick up sharp crystals.

"I'm dating a jerk!" Mideah blurts. Sniffle-hiccup.

"What'd Jason do now?"

"It's not Jason."

"What?" Gina rises and looks at Mideah. "What do you mean? I thought you and Jason were like this." She crosses her fingers.

"We still are... Sort of. Jason is Jason. You-know. He's so annoying lately." Mideah strums french-manicured fingers against her lips and confesses, "I'm talking about someone else."

Gina jerks to attention. "Oooo. Do tell." She pulls out Mideah's vanity stool to gossip sitting down. She crosses her stubby legs and leans forward.

"I met an older man." Mideah blurts and stops talking. She can't decide how much to share.

Gina tilts her head, eager for information. "And?" She motions with her hand, *keep going.*

Mideah lifts her legs from the edge of the bed, "He..." She swings them around, lays on her back and looks at the ceiling. "He isn't exactly..." She bites her mouth into a lip-less smile.

"Exactly what?"

"...Available."

"What do you mean? Does he have a girlfriend?"

"Not a girlfriend..." Dodging the question, she remarks, "he's super interesting. A pilot. Smart. Gorgeous! Rich!"

Mideah stops and wonders. *Or maybe his wife is rich? —I don't know.*

"I am falling fast for him. Faster than anyone, ever before." Her legs rise to the ceiling. She points her fuzzy pink slippers to stretch out nervous energy.

"What do you mean, *not available?*" Gina backs up their conversation to her last question.

"Well." Deep inhale. "He has a wife." Exhale. "It's complicated. I don't blame him for running around. She's such a bore. He says they don't have anything in common. All she wants to do is travel and spend money."

"Mideah! I can't believe it! You are dating a married man?" Gina is animated. "What are you thinking? He is probably filling you up with lies!"

"No Gina. This is different. He doesn't even love her. He says they will probably get a divorce soon."

"Yeah. Right. That is sooo-cliché. Huge cliché, So weak! Why do you want someone else's life?"

Mideah turns to her side and faces Gina, "Come on girl. I'm pouring my heart out. You can at least support me!" She pulls long strands of hair across her face and says, "Besides, if you saw him, you'd do the same thing."

Gina softens. "What does he look like?" She craves juicy drama. "Do you have a picture of him?"

"I do. On my cell." Mideah reaches down between the bed and the wall to pick up the phone that bounced off the bed earlier. She thumbs around and hands it to Gina to gawk at.

"Okay. Nice! I am beginning to understand the attraction. He's wearing those bedroom eyes, for sure." She looks one more time at the dark haired man on the screen, piercing her with the palest blue eyes ever. She hands the phone back. *I might do the same thing, I guess, if given the chance.*

Mideah pouts over Ted's face, lets out a lover's sigh, shuts off her phone and tosses it to the end of her bed.

"So why's he such a jerk?" Gina asks, remembering that Mideah was really upset a few minutes ago.

"You are not going to believe it!" Mideah explains, "We had this amazing vacation planned for Mexico, which I made all the arrangements for. Of course! He just called and said his wife found out, so he has to take ...her!"

"No way!" Gina exaggerates her shock. "How incredibly rude that the wife might want to take a vacation with her husband!" She persuades Mideah with sarcasm.

"Gina! Be reasonable. I am not going to tell you anything else, unless you are fair with me."

"I am just kidding. How did she find out, anyway?"

"I don't know. He wasn't sure either, says she is super suspicious of him, practically watching every move. How suffocating. He should leave her for that reason alone."

"Maybe we should go on the same vacation? As spies."

"Brilliant Gina! Wouldn't that be great?" Mideah conspires and flutters the tip of her fingers together. "Oh, we should do this. Wouldn't it be funny? Guess who knows everywhere they are going?" Mideah's face tightens again. "Urgh! It makes me so angry. That was my vacation you know!"

"When are they going?"

"This Friday."

"Four days! You were leaving for Mexico in four days and never told me?"

"I was going to let you know pretty soon."

"When? After your goat cheese burrito and margarita?" Gina changes her mind. "There is no way I can take off that soon. Looks like following them to Mexico is out of the question."

"Yeah. I suppose you are right. Hmm. What else could we do?"

"I don't know." Gina has Mideah's hairbrush and is pulling out strands of blond hair.

"He will be gone for nine days. It just isn't fair. I already took the week off," Mideah whines. "I feel like going over to his house and telling him off. Or cutting her hair off while she is sleeping."

"Really? Want to? I'll drive you over. Not to cut hair, but to yell at him. Plus, I want to see what *she* looks like."

"No. I can't do it. He would be so mad. I don't want to end it, really. I love him, Gina."

"Where does he live, anyway?"

"On Alderbrier Lane."

"Oh-wow. Fancy."

"Yeah. You should see his house. It's huge," Mideah says with admiration.

"Let's drive by it. I want to see what it looks like."

"No. I think he's home. I don't want him to see us stalking his house."

"He isn't going to be home after this Friday..."

"Gina! You sneak!" Mideah is excited. "What exactly are you scheming?"

Ted is remorseful and full of flattery, huddling with Mideah in her work cubicle. It is the day after he called to cancel their vacation. He pets her, to reassure. Ted is training her to *Stay!* He gives her treats when she does tricks.

Everyone has left for lunch. They have privacy, no need to fake professionalism. Mideah sorts through all the forms to make sure her name is eliminated from travel documents and plane tickets. She is not in a good mood during this process. Ted massages her neck and strokes her hair, so she doesn't bite. *It is all a misunderstanding. Aren't I making it up to you?* He rubs the bracelet on her wrist convince her more.

The bracelet. The bribe. Hush money. Mideah found the pretty box in her pencil drawer this morning. She doesn't know how Ted managed to put it there. *Did he go to the agency first thing in the morning? It wasn't there yesterday.*

How did he get in? Mideah was twenty minutes late for work. After a couple hours she finally opened her pencil drawer for the staple remover. The elongated, red-velvet box dazzled up at her, unexpectedly. She shyly unhinged the lid. Inside was a wide, platinum gold bracelet with a single square cut diamond, centered, similar to a watch —simple, elegant and extremely expensive.

"Meet me at the park Thursday," Ted whispers into Mideah's ear.

He is behind her computer chair. Every now and then, he peeks over the tall partition to make sure they are alone.

"Will do," Mideah agrees and touches Ted's hand on her shoulder.

He bends to her and risks a sloppy kiss.

It has been a rainy week. Mideah waits in her car, watching wipers swish back and forth. Ted runs to the passenger side and rushes into the bucket seat out of the rain. His coat drips water and makes a puddle on the leather seat. His dark hair is stuck into wet clumps. It curls across his forehead and around his reddened ears.

Mideah drives the familiar route to the cabin, unaware that she is being followed. Ted has most of her attention, the rain distracts the rest. When she makes the turn into the winding gravel driveway, the car following her parks down a two-track lane in vacant land next door. He waits.

The stalker, dressed in camouflage rain gear, walks across boundary lines, ignoring *'No Trespassing'* signs stapled to the trees that surround Ted's little brown cabin.

Warm light glows from the cabin's windows. Smoke curls fragrant patterns into the weeping sky. The stalker gropes through binoculars, watching an intimate moment inside the cabin. Deceived by seclusion, Ted and Mideah undress each other, believing that distance and the overgrown forest will hide their secret.

Instead of getting aroused, the stalker is frightened. Tall trees lean over the cabin and surround the lake. Branches look like wicked arms. They reach out and point at mysteries within the forest. One tree is shaped like a robed wizard, tall and haunted. The wizard's hand stretches and points into the water. It knows a secret. There is a jagged flash of lightning, oddly quiet, no distant rumble of thunder. Wind rattles and crackles swaying trees. The sky silently flashes several more warnings. The binoculars drop to the ground. Army boots tremor in the mud.

These woods have too many whispers. Another branch points at the stalker. Lightning strikes again to reveal something greater than the night. The trees seem to shiver in terror. Hideous evil bites at him. He cannot stay here. The stalker feels nude and childlike, so small. He hasn't stopped running since that dreaded day. He kneels to pick up the binoculars. A tiny shoe, moss covered, rests upon a rock.

Not real!

A vision?

Not! Real!

Psalms 17:8-9 (NKJV)
[8] Keep me as the apple of Your eye; Hide me under the shadow of Your wings,
[9] From the wicked who oppress me, *From* my deadly enemies who surround me.

chapter 21   leah (lee-lee)

Ya-outta see my mom's belly. It-is-huge! Her bellybutton is popping out. She let me draw a face on it. I made one with a button nose. My baby brother is living in there. Mom says he likes to kick; so I hold my hands against her to see if he will kick me. It feels like bones bumping out. Belly bones. Sometimes I put my ear on her bellybutton to hear him talking. So far, he doesn't say much, but I think I heard him burp.

Matt keeps buying my baby brother things, like a ball glove and a big yellow truck that dumps things. Oops, I mean 'Dad'. Sometimes I forget I am supposed to call him that. Dad won't let me play with the truck. He says I'll ruin it. Come on Matt, I am old enough to take care of things! I like to sneak into the baby closet and look at the top shelf to see if something new gets put up there. That's where the yellow truck is. Today I see a fuzzy blue bear. I run to my closet to see if something new is in there too. A new doll maybe? Nope. Just the same bunch of boxes. Dang. Dolls are for babies anyway, I guess.

Mom says she will go to the hospital soon and stay overnight a couple of nights. She has her suitcase ready. I hafta stay home with Grandma Gertie, who doesn't let me do anything. She makes me eat stuff I hate, combs my hair really hard and yells if I get things dirty. Heck, I can comb my own hair. She thinks I am such a baby. She doesn't come here very much. Good thing, cuz Mom gets grouchy when Grandma Gertie bosses her around. She just got here yesterday and Mom already slammed herself into the bedroom. I'm not going out there, either. I am just gonna stay in here, looking for a blue bear or something. Matt, I mean Dad, called at dinnertime and said he was working late. I was supposed to tell Mom, but I forgot. She knows though, I heard her call Dad and yell at him to 'get home'.

Okay, now I am mad too. Why do I have to go to bed at eight-thirty? That is baby bedtime. I am almost nine, so it means I should get to stay up 'til nine. When Mom came in to say goodnight, she said I could read for a few minutes. Just when I start to read the next chapter, Grandma reaches in and shuts off my light. I stuck out my tongue at her. Good thing it was dark.

When I yell, "Mom said I could read," she shut my door anyway.

I want to turn the light back on. Do I dare? Do I? It's none of Grandma's business.

When did I fall asleep? It's super dark. I hear the garage door open and see Dad drive the car close to the door. I hear Grandma's fuzzy slippers, swish, swish, swish, in a rush down the hallway. Breathy voices talk low and fast, but I can't hear what they are saying. I watch out the window and see the porch light pop on. The front sidewalk looks like a brick bridge to the car. Dad helps Mom walk across the bridge. Mom looks sorta like a ghost wearing a sweater with big jammies fluttering around her legs. Woooo. Woooo. She's a white sheet blowing in dark air. Grandma follows them and stands in trampled snow. Grandma's hands are on her hips. Her flannel nightie doesn't blow. I pretend that Grandma's huge fuzzy slippers are floaty things and she is balancing in the snowy water.

Grandma Gertie holds her arm out and points to the air, ready to say something when Matt gets Mom into the car. Instead she stops and bites the tip of her thumb, like she's trying to stop her voice from coming out. Grandma has her arms across her chest, squeezing them tight. She shivers and watches Mom sail away. Oh no! She's looking over here. I pull myself away from the window and dive under the covers. In case she checks on me, I pretend to sleep. Suddenly it's morning.

My baby brother comes home today. Grandma Gertie is on the phone a lot, telling the same story over and over, "eight pounds, ten ounces, nineteen inches long...chubby. Jodie is extremely fatigued! Poor dear. Her labor was excruciating and lasted over twenty hours. He has the cutest chubby cheeks! The nurse said she was having *'back labor'*... I think it means the baby is in an awkward position, —the worst sort of pain... Poor. Poor. Dear."

The whole time she is on the phone, Grandma Gertie makes me wash baby bottles in way too hot water and fold my brother's clothes. He didn't even get them dirty and we hafta wash 'em. Things are so weird when Grandma's here. This is so stupid. She aught-a be doing this. Or Mom.

I hear Grandma on the phone again, "Oh! You're on the way home now? What is that doctor thinking? You really should be there another night! With all those complications. Get the nurse on the phone. I need to talk to her.... Alright. Alright. Fine. We'll see you shortly."

Dang. That baby cries a lot! Everyone has to look at him and hold him. I drew him some pictures of us and put them in his teeny bed. His bed is so cute. He has puppy blankets and sheets. I went to kiss him again and the pictures were gone. Mom didn't know what I was talking about when I asked her where they went. I looked for the pictures and didn't find 'em 'till I went pee. Someone put them in the plastic trash can next to the toilet. That's so mean! They were my brother's pictures. They shoulda asked me first. I think my brother's mad too. They are not in the trash anymore. I put them in my dresser under my socks.

I am wearing my favorite outfit and look great. When people come in I walk by them and fling my hair around. Nobody even notices. They all came to look at my brother's purple face. I twirl over by his cute bed and accidently bump it super hard. The annoying baby screams to tell on me. Mom makes me go somewhere else.

All he does is cry, eat and poop, or sleeps. Everyone keeps saying, "Shhh!" Mom and Dad hold him all the time. It is my turn to hold him. I am not gonna break him. I think he likes me best.

"Dad," I say, holding a book behind me. Maybe he'll let me read it to my new brother.

"Shhh!" Matt hushes. "He was almost asleep."

I go looking for Mom. Grandma is in the kitchen putting dishes away. I won't go in there. No way. I find Mom sleeping in her bedroom and lean my book on Matt's pillow, close to her head. The book starts to slide. Before I can catch it, the corner pokes Mom's eyelid.

She jolts her head up and bursts, "Leah! Go! Just go! Can't I get some sleep around here!"

Grandma Gertie is gone now. She stayed at our house —For! Ev! Er! I get to pass out cupcakes at school today. They have a blue letter B in the frosting. Baby Boy. My teacher made me write a story about getting a new brother. She says I can read it to the class before we get the treats. I don't want to do it! Ugh! I don't! I do not!

Teacher says, "Of course you do."

I tell her, " Of course I don't."

"You want to be able to pass out the cupcakes?" My teacher leans down and looks over her brown glasses, "Don't you?"

"Maybe," I say, then mumble, "maybe not." But the teacher doesn't hear that part.

We all run in from recess. My cupcakes are sitting on the table next to Teacher's desk. After everyone sits down and gets quiet, Teacher announces the surprise.

"Leah had a special thing happen to her." She tells us, "She will be reading a paragraph she wrote about it and will pass out treats." She looks right at me and says, "Leah, will you come up here, now?"

"I kinda changed my mind," I say. No-way-in-a-shell am I reading it. Everyone is staring at me!

"Oh, you didn't change your mind." She fake smiles at me. "We all want to hear your wonderful story. And..." She looks at me again, over her brown glasses, "I'm sure you want to pass out treats today."

Everyone is looking right at me. I lean back and slide lower into my chair.

"Yeah. We want cupcakes," they say.

Up in front of everyone, I read and never look up. This is scary. I will never-ever bring cupcakes again! When I read the part about how much my baby brother poops and pukes, the kids all laugh really loud. Lester makes farting noises. *Maybe I will bring more cupcakes.*

Teacher shouts, "Quiet!" She looks at me with her same old tilted head, and says, "Are you finished?"

I wasn't. But I guess I wanna be now. I lie and say, "That's all. Can I pass 'em out now?"

My baby brother can almost sit up now. I like to prop him up and make him clap. I count how many claps 'till he tips over and I catch him. His laugh sounds like belly gurgles. I like to pet his white hair that sticks straight up. I call him Spike. Everyone pinches his fat legs and puffy cheeks. I bet he hates that. Dad likes to throw Spike into the air and catch him. Mom hates that.

Dad calls the baby Spike all the time now. He thinks he made it up, but really I did. Dad brought Spike a surprise tonight when he got home from work. It's a red baseball hat. I wait to see if he has anything for me. Guess not, cuz after he puts the hat on Spike's head, he hugs Mom and takes Spike to watch TV with him.

Mom says, "Go set the table."

I grab three plates and three forks from the cupboards and shut the drawer harder than I am supposed to.

"Leah!"

"Sorry," It really was on accident. I think. I was thinking of something and want to ask Mom about it.

While I walk around the table to sit plates down, I say, "Mom?"

I hear "What?" from the kitchen. When I don't answer, I hear, "What!" again.

"Nothing."

At my bedtime, Mom lets me read for a while. I walk past Matt to get my book. He is feeding Spike. I watch him tickle the baby's face by poking the bottle nipple on his cheeks and forehead. Spike gurgle-laughs. Matt tries to imitate spike and makes weird sounds. *You don't sound like Spike at all!*

I read until Mom comes to tell me, "Time to turn out the lights."

"Mom?" I say, feeling braver.

"Yes?" she asks, standing in the doorframe.

"Um." I squish my lips shut and bite on them. "I. Um."

I see my mom shift her weight to her other leg.

"Well?"

I don't look up when I say, "Who's my dad?"

"Who's your dad?" She repeats the question. "Why are you asking me that?"

"I was just wondering."

My mom shifts her weight. Still in the doorway, she tells me, "Matt is."

"Nooo." I say sorta whiney and try to explain, "Matt is Spike's dad. Who's my dad?"

"He is your father too." Mom says. She sounds mad.

"Ugh! Mom!" I say. This is so annoying. "I mean, who is my real dad?"

"Matt is your father and you need to treat him like one."

"But..."

Mom stops me from talking, "End of subject."

She shuts the light off. The door clicks between us. I feel like I wanna cry. Instead, I get mad and throw my pillow off the bed. *Now I don't have a pillow. So what! I don't need a pillow. I don't need anything!* I turn and lay on my belly, and put my face into the mattress. This bothers me too. So I flop over to my back and stare at the ceiling. I can't sleep without a pillow holding my head. I reach my hand off the edge of the bed. *I hope something doesn't grab my hand.* I feel around quick for something soft. *Whew! Here it is.* I hug and kiss it goodnight, before fluffing it around my head. I pull the blankets tight around my neck and curl into the warm spot.

Someone is holding me.

Psalms 68:5 (NIV)
[5] A father to the fatherless, a defender of widows, is God in his holy dwelling.

chapter 22 - ali

Reece grows impatient. He's tired of watching Ali torture herself for over forty minutes. She is trying on pants. *How hard could it be? Pick something! Anything!* He encourages her to choose from her pile.

"The last pair you had on looked really good. They all did."

"I refuse to buy those jeans! They are size ten. Maybe I'll buy these." Ali is holding a pair of jeans, tagged size seven. She didn't really like them as well as the others. She likes the darker pair, but they are marked size ten. She can't get passed the label. Size seven means she isn't as fat as she thought. Size ten means she is a pig.

"I don't get it. You are still the same size no matter what pair of jeans you put on. Maybe the size seven is extra big."

"Thanks a lot. You just called me fat."

"I did not!"

"You said the jeans that fit me are 'extra-big'. That is the same as calling me fat!"

"It's just a number! Labels are put on clothes to guide people. The numbers aren't judging you."

"Maybe not, but you are. You called me fat."

"I won't respond to that. Beautiful to me isn't skinny or fat. And it certainly isn't reduced to the label on a pair of jeans. You don't find beauty in the mirror."

"What?" Ali groans and accuses, "now you just called me ugly!"

"Ali!" Reece shrugs, shakes his head and says under his breath, "You're so beautiful."

"Huh?" Ali pretends she didn't hear his last few words.

What Reece believes about beauty confuses her. *Does he really think that? Or is he just saying it, to make me feel better?* She is afraid to believe it. *Guys don't think like that.* Nobody she knows thinks like that. *I know I'm ugly. I have a mirror and mine Does say ugly! I'm not fooled! Reece is weird, not normal. He's so confident. Does he ever care what people think? I wish people would think I'm pretty. I'm fat. I am! Fat means that I am out of control, a pig that can't stop eating.*

Her lies weigh her down. Ali misses so many chances to live. *I can't go to the party, because all my clothes make me look fat. No way am I going to the beach — I'll have to wear a swimsuit! I wish I had her legs, her nose, her eyes.* Once, Reece told her, "Ali, you are all you need to be. Quit wanting (needing) to be in the spotlight! Step down off the stage and relax. Wallflowers are pretty. And they have value, even if nobody says so."

Reece watches Ali stand like a child, pinching her lower lip, deep in thought, and blinking away tears. He knows she needs someone to reach out to her. This reminds him of the very first time he met her, when her nose was bleeding. Right now she is real, like the time she was wearing ducky pajama pants and her dad's slippers. Her expression and pose bares her vulnerability. She allows him into her space and they hold each other like little children. *This is beauty.*

Ali pays for the jeans, feeling a little taller. She bites both her lips between her front teeth to suppress a smile. In the car, Reece uses his swiss army knife to cut the tags and labels off her jeans. Labels —size ten.

He recites, "Repeat after me.... I will not be defined by what size jeans I wear!"

"I will not be defined by what size jeans I wear," Ali repeats in monotone.

"Now say it again and mean it."

"I will not be defined by what size jeans I wear!"

"Louder!"

"I WILL NOT BE DEFINED BY WHAT SIZE JEANS I WEAR!" she screams.

"Alright! That's better."

"Okay, I'm putting them on right now!" Ali quickly crawls to the back seat of his car.

"Here? I can drive you to a gas station."

Ali pretends she isn't listening, unzips and removes her pants. Reece is suddenly shy and uncomfortable.

He stutters, "I'm not even... I cannot even believe you are doing that!"

He turns his rearview mirror up to resist the temptation to watch. He keeps his eyes on the ground, grinning. He has never seen her this happy, this silly. She works fast to slip on the new pair of jeans, then climbs back to her seat. The pants are a better fit than the ones she normally wears. She notices more freedom when she moves and sits. Plus, she can fit her hands in the pockets. *Imagine that, buying a pair of jeans that fit!* Reece is proud of her and squeezes her knee.

"Hey. That tickles."

Reece squeezes more, to annoy her. She laughs while pushing his hand, then holds his wrist with both her hands to get him to stop. He reclaims his arm, returns both hands to the steering wheel and drives on.

"I've got an idea," exclaims Ali, "Let's make this... A-Day-of-Adventure. First I pick what-n-where, then you pick. We can take turns choosing what to do next."

"I'm game. What's first?" Reece has nothing planned for the day, either.

"Lunch....Hmmm. Let's randomly pick a restaurant," Ali suggests.

"Sounds good. You pick."

"Hmm. I can't think of any. Besides, that's not random. How about this, we ask the first person we see to recommend a good place for lunch."

Turning the corner is an elderly couple making their way slowly down the sidewalk. The man is holding a shopping bag with one arm and has his other arm firmly wrapping the lady's elbow. Reece parks his car nearby, then helps Ali out, holding her hand. They both approach the elderly couple.

"Excuse me, we were hoping you could recommend a restaurant for us... to eat lunch?" Reece asks.

The old man rubs his scrunching eyebrows and says, "Hmm......Hmmm, well how about...." Before he finishes his sentence, the old woman shouts, "Cupcake Daisy's!"

"I was gonna say that, Ma."

"Well, what were you waiting for? They haven't got all day."

"How do you know, Ma, did-ya ask-em?"

The old woman ignores the man, looks at Ali and says, "Go up two blocks, turn right and it's a few shops down." She studies Reece top to bottom, grabs his elbow and gives it a shake. She says to Ali, "Don't let this one get away. He looks like a keeper."

Ali pretends to ignore the old woman's comment. She tells them, "Thank you," and rushes away.

Reece yells to her, "Hey, wait for me... Wait! You're letting me get away!" She sticks her tongue out at him.

He says, "Nice jeans!"

When he catches up to her, Ali hits him with her purse. Reece puts his arm across her shoulders and glances back. Ma and Pa smile and wave. If Reece and Ali were watching, they would see the man holding the woman's hand and giving her a peck on the top of her head. What is now called 'Cupcake Daisy's' used to be the soda fountain where the old couple first met.

The restaurant is easy to find, just as the woman described. It stands out from the other stores with yellow, clapboard siding and a pink door. Iron scrollwork holds the sign over the sidewalk. The logo has fancy curving font, scripting the name, Daisy, and dotting the 'i' with a flower. Reece tries to open the door, but Ali reaches and pulls the handle first and holds it for him instead. Right away, vanilla aroma tempts both Ali and Reece to eat dessert instead of lunch.

They walk across the original, hexagonal, black and white tile pattern that borders the entry and seating area. A tin ceiling towers above them, freshly painted in pink and white, checker board pattern. Ali tugs Reece to the old wooden display case spanning one side of the room. Curved glass promotes cleverly frosted cupcakes. Everything is indulgent and festive.

Ali stands in line with Reece, near the cupcake display, admiring the masterpieces. Reece listens in amusement as Ali chooses and changes her mind, until she selects every cupcake as her personal favorite.

"Look at this one! No, I want that one! Oh, I didn't see this... for sure, it's the one. Look at the ladybug on the flower! The butterflies are so detailed. Oh, I have to buy it. Do you want the bumble bee cupcake? You like bees ...right?"

"Your turn," says the man behind them.

The server is waiting behind the counter for their order with pen and pad ready. They haven't read the chalkboard menu above and dawdle, unprepared to order.

Reece turns to the person behind him. "Why don't you go on ahead of us. We're having trouble deciding."

The man moves ahead. He recites his order, quick and certain. Ali and Reece eavesdrop. Next, they recite their choices with confidence.

Reece wonders what to do next. "Do we just go sit down?"

Ali shrugs. They look to see what the man ahead does, then copy.

Right now, Ali is not anxious about eating forbidden foods (grilled sandwich and cupcakes —anything that doesn't normally go into a salad). She is herself with Reece and doesn't feel judged. She doesn't feel the need to pretend. This social comfort is new to her, this living obsession-free with no imagined scrutiny by everyone in sight.

"What's next for our adventure?" Reece asks.

"Your turn to pick."

"HHhhmmm.... Lemme-see." Reece thinks, scratches his whiskers, drums the table with his fingertips and says, "Show me your shoes."

"Why do you want to see my shoes?"

Reece bends down under the table and grabs her foot.

"Reece! What are you doing?" Ali cannot see him, but she knows he is pretending to be a shoe inspector, checking the soles and feeling how sturdy they are.

"Are you up for a hike? I think your slippers can handle it."

"They aren't slippers, they are *mules*," corrects Ali.

"That explains everything."

"What do you mean?" Apparently, Ali doesn't get his joke.

"Why you are so stubborn."

"Thanks a lot!" She kicks him under the table with her hoof. She knows he is kidding around. And she knows it is true. *Yep, I am stubborn.*

"Easy. Donkey."

"A mule isn't a donkey."

He presses his shoe on top of her mule and holds her foot down.

"Are you ready to go?" Reece asks as he grabs the bill and tosses a generous tip on their table.

"I don't think my *mules* are ready to leave." Ali stands in a stubborn pose, hands on her hips. "They are upset that you took my bill."

"Tell them they can buy dinner." Reece winks.

On their way out of the restaurant, they see the old man and woman, Ma and Pa, seated at a corner booth. Pa takes the butterfly off his cupcake and flutters it in the air. With shaking hands, he lands it on the flower of the old woman's cupcake.

Reece holds the door for Ali. "Nice jeans."

She scuffs her mules past him. "Hee-Haw."

1 John 2:16-17 (NIV)
[16] For everything in the world--the cravings of sinful man, the lust of his eyes and the boasting of what he has and does--comes not from the Father but from the world.
[17] The world and its desires pass away, but the man who does the will of God lives forever.

chapter 23 mideah

"Should we paint our faces? I am thinking a super dark brown, or maybe even black?" Mideah asks Gina.

"Are you kidding? Maybe we should wear an orange jumpsuit or dress in zebra stripes!" Gina can't believe how naive Mideah can be sometimes. "Wear long sleeves. Pull your hair up, too."

Mideah brags, "I look really good when I am being naughty." She gathers her hair to the back of her head and loops a black band around it. "I am going to wear this, Gina. I don't feel like changing. Besides, orange is not my color."

"I don't know what to do about your hair, Mideah. It's so light." Gina is scheming ways to be invisible, to blend into darkness.

"Who knew? Being sneaky is so much fun!" Mideah folds her hands at her chest and bounces on her toes.

The girls are giddy and nervous. Adrenaline is pumping through their bodies, augmenting every emotion. All they need now are tails and pointy ears to look like Cat Women in dark, tight fitting clothes. They are on the prowl. It's time to slow down, take a breath. Calculate. Purr.

"We look like burglars," exclaims Gina. "Criminals. Look at us. Hey, I like your hat. Good going, Mideah. It covers your light hair. Maybe I'll wear one too." Gina digs through the closet basket and pulls out an army green wool hat. "How does this look?"

Mideah tilts her head, pushes her lips out, contemplating. "You'd look much better in my brown fedora." She takes the wool hat off Gina and gives her the one she is wearing.

Gina puts it on her head and admires herself in the mirror. "Yes. This does look better. I feel like a detective... Or a gangster."

They roar, bending and holding bellies. Mideah adjusts the green wool hat on her head. *Whoa! I do look good! Better than Gina.* At the mirror, both women are admiring and comparing themselves.

"Gina, will you drive?" Mideah picks up Gina's purse and hands it to her. "I drive by Ted's house so many times. The neighbors must know my car by now. We don't want to look suspicious."

"True. You can tell me how to get there." agrees Gina, digging keys out of her purse.

Mideah inhales nervously, then relaxes. "Do you really want to do this? I'm beginning to change my mind."

"I told you a million times," Gina huffs. "It's no big deal. No one will notice us. Remember? They are on *Your* vacation. Nobody's home."

"I know. I know. They're in Mexico right now, on a dinner boat over a spectacular coral reef. I should know, I made the reservation." Mideah opens the apartment door to leave. "She really owes me for stealing my trip. Let's go!"

Gina's blue Toyota creeps down Alderbrier Lane. "I always did love going down this street. The houses are so beautiful." Gina leans into the steering wheel and looks intently out the windows. "I'll show you my favorite house."

"Can you drive a little faster?" Mideah demands. "We look like idiots."

"I'm sure lots of people drive down this street to gawk at the houses. My mom and I always did."

"Yeah, but she wasn't ready to break into one of them."

"Mideah, we aren't breaking in. We're just letting ourselves into the back door and taking a tour." She pushes the gas pedal down more. "No big deal."

"Almost there." Mideah is having a hard time breathing.

"Right up there, on the right. That's my..." Gina sees her favorite house.

"Stop." Mideah says abruptly.

"What?" Gina stomps on the breaks. "You scared me!"

"Oh nothing. I thought I saw a car pulling out of the driveway. That's all."

"Are you sure?" Gina's heart beats faster. "Was it pulling out of Ted's house?"

"No. I'm not sure. I think it's the one next door."

"Whew. Now I am getting nervous." Gina points again. "I love that house."

"That's the one."

"Yes. That one." Gina clarifies. "I love-love it!"

"I mean... Gina. That's Ted's house."

"You. Have. Got. To. Be. Kidding." Gina's jaw is on the floor. "Mom and I have been in love with that house since the first time we saw it."

They drive by faster to appear nonchalant, go several houses past, then turn up the next block. Gina parks her car on a side street. And they wait in the car.

"I think we're dressed too weird," observes Mideah. "We look like we're up to something."

"I know. That's what I was thinking." Gina admits. She begins to doubt and taps the steering wheel to figure things out. "What should we do?"

"Let's park close to his house as possible, and walk up to it like we know them. Like friends."

"Girl-friends. Hee-hee."

"Gina! He's mine."

"What if he has an alarm system?" Gina worries.

"He doesn't."

"Are you positive? How do you know?"

"He told me. His cabin has warning stickers on the doors and windows. They are fakes. He calls them *decoys*. He says alarm systems can't stop a serious intruder."

"Okay. Let's hope he didn't change his mind on this house."

"We'll have to be serious intruders, that's all."

Gina drives back to Ted's house. Only a few homes have their outside lights on. Ted's house is dark, except for one dim light on the main floor and another upstairs, probably a hall lamp. Gina confidently parks her car across the street from the house.

Getting out of the car, Gina bosses, "Mideah. Act normal. We will walk right up to the gate at the side, to the back yard. If we act like we do it every day, no one will think anything of it. Come on."

"Okay. I am actually excited about it now. I am not scared a bit. He's my friend. And friends walk into each other's houses all the time. And friends use the back door."

"That's right. We are back-door friends," Gina agrees and jokes, "I wonder if our *friends* are home?"

They pass a stone wall that edges the sidewalk and tip-toe, with assurance, up the brick pavers. The iron gate has a simple latch. It lifts easy and allows them into the backyard. There is a rake leaning across the path next to a pile of sticks and yard debris. Gardening tools are sprawled at the edge of the back porch.

Mideah trips over the rake. Clank.

"Shhh!" they say, giggling.

Gina checks the back door first. Sure enough, it is locked. While she is cupping her hands and peeping into the window, Mideah rolls a large stone over, the one that looks out of place next to the brick walk. Victory! A brass key, connected to a rubber pouch, imprints the soil.

"We're in business," she cheers, dangling a key towards Gina.

"How did you find that?" Gina whispers.

"Easy. Ted has a favorite place to hide keys. He's so predictable."

They open the door and relock it from the inside. Mideah doesn't have pockets, so she stuffs the key just inside the waistband of her slacks. Streetlights brighten the rooms, allowing them to make their way through the mudroom and into a huge kitchen. Gina marvels at the stone countertops and ample cupboards surrounding the room. She opens the refrigerator. The bright beam of light startles Mideah.

"Hey! Shut that!" Mideah commands in a whispery voice. "We are not here to eat!"

Mideah turns the corner into the next room and feels along the wall for a light switch. Risking attention, she turns the dimmer knob. The chandelier glows dim. They walk around the long table that seats twelve plus people. The room is stuffy and formal.

"Does he have a huge family or something?" Gina asks. "Look at all these chairs."

"Not really. Just the twins and their big sister. She's twelve."

Gina notices a large photo in the hall by the dining room. "Oh, this must be the twins. How cute. Are they babies?"

"No. That's an old picture. They're nine. Maybe ten?"

"Wow. Is this his wife? She's really beautiful." Gina is holding a gold leaf frame.

Mideah grabs the frame from Gina and looks at it. "Yeah, that's her. It's a really good picture of her. Probably touched up, because she isn't that pretty." Mideah puts the frame exactly where Gina found it. "I think her nose is too big."

"I thought it was her best feature. It doesn't look big to me. She looks Indian, or Latino."

Mideah feels funny walking around her lover's house. Seeing this other side of Ted makes her feel shut out of his life. Being in his house turns him into a stranger. The cabin seems more like his home to her, their home. *What is this family's life like? What chair does he sit in at the table? When did he go with his wife to Aspen? They look so happy, embracing at the top of the slopes. What is his wife like anyway?* She only met her twice, early on, when Ted first came into the agency. After that, Mideah has only met with Ted. As Gina wanders off, Mideah studies photos that explode over walls. They look like the ideal family. Mideah stares at baby pictures. *They are so cute!* Jealousy is crying inside her. She wants them to be her kids. *Not right now, though. I'm not ready to lose my body to pregnancy. I am too young for stretch marks and saggy boobs.*

A dainty sweater is draped over the back of a chair. Mideah picks it up and holds it across her chest, sizing it up. She puts her nose into the yarn and smells the stale perfume. *This is what I smell like! Ted loves it. He bought me this perfume. Special. He said it's the only kind he likes, that it's sexy on me.* She throws the sweater on the floor and kicks it under the chair.

"Gina, where'd you go?"

Mideah jerks and almost knocks over a vase when she hears the toilet flush.

"I'm in here." Gina's voices echoes down the hall.

"Come on. I want to go upstairs. Lets snoop in his bedroom."

When Gina comes out of the bathroom, they never notice she isn't carrying her purse. Mideah saw it clutched under her arm earlier, just after they unlocked the back door. She almost said, *Why did you bring your purse?* But they got caught in the moment, being prowlers, entering an unfamiliar dark home —a home with different smells, different sounds and a different lover.

Upstairs, they wander to the master bedroom. Mideah risks turning on the small lamp on the dresser. She opens drawers, snooping, not sure what she is looking for, anything or nothing at all. She doesn't want to know more, still part of her needs to know. She invades *'her'* dresser, the other woman's. The narrow top drawer is used for odds and ends, mostly jewelry and hair clips. An elongated red velvet box is pushed to the corner of the drawer. Mideah opens it. A déjà-vu feeling sucks the air out of her. Inside the velvet case is an exact replica of the bracelet Ted recently gave her. Her morals disintegrate further. She puts the entire box, including the bracelet, down the side of her pants, held tight by the stretchy fabric. *How dare she wear the same bracelet as me!*

Gina is in the master bathroom, looking in drawers and reading labels on makeup and creams. She is appalled at the price tags. *$225 for face rejuvenation gel. Really?* Carefully, she replaces everything she touches. Next, she joins Mideah in the master bedroom, and finds her nosing through nightstand drawers.

Clank. Snap. Faint footsteps are heard from downstairs. Mideah and Gina freeze, like two statues flanking the bed.

Gina mouths the words, "Oh no!"

Mideah lip-syncs back, "Did you hear that?"

Gina nods.

Mideah tip toes to turn off the lamp. She scurries to Gina and huddles close. They link arms in fear.

Gina whispers, "We gotta hide somewhere. Who do you think is down there?"

"I don't know! Why are you asking me?"

"Where are the kids?"

"Ted said the girls were going to stay with their grandma."

"Do you think Grandma came here?"

"No! She's too far away."

From the sounds banging downstairs, someone is in the kitchen making something to eat. They hear the microwave hum and ding. Slam. Hum... ding! Click. The refrigerator breaks suction and jars jiggle. A drawer is pulled open, silverware clinks and dishes rattle.

This is not in the plan. The house is supposed to stay empty. Who is down there?

"What should we do?" Mideah whines. "I'm really scared. Gina! Why did you talk me into this?"

"Shut up, Mideah! I'm thinking!" Gina whispers at Mideah's shadow, "It must be someone who knows them pretty well, since they are helping themselves to all that food."

Mideah needs to laugh. The more she tries to suppress it, the worst it gets. Now Gina is infected. Their shoulders shake and hands smash over their mouth.

After regaining control, Gina says, "Let's hide in the shower until they're gone. I saw a bathroom off the hallway."

They crawl inside the confined tub/shower enclosure, feeling claustrophobic, and quietly pull the shower curtain closed. The back of the curtain smells like soapy mildew. They stand in soap scum and strands of black hair and wait with sharp ears and pounding hearts. After a while they tire of standing. Mideah sits down first, leans back and relaxes as if taking a bath. Gina positions herself at the other end. She hugs her knees to her chest. The faucet pokes into her back. Time drags.

Mideah grows angry in the waiting. *I give up! This is so stupid. What are we doing here? Why did I agree to this? When are they going to leave, anyway?*

She kicks Gina with her toe, "Hey. Let's go. Who cares if we get caught."

"No way! What if they have a gun."

"A gun!" Mideah kicks Gina. "They are not going to have a gun! Whoever it is, is armed with Cheerios and a spoon. Big threat!"

Gina pretends to hold up a knife and whispers, "Hark! Who goeth yonder? Take another th-step and I'll th-stab you with thith th-spoon!"

"Stop!" Mideah pleads. Her shoulders shake again.

"Freethe! I have Cheerioth!" Gina pretends to use the fake spoon as a slingshot.

"Gina! Stop! I'm warning you. You're gonna make me pee."

Click! The bathroom door opens, interrupting their fake bath and halting their whispers. The lights turn on, stinging their eyes. They hear the toilet seat go up. Clunk. Zip. Pounding hearts will surely give them away. Mideah and Gina hear delicate metal clinking. *Bracelets? Belt buckle? Chains?* The toilet water echoes a steady stream of relief. The toilet paper unwinds, crushes and wipes. Flush. Mideah can see the corner of the vanity mirror, but not enough. Gina watches Mideah peek through a crack in the curtain. Gina pulls the edge of the curtain back slightly to give Mideah a wider view.

"Don't!" Mideah mouths to Gina.

Gina stops, but the curtain is moved enough to see the reflection in the mirror. Mideah is ready to jump out and tackle the bathroom intruder. *There is thief in this house! Look at her! What's she trying to steal?* The intruder is an invasive species, primping at the mirror. The girl looks tough with jet black hair spiking off her head. Her face is obsessively pierced. Her eyebrows are looped with metal rings. She adjusts the ring at the end of her nose. Each time she moves, the thin metal bracelets that stack her arm make sounds like fragile wind chimes.

Mideah is ready to run and call the police, until something jolts her memory. *Have I seen her before? Where? I can almost place it. Who is she? Oh my!*

She looks like a female Ted! That's why she looks familiar. He has another daughter! The girl looks twenty something. Her eyes are bloodshot and her movements clumsy and loose —drunk-like. She is slurring words at the mirror.

Her tongue is fat. "Take thaa. You piece of #$&! What ya gone do? $#@. I hate you #@!"

She keeps mumbling curses that make no sense. Gina rolls her eyes and makes funny faces, acting out the words coming from the sink. The girl flicks her favorite finger at the mirror. On the way out, she stumbles into the edge of the door.

"##@!=% door! Get ouda maway!"

Mideah and Gina hear the door down the hall clang shut. The girl must be in the bedroom. Without consulting each other, they tear out of the tub and rush downstairs. They move quickly and quiet enough, at least for a drunk teenager not to hear or care. Gina opens the back door, leaving it unlocked. Mideah tilts the rock, stuffs the key under it and runs out the gate behind Gina.

"What a relief! I can't believe it! That was too close!" They finally breath normal.

They are glad to be sitting in Gina's car and driving down the road. After they make the first turn off Alderbrier Lane, suppressed anxiety surfaces. They can't stop laughing and almost pee their pants.

"Stop! Oh Gina. I was so scared. I gotta pee. Make sure you stop at the first gas station."

"Me too! Who was that weirdo in the bathroom, anyway? At first I thought we were so caught!"

"I know!" Mideah screeches. "Truthfully, I've never seen her before in my life! She was decked out in Goth. Awful. Her face had so many holes, I lost count. I almost jumped her. Then I realized that she looks exactly like a female Ted! No mistake, she has to be his daughter. What a loser. No wonder he never mentions her."

"I cannot believe we did that!" Gina keeps saying, as she drives to find a place to use the bathroom. "Wow. Can you believe we escaped? I cannot believe we just did that..."

On and on they talk about every detail, replaying 'The Investigation'. That is the name they will forever call it, the time they broke into someone's house and raped a wife's privacy.

After ten days, Ted returns from Mexico agitated. His wife nagged him the entire time for not being 'present'. *Hello! I'm right here. Why are you so preoccupied?* She confronted his neglect by slamming doors and giving the silent treatment, followed by name calling and accusing. They spent much of their beach and pool time in separate lounge chairs, as far apart as possible. Ted watched her feed herself drinks, while he stung her with nasty looks from across the pool. She flirted with other men, right in his face. She made him sleep on the hide-a-way bed in hotel rooms. Unrelenting in her aggressions, she tore at him with buried anger. Towards the end of their trip, she prodded him for information about seeing other women and stayed persistent, no matter how much he lied.

He thinks the worst is over. Not so! When they arrive home, his wife finds a women's purse in the powder room off their kitchen. The driver's license has a picture of a pretty girl —Ted's type. Superficial. He actually doesn't have to lie this time. He can honestly testify, he knows nothing about it. The only explanation disappoints and angers him.

Megan must have stolen it.

He has a fight with his oldest daughter over this purse.

"As drunk as I was, there is no way I would ever-ever steal!" his daughter adamantly insists. "You never did trust me! I hate you! I am leaving!" Megan runs away again. This time, he doesn't know where she is staying. And he isn't going to bother finding out.

Genesis 4:7 (NIV)
[7] If you do what is right, will you not be accepted? But if you do not do what is right, sin is crouching at your door; it desires to have you, but you must master it."

chapter 24 ali

They leave Cupcake Daisy's and continue on *The Adventure*. It is Reece's turn to choose.

As he drives out of the city to his favorite hiking trail, Ali keeps asking, "Where are we going?"

"You'll see."

By habit, she turns on the music in Reece's car. A sweet melody plays. This surprises her. *Heavy Metal or Country, maybe? What a pretty song. Not what I was expecting.*

The song carries on to the chorus and sings about Jesus. It scares Ali to hear *religious* music. *Only freaks and old people listen to this kind of music!*

She hurries to change the song, punches buttons, looks at Reece and says, "What. Was. That?"

"THAT is one of my favorite songs."

"Reeeaal-lee?" Ali drawls. "You surprise me!"

"Huh? Why would that surprise you?"

"How can I know you this long and not know your style of music?"

"We haven't known each other that long. Anyway, you never asked."

"I didn't know you were like that."

"Like what?" Reece feels stereotyped.

"You know what I mean." Ali fumbles for words, growing uncomfortable. "I didn't know you were so religious."

"What do you mean by 'so religious'?"

"Well, you have hymns playing in your car —old lady, church music."

"Old lady music?" Reece is amused. "The band you heard is four guys my age, not old ladies." He taps his fingers on the steering wheel and says, "It's worship music."

"Worship music? Seriously?" Ali wants to believe he is joking. "What do you mean by worship?"

"It's hard to explain without sounding weird." Reece contemplates, "Humph, well..." He tilts his head and squints one eye, thinking. "It's like a deep Love. Love that makes you lose yourself to God. A surrender."

"Huh?" Ali is not sure she wants to talk about this. She feels nervous.

"See, I told you it's hard to explain." Reece strums his fingertips on the bottom edge of the steering wheel. "This might sound strange to you. But it's like craving God and having him pour himself on you."

"O-kay," is all Ali can think of to say. *Yes Reece, you sound weird. Who are you? Who believes this? He definitely isn't ashamed to admit it.*

He waits for Ali to say more. She doesn't. He wonders and asks, "Don't you ever crave God's Love?"

Her face flushes. She doesn't answer. *Crave God? What is that? I want more, that's all. I just want more.*

Dead silence between them grows awkward, so Reece asks, "You okay?"

"I don't know. I'm thinking."

"You're uncomfortable. I can tell."

"It is awkward, that I am finding this out now."

"This is who I am. I don't pretend. You didn't notice. Or ask."

"How was I supposed to know? I was never friends with anyone who takes religion that far." Ali is nervous. She can't think of what to say. "I don't really mean it like that. Um. I just don't get it. I don't know. I am done talking about it."

"I can respect that." Reece says. He nudges her shoulder and they both breathe easier. He pushes the eject button on his stereo. "I'll put away my *scary* music."

He changes genre. "Here's some music I think you'll like."

She knows the song and sings. Reece joins in.

"Where are we going?"
"You'll see."
"Where are we going?"
"You'll see...."

They drive an hour away from the city and take a two-track road to an open area where three other parked cars, equipped with roof top carriers, bike racks and kayaks, similar to Reece's. A fragrant breeze rustles fresh spring leaves that cover the trees. Their faces warm in the sunshine. It seems to be the perfect spring day.

"Where are we?"

"It is your lucky day. I am about to introduce you to your soon to be favorite *go-to* place," Reece boasts.

"Your prediction is right. This will be my favorite. It's amazing!"

"Just wait, we are only getting started." He grabs her hand and pulls her along side. "Let's go!"

They don't hold hands for long. Ali pulls away by pretending to pick up a stick. She really likes Reece, but isn't ready for intimacy. Reece actually wasn't trying to be romantic. He is still trying on their relationship, despite his strong attraction to her. Ali doesn't know him well enough to realize that he is an affectionate person. He never lost the free abandon that children have, how they sit close, hug or lean on each other. If Reece joins a group, he often puts his hand on the shoulder of the person nearby without ever realizing it. He hugs. He holds. He loves.

They walk single file down the worn trail. Ali leads. She drags the stick beside her, drawing lines in the dirt or occasionally tapping a tree trunk. Reece grabs a stick and drags it, taps a tree, puts it on his shoulder, drags it...

Ali turns around, "Are you copying me?" She is leaning the stick on her shoulder.

Reece is leaning a stick on his shoulder.

Ali makes him walk in front for awhile. His pace is faster. It takes effort to keep up, so she appreciates every time they stop. The trail winds along the ridge of a river valley with trails that descend to the river. Water splashes over rocks and logs. Animals sing into the wind, croaks, chirps and clicking noises. Everything seems to echo.

The ground erodes under their feet as they slip down the path to the river. A mature birch tree hovers over the water. Ali decides to climb this birch tree for a better view. She inches her way along the horizontal birch trunk, watching the water below. She travels further out, moving her feet sideways and holding an upper branch.

"Be careful. The branch might break," Reece calls out.

"That's mean! You must think I weigh a ton!"

"No really! Birch trees sometimes rot from the inside. That branch might be hollow."

"It feels fine," assures Ali. To demonstrate, she bounces on the branch, "See, it's sturdy!" Bounce, bounce, bounce.....CRACK!

Ali shrieks. The branch falls in slow motion into the river. She slips off the branch as it hits the water. Her butt lands first, in waist deep water, wet up to her neck. She stands up dripping, laughing hysterically and shivering, waiting in the cold river.

"Aren't you going to dive in and save me?" She chides.

"No way!" I'm not the crazy one!" He folds his hands sarcastically. "I'll stand here and pray for your safety."

Ali pulls each leg against a moderate current, and with effort makes it to shore. Her mules that Reece calls *slippers* are slipping off her feet. She curls her toes tight inside their tips, hoping they stay on. He offers her his hand and lifts her onto the bank.

"Okay, I should have listened," admits Ali. "Probably the mules fault."

"Yes. I am sure it is your stubborn mule's fault. I could tell you wanted to turn back, but your feet wouldn't listen."

Her shirt is soaking wet and sticking to her skin. Reece pretends he is annoyed, "Why are you always needing my shirt?" He pulls his bright yellow sweatshirt over his head, leaving his t-shirt on and hands the jersey to her.

She changes behind some bushes and walks barefoot to a sunny spot. She lays on her back with eyes closed and hands folded behind her head.

Reece stretches out next to her. They rest in silence. Ali's mind replays their day, the clothing store, restaurant, falling in the water. She thinks about Reece, his music, favorite song. *Worship music?*

She regrets the way she acted, judging him, accusing him of taking his faith too far. She pegged religious people as judgmental and fake. Reece is the one giving her space, respect and acceptance. It dawns on her, *I am the one that is judgmental and fake.*

This realization eats at her, until she decides to apologize to Reece. *What should I say? How do I bring it up? Should I wait until later? No, right now. All I can think of are dumb things to say. He won't care if I sound dumb. It's Reece we are talking about. Crap! It wasn't right what I said. I better apologize.* The silence agitates Ali's nerves.

Reece isn't obsessing like Ali. He is resting peacefully, with a slow steady heartbeat. Praying. Ali cannot tell he is talking to God. His eyes are shut and his face is still and relaxed. He doesn't pray to be noticed. He does it to be near to God.

Ali opens her mouth several times to say something and shuts it. Finally, she turns her head and looks at him. She stares at his profile, at the stubble below his nose and chin, his eyelashes are long and thick, they rest over his cheeks. She thinks about mascara, maybe switching brands. *Why do guys have such pretty lashes?* Reece feels her watching him and turns towards her stare. Ali doesn't turn away. She holds her pose, takes a deep breath and exhales slowly.

Reece senses something is up. "What's on your mind? You look like you want to say something."

She looks away. "I feel bad about the way I treated you in the car. I mean, I didn't... Um. I'm sorry I insulted you because of your beliefs." Her words blurt out. She talks to the sky and looks at him after everything is said.

"I am not offended. I hope you're not." Reece pauses. "Sorry it came as a shock. Really, I wasn't trying to hide anything."

In the silence, Reece asks, "What do you believe, Ali?"

Ali stays quiet. I don't know. *Why do I have to believe anything? I'm strong, aren't I? I don't think I even know what Love is. Maybe I don't believe in Love? I feel left out and lonely. Can we stop talking about it? I am scared to go there.*

Because she isn't answering his question, he conveys, "I hope you know, I respect you whether we agree or not."

"You're just scaring me a little. I am afraid to ask questions. Or maybe I don't care about religion. I don't get it. I can handle things. I don't need a crutch." Ali's mouth surprises her. She wasn't going to talk.

"Are you afraid of me?" Reece asks, sincerely. "Or of God?" He stares at Ali's eyes. "What are you afraid of? ...Yourself?"

"Who said I was afraid?" Ali says defensively.

"You did." Reece looks at her, puzzled.

"When? Did I? I guess maybe I did." Ali stews for a bit. "I am a little afraid of you." She blushes and admits, "Because you're my friend, I don't want controversy."

Reece's face is innocent. His eyes stare up at her. He really wants to listen.

Reece, you look like a puppy.

Ali turns over and props up on her elbows. "I might be afraid of God. But more afraid of some other things."

"Like?"

What will people think if I start acting different. What would I tell them? I found Jesus? That's so lame! I don't want to be some dork. I don't want to be weak. I can handle life, can't I? Religion is to control people. It's made up. People can be brainwashed, you know!

Ali looks directly at Reece and confesses, "I'm afraid of what I'll turn into if I get religious. I'll lose my friends. My family will think I went off the deep end." She finally admits it. Words just spill out of her mouth. Finally, she dares to say it out loud.

"You might turn into a monkey or a frog," Reece jokes.

Ali gives him a teasing punch. Reece grabs hold of her wrist and holds it. She wrestles away from him, feeling warm and strangely happy. Their faces are close. The edges of their bodies are touching. They look at each other, awkwardly. It is the perfect moment for a kiss. The tension of passion is powerful. They both want to move towards each other. Somehow, Ali cuts through the lust and sits forward on the ground. She digs at the soil by her feet.

Reece pulls himself forward and wraps his arms around his open knees. He says, "You will turn into yourself."

Ali doesn't respond.

"You will feel held. Protected. And loved deeper than you could ever imagine."

He moves Ali's hair off her eyes and tucks it behind her ear. He wants to see her face better. His tenderness is killing her. She feels chills down her back. *I don't get how you can feel love from something out there. It seems made up. Like a fairytale. Look at you, Reece, you really believe all this —and so innocently, yet intelligently.*

"I can see why God loves you. But I am not like you."

"Like me?"

"Yeah. Loveable."

"You don't have to be cute and cuddly like me for God to love you. He's not shallow."

Ali giggles. She takes a deep breath, exhales fast and says, "He's probably mad at me anyway, with all the crap I've done."

"Really? You're that awful?" While he says this, he puts a handful of dirt on her foot.

"Hey!" Ali wipes the dirt off. "Religious people I know are so weird. They stand along the road holding dumb signs. They guilt old ladies into sending them money. One time I was at the carnival and there was this man standing on a chair wearing a burlap dress shouting, 'repent, repent'. What is that supposed to mean? It is just plain creepy. I don't want to be like that. I don't want to knock on people's doors carrying a bible. And I don't want to act like I am better than everyone else."

Reece hears what she is saying. He hates that too. "Do you think God is out to get you? That He wants to make a spectacle of you?"

"No, I was exaggerating. I am turned off by the way Christians act. They are so judgmental and they think everyone has to believe what they do."

"I am a Christian and I don't think you have to believe what I do." *But I wish you knew how huge God's love is. Huge beyond words.* He doesn't say the rest. She doesn't want to hear.

"Well, you don't count. You're too perfect."

"I'm not perfect. Far from it. I screw-up... A lot. I really need God. Sometimes it's hard to do the right thing. I want to be better. It's like wanting to please your dad. —Sort of a spiritual motivation. I get selfish. My thinking gets dirty." Reece pulls at his shoe laces and re-ties it. "God's always working on me... I wonder what He's going to turn me into?"

Ali frowns. *Wanting to please your dad? You're lucky you have one.*

Reece shifts. He's ready to get up. "I apologize. I don't mean to be a bad example. Look at God, not at me."

"You don't need to apologize to me," Ali affirms. "Yet."

They get up from the ground and stretch.

Reece asks, "Are you ready to head back?"

"I guess so."

They are almost back to the car. Ali walks slow, stepping over tree roots, branches and rocks. "Your turn. What will we do next?"

"I've been thinking about that. I'll tell you when we get to the car."

"Nice jeans. Especially the muddy spot."

"Wet jeans. I can't wait to change them. They're itchy."

"Good thing you have your other pair, because you are not getting my pants too."

"I won't fit into your pants."

"Please don't go there again. Remember your new motto?"

"I will not be defined by what size jeans I wear!" Ali shouts.

"That's better."

Reece unlocks the car for Ali and leaves to give her privacy. When he returns, she is hiding. Her pants and shirt are arranged on the window shield and car hood, imitating a person standing with one knee bent, hand waving.

Reece pretends it's her, "Hello Ali. Would you like to stay on the car to dry off?" He sees the real Ali peeking out from behind a truck. He gets in the car, starts it and begins to drive away.

Ali runs out yelling, "Wait! Wait!"

Reece rolls down his window. "May I help you?"

"Come on. Let me in."

"Ya needa ride ma-am?" Reece presses the brakes and stops the car. "Okay. Git yee-self in da car." He says in a foreign voice.

"Thank you, sir."

"So, where you be goin'? You seem lost, ma-am. Dis ol' car kin take yous anywheres. Jist says da word."

They drive away with the flat person plastered to the window shield. The wind begins to blow it's arm, making it look like it's waving. The legs lift and dance. Ali turns on the radio to add music. The pretend person moves with the beat. Eventually, the shirt blows over the car with the pants attached. The clothing lands on the ground in an ironic position, like a wounded person. They stop to gather the clothes.

"Wow, this looks like a crime scene." Reece observes, standing like an investigator over *Old-Ali*.

"Ewe. It does."

With a stick, Reece traces the outline of the body in dirt.

"Reece! I can't believe you're doing that!"

After abandoning the crime scene, Ali announces, "I know where to go next. Stop at the nearest store. Instructions will follow."

Reece smirks as he purposely passes a store and she doesn't notice. Instead, he takes her to the convenience store where his best friend, Jeff, works.

"We're here. Now what?"

Ali recites her instructions. "First, you go in and buy something to surprise me while I wait. I will go next. Don't show me what you bought until we both have our goodies. Okay? Got that?" Ali nudges Reece, thinking he's not paying attention. "Well, do ya?"

"Eye-yi, Captain." He says and fakes a huge smile. One of his front teeth appears missing, covered with a chocolate candy piece he found on his dash. "Eye-yi-yi...

"Reece!" Ali crosses her knees and doubles over in laughter. She snorts.

"Yi-yi-yeeya! What? What's so funny?" His grin enlarges as he tilts his head like a confused puppy.

"Stop!" She snorts again.

"Okay." He licks the candy off his front tooth, salutes Ali, then leaves her in the car to do his shopping.

Reece rushes by Jeff, who is behind the counter doing paperwork, heads straight to the frozen drink machine, fills a medium size glass and waits to pay.

It surprises Jeff to see a familiar face. "Reece! Hey! What's up?"

"Hey! Make it quick."

"Whoa. Why the hurry?"

"I'll tell ya in a sec. Be right back."

Reece hurries to the car and knocks on Ali's window.

"Hey! You weren't supposed to let me see that!" She says when he hands the cold drink to her. "You were supposed to wait."

"I thought you might be thirsty. I'm not done yet." He knew it. She thought he didn't follow directions.

"Oh. Sorry. Thanks."

Reece rushes back into the store. Jeff shakes his head and asks, "Back Already? What's the hurry? Is this about a woman?"

"Ya-gotta help me! Ali is waiting in the car for a surprise."

"Oh! It really is about a lady. Sly-Meister."

Reece tells Jeff a guy-length summary of what they have been doing all day and explains why he has to buy her something.

"So what are you going to give her?"

"I don't know! That is why I need your help." Reece is picking up a gadget from a box on the counter. He pushes a button and a small fan spins and blows an impressive amount of air at his face.

"Wow. This actually works." He picks up another.

"Not that!" Jeff persuades, "Come on, let's look around."

Jeff goes to a small rack of t-shirts and pushes them apart to read slogans, mostly crude humor. He holds up a pink shirt with a big green frog on the front.

"How about this one?" Jeff reads it to Reece. "Disappointed by the prince.... Want FROG."

"Rrribb-it," Reece mocks and keeps looking.

"Well? How about it?"

"We're not ready for that shirt."

"How 'bout a doll?" Jeff holds up a plastic baby with a grownup face.

"That's creepy looking."

"A fake rose?"

"Super cheesy!"

"Paddle toy?" Jeff holds up a wooden paddle with a string and red ball attached. "You could buy this and have a contest."

"No. Maybe Ali will buy that for me." Reece picks up the paddle and bounces the red ball. Jeff takes another paddle and attempts to out-bounce Reece.

This gives Reece an idea. "Hey Jeff, let's play a trick on Ali. When she comes in, talk her into buying this paddle toy."

"Yeah! I'll do that."

Reece wastes time in the kitchen gadget aisle. He tries out a cheap calculator. *Sewing kit? Tape measure?* He pulls the metal strip out and lets it retract. *I could use one of these.* When he puts it back on the hook, he spots the perfect present for Ali.

"I got it!" Reece holds it up for Jeff to see.

"Scissors? You sound serious."

"I am."

"Why scissors?"

"Private joke."

"Scissors. Humph." Jeff doesn't pry.

At the cash register, Reece puts the scissors on the counter. "Wait a minute. I forgot something."

He leaves and comes back with a card and envelope. "Can I borrow a pen?"

Reece writes in the card. Before sealing it shut, he reaches into his pocket for two silk clothing tags, cut from a garment. Size ten.

Jeff puts the scissors into a brown paper bag, folds the top neatly and staples it. "Can I have the card?" He tapes it to the bag for Reece. "Good luck, Bud."

Squirrels play and people pass. Ali watches and sips the drink Reece bought her. She notices the keys are left in the ignition and decides to listen to some music while waiting. She spies out her window to see if he is coming before putting the CD from earlier back into the player. She is curious and snoopy.

Ali listens carefully to the words that sing, "Help me Jesus... I am shaking like a leaf... won't you be my Prince of Peace..." She feels somehow left out, wants to be left out, fears what it takes to belong. *I don't want to believe this nonsense. This is a barrier. I am not sure I can get past this. We are so different.* An unexplained loneliness floods her. She feels like her back is turned to God —the God she doesn't believe in. Ali tries to justify why there can't possibly be one god. *So many people are devoted to different religions. They really are all the same. It's cultural, right? It's arrogant to think only you know the truth. Why can't I choose what works for me? We pick our heaven. Don't we? When we die, do we even remember we were alive?*

She senses someone approaching and looks out the car window. Reece is coming! Ali pushes the radio button to hide her intrusion.

Reece slides into his seat. "Sorry I took so long. Your turn. It was harder than I thought."

"Wait here. Be good and I'll bring you a surprise." Ali imitates her mother.

He watches Ali as she approaches the entry doors. *I bet she'll try to open the broken door.* She tugs three times on the door before she sees the sign, 'Please use other door'.

She is so cute and doesn't know it.

Inside, Ali walks past the tall man with curly dark hair, who is standing behind the counter. Right away, she blushes from how handsome he is and guesses he is her age. *Maybe older?* His black glasses make him look smart and artistic.

She blushes more when he smiles at her. "Hello. Let me know if you need help finding something."

Ali recites the cliché, "Thanks, I'm just looking."

She searches the back of the store, feeling shy. Jeff watches without her knowing. He suppresses a laugh when she picks up the wooden paddles. *This is going to be too easy.*

He walks up to her and says, "I think you need some help. Are you looking for the perfect gift?" almost ruining the scheme.

Ali thinks he's flirting, "Good guess. Actually, I am."

"Our store offers a variety of 'convenient' choices," he lectures like an infomercial.

"What exactly do you suggest, sir?" Ali blushes through her flirt.

"Tell me about the person this is for. How old?"

"About your age."

"Male or Female?"

"Male."

"Hobbies? Interests?"

"He's kinda outdoorsy. I guess. He might like hiking."

Might? Reece loves hiking. Kinda outdoorsy? Kinda? She's gotta know him better than this.

"Boyfriend?" Jeff pries. *How much does she like Reece?*

"Well..." Ali is slow to respond. She doesn't want to put herself in a relationship when there's a super cute guy in front of her.

"Is he competitive?" Jeff knows the answer to that.

"Probably..."

Probably? Funny. How about very. "How about these wood paddles? You can have a contest."

"Yes! That's what I was thinking."

"Excellent choice! Would you like them gift wrapped?" Jeff says proudly. He actually got her to buy them. *Too easy.* He's having fun playing this joke on Ali. *She's cute. I can see why Reece likes her so much.*

"Really? You gift-wrap?"

"For special occasions." He realizes she's taking him seriously. "We have free wrapping for customers that buy wooden paddles today. Tomorrow it will be beans."

"Whatever." Ali catches on.

While Jeff wraps it with newspaper comics, Ali looks at key chains hanging on a rotating display. She shines the flat silver metal with her sleeve. It's shaped like a cross with the words "Matthew 7:7" engraved on it. She wishes she bought this for Reece instead. She doesn't dare change her mind, because the gorgeous guy is almost done wrapping the paddles. He even taped two chocolate kisses on top of the package.

"I want to buy this too." She pushes the keychain across the counter.

Jeff looks at it. "He'll like this." *Oops! I slipped. Hopefully she didn't catch that.*

She doesn't make the connection. She's too busy wondering if she should give it to Reece. She decides as she approaches the car and pushes the keychain into her pocket. *I'm keeping it.*

Ali hops in the car. Reece is listening to the CD she snooped to hear. He sees the wrapped package. "So fancy. Is that for me?"

"You know it is! Should we open them now, or wait 'til later?"

"You decide. Your idea."

"Okay. Later. Where to next?"

"Food. I'm starving."

They drive past farms and orchards along hilly roads to a village of barns that silhouette a hilltop. Neat rows of flowers line the brick walkway in front of a gingerbread style shed. Reece leads Ali through an iron gate and past the shed, to an apple-green barn with white french doors. Ali feels like she is walking through a storybook.

The wooden plank floor creaks beneath their feet, while they shop displays of cakes, pies and pastries. Ali craves everything she sees. *I must be really hungry.*

"Reece, I love it here! I am glad you thought of this."

"I've been coming here since I was a kid, with my parents. Back then, it was only a fruit stand."

"Why didn't I know about this?"

Ali sees other people carrying around baskets, made of thick reeds, with heavy wood handles. She finds a stack of similar baskets by the door and takes one for her and Reece to share.

Reece holds up a fruit drink with flowers floating in it. "I wonder how you drink this without choking?"

"The flowers look plastic." She holds the bottle close to her face and jiggles it. Another bottle has a floating alphabet. "Kinda cool, though." She puts it into the basket and picks out another one with butterflies drifting in blue juice.

While they are paying, a voice crackles over the speakers, "Norm-Ali, your table is ready, Norm-Ali..."

"Reece! ...Ahem.... Norm, I can't believe you told them that's your name!"

The casual dining area is separate. Reece and Ali are seated in ladder back chairs, painted red. The room smells like cinnamon apples and baking bread. The atmosphere infects them, centering life in the moment. There is no dreaming of the past or wondering of the future. They are living this day.

After devouring their meals, Reece wants to split a dessert with Ali. "I *Norm-ali* eat desert. I love everything on the menu."

"How about hot apple pie, Norm? A la mode for sure! Don't-cha think, Norm?"

The waiter returns with a fancy dish of pie and caramel ice-cream. One spoon flags the top of the ice cream, near a tiny sugar coated crabapple.

Ali tells the waiter as he is leaving, "We'll need another spoon, please."

Reece scoops up some ice-cream and holds it out for Ali to eat. She hesitates.

"Go ahead. Take this. I can wait for my spoon to get here," he remarks, wondering if germs bother her.

When his spoon arrives, Reece finishes off the pie. They are stuffed. Usually, Ali would be anxious about calories, but not today, not with Reece. He brings new life to her.

Reece reaches for the bill, but Ali grabs it from him and argues over it, "It's my turn to pay, Reece. You even said so."

"I was joking!"

"We are splitting it then."

"Okay." Reece is reluctant. He was only kidding at lunch and feels uncomfortable letting her pay for this expensive meal. He wants to treat her special.

"Let's take a walk," Reece suggests as they leave. "There is a path behind the big barn. We can walk down to the fishing pond"

"Are we allowed by the pond?" Ali worries.

"It's all open to the public."

"But I didn't bring my fishin' pole," Ali says, trying to be funny, but only confuses Reece. *Stupid me. That was such a dumb thing to say. Why do I even try to be funny? I never am.* Ali wants to be witty to impress Reece. She wishes she had more charm like other girls, the pretty ones that always have boyfriends.

Why am I trying so hard? Why am I nervous? Am I falling? Reece is standing with his hands in his pockets, looking away. *I have been flirting with him all day. What if he thinks I like him? Do I like him?* Ali watches him wave at a couple holding hands. *Mr. Friendly. He's too nice for me. Why would he want me? I'm acting like a seventh grader. Grow up!*

He interrupts her thoughts and says, "Let's go to the car. I want to get something."

Reece carries the presents they bought to a pavilion that overlooks the pond. "Let's sit over there, on the dock," he suggests.

They dangle their feet over the water, while sitting at the edge of a wooden dock. Bugs chirp in unison, with an occasional gulp from frogs. Reece remembers the shirt in the store, about the princess wanting a frog. He chuckles.

"What's so funny?" Ali wants to know.

"Nothing. I thought of something, that's all."

"What?"

"Nothing. Are you ready to open your present?" He changes the subject and hands her the bag.

"No. You first."

Reece picks up the package that was wrapped in colorful newspaper comics. He pulls both chocolate kisses off, holds one and puts the other into his pocket without her seeing.

He holds up the kiss and challenges her. "I bet you a kiss that I can guess what's in this package."

"You're on. You'll never guess."

Reece contemplates losing the bet. *Girl, you aren't the one holding the chocolate kiss. Ya-lose, you'll be kissin' me.*

"You can't feel through the paper, either." She takes the package away from him until he guesses.

"Well, aren't we grabby," Reece says playfully. He pretends to have difficulty guessing. "Hmm. Let's see, too big to be a can opener, umm, my guess is..." He quickly and confidently spills out, "Two wooden paddles with red balls!"

"What! How did you know that? Were you spying on me? And how did you know there were two?"

"Nope. Didn't spy."

"Something is up.... What is it? Reece? You're hiding something..." Ali says like a twelve year old, and feels like one.

"My best friend Jeff works at that store."

"Huh?" Ali instantly blushes. *That cute guy is Reece's best friend?*

"Jeff. He's the person who helped you pick these out." Reece holds up the wrapped packages. "Before I came out to the car, I told him you were coming in to buy me something. We thought it would be funny if he talked you into buying these paddles."

Reece roars, thinking he's so funny. "It worked. You actually bought them, didn't you?" He pushes on her knee and says, "Where's my kiss?"

"Oh. Not fair!" She hands the gift back. "Paybacks!" She threatens. "No kisses for cheaters."

Reece hands her the chocolate kiss anyway, "Here's my apology."

"Ready for the contest?" Ali asks.

"Not yet. Here, open this first." Reece gives her a bag with a card taped on it.

"Did your friend wrap this too? Sorry I didn't get you a card."

Two tags fall out. "My size 10!" She looks at Reece in surprise. "You saved them?"

It feels strangely intimate to see his handwriting in a card for her. She blushes reading his note:

Chop-Chop! To all tags that lie and say you are not beautiful!

Love, Reece

Matthew 7:7

Ali is aware of the lump in her pocket, the keychain she bought him. She still doesn't dare to give it to him. And she doesn't say anything about the coincidence of matching verses. *I wonder what that verse means. I don't have a Bible. I'm not going to ask either, because I don't want to talk about it.*

Ali opens the bag and pulls out scissors, depicting their meaning immediately.

"This is so sweet. Thank you, Reece." *He pays attention to everything about me.* Ali wants to tell him how he makes her feel, but hesitates. *I am not used to being treated like this. You scare me. I don't want to like you that way.*

Reece slides his arm across her back and gives her a gentle squeeze. She rests her head on his shoulder. They listen to insects and frogs croaking. *I wonder if she needs a frog? Lord, thanks for this. Thanks for the whole day... I am not ready for it to end.*

After a while, Ali stands, "Brr, I am getting cold. Let's drive towards town. Do something else."

The country highway winds around hills. Reece drives cautiously, with head lights on. He scans the road's edges for deer. Ali is oblivious and chatty.

"Hey!" She shouts suddenly. "Turn around."

Reece's foot reacts fast on the breaks, tightening seat belts across their chests. "You scared me. I thought you saw an animal on the road."

"Sorry. I know where we can go."

Near a steel building, Ali announces, "Right there." pointing at a backlit plastic sign on a rusted pole.

"Bowling?" I bet she thinks religious people like to bowl.

"Yeah bowling. You can teach me how."

The entrance doors unlock stale smoky air across their faces. The rhythm of balls rolling and wood pins clinking makes Ali's idea seem exciting. They rent typical clown shoes, search for bowling balls and find their lane.

Reece puts *'Ali-Cat'* and *'Reece's Pieces'* for their names on the score sheet. She picks up her ball, holds it like a professional and stares at the front center pin. Her concentration and stance fool Reece. She swings the ball back, rushes forward in tiny steps, then trips. The ball falls from her hand. It bounces twice and drops into the gutter. She rushes back and sits next to him. They laugh so hard, they need to stay seated.

Reece composes himself to say, "You have to go again."

"Why? Because it was so bad?"

"No. We're supposed to go twice."

She repeats the same score. Reece's turn. He throws his first ball and knocks down three pins and throws a gutter ball the second time.

"We have something in common, Ali-Cat. We're both expert bowlers!"

Their game improves after they take a restroom break and Reece has the gutter guards put up. Like actors, Ali and Reece overstress perfect form and invent ways to roll the ball down the lane. Eyes closed. Strike! Throwing left handed. Strike! Between the legs. Strike!

The cool night air is a relief to their warm bodies as they walk to the car holding hands in the hush of late night. This day is now history.

"Race you to the car, Ali-Cat!"

That's when they notice, they are still wearing clown shoes.

Ali lays awake reflecting on her day spent with Reece. Her happiness seems endless, until she finally falls asleep. In the deepest part of her rest, everything changes. A dark cloud suffocates her with a dreadful nightmare, one that she will never recall.

This nightmare leaves a residue of anger the next morning:

She is asleep on her back with her hands folded as if in a casket. Hovering over her bed, a battle is fought in the skirts of Ali's conscience. Creatures are fighting above her life. Evil is nesting in timeless space. The darkness is real. The shadows that surround her are alluring. They whisper lies into Ali's future. Her dream tells her, *You don't have to choose anything. Pick the one you want. Hide here, where it is safe.* Evil is offering promises. It is a trap. Something is crouching behind her closed door. It wants to devour her soul. She cannot see the creature, because there is a veil of smoke in her eyes.

A bright sword slashes and says, "Step into the light! Wash darkness away!"

Ali sees a slimy shadow, cringing low, watchful eyes glowing yellow. *Am I awake?* These yellow eyes shut and disappear to blend with the darkness of the creature's body. She isn't afraid of this monster, because she believes it's her friend. He looks vaguely familiar. Her eyes are still cloudy with smoke, the breath of demons. Demonic smoke cannot be seen at night.

Zap! In her dream Ali turns on the TV. Her demon-friend is on the TV screen. He tells her, *"Anything you desire! It is yours! Fame, riches, power, knowledge, attention, happiness, pleasure."* He is tap dancing. Everyone is watching him. *"You can't please anyone... Just please yourself..."*

Zap! Ali sits in a black leather chair. The surrounding room is gray and vast. A faceless creature approaches and hands Ali a catalog.

"Choose," the creature whispers. "Everything you need is right here."

Ali flips through pages to design her life and her appearance. She fills out the order form and hands it to the creature.

The shadow looks over her choices and says, *"This is good. It's always good."*

Zap! Ali is waiting in a gray line of endless people. *"Next!"*

It is my turn already?

A beautiful woman gently scratches her red fingernails across Ali's cheek and says, *"My name is Desire."*

Desire hands Ali a basket, woven of the finest gold, riddled with precious gems.

Her voice echoes, *"Fill this basket. Everything is yours. Go ahead, put it in."*

Queen Desire helps Ali get started by stuffing food into the basket. Ali picks out shoes and throws them in, expensive clothes, money, more food, cosmetics, gadgets, hats, jewelry, gorgeous men. Ali laughs and puts in a handful of video games.

"These are for Brandon."

"No! This is your basket!" The Queen throws the games out.

Ali is weary. It's exhausting to acquire all the things she wants. She's afraid that if she doesn't put them in now, she will never get them.

She asks the Queen, "How do I put *skinny* in there? How about *pretty*? Or looking *young*? Will *forever* fit in there?"

"Anything you Desire. Look inside, there's room for more," the Queen says, wearing a half-smile.

Ali looks into the glimmering basket. It is bottomless! A black hole swirling to nowhere. An endless flush. Before she can run away, the Queen forces Ali to carry her desires.

This basket is so heavy, a burden more than she can bear.

It weighs so much more than contentment!

She is alone in her dream now. A hot light shines from the basket and pierces her eyes. In this new light, she can see the basket she is holding. It is alive and moves in her hands —a basket woven of snakes! Snakes with eyes that glow like gems! The light, that burns her eyes, is coming from inside the basket. It cremates everything she put inside —all her desires. Consumed.

Ali remains paralyzed.

The basket is calling her in next.

Help me, Jesus. I cannot drop this basket!

Matthew 11:28-30 (NIV)
[28] "Come to me, all you who are weary and burdened, and I will give you rest.
[29] Take my yoke upon you and learn from me, for I am gentle and humble in heart, and you will find rest for your souls.
[30] For my yoke is easy and my burden is light."

chapter 25 ali

Saturday with Reece was a riot! Buy nothing ever lasts. Why do I feel like crap in a few short hours? Ali woke up Sunday, haunted. She managed to drag herself through the day with her favorite companion —Food. She really believed she was renewed. She felt changed after spending the entire day with Reece. Except, Ali was back to her old habits the minute she got out of bed. She ate like a mad cow all day long. Her cravings were a bottomless pit.

Today, Monday, is ever worse. It is still morning and everything is going wrong and compiling. Ali crushes Brandon with her attitude while driving him to school, something she does not want to do! Now she will be late for class. *Of course mom couldn't possibly be late for work and her important meeting!* The air in the car fills with poison vapors of anger. Brandon is in the backseat yelling and blaming her for missing his bus. Ali rolls down the window, freezing tears onto her brother's face, an attempt to drown out the noise. Brandon bounces the back of the driver's seat with his feet to annoy his sister. She is trying hard not to explode. With anger lingering on the fringes, Ali poses calm and collected behind the steering wheel. After a few more jolts from her brother's feet, Ali rolls another window down. She locks the controls so the passenger in the backseat can't put his window up again. Brandon kicks harder. Another window rolls down. He calls her a bad word. The last window is down, blowing cold gusts that roar louder than the two siblings.

"I hate you!" Brandon screams into the wind. "You hid my video game!

I know you did it! It's your fault I'm late for school!"

"Give it up! I didn't hide anything!"

"Roll up the windows!"

"No!"

"I'm telling my Dad!"

"Tell him! He probably hid your game." *Your dumb Dad.* "He said to get a life!"

"Roll 'em up! Ali, please." More tears roll down his cheeks. "It's really cold," he whines. "Please Ali."

Eventually, Ali rolls up the windows, after ignoring him long enough to make it seem like her idea. She feels bad for making him cry, but doesn't say so. Anger trumps compassion. She drops him off farther away than necessary. Brandon thinks she is doing it to be mean. Ali does it so that his friends can't see he was crying. She wants to give him time to compose himself. As he walks away, she regrets rolling down the windows; not because it was a malicious thing to do, but because it messed up her hair.

Ali is barely late for class. Instead of rushing into the classroom, she walks past the door and around the corner to the restroom. She worries about how she looks, how she looks to others. Fluorescent fixtures, above the mirror, spotlight every flaw and cast unattractive shadows under her eyes. These lights flatten her face and double her chin. Ali hates the creature staring back at her. It's hair is flat and knotted. It's face has two new pimples. Ali squeezes the creature's belly like she is fluffing a pillow. She leans in closer to trace her fingertip across the puffiness beneath each eye, swollen from lack of sleep. She lifts up her shirt to confirm her obesity and despises how deep her bellybutton sinks into the flab. Yesterday, she ate way too much and now it shows. The clothes she selected to wear widen her mid-section. Ali fears that her muffin-top belly will spill over when she sits down and someone will notice. She surrenders her power to the creature in the mirror, the one that says she is worthless, fat and ugly.

"Hide until you are beautiful," it mocks.

She exits the restroom and makes a choice, which seems to be inconsequential. But when adding up several similar choices in a short span of time, the consequences are life changing from missed opportunities.

The very next door Ali opens is not the classroom door, but her car door. In the bucket seat, she can slouch down and let her belly spill. Nobody is here to judge her bad habits. This is where she joins the debate in her mind. (Topic: Should Ali go to class ugly, or wait until she is pretty?) Her disposition plummets to depression. She persists in self debate. *Go back to class? No, I can't. I'm late. I feel like a fat slob. I can't miss anymore classes. I better go. No!* She vacillates too long. The debate is over. Ali's next class already started. The decision is final. *Who cares if I miss all my classes today!* Ali starts her car and drives to Cupcake Daisy's to purchase over-the-counter-medication for her food addiction.

Six pretty cupcakes are boxed to go and carried out with a quart of chocolate milk. Maybe Ali will stop eating after two cupcakes? It's possible if she doesn't flood her head with lies. Maybe she already plans on eating all six. Greedy defeat.

Crumbs and crimped wrappers, printed with daisies, remain. Ali cannot figure out what drives her to this self-destruction. This heavy dose of medication isn't working. The only thing that matters is More! More! More! Ali drives to a gas station to buy candy bars, then to a fast food restaurant for grease and salt.

After all this effort, she still remembers her defects, is still angry, and still loathes herself. This is how she punishes and soothes. More! More! More! When her self abuse is over, Ali empties her hatred, anger, loathing and comfort into a plastic grocery bag. She ties the handles together and deposits the sloshing madness into a public trash can. Her chin and hands smell sour.

She has to be at work in an hour. *Pull it together, Ali.* At a nearby playground, she conceals herself in the car. She is deep in her sickness. *Wake up Ali! Don't let a reflection in the mirror have the power to steal a day from your life!* Her self-image lays her in a coffin, shaped like a blue Honda Civic, while the life she could have moves past her.

Ali wonders how far down she can sink. She considers Reece and envies his approach to life. He doesn't worry about what other people think. He is so humble. She wonders what makes him have such confidence and assurance in God? She wants him here, with her right now. This surprises her. She will slink away and hide from everyone else. Ali's spirits lift when she thinks of Reece. She breaks out of her cocoon, only to find she is still a caterpillar, slow moving and unable to fly. The clock on the dashboard reminds Ali about work responsibilities. Skipping school is easier than missing work. Fear of losing a job helps her make a better choice this time. Ali knows she must at least pretend at life, the life that exists outside her blue Honda grave.

Ali moves robotic. Her arm lifts a card to punch in. Her mules clomp to the front of the store, not acknowledging. Head down, she keeps her eyes on waxed vinyl tiles. She pins a nametag to her laundered smock and pushes through the service counter gate. It clicks behind her.

In a row are three grocery carts, filled with customer returns, ready to organize and re-shelf. Ali sorts the contents of the carts, brushing past Millie often, in the confines of their designated workspace. Gum does not mask the sour stink that trails Ali. She believes it does. She cannot smell it, only because she is desensitized, others are not.

This makes Millie wonder and ask, "Are you feeling okay today?" Her magnified eyes, framed with big plastic glasses, blink at Ali's back.

"I'm alright." Ali responds, her back to Millie.

Millie vacillates, both hands clench in the front pockets of her smock. She is ready to say something, but is interrupted by a customer holding an item to return. Ali seizes opportunity and hurries out the gate, pushing an overflowing cart. She shops in reverse, placing the items back on shelves. She lingers in aisles and keeps her back turned, looking busy when others approach. Intentional body language is effective. Everyone leaves her alone —and lonely.

Ali has a returned heating pad to re-shelf. In the pharmaceutical isle, she immediately recognizes a girl, squatting and engrossed, reading labels of herb supplements, unaware of Ali's presence. Silky hair, cut in a perfect line, slices the girl's lower back. Hair drapes over her shoulder and shields the profile of Mideah's face. Ali doesn't need to see this girl's face to know who is behind the curtain of bleach-blond hair. She's the mean girl from the coffee shop. The girl Ali envied, burning in jealousy of everything surface level —her extreme beauty. Ali remembers how she stared at this girl and her friend, discretely, as she ordered her muffin and slipped into the only booth available, the booth next to Mideah and Gina, the day she got the horrid bloody nose, the day she met Reece.

Ali doesn't know her name, and never will, but will always remember her face. In spite of everything, she hungers for the beauty Mideah exudes. Jealousy soaks Ali and turns her envy-green in the pharmaceutical isle. She remembers the humiliation in the coffee shop, the mean, judgmental words spoken by this girl and her pretty friend. Un-forgiveness erupts Ali's heart and motivates revenge. The shelf next to Ali has just what she needs to vindicate. Ali sneaks a box of vaginal cream for yeast infections, the generic one with the purposed words written in bold across the sides. She puts this vaginal cream into Mideah's cart in plain view, on top of the eggs sitting in the child's seat. She hurries out of the isle, before the squatting girl catches her.

Revenge isn't meant to satisfy, yet it gives Ali her first smile of this long, disposable day. More smiles curve her face when she empties the second cart of customer returns and witnesses Mideah talking to a handsome, wishful, flirt. Mideah pushes her cart down another isle and runs into a handsome older man, who sheepishly charms her. She sees the man's eyes divert to the vaginal cream in Mideah's cart several times during their conversation. Like a flip of a switch, Ali's mood changes from amusement to obsessive coveting. *That witch has every man under a spell! Sleaze! How many men do you need?* Ali finds ways to deride herself, after she finishes judging Mideah. She spirals down a path of self-condemnation. *It's harder for girls like me to get a date. Who wants to be with someone fat, ugly and dumb? Short legs, big feet, fat thighs, thin hair, pimples, cellulite. I don't know how to flirt. I get too nervous. I say dumb things.* She focuses her anger back on Mideah. For Ali, it is easier to blame others than change herself. *I saved her the trouble of searching for genital cream. She probably needs it! I bet she gives all her men herpes. You blond-haired disease-girl!*

Co-worker Millie is happy, humming an old hymn, bent down and neck deep in the lower cabinet reaching for something. The gate smacks Ali's bottom as she storms into the service area and rushes to the register. A line is forming in the black ribbon maze that organizes customers. Eager people wait for their turn, staring with blank faces.

She isn't surprised that Millie is unaware of this long line of customers. Millie gets distracted easily. Ali is annoyed and loses patience with her co-worker's timid, naive demeanor. She often observes others treating Millie with disrespect, and takes her shot.

"I could use some help here!" Ali snaps, then regrets it when Millie bumps her head on the cabinet trying to stand up.

Millie looks at Ali with sad eyes and a smile, simultaneously. "Of course, sweetheart." She rubs the gray curls on the back of her head, confused at Ali's uncharacteristic behavior.

"Next." recites Ali, in unfriendly monotone.

A rotund woman waddles up to the counter holding out a twenty dollar bill, "Gimmee ten, two dalla scray-atch-offs lot-tree teekits."

Ali takes the money from the woman's hand without speaking. She scrutinizes the woman, head to toe. Unfair stereotypical thoughts judge the woman's eating habits, education or lack of, and her financial situation. She unrolls ten lottery tickets off two different spools and hands them to the woman.

"Next," Ali honks in the same monotone, the voice that stays with her the rest of the work day. Millie is quiet and keeps her distance.

That evening, Ali parks in front of the garage and blocks her father's car inside. She knows it will be in his way when he leaves for work in the morning. The house is vacant and dark. Ali leans on the open refrigerator door and stares at the jumble of containers and packages stuffing every inch. She pours from a new carton of milk and leaves the gallon jug on the counter. Across the room, she spots the note her mother left leaning against the toaster:

Ali,
We are at Brandon's soccer game, going to Jack's house after.
p.s. Clean the kitchen!

Her family ate without her and left the remains scattered across the table, along with their plates, silverware and glasses. Food is piled on all the plates as if each person took one bite, then went for a walk in the woods; the three bears, Mama, Papa and Baby-bear, all waiting for the casserole to cool. When the Bears return, they will find Ali, an intruder, asleep in their bed.

She scrapes the wasted food into the trash with a vengeance. When she loads the dishwasher, grime is still on everything. She hopes her mother has to pick hardened food off clean dishes after the wash cycle. *Who cares! Why do I have to do everything?* She wipes off the table and lets crumbs spill onto the floor instead of catching them in her hand. Dirty water is left in the sink, with the glass casserole pan submerged, leftovers soaking. Egg noodles and peas break apart and float to the top of chunky, gray water that smells like tuna. The stove is left for someone else to clean, so is the exploded food, spattered and curled over the interior walls of the microwave. *This is not my mess!* She sees the gallon of milk on the counter and purposely leaves it out to spoil.

In the basement, Ali detects that her brother found his video game. *Precious Brandon! Daddy's favorite!* She picks it up and hides it, again, before stepping on the treadmill, alternating between walking and running, for two hours. Abdominal crunches and stretches follow. When she is finished burning calories, her mood is elevated. She is content.

Her happy mood continues the next morning. Before she walks out the door with her traditional mug of coffee, she leans Brandon's video game against the toaster, in the same fashion her mother leaves notes. She feels a pang of guilt seeing her car parked in the turn-a-round, where her stepdad moved it early this morning. She is last to leave the house.

Ali hasn't seen much of her family lately and denies it bothers her. She doesn't really live in their house. She resides inside the lonely bubble she emotionally entered two years ago, when food and vanity became more important than living with a family that continues to disappoint.

In Trigonometry class, a chubby girl is flirting with the boy next to her. The handsome boy appears calm. Below the desk, his knee bounces nervously. The chubby girl, with a plain face, keeps whispering to him with her hand cupped over her mouth. He can't ignore chubby girl any longer. He squints his eyes and sneers at her. The girl understands his signal and sags into her chair. Ali feels sorry for the girl. *Why is it so easy to be mean to ugly people? Not fair! You're a jerk, pretty boy.*

The professor holds a marker and pokes dots onto the white-board over his writing. He reviews past assignments to prepare students for an exam. Ali is bored. Her mind wanders. She thinks about how mean she was to Brandon, Millie and pretty much everyone she came in contact with yesterday. She replays her bad behavior and feels remorseful. Three days of bad moods. It's time to change the attitude. She opens her spiral binder to an arbitrary place and journals:

How many of my arrogant moments will people endure?

"My annoying factor must be pretty high," she whispers to herself, looking at the lined notebook page.

When the boy next to her glances, Ali leans low onto her desk. She wraps her left arm around the notebook and secretly scribbles the title: *ARE YOU ANNOYING?*

Beneath the title, she makes a list:

Arrogant Moment #1: Hid Brandon's video game.

Arrogant Moment #2: Made him cry... too many times!

Arrogant Moment #3: Road rage, honk at car in front of me (profane gesture)

A.M. #4: Made fun of Millie's cat. (in front of Millie)

A.M. #5: Yelled at Millie, made her bump her head.

A.M. #6: Put V. cream in mean girl's shopping cart.

A.M. #7: Spoiled the milk.

A.M. #8: Rude to customers

A.M. #9: Parked behind Dad again

A.M. #10: Threw away Mom's toothpaste cap. (squished middle of the tube)

... A.M. #19: Took Mom's clothes out of dryer. Threw on floor.

Ali re-reads her arrogant moments, knowing there are several more. When she gets to #6, she ponders what she wrote. Still feeling vengeful, she scribbles it out with loopy circles and writes: *Judgmental to customers! (and Millie)*

Ali discovers a Mathematic way to equate annoyance and jots down a formula. She grins as she writes, proud of her cleverness and sarcastic willingness to change.

formula:

arrogant moments ÷ hours in a day = annoying factor

19 ÷ 24 = .79

Ali laughs out loud. The boy next to her glances over again. She ignores him and turns to a clean page of her notebook. At the top, she adds a new title...

DO LIST:

Reduce my annoying factor!

Ali doodles away the remaining hour, filling college ruled lines with amateur sketches of pigs and flowers, yawning repeatedly. The chubby girl has her back turned toward her recent crush. Ali watches her wipe her eyes and sniffle. She wants to ask the girl to study with her after class, but waits too long. The girl is gone. *Besides, I am off the charts annoying... I'd probably just make her cry even more.*

Ali is a shopper this time, not an employee. She hurries to the pet isle in search of kitty treats for Peaches, Millie's beloved cat. She puts the box of chewy snacks in a gift bag decorated with a red tabby kitten. *Aww, little kitty looks just like Peaches.* The gift smells like the fish food she pinched into the round goldfish bowl she had as a child. Ali remembers her two fish, one named 'Orangie', the other she called 'Big Fred'. One day Big Fred was floating upside down in the toilet. She screamed and ran through the house.

"Mommy, Big Fred isn't in heaven! He fell in the potty!" *Gee Mom, you could have at least checked to make sure Big Fred was flushed all the way down!*

In the staff locker room, Ali hooks the looped handles of the gift bag over the collar of Millie's coat and reports to work.

"I have a surprise for you in the staff room," Ali says to Millie, offering a teasing apology, an attempt to reduce her *annoying factor*.

With a new attitude, joy grows with each deliberate act of kindness. Ali's eager to help where needed and gathers smiles from everyone around her.

When she gets home from work, she wills not to sink her ship with food. Instead, she plays a video game with her brother, does the dishes and cleans the kitchen before her parents get home from work.

Why is everyone being so nice today? Everyone's in a good mood.

Proverbs 6:25-27 (NIV)
[25] Do not lust in your heart after her beauty or let her captivate you with her eyes,
[26] for the prostitute reduces you to a loaf of bread, and the adulteress preys upon your very life.
[27] Can a man scoop fire into his lap without his clothes being burned?

chapter 26 mideah

The cabin in the woods is a graveyard for secrets. Unmarked tombs haunt the oaks. And millstones plummet sins to the depth of the lake. Not forgotten. Vengeance lingers in grace.

Mideah is pouty and childish, manipulating Ted, while sitting on the bench overlooking the lake. The platinum bracelet from the red velvet box dangles around pointy bones of her wrist. The identical bracelet, stolen during *The Investigation*, became a Mother's Day gift for Mideah's mother. Every time Mideah's wrist sparkles, it reminds Ted of how upset his wife is. The duplicate bracelet is gone, missing from his wife's drawer where she swears she left it. Good thing Megan is gone (missing),because his wife is on the warpath. *Go ahead and defend her, Ted! What am I supposed to believe, Ted? That's when I noticed it missing! While she was staying here. Do the Math, Ted! I knew that was a bad idea. We can't trust her!* Ted is also believes his daughter stole it, yet he still protects Megan from her stepmother.

Yesterday, he rescued his lost daughter by turning in the purse she stole, the one his wife found in their powder room. At the police station, he wouldn't leave his or Megan's name. He just asked the officer to return it to the owner. There wasn't much cash in the purse, just several credit cards and a driver's license with the photo of a provocative young lady. Ted put some twenties and a hundred dollar bill in it to make it look untouched. He wasn't sure if his daughter took money from it, or not.

There is something Mideah wants from Ted. She pours on her baby act to get her way.

"You know, it isn't fair the way you left me at home and took off to Mexico with someone else," she whines and tosses the stone she is holding toward the lake. Her sissy throw lands the stone at their feet. She scootches across the bench, closer to Ted.

"I said I'd make it up to you," Ted pleads. He touches the princess-cut diamond on her wrist. "I should be off to a good start with this two-carat diamond flashing us."

"You're on the right track, hon." She gives him a sexy kiss and pulls away. "But I know something that will totally put you in the clear." She lowers her chin and looks up at him, bottom lip out. "It would mean so much to me," she baby talks.

Before he can ask what it is, Mideah pours passionate kisses into his mouth, giving him one word at a time. "I..." Kiss. "Would..." Kiss. "Be..." Kiss. "Thrilled..." Kiss-Kiss. "If..." Kiss. "You..." Kiss. "Would..." Kiss. "Buy..." Kiss. "Me..." Kiss-kiss-extra sloppy kiss. "Implants."

"What?" Ted tilts his head away and looks at her. "Implants? As in breast?"

"Yes, please-please!" Mideah begs like a child.

Ted is enthralled. He is glad *she* suggested it. There is nothing wrong with the way she looks now, but it excites him to have something different —something larger and sleazier.

"Sure, baby!" He pulls her tighter. "If that is what it takes to make it all better."

"That's what it takes. And... I want it to be on *my* vacation."

"Vacation?"

"Yes, I want to go on a cosmetic vacation." Mideah handles the cosmetic vacations for the travel agency. "It's *my* turn."

"Well, you know, I will be working more this month. I'm not sure I can swing it, especially with the way things are at home right now."

"Shhh." Mideah says, gently touching his lips while he is talking. "Don't worry. I don't mind going by myself. Besides, my roommate is planning the same sort of trip. I could go with her."

Ted agrees to every detail of this arrangement. Later, he follows through financially, not even flinching at the cost. He likes this situation, keeping Mideah as his mistress, and hopes his wife will mellow out soon. On the way home from the cabin, Mideah leans against his shoulder as he drives her car back to the park. He rubs his mistress's knee. *I have it all.*

Jason, bored, picks at the fringe edging a pillow he is holding. He slouches into the couch and puts his feet on Mideah's coffee table, waiting and waiting for her to come out of the bathroom. *If you don't come out soon, we will miss our dinner reservation!*

Mideah has been complaining to Jason. "We never do anything fancy or exotic. Going to parties and bars is getting so old!"

At least she is finally returning his calls. This will be their fourth date this week. He feels redeemed.

She hurries into the living room. "I'm almost ready, Jay. Just give me another minute." She scurries around the apartment looking for her cell phone and get distracted by a full length mirror. Ten minutes later, she discovers her phone underneath the washcloth on the bathroom sink.

Jason helps Middy with her coat, careful not to bump her chest. She often complains about soreness, even more now than after her surgery. She is whiney and negative around him.

Back when he met Mideah at the airport, returning from Rio de Janeiro, he immediately noticed that something was different. She was wearing a white velour jogging suit. The jacket was zipped up higher than she normally would wear and stretched tight across her chest. Her tanned bellybutton winked out from above the wide elastic band of her pants. Her hair was bleached several shades lighter and her face, brown and glowing. Mideah appeared refreshed and —so big! Jason couldn't keep his eyes off her chest, along with every other man at the airport. Mideah held her chest back when hugging him, wide and gentle. Even then, she grimaced and readjusted her jacket. He asked her all about the vacation and hinted about plastic surgery. When she avoided the topic several times, he bluntly asked her if she had breast implants. *Yes Jason, isn't it obvious? Quit bumping me, it hurts!*

Shopping for new clothes is exciting. But Mideah misses wearing some of her old shirts. Nothing fits her anymore. She didn't think of this beforehand. Now she has trouble finding shirts that will span her chest and not sag over her shoulders and balloon around her small waist. She opts for fabrics and knits that stretch and cling in the right places. The surgery was three months ago and the soreness is growing more painful every day. Last week, when Mideah stepped out of the shower, she noticed that her left breast appeared slightly lumpy. She poked around to see if anything felt unusual. That's when she noticed a hard clump. When she called her Brazilian doctor, he said it was normal and emailed her instructions for self-massage. Today, she is seeing a local doctor, because things are progressively worse.

At the plastic surgeon's office, her new doctor photographs the unevenness of her chest. Her body is his sketch pad. He uses a black marker to draw ovals on her breasts. He stands behind her and holds her shoulders, while they face a full length mirror. The Dr. explains her condition as he points out faults on her body. She is not used to this! Normally, men gaze at her with lust and admiration. She isn't taking this well. *Look at my legs and arms! My belly is perfect. It's flat and curvy. I know one boob is sagging lower than the other. Shut up and fix it!*

Later that evening when Ted sneaks away from his house to call her, Mideah cries on the phone. "My body is ruined! You can't see me like this."

Ted reassures, "It's okay. Stop crying doll. You're so beautiful. You can get it fixed."

"You're just saying that. What am I going to do? I can't afford this!" She cries even harder.

"Don't worry. I'll take care of it."

"Promise?" She sulks, instantly turning off tears. Little does Mideah know, this is only the beginning of a series of bad cosmetic choices.

John 8:12 (NIV)
¹² When Jesus spoke again to the people, he said, "I am the light of the world. Whoever follows me will never walk in darkness, but will have the light of life."

chapter 27 reece

The library smells like old books and fingerprints. This ancient aroma intoxicates minds into focus. The library is where people go to be alone, including Reece. Today, concentrating is difficult for him. Nearby, Jason flirts endlessly with a dark haired girl. Reece eavesdrops, unintentionally. The girl seems more interested in searching for books than Jason's self-important shoes and the wristwatch he wears to exaggerate his status. Reece is dumbfounded that Jason doesn't grasp the signals the girl conveys. *Leave me alone, buster! I'm busy! Would you back up. You're in my space.*

Reece wishes they would take their scene somewhere else. Outside. He needs to finish a paper for school and thought the library would keep him focused. The girl came around the corner with a clipboard and pencil in her hand, Jason following her, putting on a show. Reece overhears the girl correct lies that infest Jason's ego. Still, Jason persists. *I know you're thirsty, how about coffee? How can you resist me? Look, I am begging you. Do I look like the kind of person who begs a girl? I know you are intrigued. See! Now there's a smile.*

Finally, the exasperated girl glances at her watch and tells Jason, "Look. I'm super busy right now. I need to concentrate. Why don't you give me your phone number and I will call you sometime?"

"Gimme your number too." Jason leans his arm on the bookcase, directly above her head. He inches his face close to hers.

The girl concedes and says, "If it means you will quit bothering me, I will give it to you."

Jason, you're a jerk! Leave the poor girl alone. Now, Reece can't stop thinking about Ali and the short relationship she had with Jason. Ali refuses to talk about it. He doesn't pry. He senses something happened between Ali and Jason. Something that scares her and makes her reluctant. He asks God to give her a man that will make her feel especially loved and cared for, someone who will honor her and put her first. At times, he wants to be that man. But he feels God holding him back, warning him that Ali isn't ready for more than a friendship.

A couple of months ago, Reece got a crazy idea to write Ali a ransom note and put it on her car. It took him longer than he thought to find the right pictures. He even asked his mom for magazines to cut from. He found Ali's car in the parking lot a few minutes before she got out of work and waited at the carwash. That night turned out better than he prayed for. Between movies, they sat on a cushy sofa in the theater lobby. Reece wanted to talk about Jason. He wasn't sure if Ali was in a relationship. Plus, Autumn told him he was jealous. *Was he? Or was he only being protective?* Another couple sat down on their theater sofa. Reece had to squish against Ali. It was the closest they ever sat. Tender feelings began to stir inside him. Finally, he was direct and asked, "Are you dating that man you were with that night? That Jason dude?" After asking, Ali's demeanor immediately changed. She leaned away on the leather armrest. All she said was, "You know Jason?" She acted surprised that he knew Jason's name. She fiddled with her hands and changed the subject. His question seemed to change the rest of evening. During the second movie, Ali was jumpy and distracted. Reece reached out to her and gripped her hand, hoping it would calm her fears. He doesn't remember much about the movie, because he prayed for her and held her tightly through most of it.

The supermarket is crowded with people hurrying to and from their cars. Reece is standing in the parking lot, leaning on Ali's car. He watches a young mother lug three children close by her side to keep them safe from cars that rush by. He guesses which person will put their cart in the coral and who will shove it aside. Ali should be getting out of work soon.

It's *Carwash Club*. They meet every Friday, go through the carwash and sample food from different restaurants. Autumn usually joins them, but isn't able to make it this time. Tonight, Reece and Ali will try out a new restaurant that is gaining popularity. Reece made reservations to avoid the typical hour wait.

He sees Ali approaching with her red smock sticking out of the canvas bag she is carrying. She waves and mouths *sorry*. She is dressed nicer than usual. Reece suspects she changed her clothes after work and put on extra makeup. He's not used to seeing her with eye-shadow and lipstick.

"I'm parked over there," Reece says, pointing.

"Okay. Let me put this stuff in my car first."

They walk across the parking lot. He holds the door for her and helps her into his car. A new perfume floats behind Ali as she eases into the bucket seat. She has her favorite jeans on and a shirt Reece has never seen before.

"You look nice," Reece compliments.

"Thanks," Ali responds with a touch of embarrassment. She wants him to notice her, but doesn't want to be caught making effort.

"So do you," she says out of obligation. Right now she doesn't really see him. Someday she will realize *Reece is actually handsome. Why didn't I notice this before?*

"We have reservations at seven o'clock," he tells her. "What do you want to do after the carwash?"

"Hmm. How about go to the pub for a drink?"

The Pub is getting crowded. Reece takes the last table available, which is small and seats two. He orders a glass of wine and Ali copies. When they are almost finished, the brass bell on the entry door jingles. Mideah ushers in through the standing crowd. Reece glances at her, trying to recall why she looks familiar, then remembers seeing her at the coffee shop a few times.

Ali resents the way heads turn to gawk at the blond Barbie doll, who suffocates Ali with her arrogance and confidence. It disturbs her that Reece has the gall to look, however innocent he is. Ali's jealous face is red and getting hotter. She doesn't want to feel this way, but cannot control the way her heart is racing. *Not her again! She is so full of herself. Of course men look at you! The way you dress, practically naked. You're so fake! Implants! Fish-lips! I wish I had legs like that. But I wouldn't be showing them off like you do.*

Ali gulps down the last of her wine and says, "I'm ready to go. How 'bout you?" She pushes her chair back, while remaining seated. "Let's go. Come on!"

Reece wonders about her abruptness. "Oh, sure. I'm almost done, couple more sips." He looks at his watch. "We have plenty of time..."

Ali stands and straps her purse across her shoulder. Reece isn't done, but gets up anyway and pushes in his chair. When he turns to follow her, he sees what is bothering Ali. *Okay. Now I get it. Jason is here. Is that why she wants to leave?*

Jason nuzzles tight against the blond Barbie that walked in minutes ago. Ali has nowhere to go but directly past them in order to leave. A drunk man isn't watching where he is going and bumps Ali so hard that she knocks into Jason's back. Touching Jason, however brief, sends Ali charging out the door and into the cool dusk.

Jason turns around and sees Reece behind him. "Hey you #*&! Watch where you're going. You made me spill beer on my woman." Jason pushes his chest out and clenches his fists.

"Sorry about that," Reece apologizes, glad to take the blame for poor Ali. *Jason, you're an idiot. What happened, Ali? What did he do to you?*

Ali waits outside the door until Reece finds her. He takes her hand and walks beside her.

After a few steps, he asks, "Are you alright?"

"Yeah. Why?" she answers and pretends like nothing happened. "I'm hungry, that's all."

"The food is phenomenal. No wonder the place is always crowded." Reece remarks.

"No kidding. I might eat the table next."

Ali stuffs herself to alleviate guilt and shame, beginning with the bread and salad and continuing through dessert. They both order coffee. Before it arrives, Ali finishes her water and excuses herself to go to the restroom.

Reece drinks his coffee while waiting. He pays the bill. He waits some more. He puts a tip on the table and watches the restroom door. Eventually, Ali comes back to the table. Her coffee is cold and shaking in her hands as she sips, not making eye contact.

Reece studies Ali, suspiciously. He questions his intuition, the same intuitions he's had on other occasions with Ali. It no longer can be ignored. He knows for sure this time. Ali slumps across from him with puffy eyes and blushing cheeks. Her nose and eyelids are red, even though she put more makeup on while she was in the restroom. He can smell it. And there is evidence on the sleeve of her black cardigan sweater. Urgency wells up inside Reece. Words to say are forming.

Ali is nervous and anxious, aware that Reece senses. He isn't looking at her. *Is he praying?*

Reece sticks to small talk to steer away awkwardness, until they are in his car. He keeps the car parked. The air is stale, so he turns the ignition and cracks the windows.

Ali patters her fingertips on the armrest, not speaking.

Reece turns to her and asks, "What's going on?"

Ali suspects he knows her secret, but fakes ignorance. "Nothing's going on. What do you mean?" she says defensively.

"I want you to be honest with me," Reece says with compassion. "I'm your friend. Talk to me."

Ali hides in silence. She stares at the floor mat, adjusts her sweater, scratches her thigh.

Reece waits for Ali to say something. Anything. But she doesn't.

She isn't going to admit it, so Reece says quietly, "I know what you were doing in the bathroom."

Ali flinches. She turns away and picks at some crust stuck on the door handle.

"Please open up to me," he pleads. "I have to say something. You know I do. I can't let you hurt yourself like that."

"I'm sorta sick today," she defends. "That's all. I ate too much and got queasy."

"No Ali!" Reece inhales deeply. He exhales, "Please don't disrespect me by lying."

"I'm not lying!"

"Come on!" Reece turns sideways in his seat to face Ali. "I am here for you, not against you. Tell me what's going on. Why are you making yourself throw up?" He reaches for her hand, but she pulls farther away.

Her entire body turns to the door, crushes against it. Trying hard not to cry, she pulls the handle to get out. The dome light comes on and exposes her more. The light burns into her lies and convicts her denial. She is still seated, but has one leg out of the car. Her right foot touches the pavement.

"Ali, please!" Reece begs. He reaches out and squeezes her shoulder. "Don't run from me. Trust me... and talk!"

Ali pulls her leg back inside and shuts the door. Physical movement and the slamming door draws out her tears. It embarrasses her when other people see her cry. She curl s into the door. *I am not going to cry about this!* She pushes away tears by holding her breath. The dam is cracking. Nothing can hold back this flood.

Ali sniffles, shakes and makes murmuring squeaks. Reece moves towards her, his eyes damp also. He wraps his arms around her and holds her head to his shoulder. He comforts her with the warmth of his body, the strength of his arms and the softness of his voice.

"Ali, I am going to help you. I'll help you find someone you can talk to. This is not something you can do by yourself. It's okay. We all struggle with something. God meets us in our weakness."

"Please talk to a counselor." He wipes her cheeks with the edges of his thumbs and says, "I'll even go with you, if you want."

Ali is quiet and reflective. Reece encourages her to talk about it. He wants her to feel safe and tells her in as many ways he can.

He doesn't understand the level of shame and mistrust Ali is experiencing. He promises to pray for her and remain open minded. "I am not going to judge you or quit being your friend. Be honest about who you are. It will *not* scare me away. I love you, Ali."

For two weeks, Reece keeps Ali accountable. He encourages her to make an appointment with a counselor. He researches and gives her contact information for three different doctors that come with excellent recommendations.

Finally, after weeks of Reece's persistence, Ali schedules her first appointment with a counselor. When she tells Reece about it, she sheepishly asks him to go.

"Of course I will go with you! I am so proud of you." Reece is beaming.

"Will you stay in the waiting room? Maybe you can come in after I talk for a while."

"Ali, I promise you this... " He reaches out and holds both her hands. "I will go to every appointment with you. Unless you tell me not to."

"Sorry I am so crazy. Don't tell anyone about this, okay? Not even Autumn."

"I'm not going to tell anyone anything. I respect your privacy. You're safe with me. You really can trust me."

"I know. I know. I just needed to say that. This is beyond embarrassing."

"We all struggle with ourselves. Don't be ashamed. Be real." Reece lowers his chin and looks at Ali. After an intimate stare-down, Reece holds her face, kisses her cheek and says, "And you're not crazy!"

I am vile, Reece. You have no idea.

Matthew 18:5-6 (NIV)
[5] "And whoever welcomes a little child like this in My Name welcomes me.
[6] But if anyone causes one of these little ones who believe in Me to sin, it would be better for him to have a large millstone hung around his neck and to be drowned in the depths of the sea.

chapter 28 jason

Profusely. His body sweats. He cannot shake a repeating dream. Jason jiggles his head and blinks his eyes to wake himself, but the dream waits for him. Even though he is tired and worn. He stumbles out of bed, in the middle of the night, to shower. The steamy water pouring over him is not washing away his memories.

Jason was six years old the day he learned to fear water. His grandpa had a cottage on a river. He remembers being angry that day, walking down a narrow path that meandered alongside the river. He wandered far away from Grandpa's cottage, at least it seemed far for a child. Down river, Jason spotted a small hut, run down and vacant. In front of the hut, an old wooden boat was tipped upside down on the sloped bank of the river. The boat was small and easy to lift. He rolled it over and pushed it toward the river. The boat gained momentum sliding down the bank. Jason hopped in as the boat reached the muddy river-edge. Immediately the current clipped the bow and dragged the boat downstream. He clenched the edges as it rocked, tipped and floated him further from home. He wanted out, but was too afraid to move. At his feet, he felt cold water soaking his socks. Water seeped through the cracks. The river pulled the boat under. Jason will never forget descending below the heavy current or the bubbles that floated

Turning Inside Out

across his face and levitated his screams to the surface.

He never saw the old man, a stranger, hobbling down the river with his cane supporting a limp on his left side. Jason remembers waking up with sticks and leaves pricking into his back and head. A scary man with gray hair and a sagging face was slapping his cheeks. Jason screamed, ending his trauma. He rolled over, sprang to his feet and sprinted up river, leaving the old man shouting and shaking his cane at him.

Jason avoided water, made excuses, stayed in shallows or walked on shore. He was a teenager when he secretly attempted to overcome this fear. He set his eyes on the horizon and walked in a trance into the calm, dark lake. When it rippled against his face and into his ears, panic pushed him to shore. Never again! His frustrated mother never understood why he was terrified of the water.

He is still afraid.

After his shower, Jason keeps the hall light on and his bedroom door slightly open, to comfort his fears. He falls asleep with wet hair soaking his pillow. His nightmare resumes:

Wind is blowing. He cannot see. Jason tries to jump over the wall of this dream, aware that he is asleep. When he falls into dreaming darkness, he is floating and unable to breath. His hair flutters above his head as he sinks. And sinks. And sinks. Deep into muddy water. His feet land on a large, flat stone. Like a bottom feeder, Jason swims deep beneath the lake surface, searching. *Where are you? Where did you go?* He calls her name. She screams. He always hears the scream. It leads him back. *What is this stone?* He gropes it, brushes off the layer of silt. *Why is it here?* The stone is flat and meticulous, formed into a circle. He walks his hands over the edges. *A stone wheel?* He finds the hole in the center. *A grinding tool? A millstone. Dead weight.*

Without warning, something is behind him. It says, "The stone hit bottom without her."

Jason turns and says, "Who are you?"

"I am the lake of fire," it answers, prolonging words that echo.

Slam! A death sensation flattens Jason to the stone. His entire body is too heavy to fight, to move. The water is too powerful for him; he knows now. He can no longer breathe. Panic. Fear. Struggle.

The lake swirls. A deceitful voice accuses, "She's not here."

"Where is she?" Jason screams. Bubbles slither across his face and rise to the surface.

"She never was here. The stone hit bottom without her. The stone will pull him under. But you..."

The lake releases Jason. He kicks to the surface in a seizure and breaks through the water gasping for air. His arms flay and slap as he tries to grip the water.

"Help! I can't swim!" He pleads, "Let me go!"

Tall trees bend over the lake, controlled by the wind. "Where do you want to go?" they ask, in a sweet mocking tone.

"I want out! I don't know you."

"But we are your trees," their feminine voices hum.

"I don't know where I am!" Jason cries.

"You are not lost," the oaks whisper. "You planted us."

Jason jerks up, wheezing for air. He feels the surface around him for blankets, confused at how cold and hard the bed feels. *Where am I?* For a moment he thinks he is still in his nightmare. Until he realizes, he is on the floor next to his bed.

He checks the time. It's five o'clock in the morning, dark and quiet. He trembles with a sensation of leftover emotions. When he flips on the light and walks out of his bedroom, he feels like he is being followed by his nightmare. *Get away from me! Leave me alone. You are not my trees.*

In the living room, Jason plops down on the couch with a can of Pepsi and bag of chips. Colorful lights flash images of dull television broadcasts—knives that can cut through bricks, the butt shaper/gut cruncher/fat burning machine, lamps that turn on when you clap. Hooray!

The next infomercial, a model with straight black hair is holding a vacuum. She demonstrates the superb cleaning ability of the machine and explains the multitude of attachments that are included with *"the vacuum of the future"*. She points at attachments with her palm up, dainty fingers putting on heirs.

The vacuum model on TV reminds him of the woman he met a month ago, at the library of all places. He was parked nearby, ready to stalk Mideah and her married man at their usual meeting spot. Jason watched a beautiful woman carry a canvas bag up the library steps. He liked the way she pulled her dark hair back when the wind blew long strands across her face. For the first time, Jason forgot the reason why he was parked and waiting. He got out of the car and walked up the steps and into the library. He found the woman leaning against a bookcase, flipping through pages of a mystery novel.

He poured his charm on her during several *chance* meetings in the library. But his charisma had no power until recently, when they exchanged phone numbers. She hasn't initiated any calls —yet. Jason obsesses through his phone messages, hoping to see her name. She challenges him, doesn't fawn over him like other women. Mideah slipped from his mind that day at the library. The day a pretty woman, with naturally even breasts and straight black hair, graced the marble steps.

Does she like me? She has to. Doesn't everyone? At seven in the morning, Jason brushes potato chip crumbs off his chest and leaves his apartment and nightmare behind. He waits by the window of a popular coffee shop, with a warm mug cupped in his eager hands, and hopes a girl with shiny black hair comes in for her regular morning coffee.

Revelation 1:12-18 (NIV)
¹² I turned around to see the voice that was speaking to me. And when I turned I saw seven golden lampstands,
¹³ and among the lampstands was someone "like a son of man," dressed in a robe reaching down to his feet and with a golden sash around his chest.
¹⁴ His head and hair were white like wool, as white as snow, and his eyes were like blazing fire.
¹⁵ His feet were like bronze glowing in a furnace, and his voice was like the sound of rushing waters.
¹⁶ In his right hand he held seven stars, and out of his mouth came a sharp double-edged sword. His face was like the sun shining in all its brilliance.
¹⁷ When I saw him, I fell at his feet as though dead. Then he placed his right hand on me and said: "Do not be afraid. I am the First and the Last.
¹⁸ I am the Living One; I was dead, and behold I am alive forever and ever! And I hold the keys of death and Hades.

chapter 29 reece

For almost a year now, Reece is purposely early to Ali's counseling appointments. He does this to express love and support. When Ali arrives, he's usually reading a book in the waiting room or chatting with the receptionist. He always stands up the minute she walks in, gives her a hug and kisses her cheek. Ali depends on this ritual. It melts her anxieties and builds her confidence. She needs to see Reece's familiar face. She feels special, knowing he gives up his time to be there. She loves it when he wraps his arms around her shoulders and holds her, when the whiskers on his chin scratch her cheek, and the strength of his chest, warm and solid.

She also knows Reece prays for her, which perplexes her. It surprises Ali when the things he prays for actually happen. *Of course they do, Ali. God always answers, but He doesn't always give us the answer we want.* She isn't sure of that. Although; there have been a lot of coincidences. She doesn't pray herself, doesn't think she knows how. Mostly, Ali doesn't really know who she would be praying to. Everyone has their own idea of God or gods. *How do I choose? It seems like all the gods have devoted people. Is there really one true God?* Ali once asked, "What about all the people that don't know about your God, Reece?"

Jesus has a way to give everyone a choice.

She calls him 'closed minded' because he won't give other religions a chance.

Reece says, "There's no reason to search anywhere else."

"Isn't that arrogant?"

"Just because I choose Christ and you don't, doesn't make me arrogant. I've had my share of doubts. I have questions too. The Bible is hard to argue against. Powerfully true. God practically had to turn the pages for me. I wasn't always willing to understand."

"What if the Bible isn't true?"

"I believe it is."

"I don't believe it's true."

"What parts don't you believe?"

"I don't know. All of it, I guess."

"Even the historical facts?"

"What historical facts?"

"The ones you read."

"I haven't read any."

Reece doesn't say anything else, so Ali quizzes more, "What if none of it is true? What if the Bible is all a lie?"

"Then we are in the same boat." Reece observes. "What if it is true?"

"I don't know, what if?" Ali sasses.

"Then you are in the wrong boat. And it might be worth your while to know what happens to your boat, if it turns out to be true."

"How do I find that out? Do I find someone who can predict the future?" She's being sarcasitc.

"Read the Bible. Believe it's true," Reece says with confidence. "It will tell your past, your present and your future."

"It was written a gazillion years ago! How does it know about me?"

"Here we go again," Reece utters. "Want to be done?"

"Yeah."

"Me too!"

"Aren't you supposed to keep bugging me about it?" Ali pokes.

"No! Bugging you? Sometimes I get tired of defending myself."

Ali feels weighed down —heavy and tired. Something has triggered the return of old habits. She has been lying to her counselor and to Reece for over a month. From the time she woke up until now, her mood is sour; her mouth is sour. She feels unmotivated and depressed. Last night, after talking on the phone with Reece, she couldn't sleep at all. Her mind felt hollow. She was incapable of thinking for the entire night and blames it on the full moon.

The last time Ali saw Reece, was over a week ago. It was in the waiting room at her counselor's office. When Ali walked in, Reece was standing at the counter talking to the receptionist. The girl was laughing hysterically. Reece would say something and she would laugh again. Ali didn't get the jokes. *What's so stinkin' funny?* Ali was jealous, seeing the two of them having fun without her. They didn't know she walked in or that she was watching them.

Finally, Ali said, "Hey."

Reece turned and said, "Ali!" with his voice full of enthusiasm. "I missed you so much!"

He picked her up and twirled her in a circle. From the minute he saw her, she was center stage.

Reece was giddy and playful. Now he had both the receptionist and Ali in stitches.

When it got closer to Ali's appointment time, Reece stood up in front of the chair Ali was sitting in.

Ali looked up and said, "What?"

Reece had his fists clenched behind his back. "Pick a hand."

"That one," Ali said and pointed to his left hand.

Reece held out his fist. "Tap on it."

Ali tapped on the top, wondering what Reece was up to.

"Ta-dah!" He opened his fist. A copper penny was in the palm of his hand. "Take it."

"It's so shiny!" Ali studied it and said, "Oh, no wonder. It was minted this year. Thanks! Is it for good luck?"

Reece had his hands behind his back again. "Pick a hand..."

"Now what?" Ali pointed to the other hand.

Reece transferred something to a different hand, behind his back. He held out an empty palm. "Sorry. It looks like I am keeping the other one."

"Another penny?" *What's this all about?*

"Hold on to yours. I'll be holding this one, praying for you."

While talking to her counselor, Ali held tight to the penny. She was careful or sarcastic with every word she spoke, hiding truth from love and healing.

After her appointment, Ali entered the waiting room stuffing tears and full of guilt from lying to her counselor. The session was a disaster.

"Hey Ali! Done already?" Reece said, full of happiness and sunshine.

She pushed tears away to fake joy. "Let's go. I'm hungry."

"Wait. Sit down. I have something else."

Ali plopped into the vinyl chair. "What now, Reece?"

Reece reached into his pocket and got down on one knee in front of her. Before he could speak, Ali said, "Oh no. What are you doing?" *What is he going to ask me? What will I say? Is he proposing?*

Instead of taking her hand, he picked up her foot and slipped his shiny penny into the tiny slot in the tongue of her shoes.

"Can I have your penny now?" He put Ali's penny in the other shoe.

When he stood up, he pulled Ali up with him. He put his hands on her cheeks, then leaned in and gently kissed her lips for the first time. He didn't plan on it. It just happened. They were alone in the room, standing close. Ali didn't pull away. It was a short kiss, but it felt intimate and loving. After the kiss, she rested her head against his shoulder and embraced his waist.

When they pulled away, Reece said, "Your shoes, or should I say mules, are penny loafers."

"So what's the penny about?"

"Every step you take... God is with you." Reece bit his lower lip and said, "Wow, that's cool. Okay. I admit it. I just now thought of saying that.

Really, I put them in there so you would think of me."

He pulled her to his chest with gentle strength. She could feel the beating of his heart, could hear it pound solid and warm against her ear. Her friend, her cherished friend, helped suppressed tears trickle through her veins —to soul.

The house is filled with forbidden food. Brandon and her dad eat so much junk. Temptation is a constant battle. Now it's the afternoon. This dead day still has no purpose.

Ali is lifeless. She hurls over a ring of porcelain. Her hair is held back with her left hand, while the other hand gets washed in warm mucus. It is detestable. It is a ruin of time. It is shameful! Ali is confirming her unworthiness.

It's all hopeless. There is no end. There is no answer. All the work, all the progress she has made, is flushed down the toilet. She hates yesterday! She hates today! She hates tomorrow! A lie told her to eat it. A lie shames her. A lie told her to hide. A lie told her she could be a goddess, sexy and alluring. Wanted. Important.... Noticed. After all the counseling, Ali still doesn't want her choices to matter. She refuses to be accountable. She believes greed is much easier.

Somehow, she feels found out. *When Reece looks me in the eyes and asks, what am I going to say? Should I lie again? I can't help it. I was tricked. I am a weak greedy glutton! I need to cover this up. I'll do better. No one needs to know about this. It is absolutely none of their business!* Ali splashes her face with cold water. While she wipes the floor and sides of the toilet, words stab her head. Ali remembers her attempt to read the Bible. (Reece told her she doesn't have to start from the fist page. She started from the beginning anyway.)

Ali is home alone. She is arguing with herself, out loud. "Why did God kill an animal to cover up Adam and Eve?" Reece's gentle voice echoes in her mind, *Blood is life, sin is death. It was about Jesus.* "How? Jesus wasn't even born yet." *It is prophesy.* "How is it about me?" She talks to herself, "I know Reece. God made a covering for me. Blah. Blah." Ali is angry. "I just don't see how blood from dead animals changes anything."

Ali calls three times to cancel her counseling appointment at four o'clock. Each time, no one answers or the phone gets disconnected. *Forget it! I just won't show up!* She calls Reece to tell him she isn't going. His phone isn't working, either. She worries that if she leaves him waiting in the lobby, he will suspect. Plus, they are supposed to go to a movie after. *Cancel that too?* Ali wants her lies to be believable, so she quickly showers and puts on heavy makeup to cover the red splotches on her face. *I guess I have to go now! Stupid phone!*

The parking lot is almost empty. Ali glances at parked cars and doesn't see Reece's anywhere. *For once, I get to my appointment before Reece! Why isn't he here waiting? He's always here.*

Ali is nervous and lacks confidence. Her movements are clumsy and abrupt as she thumbs through magazines without seeing. The receptionist calls her name.

"Have you seen Reece?" Ali asks her, worrying.

"No, not yet. Unusual, isn't it?" The receptionist is also worried. Something doesn't feel right. Off kilter. "Our phones were out earlier. Maybe he tried to call?"

"Yeah. Probably. Well, could you send him in when he gets here?" Ali asks. "I was hoping he could go in with me today."

"Sure. Let me clear it with your therapist first."

During her session, the therapist encourages truth from her. It is a tearful session, even welling the eyes of her doctor. Near the end, they both wonder, concerned about Reece's absence. The Doctor checks the waiting room, in case the receptionist forgot to send Reece in. The waiting room is spacious and empty.

When the session is over, the receptionist walks out with Ali and her therapist, locking doors behind them. TGIF-thank God it's Friday. They are last to leave.

She needs to talk to him. The generic message says his phone is out of service. *His phone always works! He is so anal about it.* Last night, they talked on the phone forever. He asked her if she is being accountable with food, and if she's taking *Loving* care of her body. Ali lied to him.

She really is trying to change and is doing her homework. But sometimes she fails. Sometimes she doesn't want any help. He knows about the appointment. He mentioned it last night. *What about the movie after?* She waits in the parking lot for another hour. *Where is he? Reece?*

Reece wants to be alone. Content. The city streets are deserted as the town still sleeps. Early morning. His roommate is gone for the weekend. He doesn't have to tip-toe around and keep lights off as he collects his gear and packs snacks in a dry-bag. *Ready!*

It excites Reece to have Friday off work. *Who cares if it's gray outside.* The air is heavy with moisture —motionless. Insects buzz amid the thin fog. The sun will rise soon. *Why's it so hot? It's June. It's four in the morning!* Reece is given peaceful conditions for kayaking.

The distant moon is fuzzy, lighting the trail. Reece has his kayak strapped to a pair of fold-away wheels. He rolls it above the river, along the edge of a steep bank. When he gets to a convenient place to launch, Reece realizes he forgot to tell Autumn to pick him up sometime after lunch. *Doesn't matter, I have my cell phone. I need to tell her where to pick me up, anyway.*

He doesn't have to paddle far to intervene with nature. Around the first bend in the river a lone buck is wading. The deer splashes in the water and wanders up stream. Reece can hear this animal approach. He sees the buck standing mighty, in silhouette, his antlers widespread and backlit by the moon. Reece remains still and lets the river carry him past the king. This buck has no fear of him. He watches Reece float by and even follows after the kayak, splashing along the river edge.

The woods rustle with critters, making big noise for such small creatures. Reece paddles with the tip of his kayak breaking through water so flat, it looks like a glass floor. God's Spirit is everywhere, truly saturating the woods, the river, the sky. Reece feels so spiritually moved, it seems like Jesus is going to walk from the woods, down to the river, holding a bear cub.

Gradually, a mellow cadence of flapping progresses from behind. A dark shadow swooshes three feet above his head. It ripples the water and sends a strong breeze across Reece's face. It soars with powerful wings, tracking the center of the river. Before Reece can recover from amazement, another eagle zips past, identical to the first. This is the closest he has ever been to the magnificent bird. Twice! *Wow! God! Thank you!* Clearly, He is blessing Reece with His creation.

Really? A third eagle lags behind before it breezes past, cocking it's head. *Did he just look at me?*

I hear the sound of rushing water...

Where am I? *Teeter-totter-bread-and-butter...* Voices. I can hear my heart beating. *Hold on buddy! Just reel it in.* I can feel the blood in my veins. Mom! I can't wake up!

Hi Reece John Wheaton.

Who are you?

Did you see the eagles?

What day is this?

It's every-day.

My eyes —they see! His head and hair are white like wool, as white as snow, and His eyes are like blazing fire.

Jesus?

Hand to hand to hand... in paper doll fashion, is Jesus holding the hands of children.

When I saw Him, I fell at His feet as though dead. Then He placed His right hand on me.

Matthew 25:23 (NKJV)
²³ His Lord said to him, 'Well *done,* good and faithful servant; you have been faithful over a few things, I will make you ruler over many things. Enter into the joy of your Lord.'

chapter 30 reece john wheaton

Mr. John Wheaton gapes at the photograph in a pewter frame. Salty teardrops wet the glass. He uses the corner of his t-shirt to wipe his eyes. He lifts the picture of Reece, himself and Grandpa closer to his face to rewind time. It was taken the day they took third place in a sailfish tournament. Holding the trophy, John stands sandwiched between his father and son Reece. Now the generations before him and after him are gone. He is left feeling scarce, amputated and no longer whole.

How does a father move past the agony of losing a son? Losing his father five years ago still hurts, especially in the spring during their annual fish outing. He can barely *exist* in this despairing moment. His brain cannot grasp the concept of recollection, cannot evoke that particular day when he was complete and centered within his family as portrayed in the photograph. His mind refuses him memories that should come easy. This shutdown of thoughts is an instinctive reaction to preserve his life. Remembering his father and son right now will tear his soul apart. John will live through the next several months sedated by lack of contemplation, a zombie going from point A to point B, only to lie awake all night suddenly remembering, then forgetting by morning.

His wife Nancy weeps through the night with tears that are on fire. Reece died four days ago; it seems like four years. He will be buried tomorrow. Nancy mourns close to the edge of endless sorrow. It is God who gives her strength not to fall over this massive cliff.

Yesterday John saw Nancy ripping her skirt and crying out to the Lord. He went to her and held her tight. She shook in his arms! Trembled! He rocked her, not saying a word. God grants him enough peace so he can bear her pain and his own. He forgets long enough to take a breath. Otherwise, he would suffocate. *Tomorrow... I don't want tomorrow. Give me five days ago! This is too heavy. I am pressed to the ground!*

Nancy asks her husband to drive them over to Reece's apartment. His roommate lets them in and leaves, so they can have privacy. John Wheaton stands back and watches in dismay as Nancy assaults the closet and dresser in Reece's room. She slams drawers shut and leaves most open. She searches the laundry whimpering and wailing. She can't find what she's looking for. This almost pushes her to madness. She will not give up the search.

The doorbell rings and rings. Nobody responds. Jeff stands patiently and waits, before the pushing doorbell for the fifth time. Reece's mom parts the curtains a sliver, enough to see the porch, and rushes to open the door. She grabs the starched linen shirt from Jeff, drops to her knees and cries into the folds. It has a sailfish on the sleeve. Jeff understands her reaction. He touches the top of her head so gently and walks away.

Nancy inhales the scent of her son over and over, until breathing leaves her breathless. After collecting herself, she drives with puffy eyes and a red nose to the funeral home. Reece will wear his favorite shirt, forever. When she clasps the cross necklace on him, she tries hard not to think of the fact —in two days these items will be shut inside a dark box with her son's body. Jesus is her comfort and assurance. Reece is with the Lord.

I will not be afraid to love again. I will love past my last day with you. I will be present in my moment with you, offering my depths. If you are here another day, I will love you again. And if you are gone tomorrow, I will know I have loved you entirely. I look at you for the last time, in the soft pleats of satin. I am holding on with every shred. Please do not close this lid! I will never be ready for this good-bye.

Ali is bewildered. *Why isn't Reece calling me?* She's angry with him, which is her preference over worry. She stops at Bluewater Adventures to see if he's working. Autumn tells her that Reece doesn't work until Monday. Ali forgot. He already told her that. He was excited to have time off, especially Friday.

...Friday. The day he didn't show up for her appointment. Ali is sure Reece met some girl and fell head over heels. *What else would it be?* Her jealousy grows as her thoughts lie, until they eat in far enough to seem true. *That's it! Who is she, Reece? I thought you were always going to be there for me? Well, I really needed you Friday!*

Ali mopes into her bag of chips. Halfway through the bag, she smashes her face into a soft pillow and sobs. She hates food! She kicks the bag over the side of her bed and crumbs spill across the shag carpet. She will walk on these chips for a month until Brandon vacuums them to help his sister.

Sunday. And still no word from Reece. Call me, Reece! Please call me! I need you so much! I'm sorry I take our friendship for granted. Reece! Where Are you?

"Ali!" Someone is shouting from downstairs. "Ali!" her mom yells again.

Ali races to her bedroom door and locks it. She is not going to answer her mom. She wants her mother to leave her alone.

"Ali?" mutters her mom outside her door.

Ali hears the door knob turn back and forth, before a polite knock-knock-knock.

"Ali. I know you're in there." Pause. "Well, you can ignore me or come out and see who's here."

"Reece!" Ali says, thinking it is him. She's certain he is leaning against the kitchen counter, eating cookies with Brandon.

Her bare feet crush BBQ-potato chips into the carpet when she rushes from her bed to check her face in the mirror. *Yes, I look like I've been crying. Reece won't care. In fact, he will be proud that I am showing vulnerability.*

Ali pushes past her mother. She bounds down the steps and composes herself before entering the kitchen.

But it is not Reece waiting for her.

Genesis 1:16-19 (NIV)
[16] God made two great lights--the greater light to govern the day and the lesser light to govern the night. He also made the stars.
[17] God set them in the expanse of the sky to give light on the earth,
[18] to govern the day and the night, and to separate light from darkness. And God saw that it was good.
[19] And there was evening, and there was morning--the fourth day.

chapter 31 ali

Reece permeates. He's all she wants to think about. Ali wants to remember everything about him, the things he did, the words he spoke. *It's His Love you crave, Ali. The Love we all crave. He made his son, ...to rise for us. I love morning. Every day, the sun comes up and it reminds me of Jesus. New light. New beginning. Hey, did you see that eagle? No other bird commands the sky like that.* Reece was always pointing to the sky, encouraging Ali to look up. *The animals surrendered their blood for man.* Why? That is ridiculous! *Because giving your life is the ultimate sacrifice.* Why have a sacrifice? *It covers shame.* What do you mean? *Nakedness —a dark soul exposed.* What does being naked have to do with sacrifice? *Adam and Eve did the very thing God asked them not to. They were ashamed. God sacrificed an animal and covered them up. Like Jesus. God was showing us Jesus right from the beginning. Page one. Genesis.* What does that have to do with Jesus? He wasn't even born yet. Sometimes Ali thought Reece was crazy, the things he came up with! *What if you had a daughter, and she was born with blood cells that cure all forms of cancer... and the Dr.'s told you she would die if her cells were taken. Would you give her life to save everyone that was dying?* Reece, you're a lunatic. *What if her baby brother had cancer? And your brother, uncle and best friend? What if everyone you loved had cancer?* Shut up Reece, I get your point! Besides, I couldn't make that decision for her. I'd let her choose. *Exactly. You do get the point.*

Ali is overcome by grief as she sits on the bench that overlooks the river. This is her favorite place on the trail, Reece's also. It is where she sat so many times with him, pouring out her heart, crying on his shoulder, splintering harsh words in his gentle ears.

Reece would slouch on this bench, extend and cross his long legs at the ankles, and wave his muddy hiking boots back and forth, listening. Never again. She feels alone more alone than ever. Questions spin, questions that have no answers. They all begin with *why*. Fairness is never a promise in this life. What seems most unfair is the permanence of Death.

"So Reece, if God is so good and powerful, why do people murder and babies die violently?" He gave us the example of perfect Love. He taught us from the beginning that someone always pays for our bad choices. I bet the hide of Adam and Eve's favorite pet covered their choice not to listen to God. "What about storms and naturals disasters?" God warns us about his wrath. Read Revelation. There's a bigger story happening, Ali. "Good people die too, even Christians." He shelters His kids from every storm. "When? Didn't you hear me? Good people die!" His shelter isn't always on this earth.

It makes Ali angry to sit without Reece on *their* bench. She kicks some dirt with her sandals. She can feel the soil settling between her toes and under her soles, little stones jabbing into her skin. This would normally annoy her, but right now she just doesn't care. She stands up and digs the tip of her sandal further, wanting more dirt, more sticks, more pain. She walks along the trail this way. Her eyes are red, bloodshot with rivers — flooded and swollen. Her fists clench as she curses the sharp stone cutting into her foot. A waterfall of tears pour from somewhere deep inside her soul, eternal tears. She believes that the pain she endures will kill her. Her heart will stop beating. Her lungs will stop breathing. But her lungs do not stop, they gasp for air instead. Her heart pounds so hard, she can see the bloody rhythm moving her shirt up-down...up-down...up-down.

"What example of Love?"

Jesus on the cross.

"I still don't get it. It sounds too preachy."

She curses more in voiceless screams and leans her back to a tree. Ali lets the bark scrape stripes across her back as she falls into fetal position to sob into her knees. All her strength is gone. She spirals to the lowest portion of her life, pinned against the bottom of the cesspool.

Ali runs out of tears. The universe is still. Nearby, a trickle of water flows between rocks and gurgles amid a flock of birds chirping. A squirrel cannot keep still. It hurries and stops, hurries and stops. Life rushes on. The wind blows Ali's hair across her face and wipes her tears. Her senses are acute. The tiniest sound is a clamor, like shouting during a funeral.

Unexpectedly, an eagle leaves the branch above her. It swoops down in a mighty force and lands in front of her. The fearless eagle looks at Ali and flies away. It left her a mouse laying lifeless. She leans in for a closer look. The mouse twitches. Ali screams and falls back against the tree, pulling her feet close. The mouse rolls over and runs off.

"What ...was that?"

Ali tilts her face to the sky as an awareness pours over her. *It's like new life, Ali. Like every year we have spring. Jesus is alive. Concurred death. So we will too.* Reece's words fit her every thought. Ali's soul awakens and overflows with an assurance of something majestically higher than herself. It isn't a voice she hears. It's more of a *knowing*, like a truth she cannot deny. It announces His presence. Peace fills the space unlike any feeling known to her. Why does she feel held, as if curled up on her Father's lap? This moment feels like time does not exist. It is *Everyday*.

"Jesus?" she asks and all is still.

Ali is certain of His presence. Rays of sunshine beam through the shadows of trees that surround her. Somehow everything she sees ...looks like Love —colorful and full of light. This love washes over her. She closes her eyes and offers a silent prayer. Her soul submits and opens up to the First, the Last, the Beginning and the End, the Highest above all things: *The Lamb of God. Light of the world.* Ali feels stronger now, protected and no longer alone.

"I am alive." This is New Birth. Life begins right here.

Her feet keep sliding as she climbs down the steep bank to the river below. The familiar birch tree leans into the water. Ali removes her sandals and shakes the dirt off. Her bare feet slide carefully across the peeling bark as she balances down the limb, closer to the water. She lowers herself onto the log. Chills crawl up her skin as she dips each leg into the icy water and washes her feet.

Revelation 19:6-8 (NIV)
⁶ Then I heard what sounded like a great multitude, like the roar of rushing waters and like loud peals of thunder, shouting: "Hallelujah! For our Lord God Almighty reigns.
⁷ Let us rejoice and be glad and give him glory! For the wedding of the Lamb has come, and his bride has made herself ready.
⁸ Fine linen, bright and clean, was given her to wear."

chapter 32 ali

Disappointed is not even close to describing what Ali feels like. She rushed down the stairs, but someone else is standing in her kitchen. He isn't leaning against the counter. And he isn't eating cookies with Brandon.

The man standing in the kitchen looks nervous and out of place, with both hands in his pockets and head forlorn. He barely looks up when Ali walks into the room.

At first she's confused. She isn't sure who it is. Until his eyes meet hers and he says, "Ali, I need to talk to you..."

"Jeff?" Ali sputters. "What's going on? Why are you here? Where's Reece? Why isn't he calling me? I have been...."

Jeff reaches out and grips Ali's shoulders. He leans his face to her and says with his voice cracking, "Reece is dead."

"What!"

Jeff catches Ali as she drops to her knees.

Her mother rushes over and helps Jeff lead Ali to the living room. Her mother cries and leans on the wing back chair where Ali is sitting. Jeff tries to explain, but cannot stay composed for more than three words.

"They found him Sunday. He was still in his kayak." Jeff is shaking as he explains.

Ali has her face in a pillow. She looks up when Jeff tells her...

"The kayak was wedged against a fallen tree, near the shore."

"What happened? Did he drown?"

"No. He wasn't even wet. He was slumped over in his kayak. Autumn found his paddle first. It was farther down the river, quite a ways down from where she found him."

"Autumn found him?"

Jeff is crying again and has a difficult time with the rest of the details. "She was on the trail that day and saw his paddle across the river caught up in bushes."

Ali's heart races, much like Autumn's must have when visioning the abandoned paddle.

"Autumn ran along the edge of the river a couple miles before she found him."

"I don't get it?" Ali stomps her foot. "What happened? Why did he die?"

Jeff bites his thumbnail. His hand is shaking. "I'm confused too. They say it was a brain aneurism. Must be his time to go."

He crumbles next to Ali.

With dry eyes and weeping hearts, Jeff and Ali stand in front of her bedroom closet. She slides hangers over until she finds the white sailfish shirt. It is spotless and incensed with the legacy of Reece.

part two

Although I am persecuted.
I am not a victim.
I am a warrior!

Psalms 22:7-11 (NIV)
7 All who see me mock me; they hurl insults, shaking their heads:
8 "He trusts in the Lord; let the Lord rescue him. Let him deliver him, since he delights in him."
9 Yet you brought me out of the womb; you made me trust in you even at my mother's breast.
10 From birth I was cast upon you; from my mother's womb you have been my God.
11 Do not be far from me, for trouble is near and there is no one to help.

chapter 33 ali

I am slouching in my car, listening to commercials on the radio and attempting to slow the anxious pace it took to get here. Somehow, I managed to get to my daughter's school early. Kids are pouring out of the cracks, a few I recognize in the chaos. My heart connects to their world when I see my only child hurry through the crowd of middle school girls. She is leaning forward with her forehead facing the ground.

"Stand up straight, Reeh. Be confident," I say out loud, but not to her —at least not this time. She is walking alone in short rapid steps, almost on tippy-toe. Thirteen is such an awkward age.

"Hey girl," I say when she opens the door.

Reeh doesn't answer. She just slides into the bucket seat beside me and shuts the door. Before I am even out of the parking lot, she buries her face into her school backpack. Her shoulders shake as she whimpers squeaky mouse noises. She takes a deep choppy breath and squeaks some more. At first she is embarrassed about her tears and won't look at me.

But when I ask, "Reeh, what's wrong?" Her reason spills out.

"Mom, I'm ugly!"

Before I have a chances to comment, she says, "And don't just say... 'no-yer-not-you're-beautiful'...cuz I don't believe you!"

Okay, she stole my line. What do I say to this? She is beautiful. I want so much for her to realize it.

So instead, I say, "Tell me about your ugliness, because I am just not seeing it."

"It's everything!" She wails more.

"Like...?"

She shrugs her shoulders. That is her answer. I wait a while before I ask again.

"Can you be more specific?"

"I'm fat!" She admits, speaking fast as if the word condemns her.

"So you think fat people are ugly?" I really want to say, you're not fat. There's nothing wrong with the way you look.

My daughter is not a bean-pole, nor is she overweight. Her tummy is soft, just right for a thirteen year old. And she is shorter than most of her friends. So of course they appear lean, with fat stretched out like taffy. Reeh is strong, athletic and super coordinated. Her body has abilities. It's designed just for her. God says, *It is good.* He would know!

Reeh thinks about fat people, to decide if they are ugly. "Fat people aren't exactly ugly." Pause. "Some are, though... like me."

"Is it important to be skinny?" I realize at times, I still need to ask myself this.

"Ah-Yeah," Her tone means: *Duh!*

"I guess I'm clueless, because I don't understand why skinny is so important." This is a mini-lie. Sometimes I am convicted of giving "skinny" too much power. You would think by age forty-one I would have this issue resolved. I mostly do. Sometimes, I am haunted by old patterns of thinking. I don't want my daughter to be like I was.

"Girls are prettier when they are skinny. And more boys like 'em." Reeh admits her envy.

"Do boys only like the skinny girls?" I'm wondering if all this is about a certain boy. *Does Reeh have a crush on someone?*

"Probably not every boy. The boys I know do," Reeh mumbles over her shoulder to the window.

I barely hear her confirm my suspicion. *Think, think, what do I say?* She hasn't shown much interest in boys, until recently. Now I am over-analyzing my daughter, hoping silence won't kill this chance for impact. It frustrates me that kids (and grownups) focus so much on appearance. It dumbfounds me that shame begins at such an early age. *Eve, why did you bite that apple!* If Eve didn't, I would have. I'd also hide in the bushes if suddenly I realize... I am outside —stark naked! In front of Adam! It's lights off for me.

"Reeh, how about this," I advise. "Why don't you just be who you are and let love find you."

"What's that supposed to mean?" Reeh sneers, curling her upper lip.

I laugh. I knew it before I said it —exactly what her response would be. I gloat inside, possibly too proud of this nugget I gave her. *Lord, please help her to remember it, when she needs it most.*

"Is this about a boy?" I ask directly. "Did something happen today that hurt your feelings?"

Reeh slouches and pulls at the fringed hole in her jeans. We actually bought new jeans with holes already in the knees. I get distracted and think about the person whose job it was to cut the holes in Reeh's brand new jeans. I look at Reeh and wonder. *Will she talk about boys with me?* I want her to tell me everything. From the moment she was born a piece of me was torn off, held and owned by her. I want every bit of her, at least right now. Someday I'll have to manage with less of her, when I am required to give Reeh to her husband and settle for seconds. I want this man to love her for who she is.

For richer or poorer, young or old, fat or skinny, happy or sad, pretty or.. Oh stop.

"Some girls told J.R. that I liked him, when I was standing by my locker," Reeh explains.

Good, she is talking. *Don't ruin it. Don't butt in. Listen.* "Oh Reeh." I respond, with sympathy.

"Yeah. It happened." Reeh picks at her jeans again. "I never told anyone that I liked him. Kayla said it when he walked by. She is the one who wants to go with him."

"Does he like Kayla?" I ask.

"Probably. She's skinny and pretty."

"Humph." Is what I say instead of, Find another boy if that's how shallow he is.

But I don't know J.R. I think Reeh might have a crush on him. "What did he say when Kayla said you liked him?"

"All the boys laughed and kept walking. Then I heard him say, *'I don't either like her! I think she's fat,'* when they all got around the corner."

"Are you sure he was talking about you?"

"Who else would it be?" Reeh sasses.

"Another girl around the corner?" I try to encourage —not that calling someone else a name makes it any better.

"Mom!"

"Okay Reeh," I am hoping she takes my advice. "You can't let people decide who you are. Tomorrow, if you see J.R. and Kayla you need to stand tall, look them in the eye and... walk on!"

I can tell she is digesting what I said. The car is quiet for a while. She discretely wipes her eyes, hoping I don't see her crying again.

"You okay?" This stuff breaks a mother's heart.

"I just don't want to be ugly, that's all."

She wants my sympathy right now. I see her struggling to believe in her beauty. She thinks that if people make her center of attention, she is valued. *Lord, help her not to believe this lie.* I reach over and squeeze her knee. She takes my hand and holds it.

"You know it isn't true. You are exactly how you should be — wholesome, fresh and beautiful."

"Mom's are supposed to say that."

"Daughters are supposed to believe it."

We swap grins. I squeeze her hand before she lets go to change the radio station. Her music is unfamiliar. Who are these bands kids listen to? I will make it a priority to learn her culture, to understand her better. We teach each other.

Reeh stays in the car while I run into the grocery store to pick up a few things for dinner. I try to think of something healthy to make, partially blaming myself for Reeh's distorted body image. I am torn. Half of me wants to help her lose weight, if it helps her feel better, the other half knows that it is a deeper issue. Reeh stirs up my past and renews my childhood pain. I must have passed my insecure gene on to my little girl. I ponder the notion that unresolved issues get inherited through generations. *Generational sin?* I will break this unhealthy chain. *Lord, please help Reeh realize while she is young, that her worth is found by knowing who she is to You —and only You!*

Mrs. Rawlings, prim and proper, promenades from behind the gourmet bread display. Her shoes and purse ensemble are a perfect match, yet out of place among local shoppers. I imagine her born with shoes that match her diapers, seventy years ago. I doubt she owns a pair of sneakers. Her shoulder length hair has thinned over the years from overuse of chemicals. It moves like a helmet when she turns her head, a stiff and lifeless idea of hair, worn dull as her conversations.

Mrs. Rawlings is prone to the delusion that she exists above us tatty acquaintances. We are not in her social circle. Although, based on the job titles of my husband and I, also the neighborhood we live in, she considers us the fringe of her society. I don't rely on her opinion to know my worth, even though she thinks it's required.

Mrs. Rawlings peeks above her superior hedge to talk to me. "We missed you at the benefit last week," she asserts, to convict me of rejecting her invitation.

"I heard there was an excellent turn-out," I say, untouched by her reprimand.

"As always." She pitter-pats her long nails on my arm. "But it would've been nice to have you and your husband as part of the excitement."

"Well, we appreciate your help in the community," I encourage, and find an escape. "I've got to run. Reeh is waiting in the car, hungry as a horse."

"Of course," Mrs. Rawlings articulates, "Run along, dear," ending our conversation in charge.

My family could benefit from a nutritious meal. Lately everything is quick-fix and starchy, not enough veggies. Healthy isn't always easy. I'm chopping and chopping. Preparing dinner takes longer than I want it to. Reeh wanders into the kitchen to snack. I hand her the carrot I just peeled.

She leans on the counter and eats it. "I'm hungry Mom. When we gonna eat?"

"I'm almost ready to stir-fry. So pretty soon." I should enlist her help, but don't bother asking. Sometimes it's nice to have the kitchen to myself.

She starts to take the lid off the rice.

"Don't Reeh." I stop her. "Leave the lid alone or the rice won't cook."

"Rice," Reeh says, disappointed. Her ideal food is chips and Pepsi.

"Go find Dad and tell him dinner's almost ready." Chop-chop-chop.

Reeh snitches veggies from my stir fry pile. She leaves the room and forgets to tell dad, *come eat.*

I should have Reeh set the table instead of shadowing the kitchen. I almost yell for her to set it. Next time. Helping out should be a habit for her by now. I make a mental note to work on this with her. I want her to recognize when other's need a helping hand. Plus, what does it say about me, that I'm the family slave? When she leaves this home, I want her ready for the world.

"Reeh, come and set the table!" I yell towards her bedroom, changing my mind about doing it myself. There, that feels better.

I hear her bedroom door open, "Mom, I'm busy."

"Whatever you are doing will have to wait. Please come and set the table."

"Huff!" Teen attitude at its best.

We both scurry to put food on the table.

Reeh leaves the room. I hear her say, "Dad, come and eat." Initiative. Good job, Reeh.

Dad pulls out Reeh's chair by habit, starting when she was little. We pray before the meal and dig in.

"How was school today?" Dad asks.

"It was okay." Reeh fibs, looking at me from the corners of her eyes.

"Was it okay? Or do you wish you had a do-over?" I say. I want her to open up and tell him about the *'ugly incident'*.

"A do-over would be nice," she admits.

"What would you do over?" Dad asks.

"Probably not stand by my locker when Kayla is there."

Wow, this is more information than we usually get. *Keep talking. We want to hear more.* I wish she didn't have a locker right next to Kayla.

"Not Kayla again," he gripes.

I want her to tell him about J.R. and that she feels fat and ugly. She doesn't say any more on the subject. I will fill him in later. He won't like the *boy-thing*! Get ready Dad, here we go.

This type of evening, when we are all home, is rare. We aren't rushing off to weekly commitments. We separate to different parts of the house, to each enjoy some time alone. We aren't the picture-perfect family who sits by the fire at night playing board-games —a yellow dog at our feet. I gave up this expectation a long time ago. We watch TV more than we should. *Maybe I will buy Monopoly.*

Motherhood hit me like a tornado, swirling me in responsibility beyond comprehension. Reeh's early childhood devoured my schedule. Arrows of guilt shot at me from all directions. *Is this the right diaper? Am I playing with her enough? She isn't saying very many words yet —it is my fault for not reading to her every day? What if I choose a bad babysitter? How can I possibly go back to work? Won't it give my child abandonment issues? Do I let her watch too much TV? What other choice? TV entertains her while I fix dinner. Plus, I need a shower sometimes!* I surrender and re-surrender to new arrows every day. Now, I try to address the guilt reasonably and give myself some slack. *Am I giving myself too much slack?*

Tonight, I need lazy alone time. I flip though the channels in shock. *Is it me? The actors are near naked. Every joke is about sex.* Another channel. *Murder and bloody violence. Entertainment?* I don't need my imagination, not with this sort of media. I feel guilty wasting precious time. There're so many commercials. Is this guilty arrow legit? I'm tired —mindless and spent right now. I see my exercise shoes by the sofa, right where I kicked them off a week ago. Wow, not another guilty arrow! *Go away. Leave me alone. I want to be lazy right now. I don't want to do anything, or think anything.* There. I shut the TV-filth off and close my eyes. My home is still. Different appliances turn...on...off...Hummm. I feel really good right now. Take that Mr. Guilt!

In the conference room, I prepare for our weekly production meeting. My senior graphic designer, Rhodie, should be in here for our pre-meeting status update. Instead, she flirts with the handsome young sales reps. They swoon over her. I see it all through the one-way glazing of the conference room. Rhodie is trading cleavage for power. She's about seven years my junior, over-qualified in looks and under-qualified for her position. I admit, I judge her with jealous prejudice. When my boss promoted her, I nearly fell off my chair. Later, I found out she's the daughter of a woman he is dating. *Really Mr. Boss? My respect for you dropped a few notches.* Luckily, his choice was uncharacteristic, which makes me wonder how it all came about? He's actually the best administrator in the advertising agency.

I watch Rhodie saunter away from her admirers in the direction of her cubicle. As usual, she forgets our weekly scheduled meeting. I call to remind her. She sits down across from me at the head of the table. Her blouse is unbuttoned and gapping open. *Miss, I really don't want this view of your bra!* Immediately, I'm distracted and angry. *Envious?* At her level, professional attire should not be an issue. My focus should be on work, not enforcing dress codes to subordinates.

"Rhodie, would you like to borrow a pin?" I offer.

"A pen? No, I brought one." She says and holds up the ink pen she was tapping on her notepad.

"A pin. A safety pin," I repeat for clarity. "Your blouse isn't staying buttoned."

Rhodie crunches her eyebrows together and curls her lip. She looks down her shirt and challenges, "No thank you. My blouse is just fine."

"No. Really, it isn't okay." I force myself to stay calm. "Could you please close it up a button higher?"

Rhodie stares at me like I'm her mother. When she realizes that I am serious, she shakes her head in protest and closes the gap. Others join our meeting. A handsome associate sitting opposite from Rhodie is having trouble concentrating. I notice her blouse is very breezy —again. I read somewhere that when we teach our children to respect others, we teach them to respect themselves. Rhodie must have never learned that lesson.

Reeh calls me, just before my lunch hour. She is in the school nurse's office. I assume she has the flu. "Reeh, are you sick?" I ask before she has a chance to speak.

"No Mom," Reeh groans, as if I am silly to think that.

"Well then, what's going on?"

"I started my period today," Reeh blurts.

"Oh my!" I feel a rush of goose bumps rush up my spine, followed by a huge sense of loss. *My little girl!*

This surprises me, even though we have been expecting it to happen. For the past few years Reeh has been fascinated with the whole reproductive cycle, full of questions. I have been open and honest in my answers, with hopes it will keep us talking during her dating years. She is the last of all her friends to get her period.

"We need to celebrate!" I exclaim. "I'll pick you up in a half hour."

I let my department and boss know that I'll be taking the rest of the afternoon off and head out the door. I hope nobody sees that I am crying. I feel like I should pick up another package of diapers, not sanitary pads. I cry again in the store. If it weren't for my denial, I'd be prepared for this moment. I am not ready to buy these! My baby! You used to sit on my lap, and I'd comb your hair. You couldn't go to bed without a stuffed animal to hug. Your shoes fit in my pocket. Your clothes fit on tiny hangers. Your Barbie dolls were the teenagers, not you. What day was the last time I twirled you? I wish I knew it was the final spin. I would have closed my eyes and memorized the way your hands felt clutching mine; then opened them and memorized the happiness on your small soft face.

Remember when Daddy would lift you up to dance; or you would stand on his shoes? Your lunch box had pink bears on it, and your hair —pink ribbons. Your bedroom used to be scattered with toys, but now scattered with clothes. I am so glad we haven't stopped reading books in bed together. I still need to hold you. I always will. This *letting-go* keeps happening before I am ready.

Reeh is sitting on a bench at the school entrance. She looks small and childlike from a distance. I park nearby and get out to meet her. We embrace, teary eyed. I kiss her cheek.

"Did you have lunch yet?" I ask.

"Nope."

"Where do you want to go? You pick."

"Let's get Chinese!" Reeh decides.

"Yum! Good choice."

We order the works —appetizers, egg rolls, soup and split the entree. This will be another special memory for us. I tell her about the day I started my period at my best friend's house. How I called my mother on the phone with the news, scared to death to tell her. My mother and I never ever talked about periods, sex or boys. This was the way of her generation — modesty. A manufacture even named a sanitary napkin with that hush-hush name. She was taught by her mother to be secretive about it. I could talk about it to my friends, but it was still an embarrassing discussion. I was shocked at ten, to find out that girls bleed. At first I accused my friend of lying to me about it. But when we saw the movie at school, when all boys had to leave to see a different movie, I realized she was telling the truth. My friend's mother explained everything to her. My mother put her shame on me, just like her mother did and so on, for generations prior. I shout *hooray* inside, for breaking the chain of shameful menses. I am sure my daughter will talk openly with her daughter.

We toast her rite of passage. Clink. "To period underwear," I say.

"What?" Reeh laughs, confused.

"You'll know soon enough," I smirk, "There's a stain that is impossible to remove from clothing. You're going to want to choose old undies to wear for the next five days."

"Ewe!" Reeh finally catches on. "Mom, I am eating!"

After lunch we go to the mall. I let her buy some pretty under garments from the *'secret'* store that has provocative graphics all over the walls. I study their posters and imagine ways to improve the signage, a habit of mine for as long as I remember. *Is this state of undress what sells their product?* I notice that no males are in the store. Outside the entry there is a seating area, strategically placed, the waiting room for men. Lazy Boy recliners are filled with men, patiently waiting for their partner —lost inside the satin and lace store.

Reeh selects the same bra that Rhodie was imposing on everyone today. We argue, because I refuse to buy it for her.

"Pick something else," I persuade. "Two extra things, if that what it takes. We are not buying that one!"

Reeh rolls her eyes and picks out two bras that are age-appropriate — cutesier, with monkeys and satin bows. *Okay-Okay. Don't start crying again.* But the pink bows on her bra are like the ribbons she used to wear in her hair —yesterday. *Yes, I swear it was yesterday!*

It is one of those nights my husband and I wake up at two a.m. and have a conversation. We didn't get a chance to talk earlier. I tell him about Reeh becoming a woman today and about the things we did. Reeh's life is on fast-forward. We try to pull it back by reminiscing in the cool moonlight. It won't be long before our daughter's bedroom becomes the guest room. *Help!* Lets pull back time further. We exchange more memories. Remember when Reeh licked the frosting off the cupcakes at Marcy's Valentine party? Remember when she *"adopted"* the stray cat that was really the elderly neighbor's? She didn't tell us where she got it. Puffball was Reeh's kitty for five months, until I invited the elderly neighbor over for coffee. Remember when Reeh brought red lipstick to pre-school? At circle time the teacher was surprised by fire-engine-red lips on every child —even the boys. Remember when...

Ezekiel 16:6-7 & 15-17(NIV)
⁶ "'Then I passed by and saw you kicking about in your blood, and as you lay there in your blood I said to you, "Live!"
⁷ I made you grow like a plant of the field. You grew up and developed and became the most beautiful of jewels. Your breasts were formed and your hair grew, you who were naked and bare.
¹⁵ "'But you trusted in your beauty and used your fame to become a prostitute. You lavished your favors on anyone who passed by and your beauty became his.
¹⁶ You took some of your garments to make gaudy high places, where you carried on your prostitution. Such things should not happen, nor should they ever occur.
¹⁷ You also took the fine jewelry I gave you, the jewelry made of my gold and silver, and you made for yourself male idols and engaged in prostitution with them.

chapter 34   mideah

The first thing Ted did with his inheritance was trade in his old wife for a younger version. *She can keep her family money. I have my own now.* He thought his old man would never die. Ted was shocked to find out he was in his father's will. Although, he was the only surviving son. Must be all those hospital visits after his father's first stroke paid off. The second stroke left his father too needy and grotesque. Ted couldn't stomach watching him eat, let alone the constant drool. *No way should I have to look at that!* Ted moved to another town; one hour away from wiping the mucus off his father's chin. *Anyway, my girls have their own families now. Why do I need to stick around?*

Ted was seriously thinking about retiring early. He had plenty to live on and didn't need to work. Vanessa talked him out of it. She refused be married to a *retired old man*. Vanessa already felt old at age thirty-four.

Her father was pretty upset, so she lied about Ted's age. "He's not that much older than me, Daddy. He will be a great role model for Trista."

Hopefully Vanessa's father never finds out that Ted's older than him. It's worth maintaining the lie by working two more years, if it means living in peace with Vanessa and her father.

"Don't even say the 'V' word, Gina!" Mideah pleads, "All I ever hear about is *Va-ness-a* these days."

Mideah is tilted back in a massage chair with her feet soaking in blue gurgling water. Gina reclines in the chair next to her and is wearing the same white terrycloth robe as Mideah.

"I'm glad you thought of this spa day, Mideah. I really need to get out of the house. My mother is driving me crazy. I'm so sick of her lecturing me about my choices in men!" Gina huffs. "She already hates Brett and she hasn't even met him yet. She says I should take some time off men, to concentrate on my sons." She hands Mideah an extra celeb gossip magazine. "My boys are grown up! They hardly ever call me. I only heard from Toby once since he started college and Ryan lives so far away. I can't just grab my purse and drive over. They're so busy, anyway."

"I heard Vanessa is driving a Mercedes now. Convertible. Ted knows how much I love convertibles. Has he ever bought me one? No! Besides, she should be driving a mini-van. Since Ted will be raising another daughter." Mideah is irritated. She turns a page of the magazine Gina gave her. "I think I might have my lips done like hers." Mideah tips the page toward Gina. "What do you think?"

"Perfect pout. Will you be going for more fullness this time?" Gina feels her bottom lip, considering going larger. "How old is Trista?"

"Anything I do will look better than Vanessa's," Mideah criticizes and looks across the room at her reflection in a large mirror on the wall. Pouting her lips, Mideah admires her face. She pushes her eyebrows higher with her fingertips and wonders if she needs a brow lift? *Too hard to tell, the mirror is so far away.*

Gina encourages Mideah by insulting Trista's mother. "Vanessa's lips are so fake looking anyway. It looks like her mouth is turned inside out."

"No doubt." Mideah agrees. "I want a more natural look. I'll stick with collagen." Mideah turns another page, "Oh. And Trista's eleven. I think. She's actually quite adorable, looks like me when I was her age."

"I'd like to get some lipo done sometime, or maybe a tummy tuck."

Gina pats her middle age belly. "I can't seem to lose this weight. Ugh! Especially since I turned forty (something). Brett doesn't seem to mind. I just want to fit in my old jeans. I wish he could see what I used to look like."

"We've still got it Gina. Just look at us. We look like we're in our twenties. Early thirties at the most," Mideah brags. "I know I look younger than 'V' you-know-who."

The attendant doing her pedicure glances at the manipulated appearance of Gina and Mideah's faces. Evidence of cosmetic work and aging are obvious, but not to Gina and Mideah's faded mirror. The pedicurist elbows her co-worker and says something in a foreign language that makes them both giggle.

In proper lighting, their wrinkles are exaggerated. Gray hair multiplies and makes a stripe at their scalp —natural hair/pretend hair. Foreheads, eyes and lips keep creasing. More brown spots appear on skin. Chins sag, along with upper arms. Noses and earlobes never stop growing. Mideah and Gina are swimming upstream in a strong current. The River of Aging pulls them downstream, instead. It's harder to keep up. *Work* done to lie about an age they should be proud is drowning their lives. Why not just float with ease and declare aging: Momentous, Vital and Beautiful!

Gina's mother constantly nags. *So what if we look our age? Does all that effort really have the power to change who we are? Does the mirror tell us lies or does our mind? It cannot reflect true beauty, so why believe it, Gina?*

"I'll be moving in with Brett in a month or so. As soon as we find a place to rent," Gina announces. She dislikes her current living arrangement.

"Don't even talk about moving into an apartment," Mideah harps. "I am still sore at Ted for not letting me keep my apartment at the Towers. He has more money than he knows what to do with! He says it wouldn't be appropriate, because he's married now. Ya-know, he doesn't even answer my calls anymore. I hardly ever see him since he moved."

"Your place is really nice, Mideah. Better than where I'm living. With my mother!" Gina complains more. "She keeps throwing my dirty clothes back in my room. How hard is it to just wash them? I do her dishes and her..."

Mideah cuts Gina off and says, "He'll be sorry. I know he'll get sick of her and come back to me." She scratches at the old polish on her nails and adds, "I haven't flown with him in over a year. Maybe I'll buy a ticket for his next international flight. He'll have a layover for sure. I bet Dave would give me the info, if I beg him the right way. Hmm..."

"Why don't you just forget him?" Gina persuades, for the umpteenth time. She doesn't understand what Mideah sees in that man. She has opportunities for really gorgeous men. Why does she keep going back to *him*? How many proposals is she going to turn down? Ted is never going to marry her. She's a side-liner, second string. She tries to tell Mideah, but it makes her upset. It is a forbidden topic.

"I told you Gina, true love is funny. It makes ya crazy. I don't expect anyone to understand. So I will not explain."

"And what about Devon?" Gina reminds Mideah, "Ted is married now, you know." Gina regrets saying 'Ted-married' the minute those two words come out.

"To the wrong person!" Mideah corrects and turns bitter. "It was bad timing. Vanessa came around when Ted and I were having a bad year. I can't stand her. She knew he was mine! Then she goes and acts all young and innocent, tricks him into marrying her. She's such a control freak, too. Ted said he can't go anywhere without her getting all the details. She won't let him call me, either. Well, she's already getting fat and they've only been married eight months. A few more pounds and he'll be knocking on my door again. Just wait, Gina." Mideah catches her breath, calms down and explains, "Devon isn't ready for a commitment. He needs a better paying job. Besides, I like the way it is right now." Mideah hates surviving in lower class. "I need to ask Daddy for a raise. Rent isn't cheap these days, especially with Ted not helping out anymore."

"You spoiled little girl!" Gina teases.

An hour later, Gina and Mideah relax in a dim lit room. Soft music plays and water trickles over smooth stones. They have cucumbers slices over their eyes and mud-packs on their faces. A massage therapist rubs oil onto their arms and legs. After this, the last treatment on spa-day will be fatter lips and poison injections. They sacrifice facial expressions for a wrinkle free brow.

Why is it so important to have a smooth forehead, Gina? Leave me alone, Mom!

Outside is cold and rainy. Mideah is alone in her apartment watching a TV show about extravagant weddings. She still imagines her perfect wedding, which grows more flashy and expensive each year. There are so many brides to outdo, now that she's older. She still hasn't found her perfect man. *Devon?* Maybe. Ted is her number one possibility. But he's getting old and stuck in his ways. He doesn't change for her as easily as when they first started dating. Getting her way takes effort and is trickier. Ted is financially gifted, so that's a major plus. *Oh they wedding they could have! If Devon made more money, maybe things would be different?*

Mideah looks in a mirror during a commercial break to analyze her appearance. *That bride had flawless skin. Is mine that smooth?* The *work* done on her face isn't what she was hoping for. It's hard to erase the years. She no longer is the most attractive person where ever she goes. She can't compete with the young beauties in the media, at the clubs, or even at the office where she works for her father. She gets her own way at work because she's a *Daddy's girl*, not because she's a *pretty girl*. She still turns heads, but deep inside she wonders if it's a guessing game —name that plastic surgery.

Feeling lonely, Mideah finds her phone and checks messages. Two are from her mother and one from a married co-worker at the office. *Dirty old man!* She was hoping for a message from Ted or at least Devon. She calls Devon's number and gets his voice message.

"Hey Dev, It's me. Get over here! I have a bottle of wine waiting..." She can't think of anything else to say. After an awkward hesitation, she says sweetly, "Okay. Bye."

Devon doesn't get her messages until the next day. He is out with the guys —buffalo wings, beers on tap and girls on lap. He is young. Mideah wants to live vicariously in his era. She dodges her birthdays as they fly at her and clings to immaturity. Growing up means letting go of all the selfish attention she craves. She doesn't understand serving others, or selfless actions. It has to be all about her. *Why wouldn't it be? I'm still pretty.*

Her father created a position for Mideah when his business became an ultra-success, fifteen years ago. She is in charge of travel arrangements for executives and the sales staff. Mideah is often bored at work, because her job is simple and not very time consuming. She spends most of her time flirting with colleagues or planning office parties.

Recently, she's been wanting to go to Denmark with her mother. When Mideah was in college, she organized and saved for a trip to Denmark —a trip that never happened. Back then, she vacationed with Ted. There wasn't time to travel with her mother. It became low priority, then forgotten.

Maybe I will surprise Mom for her birthday next year?

Mideah's idea is rekindled.

Luke 12:22-26 (NIV)
²² Then Jesus said to his disciples: "Therefore I tell you, do not worry about your life, what you will eat; or about your body, what you will wear.
²³ Life is more than food, and the body more than clothes.
²⁴ Consider the ravens: They do not sow or reap, they have no storeroom or barn; yet God feeds them. And how much more valuable you are than birds!
²⁵ Who of you by worrying can add a single hour to his life?

chapter 35   ali

I've been looking forward to our family dinner all week long. We're always running somewhere, with conflicting schedules and having four word conversations. *Bye, see you later! I have a meeting. I need a ride. Amanda's picking me up. I'm working late tonight. Church meeting, seven o'clock.* I even put candles on the table, besides the sixteen on Reeh's birthday cake. I set the table with our *good dishes*, including extra plates and silverware for salad and dessert. Who cares is there's a ton of dishes to do. I really need to let go of my practicality and use our *special* things occasionally. I dust these dishes more than I use them, which makes no sense. The table looks fabulous — color coordinated and festive. Our house is fragrant with the smell of a home cooked meal.

"Everyone! Dinner's ready!" I yell down the hall.

We rush to the table faster than normal. And tonight we eat more than normal, celebrating. Three pretty packages are waiting at the end of the table with balloons floating above them, to tease Reeh. I know she's anxious to open her presents. She can't keep her eyes off them.

"Which should she open first?" Dad asks. He's standing at the end of the table looking at me.

"Biggest to smallest." I give him my strategy. He only knows what's in one of the packages.

Reeh shakes the box by her ear and performs her guessing ritual, "Hmm. I don't hear anything. I bet it's clothes." She raises it, shakes it again and says, "A sweat shirt," then tears at the paper.

Reeh's a good guesser. She takes out a pink hoodie with the name-brand logo stitched across the chest in fat lettering.

"Love it!" She holds it to her chin and stretches it out to show us.

"Alright. This one is next. Dad hands her a medium box.

"It's heavy." Reeh shakes it." No sounds. "Umm. The box looks like shoes, but is way too heavy for that." She jiggles it harder.

"Careful," I warn, knowing what's inside and hearing a faint clink.

Reeh taps the box, contemplates and perks up to announce, "Books!"

She doesn't see my suspicious grin when she rips into a re-purposed shoe box that smells like leather. The items inside are wrapped again in newspaper. Reeh tears Sunday's comics off one.

"Olives?" She giggles. "Mom! I could never guess that!" She unwraps four similar jars of her favorite olives and lines them up in front of her.

The last present is small, wrapped in white paper with a ribbon taped around the box. It has a perfect bow on top. Pink, her favorite color. I cheated. I didn't tie the bow. I bought a child's hair-clip and attached the ribbon on the box. In my denial I believe, *Reeh could wear this bow in her hair.* Reality hits. *She's sixteen! The days of bows are over!* So, when Reeh takes it off the package and clips it to her hair, I almost cry.

"This one is lighter than that last one." She moves it through the air. "I wonder if it's jewelry, or a watch?" It doesn't make any noise, no clues. "I am going to guess. Umm... A watch?"

She's only right about the box, which had a watch at one time, the one on my wrist.

"Yup! Right once again," Reeh overstates with pride. She flicks back the lid of the tiny treasure chest. "Huh?"

We beam at our daughter and glue our eyes on her expression. This is what we want to see —her look of confused-wonder.

"Dad! This is your key chain," Reeh says, holding it up.

She rubs her thumb across the nicked and scratched metal surface where *Matthew 7:7* is embossed and fading. Dad's keychain has only one key now. She flips it to the backside and silently reads the engraving, like she has done so many times before.

'Jeff and Ali - June 6'

And below her parent's wedding date is:

'Reece - June 7'

The day he died.

Reeh presses her thumbprint over his engraved name, her namesake.

Our daughter knows some details of Reece's life-story, how it intertwines with our journey. But Reeh will never comprehend the impact our treasured friend had on both Jeff and I. He changed our lives. His memory is clawed into our hearts in a painful, yet beautiful way. God painted him into a place and time of our lives to brush against us, blending us together like a strategic piece of art.

Reeh holds the hem of her t-shirt between her thumb and fingers to shine her inherited keychain.

"Matthew 7:7. Ask and it will be given..." Reeh knows the verse well.

I squeeze Jeff's hand, remembering the day I bought it for Reece. I didn't know that the stranger behind the cash register would be my future husband. Jeff also remembers the day Reece and I came into the store, separately. I never gave the keychain to Reece. I kept it in my jewelry box for years. I gave it to Jeff on our honeymoon.

"Does this mean I get your car, Dad?" Reeh asks, optimistically. "Your key is still on here."

"I... don't... think-so," Jeff opposes.

"Oh." Reeh downplays her disappointment. "Can I borrow it then?"

"We have one more surprise for you," Jeff says with suspense.

Reeh sits straighter in her chair. "What?"

We lead our daughter down the street to a neighbor's house. Jeff hands a remote control to Reeh. "Push the button."

Reeh presses the garage door opener, suspicious of what she will find. We keep telling her to save-save-save; so that when she turns sixteen, she can buy a car. Up until now, we have been opposed to buying her one, but our good intentions softened the past couple of years. I know Jeff was secretly checking out used cars and so was I.

The garage door rattles and heaves. "Ta-dah!" Reeh's final birthday present.

She shrieks, "Is that mine?" and runs into the garage to pet the hood of her first car.

"Want to take it for a drive?" Jeff exclaims, more anxious about it than Reeh. He opens the door and sits down in the driver's seat.

"Da-add!"

"What?" He wonders, not yet realizing.

Reeh stands at his window dangling keys, "Isn't this *My* birthday present?"

"Oh." This will take some getting used to. "Alright. Just let me back it out for you."

Rewind. Reeh, seven years old, rides the bus for the first time. Daddy follows the bus to school and watches until Reeh is on the playground, safe and sound. Every day. For a week. Reeh never knew. This, Jeff never knew: For that same week, I drove to the school at the end of each day to watch her get *on* the bus. What I really wanted to do is sneak onto the bus and make sure the big kids were nice and they used age-appropriate language and content. Rewind. Jeff and Reeh at the lake... every time Reeh takes off her life jacket, Daddy puts it back on her. *Daddy, I'm six!* The water is only three feet at the deepest point of the roped in swim area. Embarrassed, Reeh swims in waist deep water, with a life jacket on and Daddy an arm's length away. Rewind. Reeh, five years old, bike helmet, knee pads, and Dad running next to her holding onto her bike while she screams, *"Let go Daddy! Let go Daddy! I can do it."*

If we have it our way, Reeh will never leave the house without layers of bubble wrap packaged around her. How do we shelter her from this new era? Both Jeff and I have instructed her for so many hours behind the wheel, giving her opportunities to drive. We taught her road sign symbols before she could read. *Green means go.* How do we protect her from other drivers on the road or when she rides with friends that distract her? This requires more letting go. *Lord, please protect our daughter from things beyond our reach. Please keep her safe behind the wheel of this car.*

Jeff backs out the car while Reeh and I wait on the sidewalk. Our elderly neighbors, who graciously lent us their garage, are peeking out their front window, eager to be part of Reeh's surprise. We invited them out but they declined, not wanting to impose. They come outside as we drive away and wave to us down the street.

"I can't believe this is mine!" Reeh cheers, over and over. "Ha! I have my own car!"

Jeff instructs Reeh from the passenger seat. "Watch your speed. Remember your turn signal. Be careful, that car might pull out..."

"I know Dad. You told me a million times!"

"I just want you to be safe."

"I will." Reeh pats his arm.

"Both hands on the wheel."

"Hey. Can I pick everyone up for my slumber party this weekend?"

"We'll see," I say from the backseat.

A chorus of crickets serenade the dark green tent that is set up in Reeh's backyard. Zipped in, are seven sophomore girls seated in a circle. One holds a flashlight near her chin, light shining upward, casting scary shadows on her face.

"Truth or dare?"

"Dare," decides Amanda. She takes the flashlight from her chin and glints the light across the circle of eyes.

"We dare you to..." The girls look at each other for ideas.

"How about run around the tent four times?" Reeh proposes.

"No, that's too easy."

"Ten times?" Reeh suggests.

"No!" The girls say at once.

"How about in her bra?" says Sadie.

Everyone laughs.

"I'll do it!" agrees Amanda.

"No. My Dad will be mad," Reeh protests.

"He won't see us. He's in bed."

"He might." Reeh lowers her head and taps her thumbs together. "Then he'll never let me have a party again." She's also worried about getting grounded from driving. Her car keys came with a set of rules.

"Alright." Reluctant voices give in.

"How 'bout she eats a spoonful of pepper?" challenges Sadie.

"Eee-uuu!"

One by one the girls crouch and climb out of the unzipped slit. They run through damp grass to the back door. Inside, Reeh gets out the pepper shaker and a teaspoon. She pours some into the spoon and passes it to Amanda.

Amanda takes the spoon and raises it to her wide open lips in a slow dramatic motion. Giggle. She mistakenly takes a deep breath before shoving the spoonful into her mouth. Pepper coats her lips and chin. It stings insider her mouth. Loud shrieking girls are bent over, holding their knees together tightly.

Amanda fans her mouth and tries speak. "Wa-ar! Wa-ar! Wa-ar!" Each word sends out puffs of pepper, like a smoker exhaling.

Reeh passes a glass of water to Amanda. Before she can swallow, her anticipated sneeze surfaces and water sprays out over everyone. This hurls the girls to the floor. They hold their bellies in uncontrolled laughter. Poor Amanda is at the sink —spitting and rinsing, laughing and coughing.

"Who's next?" Someone asks as they hurry back inside the tent.

Reeh holds the flashlight in anticipation, hoping her friends go easy on her.

"Truth or dare?" they ask.

"Truth," Reeh stammers. She quickly changes her mind. "I mean dare!"

"No. You already said truth," insists Sadie.

"Okay-okay. Truth." Reeh points the flashlight to the floor. At the center of the circle, bare feet and knees glow. Light fades before it reaches the girl's faces.

"Have you every kissed a boy?" asks Ruth.

"Lame!" Sadie hollers. "That one's obvious. Everyone's kissed a boy by now! Think of something better."

Ruth's boney body sags, weighing down from Sadie's reprimand. She doesn't make another suggestion for the rest of the night.

"Here we go." Sadie takes over. "How far have you ever gone with a boy?"

The girls pop to attention. They hope Reeh tickles their ears with a juicy answer.

Reeh hesitates. She doesn't want to lie, but the truth is embarrassing. Sadie yanks the flashlight out of Reeh's hands and shines it on her friend's face. Reeh's eyes squint and sting from the brightness.

"Well?" Sadie points the flashlight closer. "We're waiting..."

"Quit pointing the flashlight in her eyes," defends Amanda, who grabs the flashlight from Sadie and hands it back to Reeh.

Reeh cups her hand over the top. This changes the light to a bloody glow. "The truth is..." Reeh lifts her hand off and back on, repeatedly, flicking the tent from light to dark.

"The truth is..." she repeats real slow.

"Come on, answer. What is the truth?"

"I've only kissed a boy!" Reeh blurts out a lie, fast and under her breath.

"Huh?" questions Amanda. "You never told me that." They were supposed to tell each other about their first kiss.

Reeh shoots Amanda a silencing look. Amanda understands. They will talk later.

"My turn!" Sadie snatches the flashlight, "And it better be a good one."

"We'll ask you the same question," says Amanda, "How far have you gone with a boy?"

"You didn't say truth or dare yet," Sadie sputters.

"Truth or dare?" They say at once.

"Truth."

"How far?" Amanda demands.

"Third base." Sadie admits with pride. She considers herself mature and experienced.

"What's third base?" Ruth asks, shyly.

All the girls giggle. Ruth sinks.

"First base. Second base. Third base," Sadie says, while pointing first at her mouth, then lower and lower. "Home run."

Ruth gasps. Everyone else is laughing.

"Ruth hasn't gone yet," someone says.

Sadie holds out the flashlight. Ruth doesn't dare take it, so Sadie taps her knee with it.

"Here, take it. Your turn."

"Truth or dare," they say.

"Truth." Ruth almost whispers.

The rest of the girls want to go easy on Ruth. They pity her shyness, except Sadie, who beats them with a truth-question.

"Have you ever made yourself throw up?" Sadie asks, bluntly.

This time everyone slumps down with Ruth.

Rumors spread like weeds, in sixteen year old soil. Ruth looks like death itself. Her oversized, white shirt drapes over skeletal shoulders. Her face sinks into the light of the flashlight that she is hugging against her chest.

Life disappears from her eyes when she answers the question — truthfully.

"Yes."

The party just died.

Revelation 3:18-20 (NIV)
[18] I counsel you to buy from me gold refined in the fire, so you can become rich; and white clothes to wear, so you can cover your shameful nakedness; and salve to put on your eyes, so you can see.
[19] Those whom I love I rebuke and discipline. So be earnest, and repent.
[20] Here I am! I stand at the door and knock. If anyone hears my voice and opens the door, I will come in and eat with him, and he with me.

chapter 36 ali

Every time I see Ruth she looks thinner. She stirs me up inside. I worry about her and also Reeh. The last time Ruth was over for dinner, she took very small portions and moved food around her plate to make it look like she was eating. I saw her plop a forkful over the edge of the table, when she thought no one was looking. Reeh was also watching Ruth eat, actually, watching her *not eat*. I hope Ruth doesn't influence Reeh with her obsession.

Past memories are becoming walls around me and prevent me from opening up to my daughter. I refuse to let it continue. However, I struggle to take action. In Reeh's younger years, I imagined that open conversations would be easy, that we'd always be close. We are close, but not in the way I dreamed. My imagination-Reeh is supposed to rush home and tell me everything, down to the teeniest detail. She will say things like, *Mom, I took your advice and it changed my life.* Or, *I am so in love with so-in-so, president of National Honor Society.* Or... *Mom, can I help you fold those clothes while I tell you about the party last night and all the good choices I made.* Imagination-Reeh is supposed to hug me and tell me she loves me several times a day, not yell at me, saying, *I wish I had a new mother!* Remaining close to my child takes so much work and is mostly one sided effort —my side. It hurts to think that our relationship is possibly more important to me than to Reeh. *Maybe she is feeling the same thing?* What does Reeh mean when she says, "Mom, you just don't get it." Wanna-be-right-Me thinks she knows what I am not *getting*.

I had an ideal of what it should be like with my mother. My ideal never happened and was somewhat unrealistic. My mother was not capable of loving me the way I needed her to. So many of my needs were not met. *Show me Reeh's needs, Lord. Help me close this gap. Give us our missing pieces.*

Because good communication wasn't modeled growing up, It is something I have to discover on my own. Often, I have to force myself to set aside time, make the effort, ask the difficult questions, then remain calm for the answers. I want to fix Reeh, rescue her from pain, fears, self-doubt and especially from her own selfishness. I seal my mouth shut, praying, *God help me know what to say, what to do. Speak for me.* I make myself knock on her bedroom door to draw her out. "Join us, Reeh. We want you around. We enjoy you. We miss you."

I thought my old sins had died, yet they seem to be waking up in Reeh. It's as if my sins were pushed out of the womb, only to clutch onto my daughter's flesh. Just like Ruth, Reeh is looking thinner these days. The past couple of months, Reeh has been over-exercising and withdrawing socially. Each time I slide the bathroom scale back into the linen closet, it is back out again, almost every day. I stand outside her bedroom door, ready to talk. I curl my knuckles, ready to knock. But I don't do it. Instead, I find something else to do. I make excuses not to talk about the difficult stuff, the things I never want to remember. My memories push me into the dark.

At the dinner table, Jeff is sweetly oblivious. He tells us about a funny event that happened at work. He laughs and makes silly expressions. I watch Reeh push food around her plate, Ruth-style. My brain records how many bites she takes and observes how long she chews a small forkful of food while maintaining the appearance of eating.

I hold out the mashed potatoes. "Want some more, Reeh?"

"No thanks. I'm kinda full."

I swallow my words. I don't have the appropriate thing to say. It isn't the right time. Plus, part of me doesn't want to have an uncomfortable conversation. *Why do I keep finding reasons to hide?* I force myself not to avoid it altogether. *Lord, help us please! Jeff and I need your wisdom to know how to handle this. Help Reeh to see herself through your eyes, —pure, beautiful, Holy. She looks so scared, so small. Please don't let me run away from this. I'm scared too.*

"What do you have going on tonight?" I ask.

Jeff answers, but really I was asking Reeh. "I'm going out to the garage later. Maybe take apart the boat motor, see what's wrong with it."

Reeh gets up to leave while he is talking. I try to catch her before she disappears into her room again. "Where you off to, Reeh?"

"I'm gonna go running."

"How about a walk? I could use some exercise." I try to sway her.

Reeh hesitates, trying to get out of it. She surprises me by saying, "Alright."

I leave the table a mess, food and everything. I quickly change my clothes, dust off my running shoes, which I never actually run in, and wait by the door for Reeh.

Her clothes look big on her. I used to do that, shrink inside oversized shirts and sweats. She has a miniature music player in her palm and ears plugs on. *How do I get my voice down those thin wires?* I will have to talk over the music beating into her ears. That is, if I can think of what to say and speak in a tone that won't turn her off.

We don't talk for the first few blocks. Deep inside, I am a child holding up my hands wanting to be held, reaching my soul out to God. *Is this the right time to speak? Please help me open up the conversation and really listen to what she says. I am really anxious. Help me calm down. Please-please nudge Reeh to open up and talk honestly to me.* After several pleas to God, Reeh pulls the speakers out of her ears and puts them into her pocket.

"Battery's dead," Reeh says. She walks faster, nervous and uncomfortable.

When did our relationship become awkward? "Homecoming must be pretty soon," I comment.

Reeh flinches and says, "Yeah."

I wait for her to elaborate. It's way too quiet. "When is it?"

"A couple weeks." Reeh twirls a clump of hair by her ear, a nervous habit.

"Are you going?" I crane my head to see her eyes. I want her to look at me. Instead, she looks down and shrugs.

She hums, "*I don't know,*" with her lips shut.

"What's going on?" I ask sympathetically, but get no answer. So I am more specific, "Is there a boy you're hoping to go with?"

Reeh's eyes dart to me, then to the pavement.

We walk several paces before she tells me, "Yes." She is timid saying it.

"Do you think he will ask?"

"I don't know." She looks at her wrist to check the time, but isn't wearing a watch. "Probably not."

"Why don't you go with a group of girls and have fun, regardless?" Said in typical mom-fashion.

I sense a deep hurt in Reeh after this question. She bites her lip, pulls on strands of hair and looks over her shoulder, opposite me.

"All my friends have dates," she says to the wind.

"Even Ruth?" *Stupid-stupid, why did I just say that?*

"Ruth's had a boyfriend for a long time, Mom." Reeh sounds annoyed, "For three months now."

"What if we plan something special to do that same weekend, instead?"

"You don't have to fix this, Mom. I'll be okay."

I am embarrassed. She's right. I am trying to rescue her —again. I fight the urge to defend myself. I want to over-explain with a hidden message, 'I'm right, you're wrong.' Yes, I want to be right... but I'm not.

Lord, where do we go from here? Reeh is right. I want to save her from this lesson. I want to help her, please show me how. What is my role in this?

"I'm sorry. It's difficult to see you sad."

"I'm not sad," Reeh defends.

"Disappointed?"

"Mom!"

"What are you feeling?" This time I ask her instead of telling her how she feels. *Thanks, God. I didn't realize I was doing that.*

Reeh relaxes, deep in thought. I ease up also. Communicating isn't as difficult as I make it. *Was I trying to control my daughter's trust?* She doesn't feel safe to share. I will be patient and give her a turn to lead the conversation. Silence is okay.

We are almost home when Reeh confesses. "Yeah, I'm disappointed."

I don't say anything, just pet the center of her back.

As we approach the door, she blurts out, "It is just that... I'm the only one without a boyfriend." She hurries into the house. "I'm taking a shower."

Wow, finally. This is where I wanted our talk to start. I wonder if it was strategy for Reeh to divulge and run inside, so she wouldn't have to continue? Or maybe she was building up courage to speak and we ran out of time? I feel like following her around the house, begging for more information, but I won't. I look for Jeff, instead.

A wonderful surprise awaits when I walk into the kitchen. The table is clean, food put away and dishwasher running. Jeff is a very smart man — knows how to seduce a woman. I find him in the garage, squatting amongst greasy mechanical parts that are organized in a logical order only he understands. I watch him for awhile and talk periodically. When I speak, he stops working and looks at me to listen. He is really sweet about me pestering. If it bothers him, I don't see it.

"You don't have to stop whenever I talk." I don't want to interrupt his project.

"No, that's okay." He rests a wrench on his knee and looks at me.

"Keep going. I don't mind if you're not looking at me when I talk."

"It's hard for me to talk and work at the same time," he explains and stands up to stretch his back. "If you want me to, I'll come inside. I'm at a good stopping point."

"No, no. Keep going. I have things to do inside."

As I turn to walk away, Jeff teasingly pokes my rear with his wrench. I exaggerate my wiggle all the way to the door. I look back, but I already know the expression on his face. He has the best smile.

Reeh is sitting at the kitchen counter, already in her P.J.'s. She smells fresh and looks cute with her hair in wet clumps on her shoulders. She has a wonderful complexion, with seven reddish freckles across her cheeks and nose. We counted them and gave them names when she was five. She concentrates on the algebra book open in front of her. The aroma of soap persuades me to take a bath. As the tub is filling, I pour a glass of red wine and grab a few magazines. The sound of water always sooths me. I wave my open fingers through the hot water to dissolve bath salts that keep sinking to the bottom. Damp warmth fogs the mirrors and swirls at the ceiling.

My magazine withers from drips and splashes as I turn each page. I rarely read the articles. Instead, I study the photos and read the corresponding quips. *Why am I always in a hurry?* I rarely allow myself the guilty pleasure of wasting time. Relaxing baths, such as this one, are rare. When Reeh was little, if I tried to get away for a short time and bathe, tiny palms would slap the lower portion of the door. A wee voice would chant, "Mama-Mama-Mama." My get-away would turn into toy-soup, with a toddler splashing around me. We'd give each other bubble beards and soapy hairdos. After our bath, I would wrap a towel tight around her chest and tuck it into her back. Reeh would lean over the edge of the tub and wait for the drain to screech and choke down the last bit of water. Our tub made the strangest sounds. "Mama, what down daa-err?" I'd leave the tub with a landmine of toys, too exhausted to do one more thing. Sometimes, I would hear Jeff huff his annoyance on the other side of the bathroom door and toys plopping one by one into a plastic bucket. *I don't like to do it either!*

I can no longer see the magazine, though I look directly at it, even turn pages. I'm too busy thinking. *What age do we develop a body image?* My roly-poly baby girl didn't make sure she played hard enough to work up a sweat, for exactly one hour, then question how many calories burned. She didn't worry about getting chunky or about her legs rubbing together. She didn't turn her back to the mirror and inspect the size of her rump. Instead, she would put her hands on the mirror surface to touch the beautiful person in there. *Look Mama! Baby.* Reeh would kiss the *purdy-baby* in the mirror and leave a soggy smudge on the surface.

I toss the magazine onto the floor, close my eyes and slide into the water until it circles my face. All sound is clogged in my ears. Fully relaxed, I can hear blood pumping through my veins. I listen to the steady rhythm, before returning to my obsessive thoughts. I cannot stop thinking about what's going on with Reeh. Her current battle against food and body image reminds me of my own scars. The young woman I used to be is far from who I am now. It seems like young-Ali was a character from a movie I watched. Not me. Not my life. Not who I was. I experienced vast loneliness as a child, again as a young adult. *Please Lord, keep Reeh from that selfish pit that consumed my youth. Help her realize that the world is not relying on her appearance.* Life will not wait for your ideal, Reeh! This —right here, right now, is a day worth keeping! Live in it, fully. *God, use my experience to help her overcome.*

A couple of days ago, I was cleaning the bathroom and found familiar splashes under the toilet seat and on the floor —dull orange in color, chunky. My hair instantly pricked into my head. My heart pounded. *No Reeh! Don't go there. The way out is like climbing a greased pole.* I immediately blamed myself and wondered if I've been openly critical of myself, or of her. Am I letting her watch bad TV? Is allowing her to look at magazines with airbrushed skinny girls and perfect complexions tainting her self-image?

I can't raise her in a cave or on Ali-island. I lash out against myself and journey on a guilt trip, until I realize blaming myself doesn't help right now. Blaming makes me lose focus. It's more complicated than that. I will not deny what is happening, like my parents did. Something is going on in Reeh, something that warps her decisions.

My suspicions are confirmed. I know Reeh is purging. Now what? Doubt bombards every idea of how to communicate and reach out to my daughter. I thought I was healed from this. *Lord, today it feels like I am still very broken. I am digging up bones. This is so hard. Can't I just pick up toys from the bathtub?*

What is my contribution to this? Do I have super expectations for Reeh? Does Reeh senses this and perform to my expectations? Maybe it's because I have a difficult time failing. Sometimes I go to extremes to make sure people love me. It's hard to say *No*, even though I do say it. I hide the agony I feel after. Showing it would be a failure, you know! I have yet to overcome my fear of man. I kick this fear away and it rolls back to me. I hate it. I am teaching it to my daughter. I can't ask for help. I'm sure Reeh picks up on this, also.

Oh boy, where do we go from here? It isn't all my fault, but maybe some? *Sorry Reeh, forgive me for the things I am doing wrong. I am still growing, too.*

After Reeh is in bed sleeping, Jeff and I have a serious conversation about Reeh's problem. He gently tells me I am overreacting. I am not overreacting, but almost do after his accusation. He doesn't understand the seriousness, thinks family counseling is too extreme. He excels in engineering and approaches problems with an A-B-C-D strategy, in that order of course. With earnest thought, he comes up with his plan to fix Reeh.

> **a.** Cook her favorite food and make her sit at the table until she finishes everything on her plate.
> **b.** Don't let her hang out with Ruth so much.
> **c.** Exercise is good for her. Hide the scale, if you don't like her weighing herself.
> **d.** And if she doesn't do these things, we can take away her car keys.

I try to explain why his plan won't work. It is not about the food, or the friends she hangs out with. She will find ways to exercise, probably behind our backs, which will make her sneaky. Yes, we can make her lick her plate clean. But we won't be able to guarantee the food stays down.

I know Jeff wants to understand what's going on. This hurts him too. He admits that he is confused with Reeh's emotions. It appalls him to think someone would actually make themselves regurgitate, especially his own daughter. He tries to deny it. He can't, after I give him details of what I wipe off the toilet and floor. He seriously thinks she inherited his weak stomach. When Reeh was a baby, anything more than a damp diaper would activate Jeff's gag-reflux. Certain sights and smells almost make him loose his lunch.

Jeff promises to keep an open mind. He wants to wait a few days before we approach her. I know he will research eating disorders and keep a keen eye on Reeh in the meantime. We hold hands and pray for Reeh, for ourselves and for Ruth. When we roll over to go to sleep, I keep talking to God. I want to sort out the jumble in my head. I beg Him for clarity and wisdom.

My sleep is restless. I dream of big hands knocking on the door while I take a bath. I sink deeper into the bathtub. It is full of food, floating and gross.

I wake myself, yelling, "Someone answer the door!"

Ezekiel 28:17-19 (NIV)

[17] Your heart became proud on account of your beauty, and you corrupted your wisdom because of your splendor. So I threw you to the earth; I made a spectacle of you before kings.

[18] By your many sins and dishonest trade you have desecrated your sanctuaries. So I made a fire come out from you, and it consumed you, and I reduced you to ashes on the ground in the sight of all who were watching.

[19] All the nations who knew you are appalled at you; you have come to a horrible end and will be no more.'"

chapter 37 ted mideah vanessa trista

Trista is uneasy with her stepdad. His actions feel like a contradiction. Even at eleven years old her instincts warn, danger. Her chest is developing; so it's embarrassing when he accidently bumps her there. She hates to be tickled and wishes he would stop when she tells him to. Her real Dad lives far away. She only sees him two weeks each summer. Sometimes, Trista wishes she could live with him instead of her mom and stepdad. Onetime, she got brave enough to ask him. All he said was, "Pumpkin, you don't want to do that. Your mom would miss you too much." After that, Trista never dared to ask again.

Ted often follows her around (watches her), buys her clothes and electronics. He sits to close when they watch movies. She feels awkward, it confuses her. And now, since summer break started, all she wants to do is hide from him. From everyone.

Vanessa is in the garden weeding when the phone rings. It only rings three times and stops. *Well, I guess they aren't going to leave a message.* She keeps working, dripping in sweat on a hot August day. She absentmindedly wipes dirt across her cheek and brow with the back of her hand. Everything itches when her hands are dirty.

Ted has some days off. After that, he takes his last series of flights. He's in the house somewhere. And Vanessa doesn't care where or what he is doing, as long as she can have some alone time. She wishes he wasn't retiring. Three years went by fast. Ted already gets on her nerves during his time off. Plus Trista is moody lately, probably hormones. Puberty is hard on an eleven year old. *Could everyone please just leave me alone!* There goes the phone again, ringing three times. *Who keeps calling? Grrr. Leave me alone!* Vanessa is convinced it's one of Trista's friends. *Answer your phone, Trista, before it drives me crazy!*

Ted's latest splurge is a gold necklace with a scarab beetle amulet carved out of turquoise. He bought the amulet on a recent trip to Egypt, a souvenir for Mideah. The beetle carving reminds him of Egyptian tombs. Ted isn't aware of the beetle emblem's idolatry origins or transforming symbolism. A premonition? A prophesy? Her name is engraved on the back. The *'i'* in *Mideah* is dotted with a heart. *It's time to give it to her. She's so clingy. Nag-nag-nag.*

Ted has a code so Mideah can call him at home. Three rings. Click. Three rings. Click. It gives her a chance to call discretely when she needs him. Marriage vows lasted a year, before Ted and Mideah began meeting at the cabin again. Luckily, his previous wife didn't get the cabin in their divorce. Ted finessed that decision in his favor. *Boo-hoo! Where am I supposed to live?*

Mideah meets him for their monthly rendezvous. They don't meet as often as they used to. Keeping in touch with Ted is Mideah's way of getting her hands on his money. She still has beauty treatments to pay for. Daddy refuses. Ted owes her for marrying Vanessa. He was supposed to buy *her* a white dress and get teary-eyes when *she* walked down the aisle. *Me! Not Vaness-sa!*

Mideah uses her key to let herself inside. The cabin is hot and muggy. She takes a diet soda from the refrigerator and fills the glass with ice first. Soda fizzes over the ice and overflows onto the counter. Mideah overreacts and swears. She feels edgy today. In fact, she has felt edgy all week. *Ted, what's the hold up? You should be here by now.*

Mideah's imagination is wild. She worries it might be menopause. How else can she explain the weird voices in her head? She is losing control of her thoughts.

Voices invade and tell her, *"You can't just love yourself."*

"Yes I can!" she shouts and hurries to the porch.

Similar notions jab into her head. *"You are selfish."*

"No I am not! So what if I am?"

"It's all about you."

"Shut up!"

The chains on the porch swing creek and moan as she rocks slowly, holding her icy drink. Her mind is numb and ambivalent. It's the dream's fault. *Stupid dream, I wish I could forget it.* She had the same dream two nights in a row. Both times, she woke up in the middle of the night chilled to the bone. The dreams weren't even scary. *Were they?* In both dreams, someone is calling her name, whispering gently. She can't find the voice. It is soft and vague —it's like a song. She searches her house for the sound, but everywhere she looks, nothing. The voice is still calling. It bothers her. It interrupts and distracts her from herself. *Go away!*

Last night, Mideah woke screaming, "Get away from me! Go!" She buried her head under her pillow.

Why did it follow me here? She hates the idea in the voice. She only wants to worship herself.

Ted walks onto the porch and startles her. "Hi Middy!"

She almost falls off the swing. Her drink is dripping down her arm. Mideah swears and says, "What took you so long? You know I hate being here by myself."

"Since when, baby?" Ted is confused by her attitude. Mideah goes to the cabin by herself all the time and never complained before.

To lift her spirits, he announces, "I have a surprise for you."

Mideah reaches for the small box, wrapped in white satin and tied with a red bow.

Ted clarifies, "It's for your trip tomorrow. Don't open it yet."

"Oh! So sweet of you." Her entire demeanor shifts and her speech is coated with sugar and baby talk. "Come-eer. Let me give you a big huggie-wuggie."

They embrace and kiss. Mideah covertly begs for reassurance. She needs to be first in his life. They grope to their favorite spot on the floor in front of the fireplace, to repeat their monotonous love affair. It's too hot for a fire today. The floor is hard and cumbersome. Time to relocate. Ted takes his aching bones, stiff joints and Mideah upstairs to a soft bed. Besides, their fire died shortly after it was started, over twenty years ago.

This time, both Ted and Mideah have disturbing dreams —the same dream. They are haunted by a choice. Ted is locked inside a tiny room. A fire is burning his back. Mideah bleeds onto white sheets. *Whose dream is this?* Mideah walks into Ted's fire. She stains the sheets with red footprints. *Your soul has no lover.* Their breath smells like rotten mothballs, seeping from the caverns in their lungs. *Darkness will segregate. Who is the lover of your soul?*

Mideah's suitcases are packed and waiting at her apartment door. She plans on picking them up on her way back from the cabin.

Her mother, so proud to be included, is also getting ready for this trip. She is up late washing and ironing clothes, laying out ensembles —head to toe coordination, matching outfits with jewelry. By midnight, all items are checked off her *to-do* list. They will leave for Denmark tomorrow. She is ready for the trip, time to get ready for bed.

At her vanity in the master bedroom suite, Mideah's mother spins the cap off expensive anti-aging cream to revitalize her face. She dabs the paste at the corners of her mouth and sagging eyes. She applies fade-cream over scars near her ears, where her skin was stretched and removed. She carefully brushes her thinning hair and wishes the color didn't fade so fast. She hates wearing wigs. They are itchy and awkward. Although, she packed her hairpieces anyway, just in case. She will wear them when they dine in the evening. Coordinating hats and head scarves will suffice for most of the vacation.

She lounges on her back between high-thread-count sheets and places a cool gel-mask over the bridge of her nose. She must lay still all night to let the mask deliver promised results of a youthful appearance. Her husband hates this routine. He reminds her again, after she clicks off her bedside lamp, "Honey, you're not missing any wrinkles. You're wasting precious sleep for nothing."

Vanessa kneels before a row of green beans with her grandmother's red bowl held in her arms. Almost full. The sun is hot on her back. Sweat is beading across her nose. She is happiest with her hands buried in the dirt. Flowers, vegetables, shrubs, Vanessa can grow anything. She often escapes to her gardens—more than ever when Ted is home. He is gone for two weeks. Bliss. *After this, will I be able to handle his retirement?*

She thinks about how nice it is to be home alone with Trista. Summer is always too short. August is nearly gone. So far, her daughter has been spending this summer break alone or with friends. *Have I been ignoring Trista, too? I really need to make up for lost time.* Feeling guilty, Vanessa picks a handful of cherry tomatoes and eats them as she walks the path to her back door. She's going to be spontaneous and surprise Trista with a beach day. It can be their last outing before school starts. An urgency tugs Vanessa into the house.

She hears Trista talking on the phone, behind the closed door of her bedroom. Vanessa is ready to walk away, until she overhears Trista say, *"...but I don't want my mom to find out."* This stops Vanessa in her tracks and invites her to lean an ear against the cool wood door. She can hear everything. Vanessa freezes like a statue and listens to one side of her daughter's secret conversation.

"He does it when Mom is gone." Pause. (while her friend is talking)

"I know I should, but it's super weird." Tapping. Waiting. Listening.

Deep breath. Exhale. "Yes. I tell him I don't want to... ya-know....touch. He makes a game out of it. It's... It's... Forget it. I don't know what I'm sayin'. Maybe it isn't such a huge deal."

Vanessa's ear is sealed against the door. She thinks Trista is having boy problems. *Touching? Not already! She is too young for that!* She knows she's invading her daughter's privacy, but yearns to know every detail, like she did when Trista was dependant on Mommy for everything. She wishes Trista was confiding in her, instead.

The other side of the door grows quiet. Vanessa thinks the conversation is over.

Until Trista says, "Umm... It's usually when Mom is out in the garden or sleeping."

Something shifts in Vanessa's head. Her heart races. Intuition surfaces and sweats from her armpits. Her hand is on the doorknob, disbelieving. She wants more information and less information at the same time.

"He tries to get me to sit by him and then starts to do stuff."

"Yeah..."

"I know. But..." Exhale. Louder tapping.

"Mom won't believe me. She will side with him. She hasn't been married that long. I don't want to wreck things...."

The next sentence seals her doubt. Truth suffocates and kills her make believe marriage.

"I can't just stay away from him! He's my step-dad! He lives here. Duh!"

Vanessa bites her lower lip and tastes the tears dripping off her cheeks. With a trembling hand she clenches the door knob. She is unable to open her daughter's cage. *Calm down. Knock first. I cannot run from this.*

Vanessa searches for courage, "God, where are you? I need you now." It is her first of many prayers.

Trista hears someone knocking on her bedroom door.

"I gotta go..." She mutters and hangs up the phone.

Matthew 7:7-12 (NIV)
⁷ "Ask and it will be given to you; seek and you will find; knock and the door will be opened to you.
⁸ For everyone who asks receives; he who seeks finds; and to him who knocks, the door will be opened.
⁹ "Which of you, if his son asks for bread, will give him a stone?
¹⁰ Or if he asks for a fish, will give him a snake?
¹¹ If you, then, though you are evil, know how to give good gifts to your children, how much more will your Father in heaven give good gifts to those who ask him!
¹² So in everything, do to others what you would have them do to you, for this sums up the Law and the Prophets.

chapter 38 jeff

Ali confronted my denial last night. When she started talking about eating disorders, about Reeh needing help, I wasn't ready to hear it. At first I tried to change the subject, then joked with her to keep the conversation light. When Ali persisted, I accused her of overreacting. Deep inside, I had my suspicions. My Little-Reeh is hurting and I can't fix it. I really didn't see how rail-thin she has become. I don't notice her body as a young woman's. When I look at her, I see my baby-girl. Her small and boyish figure looks normal to me. I had a sleepless night of analyzing and praying about this predicament.

Early this morning, I see Reeh rush from her bedroom to the bathroom in a small sleeveless nightshirt. I just happen to be in the hall at the most opportune moment, unexpected by Reeh. I freeze in horror at the sight of bony shoulders and knobby knees whisking by. Her legs are like two sticks, spaced far apart. I feel God slapping me awake. Reeh looks ghostly and abnormal. It seems like this happened overnight. *God, forgive me, I was blind. Thank you for helping me see!*

I tip-toe over to Ali's side of the bed to see if she is sleeping. Her breath is heavy and her face looks so peaceful. I don't wake her up, because I know she also didn't sleep well last night. I am sadly humbled. My lips move without speaking, kissing the words *I'm sorry* into the air between us.

I leave for work earlier than normal. Clients are flying in from out of state. I have some preparation to do before they get here. My glimpse of Reeh's emaciated body is a rough start to my day. I am having difficulty concentrating. *God, I need your help. Show me where I am failing my daughter. What am I supposed to do? I am pleading.* Traffic is nonexistent at this early hour. The houses I drive past are dark and sleepy. I keep my headlights on bright and watch for deer. When I turn up the radio, I hear a familiar voice. *Thru The Bible with J. Vernon McGee.* An old program is airing. I'm not usually up early enough to hear his show.

McGee is talking about Jesus Parable of the Lost Sheep, "When one sheep got lost, He went out and looked for it. When He found it, He put it on His shoulders, the place of strength. He is able to save to the uttermost.

The high priest of the children of Israel wore an ephod. On the shoulders of the ephod were two stones. On them were engraved the names of the twelve tribes -- six tribes on one stone and six on the other. The high priest carried the children of Israel on his shoulders. Our great High Priest carries us on His shoulders, and we will not become lost."

Suddenly a stone flies up and hits my windshield, startling me to extremes. *Where did that come from?* I am the only one on the road. Bam! I jump in my seat. Another stone flies up and this time cracks the windshield into a small starburst pattern. The stones smash my obsessive thoughts to silence. I grip the steering wheel with both hands and lean forward, ready for another surprise. I remain cautious the rest of the way to the office.

What a relief. I was able to leave my troubles behind for a while. My all-day meetings went smooth, almost mechanical. But my memory is back, quick as two stones, when I see the reminder on my windshield. My lamb is lost. I will search for her until she's found. *Lord, help me to lift Reeh onto my shoulders and carry her back to you.*

I drive home with caution and wonder where those stones came from. It's not an easy ride. God demands my attention. It is painful to be convicted of ignoring my daughter. I don't know how I can drift so far and not realize it. Not long ago, I couldn't wait to come home, lift her up and feel tiny arms squeezing my neck. Reeh would kiss my cheek, then rub her face saying, 'you're picky, Daddy.' I admit, the past few years I've grown lazy. I am exhausted after work. I can't wait to get home and zone out in front of the T.V. It's embarrassing to admit how many hours I spend, flicking my life away with the remote control. I let my wife pick up my share of household duties. *When did I decide that was okay? God, I am a selfish jerk. I'm lost and need you to carry me back. Please give me more energy and help me make better use of my time. I need to re-connect with Reeh. Show me what to do about her eating. What am I missing? I knock at your door for answers. I need Your wisdom and insight.*

When I get home, the house smells fabulous. Something's baking in the oven. I yell out for Ali. No answer. After, I find a note propped against the toaster:

Jeff-Reeh,
Forgot to tell you about book club tonight.
Be back late. Mac-n-cheese in the oven.
Pumpkin pie. Yum!
Enjoy!
Love,
A.

I can't wait to dig in. Ali listened to my stupid advise to, 'Just fix Reeh's favorite foods. She will eat.' This gesture is sweet of Ali. Especially since we know it's a Band-Aid for the problem.

I yell out to an empty house, "Reeh! Come eat!" No response. "Reeh?" *Where is she?*

A few minutes later, while I am taking food from the oven to the table, I hear footsteps scuffing up the basement stairs.

Reeh's face is red and sweaty. "Hi Dad."

I give her a stiff hug and ask, "Hungry?"

The clumsiness of hugging her makes me wonder. *Why did I stop giving my daughter affection? How long has it been?* This used to come natural to me. I want to turn back time. I need a re-do. I can tell Reeh suspects something. She gives me a strange look when I let go of her.

I attempt to shake off our embarrassment by reciting the menu. "Mac-n-cheese, Reeh! Doesn't it smell great? And look at the pie Mom made us."

Reeh surprises me by piling her plate with comfort food. She takes seconds and even has a piece of pumpkin pie. Everything seems back to normal. I ask about her day at school. We joke about the neighbor's dog and his retrieving skills.

"What surprise did the dog leave on the steps today?"

The neighbor's black retriever is an escape artist that wanders off and hunts. He shows off his kill by displaying it on other people's porches. Don't ask me where he found the rooster I stepped on a couple weeks ago. Reeh was right behind me when it happened. According to Reeh, I screamed like a chicken, —*bawk!* We laugh again at my reaction

I ask Reeh, "What are you doing after dinner?"

"I have tons of homework."

"Do you have time to drive out to the lake? We don't have to stay long."

I am reaching out —finally. I'm a jerk for taking so long. The confused look on her face kills me. I know that I am being hard on myself. I deserve it.

"Nah. I really can't. Too much to do."

She isn't looking at me. I can tell she is afraid to hurt my feelings.

"Maybe some other time," I suggest and watch her get up to leave.

I don't encourage her to stay and clean up. This is another selfish choice of mine. I am uncomfortable and want some space. I bang around the kitchen, clear the table and put away food.

Normally, I would head to the TV or garage right now. Instead, something pulls me toward Reeh. Her bedroom door is cracked open, but she's not in there. I walk near the bathroom and hear the shower running. I don't think anything of it at first. Reeh exercised before dinner and probably needs a shower. I pause outside the bathroom door, distracted by an unrelated thought about work.

That's when I hear it. The sound shakes me, worse than the stones hitting my windshield! The shower water splashing against the plastic curtain is a mask for sound. I am not fooled. Although, part of me wants to be ignorant. I hear it again, louder this time —retching and forceful splashing. It echoes into the toilet bowl. My throat tightens and knots. I swallow hard. Without thinking, I turn the door knob to go in. It's locked. I react on impulse, at lightning speed, using the fastest technique to open a push-lock. I hit the door above the knob with force and adrenaline. The lock pops out. I swing the door open.

Reeh jerks up from her perch in horror. She glares at me and quickly curls into the corner, with her face hiding in her knees.

"Get out of here!" she screams, "Go! Leave me alone!" She cries violently and shakes. She stays compressed into a fetal ball on the cold tile floor.

I am aghast and iced into position. I force myself to ignore my gag-reflux.

"Jesus! Help us!" I say out loud. My hands are trembling. I don't know what to do. *How long am I going to stand here? Do something.*

"Reeh?" I touch the back of her hair.

Her cries diminish to hiccups. "I am just sick, Dad," she lies. "Go away."

"I know exactly what is going on here," I plead. "Look at me, Reeh."

Her head turns, but still cowers as she attempts to hide her shame from me. Her face, I will never forget the look, beat red and swollen, with slime dripping off her chin. Survival mode finally kicks in. From here, my motions are instinctive. I divert my eyes and flush the toilet. I turn off the shower and scoop my little girl up off the floor and carry her to her bedroom. I am shocked at how weightless and lanky she is in my arms. Bones. I pull back her bed covers with one arm and lay her down, like I did so many times when she was a toddler. She pulls the covers completely over her head, taut. Her head is a ball with cloth over it. I sit down next to her. The world is silent, except for the whimpering beneath blankets.

It's hard for me to wait. I want to fix this. I think up lines to get her to open up, but swallow my words before they come out. I have my palm on her fabric covered head and gently stroke with my thumb. I hope she can breathe okay in there. Reeh's movements form a pattern. She lays still, then her body shakes more tears loose. I wait patiently. *God, please give Reeh your peace. Flood her with Love. Help her trust me! I want to be able to talk to her. Help us communicate. Don't let her fool me. Help her be honest. Words, Lord. I have no words. Show me when it's time to talk. Give me something to say. I feel like a loser-dad that failed his daughter. Please show her the way back home. Show me the way back, too.*

There is motion beneath the covers. Reeh moves her face near the edge of the bed and lifts the blankets enough for air. I still can't see her face.

"I'm sorry Daddy," whimpers a tiny voice. "I know you're disappointed."

I softly touch her shoulder and lean down, "I love you, Reeh." I give her boney shoulder a squeeze. "I want to help you, sweetheart."

"I'll be alright."

"No, Reeh. Please let me help. This isn't simple. It's serious."

"You won't understand, Dad."

"I'll try my hardest," I say in earnest. "I am here right now and whenever you need me."

She doesn't respond. I wait for more to say. "I will listen. I will pay attention. I'm sorry, Reeh. So sorry. Tell me what you need from me."

In the silence, I talk to the Lord. He hears me asking. I search for Him and He is there. My soul is bowing. I desperately pound on His door!

Soon, a girlish hand with chipped purple nail polish reaches from under the covers. I take her precious hand and cover it with both of mine. God blesses us with a pure sensation of His presence. Love flows through my hands and into the heart of my baby girl. Her hand softens and goes limp. Reeh's breathing is deep and heavy. She sleeps, blanketed God's protection.

I stay beside her as long as my body allows in this reclining position. Before my joints seize, I creak my body into an upright position and painfully stretch out the knots. Ali should be home soon.

I need a hug.

Matthew 16:24-26 (NIV)
[24] Then Jesus said to his disciples, "If anyone would come after me, he must deny himself and take up his cross and follow me.
[25] For whoever wants to save his life will lose it, but whoever loses his life for me will find it.
[26] What good will it be for a man if he gains the whole world, yet forfeits his soul? Or what can a man give in exchange for his soul?

chapter 39 ali

It's official. Jeff is crazy. I'm kidding. Gotta love that guy! Jeff is usually helpful, but now he's going overboard. I actually have to ask him to take a break. *Stop. I can get this!* I am so thankful he is the man I married. His love for our family is intense. In my younger years, I had poor judgment when it came to men. Reece would battle me over my crushes and call them superficial. Reece was extremely wise for his years. Reece was blessed by God. His life was short, but full of impact. I pray for another Reece, a Godly man about Reeh's age. He will be the man she marries, I hope. *Please, God.*

Almost overnight, Reeh totally reversed her eating disorder. It was as if the comfort and attention from her dad gave her power and assurance. I thank the Lord for Jeff's response. That night was horrible for him. When I got home from book club, I could tell he was crying. It scared me at first. I wasn't sure what kind if news he was about to give me. He told me about overhearing Reeh in the bathroom and gave me a detailed account of what happened after.

He carried her. Not just to her bed, but figuratively. Jeff drew Reeh's words out and listened instead of reacting. He began spending more time with her —Dad and Reeh dates.

I don't know all of their personal conversations, but I'm sure Jeff made her feel beautiful and valued. They have a special bond, strong and unbreakable. Reeh walks tall and is confident.

There are things I need to change. Listening is one of them! *Sorry Reeh.* Now, I look directly at Reeh's pretty green eyes when she talks, like Jeff does to me. I stop what I am doing and face her when she tells me about school, friends and now boys. She talks to me more than ever. I feel guilty for not being an active listener before. I know exactly what I made her feel like. My mother did this to me —habitual answers, nods and uh-huhs, without hearing a word I said.

We are all a work in progress. God is shaping Reeh, shaping Jeff and me. Reeh is miles ahead of where I was at her age. Even though she tends to compare herself with others and sometimes believes she is less. I remind her, we all have special talents. Let someone else have the spotlight when it is their turn. It is okay to be in the audience. The audience is just as important. I am learning also. I have to remind myself to look to God for my value, not to man. I frequently need to give up my selfishness and fears, start from where I am and follow —less of me, more of Jesus. I must deny myself from the things I lust for, my idols. Oh, my numerous idols!

Reeh has been begging and begging. She wants to be an exchange student. At first we weren't sure about the idea. She goes to counseling once a week and is making wonderful progress. We don't want this to hinder her momentum. *But then, maybe this trip would help?* Tough decision. Lately, I have strong feelings against it. Jeff is ambivalent. It is only for fall semester of her junior year. *Why is this hard for me?* It really isn't that long to be gone. *Yes it is! A week is too long for me.* Me! Me! Me! Something is making me afraid, pulling me back. I am ready to cave and let her go. I am tired of arguing with Reeh. It no longer seems worth the fight. *Am I making it too big a deal?*

We have a week to decide. The paper-work needs to be completed and the deposit sent. Reeh filled out most of the paperwork. She is determined to go. We need to sign on the dotted line. *Oh, what to do?* Five months seems too long to be away from home. I am not ready for empty nest, however temporary. Reeh will be home from Ruth's house soon. I want to talk to her about so many things and make sure she is ready. *Am I ready?*

* * * * * * *

Reeh needs a few things for her trip. *Why did I agree to this?* The list seems like a mile long. I know I'm over preparing for her and doing things she should do herself. I don't care this time. This is my way to transition; my daughter will be gone for five months!

I am going down every isle in the pharmacy. I want to make sure nothing is forgotten. And, I need this time for myself. I twist caps off the latest shampoo bottles, smelling new fragrances. Unexpectedly, I am bombarded. It is too late to hide. She's already approaching me. I have no getaway, no excuse. I don't know how I missed hearing the pitter-pat of those wood heels, bright pink to match her head scarf and handbag. She is dripping in money today, glittering fingers and earrings, several necklaces and bracelets. Her clothing is labeled properly with prestigious signage — Versace, Dior, Chanel, Coach.

"Ali, dear! Aren't you lovely today." Mrs. Rawlings flatters. "Your sundress is adorable! My daughter would *love* it! I'm not finding clothes that shade of green. It absolutely enhances your skin tone!"

She flashes her hands in front of my face, hoping her rings make my eyes sparkle. Her perfume is strong and overbearing. It reminds me of Millie.

"This dress is really old. I am sure the color must be out of style." I try not to sound sarcastic saying it.

"Oh my! No wonder. I haven't seen that color for ages." Mrs. Rawlings' eyes travel across me, comparing the price of my clothing to hers. "How was your summer? Did you do anything particularly exciting?"

I am distracted by her coloring. Her skin is orange, Oompa-Loompa orange. Her lipstick is bright pink to match her shoes, but clashes with her orange skin. *Spray tan?*

"Summer certainly went fast. We took some weekend vacations. Camped a few times. It was nice"

"Camping!" Mrs. Rawlings places her long fingernails over her heart. Her diamond is almost gaudy with extravagance. "Not *my* idea of a vacation.

Hotels only, for me! I need a soft bed and clean linen. Absolutely." She clicks her tongue. *tsk-tsk-tsk.*

I am not offended by her reaction. It's Mrs. Rawlings we're talking about. She rarely comes down from her perch.

I love camping and tell her, "We enjoy the outdoors. Sleeping under the stars. Hiking. Jeff and Reeh love fishing. They could spend an entire day in a rowboat."

"Just dreadful!" She says, shaking her head. "Soon I'll be abroad. Staying in luxury hotels. I'm too old for rowboats. I need pampering." Mrs. Rawlings taps her lips with one finger and decides, "Well of course, I'm not that old. Yesterday, a clerk thought my daughter was my sister. She's about your age. My sister! Can you believe that?" Sigh. "So much to do, getting ready for travel is... Ex--hausting."

She is hoping I ask about her trip, or tell her how beautiful and young she looks. Her ego growls with hunger. She craves brag material. I don't want to waste anymore *Me* time on this person. Selfish —I know, but honest. *Hey, wait a minute. Who is the one being selfish here?* She focuses all attention on herself. How does a person get that old and remain so self centered? I don't brag about Reeh and the glamorous trip she will be taking. Besides, my words usually fall to the ground, squished by expensive shoes when I talk to Mrs. Rawlings.

"Have a nice vacation," I say and bend over to smell some shampoo. "Ooo, this one smells yummy."

"Now dear, this is not the place to shop for shampoos. You are better off sticking to the salons where more reputable brands are strictly sold."

"My hair cannot tell the difference," I tell her. I am secretly glad that my hair is extra shiny and smooth today —as if it matters. I guess I have some shallowness to deal with. I am a continuous piece of work.

"Ali, darling," She says, clutching her purse. "I better run, so much to do before our extensive travel. Too-da-loo."

Mrs. Rawlings walks away with her chin lifted, stomach- in/shoulders- back. Good posture. *I am elite.* Some people actually believe that.

****

"Mom! Quit crying," Reeh begs. "I am only going to be gone a little while."

"I know, Reeh," Sniffle. Sniffle. "This is sad for me. Someday, you will see how hard letting go is." I hug her until she wiggles away.

"Mommy, you're smothering me."

"So?" I defend. "Can't a mother cuddle her *only* daughter before she leaves her for a *Really-Really* long time?"

"I don't leave until tomorrow," Reeh reminds me. "And I'm not gonna be gone *that* long." She talks with assurance, but I know she's faking.

This past week, Reeh has been nervous. I can tell she is having second thoughts. Now that Jeff and I are confident, Reeh isn't. We traded emotions. After we finally signed the papers and said she could go, Reeh regressed a little. She calls us Mommy and Daddy again. I haven't heard that from her in years. She even tried to talk us out of allowing her to go, by telling us horror stories of other exchange students. She is worried about not knowing their language. I wonder about that, too. Reeh took a crash course in German this summer. The coordinator for the foreign exchange program assures me that this will not be an issue, that speaking the language is not a prerequisite. *But she will attend school overseas with limited language skills. How will she learn?* Again, Reeh's coordinator assures me, this happens all the time. She says the kids pick up on the language faster than I can imagine.

I want to pack my bags and go with her. My eyes are puffy and red from crying all night. Something doesn't feel right about this trip. It haunts me. Last night I had a recurring dream from childhood. It was so long ago; I truly forgot about it until now. It feels like a sign, a signal to change our minds. We have to go through with it. It took such effort to be prepared, not to mention the financial aspects. Foreign exchange is not cheap. A family is waiting for Reeh to arrive. I feel pressure, similar to a bride that walks down the aisle and realizes she is making a huge mistake. How does a bride gain the courage to turn around and run out the door? Jeff and Reed are loading up the car. I am in the kitchen, scraping food off plates.

Turning Inside Out

Jeff pops his head around the corner and says, "Hey, can't that wait? I'll help you when we get home."

"Okay-okay," I am trying not to cry. "I want to soak these dishes."

Hot water is filling the sink. Chunks of food are floating in it. *Yuck. I can't soak the dishes in this water!* I submerge my hand to scoop the chunks out. "Ouch!" The water is scalding hot. My right hand turn red instantly.

The dream!

Children are lined up to eat, waiting in two lines. Bread is in a silver bucket. Water is in a red bucket. Reeh is at the end of one line and facing the wrong way. She won't turn around. All the other children are facing the bucket at the front of their line. Not Reeh, she is holding a stuffed animal against her chest and has a spoon in her other hand. Her legs are bent, her body leaning forward. She is getting ready to sprint out of the line. A tall man, wearing laced up military boots, walks over to the silver bucket of bread and kicks it as hard as he can. The bang echoes and the children scatter. Chunks of bread fall into the red bucket and the water starts to boil. I run to the red bucket, pick it up and pour it onto the man's back.

My dream switches to snapshots. Reeh is on the playground, swinging high as she can, looking back in fear as she soars into the sky. *Snap.* Reeh is under the table, hiding from military boots that stomp around it. *Snap.* Reeh is locked in a burgundy van, pounding on the windows and screaming. *Snap.* Reeh is waiting by a picture window repeating, "What did you get me, Mommy?" *Snap.* I am dragging Reeh out of a car, peeling her fingers off the seatbelt she has an iron grip on. She is yelling, "Don't make me go, Mommy!" I gather the little girl in my arms and promise her, "We will never-ever go there again." When the child looks up at me, I realize it isn't Reeh.

It is me.

Luke 7:44-48 (NIV)
⁴⁴ Then he turned toward the woman and said to Simon, "Do you see this woman? I came into your house. You did not give me any water for my feet, but she wet my feet with her tears and wiped them with her hair.
⁴⁵ You did not give me a kiss, but this woman, from the time I entered, has not stopped kissing my feet.
⁴⁶ You did not put oil on my head, but she has poured perfume on my feet.
⁴⁷ Therefore, I tell you, her many sins have been forgiven--for she loved much. But he who has been forgiven little loves little."
⁴⁸ Then Jesus said to her, "Your sins are forgiven."

chapter 40 leah (lee-lee)

Here we are at the airport. I was hoping we would get a flat tire and miss the plane. It didn't happen. Actually, we are super early. I am passing the time by watching other people and guessing where they are from, where they are going, and what they will do when they get there.

I see a trio approaching. Something about them seems familiar. I am intrigued; so I watch as they get closer and closer. A distinguished pilot is rolling a suitcase alongside a thin blond woman and an older lady. The blond looks radiant in the distance, but the closer she gets, the older she grows. Her hairstyle and clothing do not match her lined face. She is dressed too young, wearing a skirt that is ultra short and way too tight. Her chest is enormous. You can't miss it. If I wasn't so occupied staring at the blond (judging her, if I am honest), I would notice the orange face of the third person and make the connection. I've seen this blond girl before. *Where? Does she look like an actress I saw in a movie? Or do I know her?* As the trio gets closer, I am ready to jump out of my seat and duck behind the nearest column. I don't want to face these people. I am so glad Reeh and Jeff are getting something to eat. It makes it easier to blend and hide. *Why am I acting like such a coward?* I am an adult. Adults don't run from people they don't want to talk to. *Do they?* I scurry farther away and stand rigid behind a fat column.

"*...Please do not leave your bags unattended. All bags unattended will be...*"

"Oh drat!"

I come out of hiding to *attend* Reeh's bags, praying *Lord make me invisible. What? Be brave? But invisible would be much easier.*

"Ali dear!"

"Drat again." I whisper it this time. I turn around and say, "Mrs. Rawlings? Fancy meeting you here. What a surprise!"

Mrs. Rawlings starts bragging right away, stops midsentence and says, "Where are my manners? Have you met my daughter, Mideah?"

"I don't think so." She looks vaguely familiar. I've seen her somewhere, but my brain isn't connecting the dots. "Nice to meet you, Mideah." I hold out my hand to greet her. Mideah squeezes my hand so firm that it almost hurts.

"And let's not forget about Ted. He is *our* pilot." She emphasizes his position, in perfect namedropping style. "He will be flying *our* plane."

The man holds out his hand to shake mine. When our hands embrace, he studies my face and says, "Lee-Lee?" He cups my hand in both of his and holds it tighter. He isn't letting go. "Leah? Is it really you? Good to see you!"

I want to scream and yank my hand away. I am frozen. My hand burns from the water! I read the name on his identity badge, *Ted Daverman*. I look past the lines on his face and my memories are resurrected. His dark beady eyes exhume my past.

"Mr. D..." I say, so quietly that nobody hears. My head swirls fast. I see black spots in my vision.

My stomach is turning inside out.

I tip sideways, falling. Mr. D. wraps his arm around my back.

"Let go of me!" I snap.

Suddenly my head is clear. *I remember. I remember everything!*

How dare he use my childhood nickname! I buried this name with my lamb, next to Reece, nestled in the pit of his arm. Reece helped me walk away from that time in my life —the time I was nicknamed Lee-Lee. Reece and I had many discussions, digging up bones from my past. He would listen to me bleed tears into my pillow.

Reece would go to my bedroom dresser, pick up my lamb and hold it on his neck.

"God loves you like this, Ali."

He would stroke its cheek and kiss it, then bury it under his arm.

"He will protect you. He'll hold you in the shadow of his wing."

I take deep breaths to calm down. Mrs. Rawlings is oblivious to my reaction and immediately turns the conversation to her status report.

"You know, Ted...," she begins and stops to correct herself. "Mr. Daverman will *honor* us by flying his last flight. He is about to retire."

She touches the metal wings on Ted's chest. "Yes, yes. He will be staying abroad with us, giving us *our own* personal tour of Denmark." She winks at Ted and flirts, "It will be such a treat. Just think, at nine forty-five we will all be in the air together."

Denmark? Nine forty... That is my daughter's flight! I back away, without a word.

And run!

Mideah buttons her white blouse. The fabric gapes apart at her cleavage. Her black lace bra seeps through the translucent white fabric. She doesn't care if her spandex skirt creeps up when she walks with long strides. She likes it tight fitting. Red panties is the cure for that problem. *If it's on my body, it has to look sexy. Otherwise, why bother?*

Mideah rushes to get out the door on time. She left her purse at the cabin last night and didn't notice until the last minute. Now she has to drive all the way to the cabin, plus drive out of the way to pick up her mother. *Mom better be ready! What am I thinking? Mother will be pacing the floor and looking out her window every five minutes.*

The cabin smells dead when she opens the door, like a decomposing animal. *What is that smell? It didn't stink last night. Did it?* Mideah puts her nose into the bend of her arm and breaths through her mouth. She searches for her purse fast as she can and locks the door behind her, never investigating the stench. Her cell phone rings when she gets into her car. She glances at the screen before answering.

"Hey," she says, sounding bored.

"Mideah!" Ted is anxious.

"What now?" Mideah is annoyed for no reason.

"Vanessa is pissed!"

"So? Why are you telling me this?"

"It's really weird. She won't say why. She's asking all kinds of questions. Wants to know exactly where I am going and exactly when I'll be home."

"Big deal. What's her problem? Get rid of her. I told you, she's a control freak!"

"No. Something's up. I can tell." Ted is tapping his hand so fast, Mideah can hear it through her phone. "I don't know. She mentioned police, or detective ..." He coughs nervously. "She says I'm in deep. Whatever that means."

"What a wacko! You know what I think. Do I need to say it again?"

Ted swears into the phone, venting. "This is bad. I'm thinking about not coming back, living overseas or somewhere reclusive."

"Would you calm down! You are overreacting." Mideah rolls her eyes and takes a peek at her lips in the mirror. "Now *you're* being wacko." She holds the phone to her ear with her shoulder and reaches into her purse for lipstick.

Ted exhales. "You're right. I *am* being crazy. I can't wait to get out of here!"

He hangs up.

When Mideah and her mother meet him, he acts like the anxious phone call never happened. Ted even goes out of his way to flirt with them. He kisses their cheeks and unloads their luggage. He pays the valet to park Mideah's car, before they walk down the endless concourse to their terminal.

"You are not going!" Ali is obstinate. "I. Do. Not. Want you on that flight!"

Mascara is smeared across her wet eyes. Ali's hands are shaking and her legs can barely hold her weight. They are making a scene near the airline food court.

"Calm down, Ali," Jeff says softly and pulls her close to his side. "What's going on?"

"This isn't going to work. Reeh shouldn't be going to Denmark. I can't explain it."

"This is so stupid," Reeh snarls. "Geez Mom, don't freak out on us."

"Ali, I don't understand. What happened? Why are you shaking?" Jeff is concerned. His doubts surface and provoke him to support his wife. "Reeh, we might need to postpone this for a few months. Let me talk to your mother."

"Dad!" Reeh's demeanor is instantly bitter, "This is not fair! I can't believe it! This sucks! I hate this!" She stomps away and plops into a chair with her back to her parents.

Jeff turns to Ali. "Why don't you think we're doing the right thing?"

"What do you mean? Which right thing?"

"Letting her go."

Ali gulps in a lungful of air and pushes it out fast. "That's not the *right thing* I was thinking of. I am so afraid right now. I can't explain it. Can we pray about this?"

Jeff wraps his long arms around Ali's shoulders and rocks her, "Definitely, we should. He whispers into Ali's ear. *Lord, show us what to do. Please protect our daughter from harm."*

Out of the blue, Reeh's name is called over the main speaker, almost inaudible. Reeh curls her lip in confusion. "Huh?"

They rush to the nearest security to find out what is happening. Two guards escort them to a conference room to question them. They have to participate in a full body scan. Ali's purse is emptied, as well as Jeff's wallet. Their shoes are x-rayed. Apparently, leaving your bag unattended looks very suspicious. Ali is embarrassed and over-apologetic to her family and to the security staff at the airport. Finally, they are allowed to leave.

* * * * * * *

Mideah is disgusted! *That jerk should have watched what he was doing.* She is in the tiny bathroom on the plane, trying to stop her nose from bleeding. A hefty man accidently elbowed her face. She was standing behind him while he was shoving his carry-on bag into the plane's overhead cabinet. The front of her blouse is crimson, splotched with blood. Mideah is so angry. She has nothing to change into, until baggage claim which is hours away. When she comes out, everyone is staring at her and not because she's beautiful, this time.

The flight attendant remedies the incident by moving both Mideah and her mother to first class. Mrs. Rawlings is appalled that they even had to associate with the lower class on this flight. *We are intimate friends with the pilot, after all.*

They settle into roomier seats and immediately get served a stiff drink. Pillows and blankets are readily available. Mideah covers her chest with a creamy wool blanket to hide the blood stains. She studies her mother, who is fully tilted back in the seat, eyes closed and robotically holding a drink in her fist. Mideah fears the wrinkles sagging down her mother's neck. She doesn't want to look like that when she is old. Mideah checks the folds under her own chin to see if they are getting flabby. Her bare neck reminds her, *My amulet! I forgot to put on the necklace Ted gave me last night. It's supposed to give me good fortune.* She ropes the platinum chain around her neck and presses the turquoise beetle against her heart. She rubs her false god for safety. She closes her eyes, ready for the days ahead. But she cannot relax. *Why won't my heart stop pounding?*

Shortly after the First Officer drinks the hot chocolate Ted gave him... Ted removes his grandmother's cross from his pocket and smashes it into the cockpit floor with the heel of his wingtip oxford. *I don't hear you, Grandma!* He never believed. Never needed to. Never wanted anything more than desire. He isn't going home. He doesn't know his destination. He believes that he can decide his own destiny. His after. His tomorrow.

The plane lifts, angling into the sky. It disappears into the clouds, like a navy blue dress on a dark night. Abruptly, the plane takes a sharp turn and dares a ghastly fate. The passengers lunge sideways in their seats. The left wing dips low and leaves everyone hanging in an awkward position, with seatbelts stressed. Fear groans out of every soul for what seems like eternity.

The plane spirals downward through white clouds —flushing all hopes for recovery.

<><><><><><><><><><><><><><><><><><><>

When I watch the sun rise into fuchsia clouds to birth a new day, I hear Reece repeat, *Every day when the sun comes up it reminds me of Jesus. New light. New beginning.*

Jeff, Reeh and I are up early, eating cereal in silence and fretting over missing the plane last night. Reeh scowls behind her cereal bowl, darting us with her anger. Finally, Jeff turns on the small TV in the kitchen. We listen to the news... never expecting.

I believe that moments in my past, good and bad, have a greater purpose. A fragment does not make sense, until you see the whole. God uses our lives. He weaves us into His perfect plan, redeeming the broken pieces of our lives.

God will turn us inside out. Redeem.

Genesis 50:20 (NIV)
[20] You intended to harm me, but God intended it for good to accomplish what is now being done, the saving of many lives

the absence of light:

Abyss: What happened when the plane crashed?
Mideah: I saw someone. He was bright, like light. It might have been Jesus. But I don't really know what He is like.

Abyss: Did He come for you?
Mideah: Probably. I was alone. I saw Him in the distance. He was moving towards me. I watched Him for a while. His light was burning my eyes.

Abyss: Did you hide?
Mideah: No! Why would I hide?

Abyss: Did He talk to you? Did you say anything?
Mideah: Neither of us spoke. But words were surrounding me. When He was near me, He held out His hands. I turned and looked away.

Abyss: Because you are ashamed?
Mideah: No! Why would I be ashamed? It bothered me. That's why I turned the other way.

Abyss: Did you to follow Him?
Mideah: No. I didn't feel like it. He moved past me, silently. I felt a soft breeze on my back. My body felt dry and prickly. I became paralyzed and couldn't breathe. I tried to turn around. I couldn't move! Couldn't talk! I felt like a pillar of salt. I looked down and saw bloody footprints leading to where I am standing. My blood is staining my wedding carpet! Will someone wipe this up!
Why does it keep getting darker? Who are you, anyway? Why won't you answer me? I can barely see myself. When will it be morning? Well?
Abyss: Never. God saw that Light was good. He separated the light from the darkness.
Jesus: *How* can I give you up, Mideah? *How* can I hand you over, my child? You will bear the consequences of your lewdness and your detestable practices. Free will. You made this choice. Chains. Darkness.
You: I choose Jesus, son of God. Light of the world. Lamb of God. Prince of Peace. Bread of life. Comforter. Counselor. Savior.
Cover me, my sins, with your sacrificial blood. Amen.

ABOUT THE AUTHOR

Lisa Feringa lives Suttons Bay, Michigan, (surrounded by a beautiful landscape of water, dunes, hills and the sunrise) sharing life with her husband, Steve and daughter, izzi. Wife. Mother. Daughter. Aunt. Friend. Architect. Writer. Artist. Wanna-B-Inventor. This is her debut novel.

Made in the USA
Lexington, KY
22 February 2014